Thomas Rosco Rede Stebbing

The Naturalist of Cumbrae

A True Story Being the Life of David Robertson

Thomas Rosco Rede Stebbing

The Naturalist of Cumbrae
A True Story Being the Life of David Robertson

ISBN/EAN: 9783337025533

Printed in Europe, USA, Canada, Australia, Japan

Cover: Foto ©Raphael Reischuk / pixelio.de

More available books at **www.hansebooks.com**

THE NATURALIST
OF CUMBRAE

A TRUE STORY

BEING THE LIFE OF
DAVID ROBERTSON

BY HIS FRIEND
THE REV. THOMAS R. R. STEBBING, M.A.
LATE FELLOW AND TUTOR OF WORCESTER COLLEGE, OXFORD

LONDON
KEGAN PAUL, TRENCH, TRÜBNER & CO., LTD.
1891

PREFACE.

THOSE who read the following life will, I believe, not think that any serious apology is needed for its having been written. The subject of it has endeared himself to a large circle of friends; his character has proved itself through a long life admirable for sincerity and unselfishness; his career is marked by the successful and, in many respects, surprising conquest of difficulties; his natural history pursuits have had results of great interest and value. From his own lips and published writings, from a long series of manuscript note-books and a great store of correspondence, trustworthy materials have been available for the narrative. By many curious changes of fortune and a variety of humorous incidents, the course of the biography is enlivened; by the attractive details of scientific research as well as by the lessons of the life itself it is made instructive and profitable.

It is due to no vanity on the part of the hero that this record of his adventures sees the light. He had repeatedly refused either to indite such a relation himself or to entrust the conduct of it to another. He had even arranged that the materials on which much of it has now been founded should be burnt whenever his own more immediate control over them had ceased. His yielding at last, and allowing the story to be now told, has been, like so many other actions of his life, far less to gratify himself than to oblige his friend.

In the book at large an occasional Scotticism will, no doubt, be pardoned, as tending to give local colour to the life of a Scotchman. Every one knows that "a burn " in Scotland would in England be a brook, and most persons will be able to guess that a Scotch " dyke " is not a valley, but a wall or hedge, that a "decent " family means one that is honest and respectable, and that a " clever " young man designates not necessarily an intellectual genius, but a youth suited for the purpose in hand. Here and there, it may be, a phrase not Scotch, nor yet exactly classical English, has kept its place as too expressive or too quaint to be omitted and lost.

CONTENTS.

——◦◇◦——

CHAPTER I.

CHAPTER VII.

CHAPTER VIII.

CHAPTER IX.

CHAPTER X.

CHAPTER XI.

CHAPTER XII.

CHAPTER XIII.

CHAPTER XIV.

Contents.

THE NATURALIST OF CUMBRAE.

CHAPTER I.

BIRTH AND EDUCATION.

DAVID ROBERTSON was born in Great Hamilton Street, Glasgow, in the year 1806. His birthday was the 28th of November, reckoning by the Old Style, which, it is curious to notice, his friends still used, although the New Style had been introduced into our calendar by Act of Parliament fifty-five years before.

The year of his birth was memorable in Glasgow on two accounts. Prior to this the citizens had no other supply of water than from twenty-eight pump wells in the streets, and, as some of these wells were very limited, and the water often of a bad quality, a number of the inhabitants now procured an Act incorporating them as the Glasgow Waterworks Company. The population of the town having at this time risen to about a hundred thousand, such a measure was evidently by no means premature. The public spirit of the people was at the same epoch exhibited by their being the first in the kingdom to erect a monument to

B

Lord Nelson, who had fallen the previous year in the battle of Trafalgar.

With such grand doings, however, the family in Great Hamilton Street was not in a position to be much impressed. Three weeks after David's birth, his father, James Robertson, died, leaving his wife and three children unprovided for. The eldest boy, James, was only about five, and the other child, Jeannet, about three years old.

After the death of the breadwinner, the household was still maintained without external assistance, solely by the mother's industry, frugality, and careful management. Sad and toilsome as this part of her life must have been, her efforts had their reward ; and it is pleasant to know that she herself survived to the ripe old age of ninety-six.

The widowed mother found her baby very restless at night, never sleeping long at a time—a regular *wake-wife ;* not cross and peevish any more then than since, but simply restless, as became an infant destined to scientific research. This wakeful habit has continued from infancy to age, so that, content with little sleep, and with the power to rouse himself at any time desired, Mr. Robertson cannot remember ever over-sleeping himself, or, as they call it in Scotland, *sleeping in.*

That he made it a point of honour and conscience in his various employments not to be overtaken by such a fault, may be judged from the precautions which, it will be seen, he sometimes took to assist his natural faculty.

In addition to this more or less useful restlessness,

he has always, as far back as his memory serves, been troubled with dreams, and those seldom of a pleasant character, but often attended with a very disagreeable sensation as if of nightmare. Sometimes a frightful sound would seem to attend a terrifying incident in these visions of the night, startling his ears as though a railway train had rushed close by or through them. This always wakened him up in a tremor, with his ears ringing loudly; and though within the last few years these noises in the head have almost left him, the dreaming nightly never has.

In his early days children were not put to school so soon as they are now, so that in the leisure of his childhood he would have had time to display a precocious love of natural history, had it occurred to him to do so. But, looking back over seventy-eight or eighty years, he does not recall anything that would especially indicate or augur a partiality on his part for the study of animals, great or small.

In common with most boys that have the chance, he was fond of chasing butterflies, catching minnows with a crooked pin on the end of a thread, hunting for birds' nests, and harrying bees'-bykes (the homes of the wild bees). Like many other lads of his own age, he had a great desire to bring up some of the young birds that were captured, though the fostering was more often a failure than a success. One of the amusements in which he took part was trapping birds in snow time by a noose of horsehair or by getting them enticed under a riddle—that is to say, a wire sieve with coarse meshes. In his own home, catch-ing mice alive under a quart basin with a bit of cheese

tied to the end of a thin piece of wood was an occupation much to his fancy. In this case he had his
mother's approbation, as the mice were lodgers she
much preferred to do without.

Simple and commonplace as these pastimes were,
they exercised wee David's ingenuity, and gave some
promise of the zeal and skill which in later years he
has so conspicuously shown in hunting and capturing
the various small deer which lie fossilized in beds of
clay and sand, or which live in the waters of pool
and marsh, of loch and ocean.

As far as David himself was concerned, the mice
which were caught alive would have been allowed to
live. He never took pleasure in killing any animal,
and always detested the act of boys taking the eggs
from birds' nests for the sake of playing at what
they called "blind-smash."

In this cruel game, a number of eggs were placed
on the ground at certain distances. One of the party,
being blindfolded, then advanced towards them and
struck at them with a stick, the object being to see
who would break most eggs with the allotted number
of strokes.

In modern times, the same sort of game is harm-
lessly played by pinning on to a suspended sheet the
picture of a donkey without a tail, and distributing to
the company copies of the missing tail, to be affixed
with as much accuracy of position as any one can
manage with his eyes blindfolded. From this peaceful alternative, however, the delight of smashing
something is absent.

David's humour, even in childhood, did not incline

him either to blind-smash or to any other form of unreasoning violence and destruction. He had much more pleasure in a living mouse than a dead one, and at last a good excuse presented itself for keeping one of his favourites alive.

One day, being with his mother at the herd-market in Glasgow, he there saw a little toy-cottage with a mouse driving a large wheel on the side of it. The motion of the wheel set a shoemaker to work. He was in raptures with it. Here was a use for his mice, or at any rate for one of them. He begged his mother to buy him the mill with the mouse, but could not prevail on her to do so. Therefore, on reaching home he at once set to work to reproduce the whole contrivance for himself. Many another child might have conceived the idea of doing this, but very few could have succeeded in carrying out their intention.

For making his treadwheel, little David had the bottom of an old broken birdcage. This supplied the light wood needed for the two sides of the wheel. For the passage of his mouse from the cottage into the wheel, he bored holes in both by the help of a red-hot poker. He found no difficulty in cutting some wire into proper lengths for the bars, but to receive the wires holes had to be made in the thin wood near the edge, which was no easy task, as the wood was only too ready to split. To meet this emergency, he heated a knitting-needle of the requisite thickness, and so accomplished his purpose. Although this was a tedious business, time was no object to him then. The wires were soon put in, a mouse was procured for motive-power, the shoemaker was set on his bench, and it need hardly be said that the working of the machine which his own hands had made gave a far greater delight to the child than he would have derived from anything of the kind which his mother's money could have purchased for him.

When close upon seven years of age, David was at length sent to school. He could not have been sent much earlier, even had it been customary, for after the measles, to use the expression of the country people, the dregs fell into his eyes. It was feared for a time that he would lose his sight altogether. His eyes were long sore and longer weak, and were never afterwards able to bear prolonged fatigue, although it must be allowed that they have done a vast amount of work, and are still very serviceable. Before going to school he had learned the alphabet and a little of what was called the "wee spell," being taught so far by his mother, whose teachings, moreover, ever impressed upon him the duty of speaking the truth, of keeping his word, and of not getting into debt.

At school he was soon promoted to the "big spell," then to the Book of Proverbs, and from that to the New Testament. On the second day after this promotion, at the first reading lesson he got up to be dux, or head of the class. The teacher was rather surprised to find him there so soon, since the class contained between twenty and thirty boys. "David," he said, "if you keep there till night, I will put you in the Bible to-morrow." That the condition would be fulfilled, the teacher himself had probably not the least expectation, but what he had said put the whole class on the alert to have the new-comer down, while David was equally resolved, if possible, to keep up.

As the pupils read their chapter straight through, verse about, he knew in advance which verse would naturally come to his turn as dux, and took care to be well up in it; but, in case the master might change the order of beginning, he learned the whole chapter as well as he could, often running up to the teacher's desk to ask the meaning of difficult words. As it turned out, he managed to keep his place both in the forenoon and afternoon. Next morning he took a Bible with him, and, since both this and his inquiring glance explained his expectation, the teacher said, "You have managed so well that I cannot draw back from my word, although you might be as well for a time in the Testament." Having thus advanced through the classes which took their titles from having their reading-lessons respectively in the Book of Proverbs, the New Testament, and the Bible at large, he was next promoted to the privilege of learning to write. He had just done one page of long strokes, when his mother, requiring to have him as soon off her hands as she could, obtained an engagement for him to herd cows during harvest-time. Thus, when he was only eight years old, ended his twelve months' schooling.

Many a man who has become illustrious in literature or science may well ask himself what his own performance would have been had his ambition been checked at the outset, and all the culture of his mind abruptly brought to an end almost before it had well begun, in the unripe years of childhood. With even a moderate measure of early education, it is all but certain that David Robertson would have come to the front much earlier than he did, and that he would have taken a more independent position than he has done among scientific authorities.

If education has the value that almost all the modern world is willing to allow it, the want of it can scarcely be anything else but a drawback. Still, an active mind, even without printed books and professional teachers, reads and learns, and becomes a treasury of observed facts which to others are often only remembered statements. Had our friend David stayed a few more years at school, he might eventually have written some great books, of which there are already a good few in the world ; but his life would probably have been commonplace, and he would have had little time for the exceptional work which he has done in zoological collecting, in observing the habits and customs of marine animals, and in assisting and spurring on other workers in natural history.

CHAPTER II.

HERDING AND HORSE-BREAKING.

IN the early part of the century it was the custom
with the farmers in South Lanarkshire to hire a
strong girl who could milk the cows and who could
shear, that is, take her part with the reapers in
harvest, a small boy being engaged to herd during
the time the girl was occupied in harvest work.
It was to become such a deputy that David was
withdrawn from school. It happened to be a late
harvest, and the cows were put out in the morning as
soon as it was light. About an hour after daybreak,
a cog or wooden bowl of porridge made with whey
was sent out to the little herd. The cows were
brought home at 10 a.m. and milked. The boy then
got a piece of oat bread and some "float whey," that
is, the curd skimmed off when the whey was brought
to the boil. The cows were then again sent out to the
field, and the herd with them, whatever the weather,
wet or dry. About two o'clock his dinner was sent
out to him. It consisted of broth, with potatoes and
a piece of butcher's meat or cheese. The broth was
called kail, or, we ought rather to say, *were* so called,
for in the northern idiom broth, kail, and porridge are

used as plural words. The cows were brought home about sunset, and were milked at 8 p.m. When this had been done, supper was had, after which the farm people retired to bed.

On his first night the new lad was taken up to a loft over the kitchen and led to his bedside. There was no light. He was told to lay his clothes on the floor where he could find them in the morning. During the five or six weeks of his sojourn at this farm, he never saw the apartment that he slept in, nor what it contained. He was called up in the morning before it was light, and it was dark long before he went to bed. His shelter on a wet day was a check worsted plaid. No matter how wet the day had been, none of his clothes were put to the fire to dry, except his stockings, which were hung on the side of the " swee," the support generally used in farmhouses of that locality for suspending the cooking-pots over the fire. What was worst, before the harvest was over, snow came on, and the boy's shoes were bad and out at the toes, so that the snow got in. At this time, too, the cows were milked in the morning before they went out, so that the herd was out all day with them, having his breakfast before starting, and his dinner in the field.

It is true that he had not come from a luxurious home or been pampered by any superfluous indulgences in his bringing up, but even so there were many elements of contrast between his present position and the life he had been previously leading at school and under his mother's wing. A child of eight years old, not over-well clad, and with his feet sometimes half frozen, forced to spend his whole day out of doors, and coming back at night to the sorry comfort of an unlighted loft, presents a rather pitiful picture to the imagination. Hardy and courageous as he seems to have been, he could not help feeling this a bad beginning of providing for himself.

From the place just described he went to a Mr. Thomas Young, occupying a moorland farm, called The Logach, in the parish of East Kilbride, Lanarkshire. Here both master and mistress were more considerate. He was four or five years altogether in the service of Mr. Thomas Young and his son, Mr. John Young, who had a neighbouring farm called Ardochrigg. During that time he was in succession cow herd, quey or heifer herd, and sheep herd. It was with the son that he was promoted to be sheep herd, when he was between ten and eleven years of age. The farm was small, and the flock was not a large one, but none the easier to manage on that account, more particularly as the whole flock was sold off every season, and the farm re-stocked with wethers, or hog-lambs, as the farmers called them.

The lambs, when first brought to the hill, were very difficult to herd for a time, till they got *wonted*, that is, accustomed to their new quarters. The first thing in the morning by break of day they would be up and away, and always with the wind in their faces. Many a night, when a fresh flock had been recently brought to the farm, the young herd never got to bed, but had to lie on the haystack with his plaid about him for fear of sleeping in. After a time the sheep would become more settled. Still, as the farm was small, with no fences on any side, they required constant watching. While our David was a herd boy, he was sure to have an attack every Sunday night of the rush of noises in his head while sleeping, to which, as before mentioned, he was subject. The reason for his having it on that night more constantly than on others was perhaps that he had had more food that day and less exercise than usual, but his own boyish reflections led him to regard it as a punishment for some Sunday misconduct.

One season his master bought a young colt along with the lambs. It was one of the ugliest creatures that could be imagined, but as it improved in condition it improved in appearance, though it never became a beauty. David often gave it stalks of corn, and occasionally shared his oat cake with it. He and the colt soon became great friends. In the second season of their companionship, he tried one day to get on its back, but it met this attempt by sitting down on its haunches, and letting him slide off over its tail. However, by coaxing, and by sometimes laying his plaid upon it, and sometimes a little turf in addition to the plaid, he gradually overcame its reluctance to being mounted.

As the creature, though thin in the body, was long in the legs, it required some advantage of the ground to enable David to gain his seat. Moreover, as there was neither saddle nor bridle, it needed some skill to sit the animal, considering in general the speed at which it ran up hill and down brae, and in particular the quick turns it made when it came to a ditch that it did not venture to leap. When suspicious of a ditch, it generally slowed a little before reaching it, and the rider was prepared against a sudden turn ; but sometimes it would go bounding forwards to make the leap, then, seeing it more formidable than it had expected, would make a sudden stop or swerve abruptly on one side, with the result that might be expected to the boy on its back. What was most surprising and no less agreeable to the latter was that the colt, after thus throwing him, would stand still till he got up off the ground or out of the ditch, as the case might be, and remounted. No serious accident happened, though, on the occasion of one of these halts, which was more than usually sudden and unexpected, it is probable that David's neck was saved by the circumstance that his head, instead of being dashed upon the hard ground, was plunged over eyes and mouth into soft mud.

He rode the colt long without bridle or rope to guide him. His stick was sufficient, according as he held it up to one side or the other of the animal's head, to turn him the way he was wanted to go. Wishing him to stop, he pulled at his mane and lay backward ; wishing him to gallop, he lay forward and pressed his heels close to his sides. The creature soon came to understand what was desired, and, when in a willing mood, was easy enough to manage. Sometimes, however, he preferred taking his own way, and in such cases the rider was much at his mercy. A time, indeed, arrived when the colt began to think himself the best judge of what was proper for him to do. For the better control over him, a kind of bridle was then contrived, with a piece of round stick for a bit, and a cord for reins, apparatus which could be pocketed when not in use. One incident in the history of this moorland Pegasus must be given as Mr. Robertson himself relates it :—

"At this time the animal was still wholly in my charge, without any restriction as to riding him, and they rather thought that I was too good to him, as they knew that I often took him little presents to eat. It was never known what he could do, till one day the mistress, as expected, was taken ill, and a messenger was sent off on horseback to Strathhaven, about four miles distant, for the doctor. As her illness increased, and there were no signs of the doctor coming, her mother became alarmed lest her daughter should die before he arrived. It was known that the doctor's horse was renowned for speed, and that it had had time enough to have reached the house, so that, from his not appearing, it was feared that the doctor might have been called away to some other part of the country.

"It so happened that, when I came home that evening, I had brought the colt with me, and I was sent off to meet the doctor and hurry him forward with all speed. Away I went at a moderate gallop, and, before I had gone much more than a mile, met him coming along at a good trot. I told him that, if he did not hurry, my mistress would be dead before he got there. The single cart-track was all we had of a road, and he told me to get out of the way with my cuddy and let him pass. 'My cuddy!' thinks I, 'we will see.' Within about half a mile of the house there was a gentle incline uphill, and I

followed the doctor as well as I could, although I did
not try to get close to him, but rather kept a little
back, knowing that there was only one place with
room enough to pass between where we were and
the house. When we reached the top of the incline,
it was very steep down the other side of the hill,
and at the foot we had to cross a ford, and here the
road widened considerably on both sides of the burn.
It was here that I had a strong desire to pass the
doctor and show him what the beast could do that
he called a cuddy. So down we went at full speed,
and we both plunged into the water of the burn at
the same time, but I was the first to gain the road
on the other side. We had then only about two or
three hundred yards of a gentle incline uphill to
the house, where the master was at the garden wall
watching us coming. By the time we reached the
house I was two or three lengths in front, to the
chagrin of the doctor and the pleasant surprise of my
master. The colt was taken more notice of and more
cared for after that, although he still fed on the hill
and remained in my charge."

It was the custom at that time among the farmers,
when a marriage took place, for those who had the
best horses to run a race that was called the Broose.
The name was perhaps derived from the circumstance
that the winner in old times was rewarded with brose
or broth. In preparation for the race, those who were
to ride stood ready mounted outside the bride's house
or the minister's manse, as the case might be, and
the forthcoming of the newly married couple was the
signal for starting. Whoever first reached the young

folks' dwelling-house was presented with a bottle of whisky, with which the happy winner returned to meet and treat the bride and bridegroom and the company. On one of these occasions, there being some talk of the horses that were to run, David's master said that he had a little rough colt (meaning that which the doctor had called a cuddy), brought up among the sheep on the heather, that would beat the best of them, and that could be ridden by his herd without saddle or bridle, boot or spur.

After some good-natured chaffing, it was agreed that the colt should run, and, as the chief interest was in the speed of the animal, and as there were several turnings in the road to be traversed, it was agreed that the use of the pocket-bridle should be allowed. The time came, and David was mounted on the colt, barefooted, but wearing " huggers," which are footless stockings worn to keep the legs from " hacking," that is, suffering from chaps and chilblains. The start was what he most feared, for his dear Donald was not used to being put so suddenly to speed, and the bustle was altogether strange to him. However, he got away pretty well, second of the five that started. He seemed instinctively to know that he was wanted to be before the others, and did his best without pressure, going to the front as soon as the road offered an opportunity, and reaching the goal a long way ahead of all the rest. Great was the hurrahing when his young rider returned and met the company with the bottle of whisky. He was pressed to stay to the feast and share the merriment ; but, considering his habiliments, he preferred to go home. A large piece of pie was sent him, which he candidly confesses to have enjoyed more by himself on the hillside than he could have done in the gay company of the marriage-party.

This affair and the defeat of the doctor's blood horse placed Donald's speed, as a racer, at the top of the list against the whole countryside, and enabled his owner to get a good price for him.

CHAPTER III.

SPORT AND DANGER.

As may well be supposed, parting with Donald was a great grief to his trainer, who not only lost the pleasure of riding him, but, what he valued still more, his companionship. No doubt the colt itself had even greater reason to regret a change which involved its separation from so considerate and sympathetic a friend.

David, however, on his part, though regretful, was not of a temper to be downcast and disheartened by the inevitable. To use a Scotch expression, his loss did not cause him to weary, nor indeed, during all the time of his cow and sheep herding, did he ever find time to weary—to fancy that the times were out of joint, to be bored with existence, or to ask himself the question whether life was worth living.

Though, as we have seen, he was ready upon occasion to join in competitive strife and indulge "the last infirmity of noble minds," he was equally content to find satisfaction in treasures which no one could grudge him. The skins of adders, moles, and mice were prizes to him, and it was not his fault if any escaped that came in his way. He knew the habits and calls and nests of all the birds on the moorland of his neighbourhood, and, since still in old age he can musically imitate many of their cries, it must have been pleasant to hear him piping them out with fresh boyish voice, in the wantonness of youthful spirits, upon the unfrequented hillside.

He became very expert at catching trout with his hands. The mode of capture was called "guddling," and the operation was conducted by the sportsman's lying down over the bank of one of the moorland burns, putting his hands wide apart into the water under the overhanging turf, and bringing them very slowly together. If this is done with sufficient care, when the fish is touched it seldom offers to move away. But the hands must be worked gently about it till you have it fairly within them ; then give it the grip. Otherwise, if you come on the fish too suddenly it is sure to start off. Rod-fishing was seldom tried in these narrow moorland burns except when they were in flood in August and September, when the trout came up to spawn. Then, with a worm for bait, and a strong hair-plait line, as soon as the cork was seen to bob or sink under the water, there was no playing with the fish, he was " wapped," that is, pulled out of the water at once.

On the moorland farms the grouse took heavy toll from the small fields of corn, attacking the crop as soon as it began to ripen, but more particularly after it was cut. This gave cause to a great deal of poaching by the farmers themselves. The birds came to the corn only in the morning at the break of day, and in the afternoon a little before sunset. In the afternoon the full light made it difficult to get near them, as there was always one bird or another ready to give notice of any dreaded object approaching. Of the manœuvres and contrivances for outwitting the grouse Mr. Robertson gives the following account :—

"The way of getting within shot was to creep on hands and knees, keeping the stooks between you and the birds as well as you could, till you were near enough to shoot. If one of them got the least glimpse of you, it would give the alarm note, one chuck or so, for the others to be on the look-out. When the danger became more visible, two or three chucks were given, and when the bird was satisfied that the danger was real, it would utter a rapid series of chucks. Then not a moment was to be lost, if you were at all within reach, for they were sure to be off without further delay.

"A common practice was to hide within a stook, or to set the sheaves round one's self in such a position as to afford the best view of the place to which the grouse were most likely to come. This was best done in the morning, as the birds came in before it was quite light. On one occasion one of the neighbours close by had concealed himself within a circle of sheaves of corn. Another, coming stealthily up for the same purpose, and seeing the top of the first man's nightcap peeping out of the corn, thought it was one of the grouse, and fired at it. Many of the pellets went into the man's head and neck, but, as the other had fired from a considerable distance, fortunately no dangerous wounds were inflicted. The sufferer, however, was never again found concealing himself in a cornfield.

"Another less noisy method of taking the grouse that was practised was by means of rat-traps. A neighbouring farmer had thirty of these, so that he had a better chance of getting game than my master, who was not willing to buy more than the one he had. It was found that when a bird went into the trap, except when caught by the head, it made such a fluttering that it frightened all the others away. It was the same with shooting—the first shot made the whole flock take flight, and they seldom or never returned till the afternoon or the morning, as the case might be.

"I saw that with more traps a greater part of the field could be covered, so as to make pretty sure of getting at least one bird night and morning. I had been accustomed to catch such birds as sparrows and blackbirds with a single horsehair, and thought that the same plan would do for grouse if more hairs were used. Accordingly I prepared a few snares, with six hairs formed into a noose, attaching the hairs to a card about six inches apart, and fixing the snares over the stook of corn in the most likely way for the birds to get into the loops. I found that this answered much better than the rat-traps, besides being of little or no cost and easily carried about. I soon had as many as would cover that part of the field that the birds were most wont to come in at. With the new snare I was very successful, generally having one bird each night and morning, but seldom more for the reason above stated, that the fluttering of the captured bird scared away all the rest. The birds taken were sold to the egg-cadger, a person

who came round weekly with a pony and cart, buying
eggs, fowls, hares, and the like. Sixpence, eight-
pence, and ninepence apiece, were about the prices
he gave for the grouse. None of this came to my
fund, except that sometimes, when the take was
good, I got a sixpence or a shilling. With that I
was quite content, as I got other compensating con-
cessions contributing to my pleasures while others
were at harvest work, at which I also should in
ordinary circumstances have been engaged, since it
was the custom that both cow herd and sheep herd
should give all the aid they could at hay and harvest
time."

The shootings on these small moorland farms were
let by the season, and little or no protection was
given to the game after the 12th of August till nesting-
time. The shooting season seldom lasted more than
two or three days, so the farmer after that time was
left, with little fear of interference, to pick up what he
could, and that with the grouse could only be done at
all successfully by trapping on the corn during
harvest.

As soon as the corn was cleared off the fields, there
was no more trapping grouse. Little more was
thought of sport till the winter, when the snow
covered the ground. Then the hares came to the
kailyaird (or kitchen garden) after nightfall, and there
they were watched, and shot from the window or
other hiding-places under cover. This could only be
done with any degree of success on moonlight nights.

Another mode of hare-hunting was tracking the
animals on the snow. To prosper in this, some

knowledge of their habits was required. The hare would generally retrace the track it came by, often doubling two or three times on the same track, then making two or three great leaps off to one side and burying itself in the snow. In following one of these tracks that had more than one set of footprints, it required careful watching to see the point at which the hare had leaped off. When this was discovered it was almost certain that the hare was lying quite within gunshot.

The old moorland farmers, Mr. Robertson says, believed strongly in the hare as a weather prophet. When the hares did not come down to the kailyairds or low grounds in time of snow, it was deemed a sure sign of approaching thaw, although this might be two or three days before the thaw actually came, and when no other appearance of the weather tended to induce the expectation of it.

Although winter brought its own pleasures and amusements, the sheep herd had more to do in that season than in the summer. In a general way, when the lambs had become accustomed to the hill, he only went and counted them in the morning, seeing that they were all well and where they should be. But in rough, uncertain weather, more supervision was needed.

One winter day in particular David had good reason to remember. It had been snowing the night before. He had been out with the sheep all the forenoon, and went out again to them in the afternoon. The snow again began to fall, and the storm rapidly increased. At length the drifting snow be-

came so thick that he could not see a step before
him, nor in walking was he able to avoid the swampy
ditches and deep "hags" that lay between him and
home. Moreover, it was fast getting dark. He had
not proceeded far on his homeward route, when he
tumbled over into one of these so-called hags, which
are deep water cuttings in the moss. Fortunately it
was dry where he fell, with a sloping bank down to
the water. Under such banks the sheep often take
shelter, and through their constantly rubbing themselves against the mossy wall, by degrees a hollow is
formed. As there was much protection, therefore,
beneath the overhanging bank, young Robertson
thought he would remain a while to see if the storm
would blow over. His feet, and indeed his limbs in
general, were quite dry ; so, rolled up in his plaid, he
fell sound asleep, and did not waken till near midnight. By this time the storm had much abated, and
the moon had risen. The first thing he heard when
he got up was the people of the farm hallooing at
the top of their voices. He soon made a response,
and there was no little joy at the meeting which
forthwith followed, for his people never thought that
they would find him alive.

No doubt there would have been grief enough
among those unpolished peasants over any lad, even
a commonplace or a cross-grained one, that might
have perished on the snow-covered moor in the performance of his duty, but it is very certain that so
to have lost the ready-handed, kind-hearted David,
would not only have cast a gloom over the circle
for the time, but would have long haunted their

minds with sorrowful remembrance.   As things
turned out, the alarm that had been felt about the
loss of the boy, and the delight conspicuously shown
at his recovery, must have awakened on both sides
some extra tenderness of each to other.   It is agreeable to notice how nature, in the hardest and
roughest lives, can provide compensations, when we
contemplate the tired herd-boy placidly sleeping on
the moor in the darkness and the storm, a counter-
part of Shakespeare's finely wrought picture in that
apostrophe to sleep, which he puts into the mouth of
Henry the Fourth :—

> "Wilt thou upon the high and giddy mast
>   Seal up the ship boy's eyes, and rock his brains
>   In cradle of the rude imperious surge,
>   And in the visitation of the winds,
>   Who take the ruffian billows by the top,
>   Curling their monstrous heads, and hanging them
>   With deaf'ning clamours in the slippery clouds,
>   That, with the hurly, death itself awakes ?
>   Canst thou, O partial sleep, give thy repose
>   To the wet sea-boy in an hour so rude ;
>   And, in the calmest and most stillest night,
>   With all appliances and means to boot,
>   Deny it to a king?"

CHAPTER IV.

THE FOOT RACE—TAILORING.

AT this time, before railway trains were running, the cattle bought at fairs in the north passed over Mr. Young's moor in great droves on their way to the south. Mr. Young's farm was the first on the road entering moorland, and by an old Act, cattle from these fairs had a right to rest on the hillside for a short time, but the drovers mostly agreed with the farmer to have them stay all night. In that case they had to be herded, to keep them on the right moor. David was always employed for this purpose, because he knew the ground. His hire for this extra work was generally a shilling, sometimes one and sixpence. This at that period was thought ample for the night's watching.

In those days pockets in the clothes of young lads did not seem of so much importance as they do now. There was much less to put into them. In the belief that silver coins were far too precious to be trusted in any pocket that he had, and for better security, he used to roll every shilling and sixpence that came into his possession round and round with thread till the coin was quite covered. Then he sowed them one by one, as he got them, upon his jacket for buttons. These buttons were regularly inspected to see that all was right, and, in fact, he had richer buttons on his coat than any one in the countryside. They were always taken off at term-time and added to his fee, that is to say, at the half-yearly paying of his wages, to be spent on clothes and other small necessaries. There was generally a small surplus left over, which was invariably sent home to his mother, who, on her part, never accepted it without anxious inquiry whether it could really be spared.

About this time David went with his master to a fair, held in a small village called Darvel, in Ayrshire. The sports were chiefly jumping, racing, and throwing the stone. One of the races was for boys of about his own age, which was then twelve years. The boys had to run stripped of coat and trousers, the entry-money was a shilling, and the first prize a sovereign. Mr. Young said that he would pay the shilling if David would run. He accepted the offer, and in due time thirty boys bounded off for three times round a green field. Before the first round was quite finished about half a dozen had dropped off; by the time the second round was ended, more than half had given up, and before the winning-post was gained, four only were running and all pretty close together. In the end David won by about a dozen yards, the other three being so close together that, to use a conventional expression, they might have been almost or altogether covered by a sheet.

Upon his arrival at home, there was a consultation what was to be done with his pound. His mistress offered him as much of her home-made woollen cloth as would make him a coat, and this offer was accepted. The custom in those days was for the farmers to get the tailors to the house to make their clothes. It was said that this custom arose from a desire to keep the tailors in the straight path of morality, so far as possible, by having the exact length of cloth required cut in the presence of its owner. At the time spoken of the household did not happen to require the tailors. Nevertheless, the owner of the pound was anxious to have his coat. But, as they neither knew the length of cloth required, nor felt disposed to send the whole piece for the tailor to take what was necessary, there appeared to be no help for it but to wait. It is said with some truth that all things come to those who know how to wait, but the waiting policy is not very acceptable to the ardent temper of the young, and perhaps would not be over-wholesome for them if it were.

Anyhow, without weighing the maxims of pro-verbial philosophy, David, who had had a good deal of practice in mending his own clothes, conceived the bold idea of making the coat himself. This piece of presumption he mentioned to his mistress, but she would not hear of it at all, telling him that he would only destroy the good cloth. His own belief was that, by taking to pieces the coat he was wearing, which was a good fit, he could shape the new one by it. In regard to the mere sewing part of his task he had no fear. This idea he brought before his mistress. She saw that the thing was barely possible, but did not believe that he could carry it out, and still urged that he would only spoil the cloth. However, he was strong in the belief that he could manage it quite well, and at once commenced to open out the coat that he was wearing, taking the precaution to mark the pieces with figures that joined each other.

Having got the sewing all ripped out and the pieces carefully folded up, he took them to his mistress, and showed her how easily each piece could now be shaped from the old one. Seeing that he was so determined to do it, and that there was at any rate some prospect of his succeeding, at a convenient time the cloth was brought out, and she helped him in the shaping, each piece being marked as it was cut out to agree with the duplicate of the old coat. This done, new and old were carefully packed up and given wholly into his charge, with a notice that his mistress would have nothing more to do with the matter, and that the responsibility was now wholly on his own shoulders. As he had not calculated on receiving any extraneous help, that information gave him no uneasiness. It being summer-time, his work-shop was the hillside, but, as the time was not all his own, he did the sewing only as fair opportunity offered. By dint of perseverance, he got on bit by bit tolerably well, and within a month he had the coat finished. It might have been done sooner, but that, knowing what criticism would be bestowed upon it, David took great pains to make the work, so far as he could, an exact copy of the original. He first brought it under the notice of his mistress in position upon its maker's and owner's back, and great was her astonishment, upon a close inspection, to find it so well done.

She said that no tailor could have done it better. It wanted just one additional touch. This was to lay the seams down with a hot iron. This finishing performance, which the young workman could not very well have carried out on the open moor, he was enabled to execute within the house. The buttons required had been supplied from an old coat of his master's, and the thread was his mistress's own spinning and dyeing, so that this work of art concentrated upon it the interest and respect of the household at large. It may indeed inspire the youthful members of many a family, in which strict economy is necessary or desirable, to emulate so praiseworthy an example of ingenuity and perseverance.

David's labours, however, in the matter were not yet at an end. He had the old coat to make up afresh, which took him longer than making the new one, and was a more troublesome piece of work, because of the old seams and abrasions of some of the parts. As already mentioned, he had become skilful in mending his old clothes. He did not lay the patch a long way over the hole and sew it down, as was the custom of the housewives, but he cut the piece out round the hole, as he had seen the tailors do, making allowance for what would be taken up by the seams. He found the habit of mending his clothes for himself of much value in saving his earnings, and he always bore in mind the old proverb that a stitch in time saves nine. One point of thrift he failed to acquire, and that was any taste for knitting stockings. It was practised by all the country farmers, and he was in fact allowed yarn as a perquisite for the purpose but he always felt knitting very monotonous, and took no pleasure in any part of the business, except in putting a new heel to a stocking, in which there is something to keep the mind awake.

CHAPTER V.

SMUGGLERS—MISHAPS—LIFE ON A MOORLAND FARM.

WHEN David was nearly fourteen, the time had come when it was proper for him to have an increase of wages. He was already receiving much more than an ordinary herd boy of his class would cost Mr. Young. He now, therefore, obtained an engagement with a neighbouring farmer, who also kept sheep, but on a somewhat different principle. Here only ewes were kept, and the lambs sold when ready for market. David's duty was to look after the sheep every morning, and to assist with the farm work.

Smuggling, the name given to illicit distilling of whisky, was then common on the moors in that side of the country, and the farmers gave assistance with their horses, carting anthracite, or "blind coals," as they were called. These, having no smoke, did not betray the whereabouts of the smugglers when working by day. The malt and barm were brought from Glasgow. At that period there was no duty on the malt, and it could be carried openly at any time, but when the moor was approached it was generally after dark.

When David had been about a year in his new place, one of these smuggling booths settled down on the march, that is, the boundary-line between one farm and another. This had to be attended to, for if one of these places were found on a farmer's ground, he was liable to a heavy fine. David's master had arranged with the smugglers to do their carting as far as it was convenient, and, as he generally worked with the horse, he at first did their work himself. But as David knew the moor well, he had often to go with his master on night work, and at last nearly the whole of it fell to his share. This night work was no easy matter. They often had to go a long way through the moors in the dark without a trace of a road, and it required one well acquainted with the ground to be able to pick a way that a loaded horse and cart could travel. Being sheep herd, and having consequently a good knowledge of all parts of the moor, David was pretty successful at the work. It was no unusual thing for the horse's feet or the wheels of the cart to sink so deep into some soft place that it was difficult or impossible to get them out, until the cart was partly or wholly unloaded. The worst trial he ever had was on one very dark night. On the black peat moss, it may be remarked, the darkness is greatly increased, and on this occasion it was so great that he could not see in the least where he was walking. The cart was loaded with three bags of malt. As they went along, on a sudden over went cart, horse, bags, and all. He was far from help, and the horse could not be left lying while he went to seek for any, so he had to try what he could do unassisted to get him up.

D

With much difficulty he managed to set him free. The animal was very tired, and had had some experience of this kind of work, so he did not struggle much to rise till the word was given him to do so.

With the horse clear, it would have been possible to have gone for help, but our young carter thought he would first try what he could do by his own efforts. He found that the cart was lying on one side and in a favourable position, and as it was, like most carts on the moorland farms, a tolerably light one, he was able to turn it over without much difficulty, the upturned wheel serving as an assisting weight to bring it down to its proper position. He then had to try and find what the character of the ground was that had caused the mishap. He soon found that he had got on to the side of an old turf wall or dyke, as it is called in those parts. He then knew exactly where he was, and that the worst of the way was over. But the three bags were yet to be hoisted on to the cart. He could not, owing to the size and weight, take one of them in his arms and lay it in the cart, nor had he any convenient way of getting one on to his shoulders. To meet this difficulty, he set one of the bags up on end, then lay down beside it and pulled it down on to his shoulder. But when he attempted to rise with it, that was more than he could manage ; he was too much exhausted by the efforts he had made in freeing the horse and righting the cart. Still not wishing to give in, he crawled on his hands and knees with the bag upon his shoulders till he reached the cartwheel. Laying hold of the spokes he raised himself up little by little till he was in an erect position, and then could easily throw the bag into the cart. The other two bags were deposited in it in the same way.

Another misadventure that he had was of a more dangerous character. It shall be described in his own words.

"It looks," he says, "more like fiction than reality, but is none the less true. One fine summer morning shortly after the break of day, I was going home from the moor with the empty cart. I had been up all night, and was very tired. Our way was along the bank of a burn. I was sitting on the edge of the cart, in a state between sleeping and waking. Meantime the horse had come too near the edge of a waterfall, and, as I felt the cart going over, I myself sprang over into the water. The horse and cart came down at the same time, and, most wonderful to relate, in tumbling over sideways both had made a complete somersault, the horse falling on his feet and the cart the right side up, with nothing broken, and no hurt to the horse or myself. The fall might be ten or twelve feet, into water about three feet deep. No doubt the depth of the water helped to save us, but had I been sound asleep and not felt the cart going over, or had I not leaped timeously beyond where the horse and cart fell, I should in all probability have been smashed under them. Fortunately there was a gradual slope from the burn to the level ground, so we made our way out safely, with nothing more than the fright. Riding on a horse, you may trust him and sleep on his back. He will not go over a precipice or run against a post, but he does not seem able to calculate for anything beyond himself. He gives every attention to where he puts his feet, but he never takes into account the wheels of the cart behind him."

In these night wanderings over the moors David's attention, as became an incipient student of nature, was often taken upon dark nights with the luminous state of the soft peaty ground.   One very dark night he was going with a horse and cart over a turfless track of this description.   The horse's legs and his own and the wheels of the cart seemed to be all in a glow of fire.   Nothing, indeed, was to be seen, he says, of the horse and cart but the legs of fire of the horse walking in front and the wheels in the same state following, with his own two fiery legs going side by side—a sight not readily to be forgotten.

In the novel called " Clara Vaughan," R. D. Blackmore describes an incident of this kind as occurring during the escape of Charles the Second after the battle of Worcester.   At nightfall in the New Forest the fugitive king and his escort had lost their way, when one of them, Major Cecil Vaughan, espied a faint gleam familiar to him of old in the waste land round his own estate.   "To an accurate eye there could be little doubt as to the source of the lambent light—flame it could not be called.   It played in a pale yet constant stream on a certain kind of moss, known to botanists, not to me, for the waste lands have been reclaimed.   This light is to be seen at no time except when the air is charged with electricity."
" That strangely sensitive moss follows the course of the sun, and therefore the lambent light can only be seen from the west.   So all the time he could see it—the others never saw it at all—he knew that they

were wending from west to east, which was their proper course."

By the botanists this luminous moss is placed in a genus called *Schizostega* or *Schistostega*. If it be true that it is only to be looked for in damp caves or on exposed moors when the air is in an electrical condition, it will seldom be sought except by the zealous specialist.

The explanation of this curious light, given in the " Class Book of Botany," by J. H. Balfour, agrees very well with the use which Major Vaughan is said to have made of it, as indicating the points of the compass, although one might suppose that the shimmering gleam of the departed sun, which lighted up the moss, would have been as good a guide. " The light," it is said, "given out by some mosses, as *Schistostega osmundacea* and *Mnium punctatum*, depends on optical appearances, and has nothing to do with the development of light from the substance of the plants. In the former, the cellules of the germinating plant swollen into little globules, and in the latter the small drops of water on the leaves, produce a glimmering by a peculiar refraction and reflection of the daylight. The light of *Schistostega* is a delicate emerald green." *

On another occasion David was the victim of a rather more perilous luminosity. This incident he describes as follows :—

" Having to start for coals by three in the morning, and having been early up the morning before, I was afraid of sleeping in, and thought it best, instead

* " Class Book of Botany," third edition, 1870, p. 675.

of going to bed, to take a nap on a chair before the
fire. With a foot up on each hob, I soon fell sound
asleep. By-and-by the fire kindled up and set light
to my moleskin trousers, though through drawers and
stockings for some time I did not feel it. Waking at
last, I tore at the burning cloth, and then rushed out
to a small stream close by the house. I was wild at
the loss of my trousers, as they were the only available ones I had at the time. As all was over quickly,
none of the inmates knew anything of what had
happened.

"When I again sat down before the fire, placing
a foot up on each side as before, the burned leg
was quite bare up over the knee, but I did not see
or feel anything wrong with it. After a while, however, I noticed the skin under my knee begin to
wrinkle. It was now near the time that I was to
start for the coals, which, without trousers, could not
be done. When my condition was made known,
I was supplied with another pair, and, although they
were not the best fit in the world, they served for the
time. Soon after starting I felt my leg a little
uncomfortable and tried riding in the cart, but, the
road being rough, riding was worse than walking.
Blisters rose and broke, and by the time I reached
a village called Darvel, about three or four miles
from home, the pain was most excruciating. Here
I went into a house and asked if they would give me
anything to roll round my leg, which I had got
burned that morning. At the sight of it they expressed the greatest sympathy, and wondered that
any one would let me leave home in such a condition.

I explained that nothing appeared wrong with it when I started. After having it well dressed, I reached home with much less pain. Next day I was fit for nothing, and after that was laid up for some time, with the disagreeable prospect before me that in the healing one leg would be left shorter than the other. It was a very discouraging thought to me that I might thus become a cripple for life, and to avoid this, if possible, I persevered, in spite of great pain, in keeping the damaged leg stretched out to the utmost. Placing my two heels to the footboard of the bed, there I kept them night and day till the danger was past, and as a reward for my martyrdom the contracting action was overcome."

There were many raids made on the smugglers by the excise, although in most cases the smugglers had timely notice of the approach of danger, and it was wonderful how soon they could make a clearance of their valuables, that is to say, of all the plant used in distilling.

In one instance within our hero's experience, two or three hours after dark the smugglers were surprised and made prisoners by the excise officers and a small company of soldiers. Two farmers' wives, who happened to be paying a visit to the bothy or smugglers' shed at the time, were also seized. The still had just been filled with what they called singlings, for the second or final distillation. The smugglers agreed to run it off for the excisemen, wishing, so far as they could, to appear friendly with them. A cart was wanted to carry the spoil away, but, it being so late, it was thought best by the excise

officers to wait till morning, when they would be able
to see where they were being taken, as otherwise it
was possible they might intentionally be led into a
quagmire and be plundered in the dark.

During the night both soldiers and excisemen were
taking a "wee drap" to keep them cheery, and the
night passed with friendly jokes on both sides, whatever the prisoners may have thought inwardly about
the humour of the whole affair.

As soon as daylight appeared, the two excisemen
went to procure a horse and cart, and were directed
to a farm where they were not the most likely to
obtain what they wanted on the shortest notice, the
prisoners having some obscure hope that something
might yet be saved. As the officer in command of
the soldiers had received strict charge, when the
excisemen left, to take care of the prisoners, these
had no hope of making their own escape. In the
absence of the excisemen, the officer was careful of
what spirits he himself took, and did what he could
in an easy way to make his men equally careful; but
the drinking-measure—the end of a cow's horn—
was an ample one, and the spirits were stronger than
the men were used to drink, and these things had
their effect.

In the mean time the smugglers very civilly offered
to give their assistance in carrying their confiscated
goods and chattels some little distance out to a place
which the cart could approach. Their offer being
accepted, they had the opportunity to roll "the
valuables" into a deep ditch where they were not
easily to be seen. The soldiers, it was clear, had

become sympathizers, and the officer believed, or in his helpless position pretended to believe, that the smugglers were giving their help in good faith, and that his only duty was to make sure that the prisoners did not escape. When the excisemen returned with the horse and cart, and saw the general state of affairs, and that there were only a few of the empty worthless movables piled up to be taken away, they were glad to get the prisoners and drunken soldiers into the cart without anything else, letting the two women go free, and sacrificing the spoils, for which indeed the small country cart, filled as it was with living occupants, would have had no room.

It may be guessed, perhaps, as well from other incidents of the narrative as from the ready sympathy between farmers, soldiers, and smugglers in defeating the law, that there was but little prosperity in that part of the country. The farmers had often much difficulty in making their rents out of the farms, and David's master at length determined to give his up, and wait for the chance of getting a better one. His herd, therefore, and other labourers, had to look out for fresh employment.

The conditions of life on a moorland farm at this period and in this district may be better understood by a description of the general type of the farm buildings themselves. They had no ceilings or stair-cases. The byre, the kitchen, the spence, the barn, and the cartshed, formed a continuous line, with no rooms behind or above them, unless sometimes a loft reached by a ladder. One passage, leading from the front to the garden at the back, separated the kitchen from the byre, the entrances to these two facing one another in the centre of the passage. The horses occupied the right-hand corner of the byre, to which they were often introduced through the house passage, while the cows were brought to their stalls through an opposite opening which looked out upon the dunghill.

The kitchen had a small window in front and another at the back, with a place for the peat fire opposite the doorway. The smoke from the peat, as it found its way through the opening in the roof, blackened and polished the rafters. The spinning-wheel, which was ever a part of the dowry of a farmer's bride, had its place in the kitchen. Sometimes the swee, a sort of crane, was attached to one of the walls at a corner, and by this contrivance the huge caldron or cooking-pot could be moved from the fire to a bench at the side of the room and back again. To supply the want of a swee, the pot was sometimes furnished with a peculiar handle, called the "bool" of the pot. The handle near to where it joined the bowl had two circular openings through which a pole could be run, and by this means two of the maids could lift the weight conveniently.

Any one entering the kitchen passed between two box-beds, one of them apportioned usually to the farmer and his wife, the other to some member or members of his family. By the sliding shutter the occupants could be completely closed in. The beds were raised a foot or so from the floor, and the dogs slept under them. In the spence, a room adjoining the kitchen on the right, the few things that might be regarded as household gods were kept; and there also the farm-servants, if there were any, might find sleeping-accommodation. Meals were in common. Master, mistress, and men fed together, and fed alike. For breakfast there was a large bowl of porridge set on the table, with a basin of sweet milk beside it, and a heap of large spoons, such as in those parts were fashioned by the itinerant gipsies out of rams' horns. As soon as the spoons had been scrambled for, each was eagerly dipped first into the basin of milk and then into the bowl of porridge, being conveyed thence to the mouth without the intervention of a plate. Oatcake and occasionally bacon or salt pork completed the repast.

When the nine-o'clock breakfast was ended, the mistress set on the broth for the two-o'clock dinner. In consuming the broth, the family spoons came again into requisition. From the beef which had been boiled in it, the farmer cut off a slice and passed it on the end of a fork to one of the party, and so on in succession till all had been served, each contentedly taking the allotted portion with the fingers. For beef was sometimes substituted "braxy" mutton, which formed, and still forms, acceptable food to the farmers, although it was prepared from sheep of which the life had been shortened by disease. The special methods of preparation adopted made it perfectly wholesome as food, and by many the flavour was well liked. At six o'clock there was supper of porridge and milk.

In winter-time the hours were varied. Breakfast was at eight. Bread and cheese were sent out to the men in the field at noon. Dinner was at four o'clock, when work was over for the day. Supper was at eight, a meal much enjoyed. Potatoes which had been scraped before boiling were transferred from the saucepan to a large bowl in front of the fire, the household forming a semicircle round it. Either with a large fork or the wooden "beetle" the potatoes were mashed up, milk was poured upon them, and then the ram's-horn spoons soon emptied the bowl. Neither in winter nor in summer did the programme include any consumption of beer or wine or spirits. The food, it must be understood, was nourishing in its quality, abundant in quantity, and well cooked to suit the tastes of those who used it and throve upon it. The simplicity of manners at meal-times made up in part by the saving in time for the want of refine-ment, and there was no cause for grumbling where master and man dipped in the same dish with one another.

The literary resources of such a farm were very limited. The regulation stock of books comprised only the Bible, Bunyan's " Pilgrim's Progress," The Shorter Catechism, and Brown's " Proofs." The last work contained the passages of Scripture on which the statements of the Shorter Catechism were grounded. To this library David by some chance was able to add Mungo Park's " Travels," and it will be seen later on that this book made a deep and lasting impression on his mind. In those early days, however, his fondness for reading so secular a book on the sabbath was looked upon with much disfavour.

From " The Monastery," by Sir Walter Scott, a tale of the Reformation period, some sentences may be quoted which illustrate the description above given of life on a lowland farm. Scott does not mention the " swee," but he says, " Tibb watched the progress of scalding the whey, which hung in a large pot upon the *crook*, a chain terminated by a hook, which was suspended in the chimney to serve the purpose of the modern vane. The children," he tells us, " rushed into the spence (a sort of interior apartment in which the family ate their victuals in the summer season)." The spens, or spence, indeed, is variously explained as a dispensary, parlour, or pantry, a spare room, or a guest-chamber, and was probably made to serve many purposes. As to social intercourse, Scott says, " The idea of the master or mistress of the mansion feeding or living apart from their domestics, was, at this period, never entertained. The highest end of the board, the most commodious settle by the fire—these were the only marks of distinction ; and the servants mingled, with deference, indeed, but unreproved and with freedom, in whatever conversation was going forward." Scott, it should be observed, was writing of the sixteenth, not of the nineteenth, century.

CHAPTER VI.

THE LOOM AND THE QUARRY—FARM-WORK AND SELF-EDUCATION.

DAVID'S mother had always wished that he should learn a trade of some kind, whether he kept to it or not. If he did not regularly pursue it, still it might stand him in good stead at some time when no other employment could be procured. Although personally he had no wish to learn a trade, there were several things that inclined him to the proposal, and chiefly a desire to learn to write. That desire was much intensified by the circumstance that he had an impediment in his speech, which was a great hindrance to all intercourse with others by word of mouth. The difficulty which he had to make himself rightly understood gave him much pain, and often, when the proper word refused to come out, rather than stick altogether, he would use another word more easily pronounced, though it might be far from the right or most appropriate one.

In after life among his friend she often referred to this hesitation as "my hamper," although it must be admitted that it has never hampered him either in acquiring friends or in making his meaning and goodwill known to them. No doubt it influenced the character and extent of his vocabulary, by inducing him to employ the simplest words at his command, and a few with a great variety of application. Especially the verb " to get," in his familiar writing, displayed a versatility almost beyond belief. To save the reader the trouble of guessing, some instances may be mentioned in which this verb can be quite legitimately employed. Thus we say, to get on or off, in or out, up or down, to get on in life or up in the world, to get a meal, to get to school, to get a lesson, to get out a word, to get stuck, to get hold of a stick, to get a whipping, to get an answer, to get understanding or riches or into difficulties, to get ill or well, hurt or upset, settled or unsettled, to get insured, to get married, to get children, to get old, to get home. In fact, there are but few circumstances of life in the description of which this verb might not be naturally introduced, and perhaps but few paragraphs of any English book which might not easily be modified so as to embrace it.

In his later life, as might be expected, Mr. Robertson gave up the nervous habit of using a wrong word to supply the place of the right one that would not readily slip over his tongue. He then resorted to another device, which gives a curious quaintness to his conversation, without in any degree interfering with its intelligibility. He interposes, where it suits him, certain stock words, which have no concern in the sentence, but simply fill up a gap or apparently act as a kind of roller over which the impeded word may glide out. To give a single example, when wishing to say, "I remember an American book," he will say with perfect fluency, "I remember *of* an American *also* book." While still a lad, he felt that his stammering would always be a great obstacle in the way of his going into any business for himself. He therefore resolved to learn to write, thinking that in many cases he might be able with advantage to make his pen a substitute for his tongue. Had his stammering not induced him to acquire the art of writing, he is disposed to think that he might have remained a labouring man all his life. However that might have been, he gratefully acknowledges his indebtedness to the impediment in his speech for its leading him on to seek another power of expression. One may be excused for drawing the obvious moral, that half, or haply far more than half, of the hindrances and drawbacks over which men repine as spoiling their prospects in life, might, with a little courage and discretion, be made stepping-stones to success. Even where they are of such a nature as to cripple all energy and enterprise, in regard to these the captive cavalier, softly singing to himself in his bondage, has taught us that—

> "Stone walls do not a prison make,
> Nor iron bars a cage ;
> Minds innocent and quiet take
> That for a hermitage."

Taking his mother's advice, David, who was now about seventeen years of age, arranged to learn weaving. His elder brother, James Robertson, took him on easy terms, and he made good progress.

The new arrangement enabled him to go to an

evening school during the winter months to learn writing, upon which, as already explained, he had set his heart. When the school available to him opened for the evening classes, on the first night only four pupils came forward, on the next night only one more appeared, and the third night brought no addition to the ranks. This was so discouraging to the teacher that he gave up the evening classes altogether. As may be imagined, this was rather disconcerting to young Robertson, who had remodelled his plan of life to a great extent with a view to them. Having resolved, however, to master so much of the art as might serve his purposes, he now bought some round-hand copy lines and some half text, and lost no opportunity of practising. At the same time he got hold of an old letter, the writing in which took his fancy, and he soon left the copy lines to imitate the style of the letter, which he so far succeeded in doing that he could for long after trace an imperfect vestige of the original in his own handwriting.

Weaving, taken up as it had been to subserve a different purpose, was not to his mind. It gave no prospect of advancement. His thoughts often recurred to the saying of a daft woman, who, looking in at a weaver's window, and making her arms go as if she were weaving, cried, "Trotilty jig, trotilty jig, it will be a long time ere you get to heaven off trotilty jig." When he had been nearly a year at the trade, he made up his mind to leave it. He then first engaged with a Mr. Nelson, of East Kilbride. The work in this employment was to remove the soil off

E

limestone, to uncover the limestone for the operations of the quarrymen. The soil had to be wheeled away in barrows to a distance of about thirty yards. This length was divided into three stages. One man filled the barrow, another took it the first ten yards, another the next ten, and a fourth the remainder. The object of this arrangement was to prevent any waste of time between the filling of a barrow and the emptying of it. As David's hands had become much softened at weaving, by the end of the first day of the new work there were several blisters on them. It was the custom at such places, when a new hand was engaged, for all the workmen to do their utmost to overload and oppress him so as to force him to leave. In the case of a young hand they often gained their point.

By the end of the third day all David's fingers on both hands were a mass of sore blisters. In the morning, and after meal times, freshly taking hold of the barrow was, he found, like taking hold of a red hot iron, leaving the handle of the barrow marked with blood. After the first pressure the pain, however, became much less. But the more his sufferings were seen, the more he was loaded, especially by a big soft navvy, when it was his turn to fill the barrow, for all the men changed places once between each meal. There were occasional hints that David might last out till Saturday, while some were willing to bet that Friday would not see him on the ground. These remarks only determined him the more not to give in. He had had blistered hands before without stopping work on that account. Saturday night came,

and when giving him his wages, Mr. Nelson, the contractor, said, " I suppose that you have had enough
of this work, and that we will not see you on Monday? "
Young Robertson asked whether he did not require
him, to which he answered, " Oh yes ! if you wish to
come." No more was said, though David could see by
his looks that the contractor little expected him to
re-appear. By this time his hands were feeling better,
and the Sunday's rest improved them still more.
Consequently, to the astonishment of all, he was
among the first on the field on Monday morning.
The men then seemed inclined to favour him, in
admiration, perhaps, of his pluck and perseverance ;
and at any rate he had no longer any cause to complain.

He did not, however, stay long at this work, nor
from the first had it been his intention to do so. It
was merely a stop-gap, and an employment so very
unromantic that a man of less simplicity of character
would perhaps have suppressed all mention of it.
But Mr. Robertson is free from any false shame of
this kind. In May of this present year, when he was
taking me out for a dredging expedition, on our way
to the boat with a load of pails, bottles, nets, and
dredge, the latter with its heavy chain and rope had
to be wheeled in a barrow. Naturally I offered to do
the wheeling, but my friend of eighty-three positively
refused to allow it, laughingly exclaiming, " Oh no !
I am used to it. You remember the time at the
quarry."

During this rather unsettled period of Robertson's
life, a little incident occurred which may have helped

to foster his taste for natural history, and from which it may also be inferred that he had inclinations very ready to turn to literature and science.

A young man, named John Hamilton, of about his own age, arranged with him to go for a month or so to the harvest. Not much caring whither they went, they set off eastward, and obtained employment at a farm called Spindlehoe, in the neighbourhood of Uddingston. The farmer had but few labourers, and they were all exceptionally good shearers, or, as we should say, reapers. There were two to each ridge. As Hamilton had not had much experience in the harvest-field, it was hard work for Robertson, with an unskilled mate, to keep up with the others.

The two friends took lodgings in the neighbourhood of the farm. Hamilton was a young man of a literary turn, and, as David was by no means averse to reading, they soon discovered that there was a good library at Bellshill, not far off. They applied for and obtained, first, Buffon's " Natural History," then Goldsmith's " Animated Nature," and lastly, Homer's " Iliad," not in the original Greek, but probably in Pope's version. These books they read of an evening and on Sundays.

In the same house was another lodger, a man of about fifty, who professed to hold the creed of the old covenanters, and who did not by any means impress the two boys as being a person in whom amiability was carried to excess. He had been in the house rather more than two years. The lads had very little conversation with him. He seemed to shun them. They saw that he had nothing in common with them, and they did not court his company.

At last the spirit moved this solemn person to disburden his soul to the landlady. He told her that his fellow lodgers were two very bad young men ; that he did not think it was his duty as a Christian to stay in the same house with them ; that from morning till night, on the Lord's day, they had read books which no one but depraved heathens would read ; that he had never seen them with the Bible or " Pilgrim's Progress " in their hands ; that he himself had been a long time in her house, and that it was not a little that would make him leave it, but that it would be an offence to his Master to stay and sanction such proceedings. He concluded by saying that she knew best herself what should be done, but that he would advise her to remember that she would one day have to answer for it, if she harboured in her house two heathens fit to corrupt a whole countryside.

The landlady told the lads of the sermon that had been preached to her on their account.

" Well," David said, " he has been a long time with you, and may continue still longer, while we can only be here for a month or so at most. To-night, when work is over, we will look out for other lodgings."

" No," said the landlady ; " you need not look for other lodgings as long as you are satisfied with my house. Let him go when he likes. I care not although he leaves to-night. Do you know what he wanted me to do—the old hypocrite ? He bought some old cheap oatmeal that he cannot eat himself, and he wants me to sell it to you for good meal, and

to say that he got it from a farmer for wages, and
that he had more of it than he could use. The truth
is, the lying rascal bought it from a shopkeeper in
Bellshill that was selling it for the use of hens. I
told him to sell it to you himself. That is the godly
man that was afraid to anger his Maker, and told me
to mind that I would have to answer one day for the
kind of lodgers I was keeping! I told him that if he
were not pleased with the house, he could leave it,
for I saw nothing wrong with the decent, quiet lads
reading books on God's own works; that my own
father read a great many of these books himself;
and that, as long as the young men were willing to
stay, I·was willing to keep them."

She further added that her lodger had no intention
to leave ; he knew he was too well off where he was ;
that he had tried the same thing before with other
lodgers she had had. " He wants," she said, " to have
the whole house and fire to himself."

Seeing how matters stood between the honest
landlady and this Monsieur Tartuffe, Robertson
stayed on throughout the harvest-time. At the end
of the second week, Hamilton, finding the work too
hard for him, was obliged to give it up and go away.
The two friends had shared between them the
expense of a single bedroom. When Robertson had
to occupy it alone, his hostess kindly offered to take
only the share that he had previously paid, well
knowing how ill he could afford to pay double. It
may well be that if anywhere the history of good
actions has a lasting home, "this that this woman
hath done will be told for a memorial of her." It is

no wonder that she and David parted good friends. He left the ill-conditioned lodger to improve under her influence.

At the age of eighteen David hired himself out as a farm-servant with a Mr. McAsland, at a place called Newlandmoor, in the neighbourhood of East Kilbride. Mr. McAsland was not himself a farmer, but he retained as managers two brothers, from whom he had bought the farm. They were both strong young men, the one six feet and the other six feet two inches in height. They had been left the farm by their father, and had run through their means, not by intemperance or speculation, but by careless inactivity, and were not particularly well qualified to manage what they had undertaken. It was under their direction that David had to work. Mr. McAsland's daughter, a clever, sensible young lady, superintended the management of the house ; and, although she had not been accustomed to such work, was considered to do it exceedingly well.

It was part of young Robertson's employment to take the milk to Glasgow. The horse in the first instance employed for this purpose was very slow, and took a long time to get there, and as long to get back for home work. In course of time the laird, as the proprietor was called, purchased a fine mare, warranted to be an excellent walker, as in fact she turned out to be. But the mare was so exceedingly difficult to work with, that those who tried the task would have none of it, and there seemed nothing for it but to part with her. Yet she was so good a walker, having no match upon the road, that David pleaded for trying her a little longer. This was allowed. In a short time he entered into her ways, and found little or no difficulty in working with her.

The managing brothers, seeing by this circumstance that he was finding more favour with their employer, and having more responsible work with the mare, now began to try every means to be rid of him. They had nothing really to say against him further than that he had not the pith in him to do a day's work, and considering his age there might be some semblance of truth in such a suggestion. Nevertheless, the laird did not appear to pay much heed to their remarks. He was in the habit of going to Glasgow every Tuesday morning and coming back every Friday evening, and he was mostly out with his men in the field on Saturday and Monday.

On one occasion they happened to be carting peat moss from the lower end of a field up to a higher part, to be spread over some tough clay soil. Each of the three worked a horse and cart, and had just time to fill the cart, while the other two were out emptying theirs. As there was not room for more than one to fill at a time, it was proposed that the cart which was being loaded should move off, whether full or not, as soon as another cart returned. No objections were made, and this would be a means, the brothers said, of keeping the whole party more constantly at work. The brothers, as already intimated, were heavy powerful men, and each began to fill his cart with all his strength, emptying it likewise with all speed, and whipping the horse back so soon, that David had not time fully to load his cart, but had to leave, according to arrangement, with only part of a load. He then perceived that the object of the arrangement was to show how much more they could do than he could, and to depreciate him by the contrast. They began to chaff him, saying that his cartfuls would be mistaken for molehills. He made no attempt to compete with them under the conditions of the moment, knowing well that they would not work in the same way in the master's absence. He merely said that to make his small cartfuls more easily seen, it would be better for them to empty their carts on separate ridges, and that they would see better in that way how the comparison stood by Saturday. The brothers thought that there was no occasion for this, but the laird had been hearing and seeing all that had been going on, and for some reason of his own at once sanctioned the proposal. It was adopted without further delay, each unloading his cart on the ridge allotted to him. When the first ridges were filled, they were to follow on with others in the same order.

Next morning the laird, as usual, was off to Glasgow. When work began in the field, the brothers were not showing the same zeal as they had done the day before, while David went on as usual. Accordingly on Saturday, when the laird made his appearance after breakfast, he saw that David's ridges were not the worst clad. Nothing was said, but he seemed to understand well how matters stood. There was no more chaffing on that score, and things went on pretty smoothly, as it was seen that the laird could judge for himself, and that David was allowed in a great measure to have things done as he thought they ought to be done.

About this time a highlandman came to the farm asking for work. The laird, being himself a native of the Highlands, inquired of the man what part of the country he came from. It turned out to be the very place to which the laird himself belonged, and the man's name was McAlister, which was said to be the real or at least the original name of the laird, who had changed it to McAsland. The laird had had a brother who left home when a young lad and had never been heard of since. This he mentioned to the highlandman, who noticed, and did all he could to strengthen, the laird's obvious suspicion that he might be this long-lost brother. He was at once engaged, and much favoured. But work was not Sandy's forte. He became a regular spy, conveying tidings of his mates' doings to his master, with little compunction regarding the truth. But he had not the ability to hold the advantage he had won. It was soon discovered that he was a confirmed and unscrupulous liar, and unfaithful in the extreme to his best friend, the laird.

Sandy had told so many unlikely and impossible stories that the household in general had ceased to believe anything he said, unless it was known to be correct on other grounds. Among other things, he had often boasted how well he could play on the fiddle, and that no one in the Highlands could match him at the bagpipes, and that he possessed beautiful bagpipes, which he had left in Glasgow with his landlady.

The laird had no knowledge of farming himself, and

was very penurious, and suspicious that he would be taken advantage of. He had been told how wasteful servant men were with horses' food, and to prevent any such extravagance he had the allowance of corn measured out for the week. The allowance might have been enough for half-worked horses, but was far from being so for those in full work. In consequence, the animals soon began to lose flesh. To remedy this as far as possible, David, who was quick in sympathy with animals in general, and with horses in particular, rose every morning between three and four o'clock, and gave them a feed of the unwinnowed corn from the barn. Sandy found what he was doing, and told the laird. What followed Mr. Robertson thus describes :—

"One morning when I was coming from the barn to the stable, the laird came out from his hiding-place and caught me by the neck, and said—

"'You thief, you are stealing my corn.'

"'And giving it to your horses,' I said.

"He replied that I had no right to do so, and that it was against his orders.

"That was true, I said, but that I had done it with the best intentions for his interest, and that it was not, as he seemed to think, any advantage to me, but a great deal of unpleasant trouble, and that the only solace I had had was that I was doing good to his horses, and, as I thought, benefiting himself. I said too that, for all that I was giving them, they were still not in the condition that a farmer's horses should be ; and if they did not get their proper food they could not do their proper work.

" 'Well,' he said, 'if you will promise not to waste, I will give you the keys.'

" I replied that I had never done anything to my knowledge contrary to his interest since I had been in his service.

" He answered that he had never had reason to doubt me ; adding, ' There are the keys, and use your own discretion.' "

That little sketch is a gem in its way. It finely exhibits the force of conscious integrity in trying circumstances. Out of an incident that might have been almost tragic in its effect upon a young and sensitive spirit it evolves an innocent and reassuring triumph, and, without noticing how the mischief-maker had been discomfited by the very success of his plot, it contrives to leave on the memory a kindly impression even of the close-handed, narrow-minded laird, since it is undoubtedly one part of virtue in a man himself to be able to recognize virtue and trust it in his fellow man.

Ever, when the subject turned up about Sandy and the bagpipes, the laird endeavoured to support the notion that he really possessed them, while the others always in a jesting way doubted the probability of their ever seeing Newlandmoor. They said that they should above all things like to hear Sandy playing the bagpipes, considering that he was so wonderfully fond of music, although they had never heard him sing, whistle, or hum a tune. The laird seemed annoyed at their continually doubting Sandy's veracity, and they began to think that at last he was himself beginning to doubt the truth of the stories that Sandy had told him. The next time that the bagpipes were questioned, the laird said, "We will put it to the test, Sandy. You shall go down to Glasgow with me to-morrow, and then you can show them whether you can play the bagpipes or not." Sandy did not seem overjoyed at the proposal. When at Glasgow, he took the laird to the Venal in the High Street, and, although he had, according to his own statement, lived in the same lodgings for two years, he could not find the house, and no one had heard of any one of the name he gave being in the Venal. This satisfied the laird. One thing after another now came out against poor Sandy, till he was dismissed in disgrace.

Somewhere about this time an account came in to Mr. McAsland from the miller, for corn which he had ground. As David had always taken the corn to the mill, and brought the meal back, the account was shown to him, to see whether he remembered taking to the mill what was charged for. He took the account to look it over at his leisure at night.

Now it must be explained that he had been trying to learn book-keeping, and for that purpose had three small books ruled with money columns, a day-book, a ledger, and a cash-book. He had made an attempt to include the transactions of the farm, so far as he personally had anything to do with them. Thus he had entered how many times he had been at the mill, with so many bags of corn, and when he had been back for the meal, with dates to all the entries. But there was one load less in his book than there was in the miller's account.

This book-keeping was a new discovery to the laird, and he wished to know for what purpose David was keeping the accounts. When he explained that he was endeavouring to learn the process, the laird raised no objection to his carrying out his object, but wished to see the books again when they were filled up. He was also anxious to know whether the correctness of the entries could be fully depended on. This being guaranteed, he refused payment to the miller for the load that was not entered in the book. The miller was quite wrath at having his word doubted, but the laird would not pay, nor yet would the miller make the required deduction. At length David's books were produced as proof, but the miller held that they would not be accepted as such, since they had only been used for practice in order to learn, and under no responsibility. He maintained that no court would hearken to such evidence. But another circumstance came out, fatal to the miller's contention. Upon closer inspection of the entries it was observed that David had been at Glasgow on the very day for which the miller had made the entry for the disputed load. As this fact could be easily attested, the miller had to give in. In this instance, therefore, David's attempt at self-education won him some credit with his master, to whom it had proved of definite pecuniary advantage. But, it will be seen, he did not regard such attempts by any means with unmixed favour.

It was the recognized privilege of the farm-servants in that side of the country to have nothing to do on winter nights after dark, except that the lads had to clean and supper the horses, and the girls to supper and milk the cows. The rest of the time they could knit, or mend their stockings, or do anything else for themselves. Of this privilege the laird personally did not approve, but as he was seldom or never in the kitchen after nightfall, the servants' doings at night were never interfered with. At this time David's active mind was much in earnest about learning arithmetic. It so happened that a gentleman from Glasgow, who was paying his addresses to Miss McAsland, came to the farm to see her every other Saturday, and stayed over till Monday. As Miss McAsland was often in the kitchen superintending, the gentleman was also a good deal there on his Saturday nights. He was a great help to David with his sums. Every time he came the learner was always ready for more help, and the gentleman was always ready to give it. He promised to bring David some books that would help him ; but, as he happened to tell the laird of his intention, he was strictly forbidden to carry it out, on the ground that it would turn the lad's head from his work. The laird was, as young Robertson thought, very peculiar in some things. His men might do anything, however trifling, in their own odd time or out of it, if it was for him, but nothing essentially serviceable to themselves could be allowed. His creed was that no man could justly serve two masters ; and no doubt, under such a phrase, forgetful of its true import, he concealed from his conscience the narrow selfishness of his own conduct.

There was a fair held in East Kilbride once a year. It was called Sheep Friday, being the remains of an

old sheep market which had now dwindled down to
the attendance of a few scores of sheep and a few
cows from the neighbouring districts. The fair,
however, was largely attended by farm servants as
a holiday, when jumping, throwing or putting the
stone, and other such sports, were much practised.
At one of these fairs David noticed among the sheep
for sale a pretty little parti-coloured lamb, and took
a fancy to it and bought it. He knew that the laird
would not allow him to take it to the farm as his
own on any terms, so he arranged with a farmer
whom he knew to grass it for him for six months.
He did not keep the transaction a secret, and as soon
as the laird heard of it, he went to him, and a conversation followed on this wise :—

"He began, 'I understand that you were in the
trading way on Sheep Friday;' and he added, 'As
you have entered into business on your own account,
it must abstract your mind from your duties to me.'

"'Well,' I said, 'if you think so, I shall remove
that objection. The party who has the lamb will,
I believe, take it off my hands at the price that I
paid for it, and if not, he can have it at what he
thinks it is worth.'

"He said, 'You can think over it.'

"I answered, 'I have already done so.'"

There was no more said about the lamb. David
went to the farmer who was taking charge of it, and
received from him a little more than he had himself
paid for it, so that he was no loser in a money point
of view, though the affair was vexatious.

Although he had been kindly treated the few years

he had been with Mr. McAsland, he saw that he could do nothing for his own improvement, however closely he attended to his master's work. He was most desirous to have as much command of reading, writing, and arithmetic, as would lift him above the position of a common labourer, if ever he obtained the chance of rising. So he now had his mind made up to leave Newlandmoor at the first term, that is to say, at the close of the current half year, and to try and get into a place where he would not be so much bound down. When the time came to give notice of leaving, he was much pressed to remain, with an offer of a good advance in wages, but nothing would induce him to stay.

He was about twenty-one years of age when he engaged with a Mr. Thomas Ballantine, a farmer, about three miles south of Kilbride, his work being much the same as what he had had with the laird. His new master had been at one time one of his fellow workmen. On this farm also there was a "laird." It was not, however, the master, but a young man working under him, who was so designated half in joke, because he was heir to a farm in prospect. This young gentleman was the fortunate possessor of some of Walter Scott's novels, and added to David's happiness by allowing him to read them.

A humorous incident connected with his farm life may here be mentioned. There was a man among them far too fond of going out on the spree. Intemperate mirth would then give way to melancholy and despair, displayed by repeated threats that he would hang himself, or cut his throat. Young

F

Robertson, preferring farce to melodrama for home consumption, at last grew tired of all this, and took an opportunity, when the man was in the tragedy vein, of offering him a knife, saying, " Don't be always talking of it, just do it, and have done with it." "Ah," said the fellow, "you would like it, wouldn't you?" But he did not accept his companion's kind offer, nor did he ever again propose to do himself an injury when David was present.

In his new employment it was agreed that David should be allowed to go on winter nights at eight o'clock, after he had suppered the horses, to a night school at a place called Millwell, perhaps about three miles or so distant, to take lessons in arithmetic. The book used in the schools of the district was "Gray's Arithmetic," in which he had already made some progress, so that he did not need to go every night, but only when his calculations had been brought to a standstill by some stumbling-block. When he went, it was not to take a seat in the school, but just to have his difficulty explained, so as to see how the answer to the riddle came out. This seldom took more than a few minutes, nor did he often need to consult the oracle again sooner than in two or three days, by which time he might have met with some fresh difficulty which he could not master. On the road to school there was a burn to be crossed by stepping stones. In the dark the stones could not be safely used, and often the burn was swollen above them, so that on almost all occasions he had to strip off his shoes and stockings and wade across. As this was many a time when the snow was on the ground, such a foot bath was not particularly pleasant, and it had to be repeated on the homeward journey. Nevertheless the wader was young and hardy. On resuming his shoes and stockings he was rewarded by soon feeling a healthy glow in his limbs. If it was the pursuit of knowledge under difficulties, the chase was not unfruitful. By the end of the winter he had been nearly through Gray's book, and had equipped himself with an accomplishment of solid value, for, as he had to think out most of the problems for himself, he had won, so far as he had gone, a pretty good grip upon the subject.

CHAPTER VII.

COLLEGE—TEACHING—DYER'S WORK—ILLNESS.

IN the year 1830, Robertson's wish to better his
position led him to make what would be thought
almost anywhere but in Scotland a surprising change
in his manner of life. About this time two of his
old playmates had entered college at Glasgow as
divinity students. David, who till now had been a
farm labourer, began to think that he might succeed
in the medical profession, and consulted some of his
friends about it. Of all, however, to whom he mentioned the project, not one gave him the least encouragement, but the reverse. He was too old. He
was twenty-four. He would have to attend college
for seven years. He had not the means to carry him
through. It is little wonder that sober-minded friends
should have discouraged what must have seemed so
rash an enterprise, for it is not every razor that will
cut through a whetstone, however boldly handled.
David himself had some serious doubts as to the
prudence of the step. Yet it appeared to him that,
if he remained at his present work, by the end of
seven years he would in all likelihood have made no
advance, whereas if he could struggle through the

seven years at college, he might raise himself above continuous manual labour, and be able to provide something against old age.

His first intention was to do farm work during summer and go to college in winter, but before committing himself wholly, he went to Glasgow, and called on Dr. Robert Hunter, Professor of Anatomy in what was at that time called the Andersonian University, although it was subsequently agreed that the title of University should be relinquished by this place of education in favour of the Glasgow College, now known without risk of confusion as the University of Glasgow. In Brewster's "Edinburgh Encyclopædia," an article upon Glasgow, published in 1816, gives the following particulars, which are still of interest :—

"The buildings for Anderson's institution are situated on the west side of John Street. The ashlar front is relieved with mouldings, terminating in a balustrade and pediment. The roof being formed into a dome, has a very fine effect. The great hall is of a spherical form, and seated for five hundred persons. The library, laboratory, and apparatus apartments, are fitted up with every convenience.

"The late celebrated Mr. John Anderson, Professor of Natural Philosophy in the university of this city, by his last will, disposed and conveyed his valuable apparatus, museum, and library, and his other effects, to eighty-one trustees, whereof nine were to be tradesmen, nine agriculturists, nine artists, nine manufacturers, nine physicians and surgeons, nine lawyers, nine divines, nine natural philosophers, and nine kinsmen or namesakes, for the purpose of establishing a college in this city, for the arts, medicine, law, and theology. At the professor's decease, his trustees were incorporated by charter, in 1796. Pecuniary and other considerations have hitherto limited the plan to physical science, comprehending natural philosophy, chemistry, materia medica and pharmacy, mathematics and geography. Popular and scientific lectures, from its commencement, were continued to be delivered to both sexes in this institution, by Dr. Garnet, with great approbation, till in 1799 he received an appointment in the Royal Institution of London, which had been formed on the model of this primary institution. Dr. Garnet was succeeded by Dr. Birk-beck, who, in addition to the branches taught by his predecessor, introduced a familiar system of philoso-phical and mechanical information to five hundred operative mechanics, free of all expense, exclusive of the exhibition of an extensive apparatus. Particular models, illustrative of the arts, were introduced. A subscription library, for the use of this class, has been productive of beneficial effects."

With the "celebrated Mr. John Anderson," who thus started a movement of considerable social importance, we need not here further trouble the reader, though there will be another occasion for referring to his rather whimsical will. David Robertson, having obtained an interview with Dr. Robert Hunter, said that he had come to ask his advice with regard to the likelihood of his success as a medical student, consider-ing his age and particularly the impediment in his speech. The professor very kindly took great pains with him, making him read and answer questions and utter such words as he rightly considered difficult for a stammerer to pronounce. He then said that he had had several students with worse hesitation in speaking, who had nevertheless succeeded well ; that he had not the least doubt that, if Robertson acquired the requisite knowledge, he would find a way to communicate it ; that his success would depend on his own industry ; and that, as to his age, that would only make him a few years later in finishing his studies than he otherwise would have been.

David was satisfied with what this clear-sighted friend told him, and without further wavering resolved to make the venture, however it might turn out. It should be borne in mind that Latin was not then considered of the same importance to the medical man as it is now. To be able to read the pharmacopœia was all that was required.

He now arranged with his old playmates referred to above, Robert Miller and John Miller, to try and get a room that would accommodate all three of them. If that could be obtained, they thought that they could manage much more economically than in separate lodgings. They were able to hire an attic with two apartments, abutting against the Cross Steeple, with two windows looking on to the Trongate. They could step out of the windows on to the balcony which ran along the front of the building, and look over and see what was going on in the street below. Bedding David obtained from his mother, and they procured in the town the rest of the not very elaborate outfit which they required.

These little matters being settled, Robertson commenced his studies under Dr. Hunter, the professor of anatomy, by whose advice he had adopted his new career.

The three students managed very well in their new quarters. If they had none to help, neither had they any to disturb them. Each took his turn at cooking and such domestic duties as fell to their several shares. The rooms were very convenient, with water on the stairhead. A little girl who lived on the same landing went on any errand that they required.

There was one difficulty for them in the circumstance that there was only one key to the door, and they mostly came in at different hours. To obtain two other keys to fit the lock would have been some trouble and expense. To meet this difficulty, Robertson thought of a plan that would answer the purpose as well as additional keys, and that would be more secure against pick-locks. On the inner side of the door there was a wooden bar that could be shot into a keeper attached to the doorpost. To two points of this bar he attached cords, by which it could be drawn into and out of the keeper. The ends of the cords he put through holes in the door, so that the bar could be worked from outside. A piece of wood for a latch was also arranged to fall behind the bar when in the keeper, and this latch had to be drawn up by a cord of its own before the bar itself could be drawn back out of the keeper. Under this arrangement, unless the latch were raised, it was of no use to pull at the bar, and, even with the latch raised and held up, pulling the wrong cord would only keep the bar fast instead of releasing it. Moreover, the passage in front of the door was not very well lighted, and the ends of the cords, being placed as far asunder as could be managed, and projecting outside as little as possible, were not readily seen. To pull the cords in the proper order was easy enough for those in the secret, but sufficiently puzzling for any stranger bent on mischief and liable to be surprised in the attempt. The plan answered the purpose of the three students exceedingly well, and they had neither the trouble of carrying keys nor the risk of losing them.

As the summer season was now near its close, the elder of the two brothers, Robert Miller, and Robertson thought that they might add a little to their finances by commencing an evening-school for writing and arithmetic.

The step from the cart-wheel to the college was good, but the farm servant commencing schoolmaster, in order to pay for his own schooling, gives an even more delicious picture of cool courage and a still more striking specimen of the unexpected.

They rented a moderately large single apartment on the ground-floor in a close in the High Street a little above the Cross. They had been fortunate enough to hear of a person who had some old school furniture for sale or hire. They arranged for hiring it on moderate terms. They then thought that, if they could sleep in the schoolroom, they could save the rent they were paying for the attics, and, as may be supposed, they had good reason to appreciate the old proverb, " A penny hained is a penny gained."

The change from the attics was the more necessary, as the younger of the brothers, John Miller, had taken to himself a wife with a view to bettering his position, so that the rent now fell upon two instead of three. Although it was not a heavy rent in itself, the change of incidence was quite sufficient to tell heavily on their small means.

In the new room there were two large wall-presses, the one suited to hold their food, the other their cooking apparatus. They had heard of folding beds, and thought that, if such a one could be procured, they would be completely equipped. Hunting among the brokers' shops, they chanced to find what they wanted—a bedstead, which, when folded up, looked like a wardrobe. The first thing they did was to paint on it " Academy Library." This innocent piece of deception does not appear to have troubled the conscience of either the medical or the divinity student. On the contrary, they rejoiced in it, and felt that they were now all right. They folded down their bed at night-time, slept comfortably in it, rose in the morning, folded the bed up again into an Academy Library, washed themselves, made break-fast, and were ready to go to their college classes. They both shared in the domestic work as before. It was important that this should be done in the shortest time possible. In the matter of boiling potatoes, Robertson found, by experiment, what quantity of water was required to "boil dry," that is, entirely to evaporate just by the time the potatoes were sufficiently done. The small quantity of water needed only a little time to reach the boiling point,

and the high heat was all the sooner applied to the
potatoes. To increase the temperature, these were
wrapped in a wet cloth, and a weight was put on the
close-fitting lid of the pot. Practically, the young
housekeeper seems to have made an independent
discovery of the process well known to housewives as
that of "steaming."

David's colleague, Robert Miller, wrote a beautiful
hand. He prepared, as specimens of his writing, a
number of large cards, announcing the opening of the
school. They got them put into a number of shop-
windows about the neighbourhood. The fine handwriting attracted notice, and, starting with a few
scholars, they soon had a pretty good class. Robert
Miller took the writing, and David Robertson the
arithmetic. They got on very well, and at last had
little space to spare for more scholars.

When the winter session was drawing to a close,
and the evening school with it, Robertson had to
consider whether it would be possible for him to
continue his college classes during summer. It could
not be done without income from some source or
another. He thought of many things. The great
difficulty was to meet with such an employment as
he could leave during his class hours, and also one
that would not make his clothes unpresentable at
college, seeing that his changes of raiment were far
from numerous. After several applications, he obtained
an engagement with a Mr. Douglas, dyer and
renovator.

Although this occupation was taken up merely to
put bread into his mouth while he was preparing for

a professional career, it is evident that he gave himself to it with his usual conscientious earnestness. There is no need to ask his own opinion on this subject, for, besides subsequent events which speak very clearly on the subject, there still exists an old note-book, in which he entered descriptions of the processes used in the trade ; and this book testifies to the method of a man determined to be master of his subject.

Naturally, under the arrangement made with Mr. Douglas, his wages were very small ; but that was compensated for by his being free at all his class hours.

Lodgings were the next important matter to be looked after. He thought of a very decent family, named Malcomson, on the Calton, to which he had been accustomed to take butter and milk when he was with the McAslands. He called on Mrs. Malcomson, and told her what he wanted, and that he could not afford to pay much. He was not altogether a stranger to her, having, as just mentioned, supplied her for a considerable time with farm produce. She had three boys at school, and she said that if he were willing, and could spare a little time night or morning, to help the boys with their lessons, that would pay for his lodging. He said that his spare time was not much, but that he would do what he could, and would prefer to pay something besides. She answered that that matter could be settled afterwards. He considers that he was fortunate in getting into this house. Perhaps good character had more to do with it than good fortune. Both Mrs. Malcomson and her husband were exceedingly kind. Knowing his circumstances, she made every penny go as far as she could, though indeed there was not much to decide on. His food, although abundant, was of the plainest kind. Markets at that time were in his favour. Potatoes were being retailed at sixpence a peck, a measure which contained two stone and a half, or, in, other words, thirty-five pounds' weight. Buttermilk was a penny per Scotch pint, equivalent to two quarts English measure. Butter was ninepence a pound. Oatmeal was about the same price as it is now, from two shillings to two shillings and fourpence a stone. Tea was not included in his dietary, nor butcher's meat of any kind ; and, during all his time at college, the cost of his food never exceeded two and sixpence a week. To modern notions this might seem pretty near the starvation point ; but Mr. Robertson says it was not so. He had always as much as he could take, and it kept him in robust health.

At this time cholera first made its appearance in Glasgow. Medical students were offered a guinea a week to assist in attending upon patients. To a young man whose resources were so small as David's were such a sum was a great consideration. He offered his services, and was accepted. But there was one reason which made him hesitate about using the opportunity, namely, the risk he would bring upon the family with whom he lodged. He acquainted his landlady with what he proposed to do and suggested that it would be better for him first to look for lodgings where the risk would be less. His friend Mrs. Malcomson saw the danger for her own family, but she observed that the risk would be still greater for himself wherever he went to lodge, and pointed out that he must also consider the result of his coming in contact with the workers at Mr. Douglas's establishment, where he spent the greater part of his time. In the face of so many obstacles he made up his mind not to attend the cholera hospital.

Some time after this he caught a fever, and was very ill. When he had reached the recovery stage, with every prospect of getting well, the doctor judiciously pointed out that there was much more danger now of his communicating the disease to the family than there had been in the first stages of his illness, and recommended that he should be taken to the infirmary. His landlady would not hear of the proposal. She said that, if the case had been with one of her own family, she would on no account have sent one of them to the infirmary, neither would she send him. He would have liked well enough to have stayed where he was, but, seeing the danger of illness, or even death, to which he might be exposing the family of his kind landlady by staying, he insisted on being removed, and this, after some further arguing, was agreed to.

Unfortunately, just after his removal to the infirmary, he had so serious a relapse that little hope was entertained of his surviving. He was for a considerable time unconscious, and his recovery was slow and tedious. As a medical student, he received not less but, if anything, rather more than his fair share of attention, and had, moreover, the privilege of a bedroom to himself.

When at length he was a little better, he was much disturbed with the appearance of people coming into and going out of his room, and had a difficulty in distinguishing between real persons and the imaginary. The doctor explained to him that this was caused by weakness and the state of his brain, which could not distinguish between the image of the eye and the image of the mind. It was not that the appearances caused him any fear, but they kept him from sleep, for he saw them even when he shut his eyes and in the dark, although they were more lifelike in daylight, and when his eyes were open. His bedroom was very quiet, a thing favourable to his condition at one time, but afterwards too lonely, as he saw the nurse only a few times a day and the doctor on his routine visits. To help to take his attention off the fancies that disturbed him, he was now therefore removed to the large ward among the other patients. There he had much more of reality to engage his mind, and had visits from the nurse more frequently. The phantoms soon became less and less frequent, till they left him altogether, at least in the daytime when his eyes were open. By degrees he was once more greatly improving in health, being able to walk about the ward and take his food with some measure of appetite.

After so protracted a stay in the infirmary he began to long for home, and told the doctor of his desire ; but the doctor said that it was too soon for him to leave, and when next day the impatient patient again argued the subject, he still held that it would be safer for him to stay where he was for a few days longer. After two or three days' interval, one morning he dressed himself ready for leaving. When the doctor came round and saw his intention, a colloquy ensued, which Robertson had good reason to remember, and which he records as follows :—

"The doctor said, 'If you go now, you will most likely be back again.'

" I answered that if I were once home, I would not be back again, come what would.

" He wished to know if I had any complaint of not being properly attended to.

"I said that I had none, but the reverse ; that I had been very kindly treated, and every attention had been paid me, but that I had taken a longing to be at home, and to go out into the green fields which were close to my mother's door.

" ' Well,' he said, ' you must take care.' "

Accordingly David left the Royal Infirmary and made his way home in a coach to Merns, the village in which his mother had been living for some years past, at a distance of about six miles from Glasgow, on the road to Kilmarnock. It proved to be a case of most haste, worst speed, as the experience of the physician had foreseen. Although on reaching home David felt tired and nothing more, after he had got to bed an unpleasant pain began to make itself felt in his neck at the back of his head. By the morning the pain was much worse and extending upon his head. A doctor was called in, and he at once pronounced it to be erysipelas of a bad kind, as it turned out in fact to be. It crept up over his head, causing great pain, down over his brow and face, shutting his eyes quite up in its progress down to his neck, whence it had started and where it stopped. There was as little hope of his getting through with the erysipelas as there had been at one time with the fever. The doctor said that, if his constitution had not been unusually good, he could not have survived the last attack. He was again very much reduced, and this time it was long before he had any desire for food ; and between the two, fever and erysipelas, it was fully a year before he could return to his college work.

Many of his certificates of attendance at lectures are still in existence. It is largely due to wifely care that these cards have survived the changes and chances of between fifty and sixty years. Apart from any biographical interest, they have a value as showing that the training of a medical student in those days was no perfunctory affair, opening the door of the profession to any chance comer.

The certificates vouch that David Robertson attended courses at the Andersonian University, in Anatomy, theoretical and practical, under Dr. Robert Hunter, from May 4 to October 26, 1831, from November 8, 1831, to April 25, 1832, and from May 8 to October 25, 1832 ; lectures on Surgery, under Dr. James Adair Lawrie, from May 8 to October 30, 1832 ; on practical Chemistry, under Thomas Graham, F.R.S.E., from May 8 to August 1, 1832, and from November 5, 1833, to April 25, 1834 ; on Materia Medica, at the Glasgow College, under Dr. Richard Miller, from November, 1832, to April, 1833 ; and that he attended Dr. Lawrie on his daily visits to

G

his patients in the Glasgow Royal Infirmary for a period of three months prior to February 1, 1835.

He adds from memory that he also attended the lectures of Dr. Brown, Professor of Midwifery, and served the required time as a dispenser in Dr. Forman's shop, in Bell Street. The certificates are merely formal, but on one of them Dr. Graham goes out of his way to add a special note that his pupil had " pursued the study of chemistry with unremitting assiduity."

CHAPTER VIII.

IT will not have been forgotten that, to support the expenses of a long college career, Robertson had become assistant in the establishment of a dyer. Here as elsewhere he seems soon to have found himself on a footing of familiarity and confidence. Mr. Douglas and his family often went to the seaside, many delightful points of which are so easily accessible from Glasgow. One very pleasant spot in the Firth of Clyde is the island of Great Cumbrae, not unknown to fame for the cathedral and theological college, built at great expense by the late Earl of Glasgow, but now for some reason left in melancholy disuse. On the southern shore of this island is situated the favoured watering-place, Millport, with which Mr. Robertson's scientific pursuits and many happy days and years of his life have been connected. This is how his acquaintance with it began. It was to Millport that Mr. Douglas often resorted with his daughters, and David, when not engaged to visit his mother, was not unfrequently invited to go with them.

What with helping boys in their lessons, steeping

faded fabrics in the dyer's vat, practising surgery, and studying medicine, Robertson must in general have had his hands pretty full, and these off days, among the sea breezes and charming scenery, enlivened too by feminine companionship, must have been very refreshing.

Shells were plentiful in the island then as they are still, and gatherings were made, but it must be confessed they were devoted to a not very scientific object. With *Littorina obtusata*, a species of periwinkle, and the dog-whelk, *Purpura lapillus*, Robertson worked out, upon a signboard six feet long, the name of his employer and his occupation, setting off the inscription on a background of other shells, and flanking it with figures, one of which was a chameleon, wrought in a kind of mosaic, this animal of changeful colouring being chosen as emblematic of the dyer's trade. When the signboard was put in the window, so many persons used to congregate on the path to look at it that the police said he must remove it. This he refused to do, since it was in a perfectly legitimate position, and it was their business, he told them, not his, to keep the footway clear. A different view of the position appears to have been recently taken in America; for, when an enterprising advertiser in New York took to dressing the heads of a party of seven sisters in his shop window, the authorities interfered, owing to the crowd which assembled blocking the thoroughfare, and we are told that, the question being disputed at law, "the court considered such an exhibition highly sensational and the consequent obstruction a public nuisance." This,.

however, is a piece of judge-made law, not easily reducible to any fixed principle.

In those days Robertson had not learned to value marine objects as treasures of natural history, nor did his various employments leave him much leisure for that pursuit. Still, even then it had its attractions for him. The first glow-worm, *Lampyris noctiluca*, that he had ever seen, he obtained at Millport. It was a great prize to him. He had many a night's hunt for more specimens of it. They were by no means common. Few of the natives had ever either seen them or heard of their existence in the island. He was much interested about the source of the light, finding that it proceeded from a part of the body on the underside of the abdomen, which the insect turned up when it showed the light.

The branches of science, however, to which his attention at this time was more especially directed were anatomy and chemistry. The various processes which the dyer makes use of could scarcely fail to interest so observant a mind in chemistry, and if the readers of this biography were likely to be in any great proportion dyers and renovators, there would be some satisfaction in quoting from the five hundred and fifty notes and recipes in his common-place book, which testify to the close connection between the trade and the science. But analyses of indigo and cochineal, the description of madder, its uses, and the mode of preparing it, or even the simple directions for dressing silk and satin ribbons and restoring crape, would here be out of place. The technical details for changing a Prussian-blue jacket to brown, and a dark claret silk gown to a fine ruby colour, would appeal only to the specialist.

While chemistry attracted him on the side of his trade occupation, anatomy seemed to be an essential and principal branch of his study as a medical practitioner. This also suited his natural inclination towards zoology. Dissecting animals of various kinds occupied a good share of his spare time. In place of the skins of moles and snakes which had pleased him as a boy, he now had skeletons of mice and birds and frogs.

It had been mentioned at one of the college lectures that the frog's heart continues to beat some time after it is taken from the animal. It will be borne in mind that no scruples had as yet arisen among the general public, and still less among medical students, on the subject of vivisection. Accordingly, one day having procured a frog by the side of a little burn or brook, he bound it down on the grass and took out its heart. This, as the lecturer had told his class, continued to beat after its separation from the body. "But what followed," Mr. Robertson remarks, "was rather astonishing. The animal, being released, leaped into the water and made its escape! This is a fact that few people will believe, and I have seldom ventured to speak of it." It was undoubtedly a heartless proceeding on the part of the frog!

In about a year after his recovery from the illnesses mentioned in the preceding chapter, Robertson was well through with all his classes. He was now over thirty, and in one sense of the word had life yet to begin. In the apothecary's shop he had had a good opportunity of dispensing medicine to persons of various ranks and conditions. With the Royal Infirmary he had become acquainted in more than one capacity. He had satisfied all the preliminaries for obtaining his diploma, and for the examination, which he had no doubt of being able to pass. But for some time past there had been a disturbing element in his mind. Surveying the profession from more than one point of view, he had begun to perceive that "it is not all gold that glitters." To use his own words about this critical period :—

"I had reasoned with myself," he says, "that I had not any means of my own to make an independent start, and that, if I struggled on till I was able to do so, the class of patients I should have, at any rate to begin with, would be much more numerous in their persons than their payments. Then there was another phase of the matter to be contemplated. In all the duties of the profession one is brought face to face with pain to a more or less distressing degree, nor is there any hour, night or day, that one can call one's own. But the greatest consideration with me was that all depended on myself. On the other hand I thought that, if I got into business, even in a small way, it might by industry and close attention increase and enable me to employ other hands as well as my own, and should illness or death overtake me the business might be carried on without me. I was in good favour with my employer, Mr. Douglas, and his family. I had entered into an engagement with one of his daughters. He had, besides the dyeing establishment, a china and earthenware shop in Jail Square, Glasgow, in which my betrothed was an attendant.

"All had advised me, as before stated, not to enter the medical profession, and all now advised me to abide by it. But my determination was fixed, and nothing would now induce me to become a medical man.

"I had set my mind on having a small shop in the same line as that in which my betrothed was already employed. She could manage it and I would continue in my present employment, which now would have all my time, and I should have more wages, which would enable me to keep the house, leaving the profits of the shop to pay rent and improve stock. A shop and upper flat for dwelling-house were taken on the west side corner of Jail Square, at a rent of twenty-five pounds a year. I was free of debt, but my whole stock of cash was only seven pounds, to marry, to furnish my house, and stock my shop. Still I did not despair. I had had a good lesson in economy, and I had no pride to sustain, and I had confidence in our combined energies."

It may be guessed from this recital that it was not infirmity of purpose that made Robertson, at the eleventh hour, so to speak, give up the plan of ambition to which he had devoted so much energy and self-denial. Though he mentions various sage reflections as affecting his decision, it is probable that he asked his heart one famous old question which outweighed them all, "Will the love that you are rich in make a fire in the kitchen?" Clearly a young medical man with a crowd of pauper patients could not hope to support a wife merely by the wealth of his affection, and even the influx of fees might, as he prudently foresaw, at any moment be prematurely ended by one of the many accidents to which his profession would expose him.

It must not be supposed that he was in any way influenced by want of ability or knowledge. So far from that being the case, he was so highly thought of by his medical teachers that they pressed him at any rate to pass the examination for his diploma, for which they knew him to be perfectly well prepared ; but he declined to seek an honour which seemed to his mind to demand a return of services which he would not be in a position to render.

Proverbial philosophy pronounces rather strongly against those restless persons who try first one thing and then another, and never seem to settle or succeed in anything. The poor results which such men often have to show at the close of their muddling lives are considered a proof that change is mischievous. But the same argument might be used with tenfold force against remaining stationary, in proportion as the numbers are far greater of the men who spend all their lives in the narrowest grooves with results equally poor. Lads are sometimes forced, by the mistakes of themselves or of their friends, or under some fancied necessity of circumstances, into professions or positions for which they are unfitted or in which they are unhappy. Once there, there they remain as if spell-bound, not knowing that the new cord and the green wyths and the weaver's beam that holds the web into which the very hairs of their head seem to be interwoven, are all phantoms, imaginary fetters that would disappear from a man that would open his eyes.

Be the matter of principle what it may, Robertson never found cause to regret either his bold resolve to become a physician, or his almost bolder resolve, by a fresh change of plan, not to become one.

Though his capital was very small, in those days there was much more of the coarser kinds of earthenware sold than there is now, and a few pounds' worth, in common saleable things, made a considerable show. He painted and lettered the outside of his shop in his own spare time. Miss Douglas's family supplied the little household furniture that they at first required. The fittings of the shop and counter belonged to the landlord, and with a few alterations suited their purpose. The marriage took place in a very quiet manner. There were no grand relations to offer the use of a country seat for the honeymoon ; there was no spare cash to enable them to spend it in a series of strange hotels either in Great Britain or abroad. But they spent it very agreeably, nevertheless, doing the most they could for the welfare of their new undertaking, and putting things in the best possible order for the opening day.

CHAPTER IX.

A YOUNG wife and a new business, calculated as they were to absorb his attention, did not wholly abstract Robertson's from more strictly intellectual pursuits. It was about 1837, the year of his marriage, that he began to be a naturalist, if we may appropriate that term to the man who studies and observes, collects and describes, not with any commercial or professional aim, but for the advancement of science either in his own mind or the minds of others. The commencement he made was by attending a course of evening lectures on Geology. These were delivered by Mr. John Craig, author of " The New Universal, Technological, Etymological, and Pronouncing Dictionary of the English Language." At that time Robertson had not entertained any particular preference for one branch of natural history over another ; but as the carboniferous shale heaps were plentiful where he had spent most of his early days, and as he had, although without any very definite aim, gathered fossils from them, he now felt the more interest in these lectures. At the close of the first season they were given up, and so also for a time was his study of geology.

The catching of butterflies, which attracts and

introduces so many to entomological studies, had never aroused any particular enthusiasm in David. It was therefore quite by way of exception that one Sunday morning, when his wife and he were taking a walk on Glasgow Green before church time, he caught a red butterfly and a white one, *Vanessa urticæ*, the small tortoise-shell, and *Pontia brassicæ*, the large white butterfly. For want of any more suitable receptacle, he stuck them with pins on the inside of his hat. He and his wife then went to church, and had been in their seats for some time when he noticed that a lady appeared to be looking at him with a kind of mischievous smile on her face. He then remembered the butterflies, and to be sure, there they were both fluttering on the crown of his head. Neither his wife nor he stared much at the people in church for the rest of that forenoon, nor did they venture to show their faces there again in the afternoon. No catching of butterflies on Sunday has to be chronicled hereafter.

His chief thoughts at this period were not devoted either to fossils or insects. Early in the morning he used to go to one or other of the Firestone potteries, to select such goods as were wanted for the shop. He never ordered more than there was cash in hand to pay for. By and by some of the travelling dealers began to drop in for odd things. There were always some new shapes or patterns being made at the potteries, and for these the demand was often greater than the supply. Robertson being a confirmed early riser, and going the first thing in the morning when the ware was taken out of the kilns, could generally get what he wanted. The fact of their having such goods in stock drew more and more of the peddling fraternity to them for these novelties. Still there was not sufficient variety to obtain their whole custom, and for giving them a part of it the pedlars met with black looks at the other shops from which they were still obliged to procure some of the articles they needed. At the same time, the work was becoming too much for young Mrs. Robertson to manage.

For David to give up his situation and the pay it brought in was a serious matter, but there was no help for it. His father-in-law had a small printing-press, which he was willing to let him use, and which he turned to account as follows. With it he printed some hundreds of small bills, which cost him little more than the price of the paper. They were only about four inches square. In them it was stated that the lowest price would be asked and that no abatement would be made, so that the child or inexperienced person would have the goods at the same price as the most experienced dealer. His plan was to begin to distribute the bills first on the south side of the Clyde, commencing at the east, and taking street by street westward, till he had gone over the whole south side of Glasgow. He engaged four clever boys and went with them, sending two up each side of the street to take house about, and serving them with parcels of bills during the progress of the expedition. They left home after breakfast and did not return to dinner, but got some milk and bread on the way. By the time they quitted their circuit for home, they had reached as far west as Jamaica Street Bridge. The bills they

had distributed presently increased the trade so much
that he had never need or time to go out with more.
He was now at the potteries every morning, but still
laying off his orders just to the amount that he had
cash to pay for them.   He had resolved on no account
to be misled into getting into debt, and kept his
resolution—surely one of the chief secrets, not for
building rapidly a mighty fortune, but for securing
temporal happiness and peace of mind.   Under this
system their business grew, and their regular and
prompt payments gained favour that was of much
advantage to them.

His wife's sister, Grace Douglas, having married
Mr. Daniel McDougall, she and her husband took
over Mr. Douglas's china and earthenware shop in
Jail Square next door to them.   They forthwith
became great rivals, though very friendly ones.   The
two houses did not follow the custom general in the
trade, of giving their orders by letter.   The two
brothers-in-law went personally to the potteries and
carefully selected what they wanted.   When particular things were scarce, as was often the case, by being
on the spot they were sure of securing a good share,
as Robertson had found in his earlier experience.
There was a pottery at Cartsdyke, near Greenock,
which they both attended once or twice a week.
Since it was obvious that in such cases one could
very well do the work of both, they thought that it
would be a great saving in many ways if the two
houses were in partnership.   After due consideration
this was agreed to, and the firm became Robertson
and McDougall.

Up to this time the business had been confined, with few exceptions, to goods from the home potteries. This laid them under great disadvantage, from their not having the variety of English goods which some competing firms were able to offer. Though their trade was limited to the commoner class of goods, their dealings were in a great measure wholesale, supplying the small shops and itinerant dealers. As with the growth of their trade they felt the want of English goods more and more, and as the new alliance made the absence of one or other of the partners feasible, it was now resolved that Robertson should go to the Staffordshire potteries. He did not know much about the goods that he was to purchase, further than what he had seen in other places of business in Glasgow. They had, moreover, very little capital to spare from the immediate requirements of their trade at home. But, as it was only a few odd leading things that they wanted, and a few samples of anything new, that they could order from if they saw they were likely to take, it was not much money that was required. The chief object was to find out where and by whom such and such things were made so that they could order when needed. Accordingly the senior partner left home with twenty pounds.

In 1841, the year of this expedition, trains were not yet running from Scotland to England, and the passage from Glasgow to Liverpool was commonly by steamer. The boat that Robertson went by left on a Saturday, at 8 p.m. The night turned out to be rather stormy, and, as he had never been on the sea further than from Glasgow to Millport, about forty miles, the greater part of that distance being in the river Clyde, he was no great sailor. By the time they reached Ailsa Craig, he was frightfully sea-sick, and feeling as if he did not care whether the vessel went to the bottom or not—a sentiment with which so many of us know how to sympathize, although it is said that any actual display of a disposition on the part of the ship to go down puts the sentiment to flight, and makes the sufferer really anxious to keep afloat.

The vessel arrived safely at Liverpool about 8 a.m. on Sunday, or as David had been accustomed to call it, Sabbath morning. Although he took a comparatively liberal view of the privileges of that day, and had once even been lured into capturing butterflies in the course of it, none the less was he now much surprised to see the windmills all going at full speed, and, when he went ashore, to hear the clank of hammers and the noise of machinery in the workshops, and to notice other places of business open. Upon inquiring, he found that certain trades kept their places open on Sunday till breakfast time, and some others for the greater part of the day.

He had Sunday to spend in Liverpool, and had time to take a walk in the suburbs. There he was still more surprised to see men working in their gardens, others going with their baskets and rods to fish, birdcatchers with their cages and call-birds, and in general a scene showing that Sunday was not viewed in the same light in England as it was in Scotland.

On Monday, by rail and coach, he reached the

Staffordshire potteries. The account of his adventures there must be given in his own words :—

"Here," he says, "my hardships began. A milky way of potteries! I had no guide to help me to find the things that I wanted ; besides, I had very little knowledge of the trade, only there were a few things that I knew that I specially wanted, and was resolved to hunt till I got them. Each manufacturer in general was confined to a special class of goods, which made it much more difficult to find what you were in search of. The first place that I went into, the salesman attended with open book in hand to take my order, but they did not seem to have anything in my way. After calling on a few others with the same results, I at last came to one place that had some of the goods that I was seeking for, and I there gave a small order. When it was paid for, I asked the young man who served me if he knew where such and such things were made. He said that it was against their rules to give any information regarding what other manu-facturers made, but, if I went to a Mr. Hamilton's, I would get several of the things that I had named.

"As soon as I entered Mr. Hamilton's warehouse, I was delighted to see the chief things that I was in search of. I was attended to by Mrs. Hamilton, a very courteous person. She soon saw that I did not know much of the trade, but not like many under the same circumstances who take advantage of those who cannot judge for themselves, on the contrary, she seemed to try only to put things into my hands that would suit my market. It was here that my chief opponent got most of his goods, and, from some

H

remarks that she made, he was no great favourite. He had been making a great stir selling gold-gilted teapots at two and sixpence and three and sixpence each, which were considered a great bargain. They were what is called 'seconds,' that is, goods less or more imperfect. I noticed the same on a large shelf near the ceiling. I asked the price of them. She answered, if I took them all I could have them at sixpence-halfpenny each. The price astonished me, and I said at once that I would take them all. They were taken down on the floor, and the number and the bulk far exceeded what I had calculated on, and would, I feared, take more than all the money I had brought with me to pay for them.

" It was now closing time, and Mr. Hamilton had come in from the works to take his good lady home. They asked me where I was staying, at the same time inviting me to go home with them to tea. I accepted somewhat reluctantly, seeing that I was quite a stranger to them, neither had anything been said of the position that we were in at home. After tea I was surprised to find that they had sent to the hotel for my luggage, and that I was to stay over the night with them. I did not sleep much that night, thinking on the large lot of teapots and the little that I had to meet all my demands. Next morning, when we went over to the warehouse, I said to Mrs. Hamilton, if she would pack up the teapots and lay them aside till I got home, I would send the money, as I would require the most I had for other goods. She said that I might let the whole of their account stand till I got home. One thing

I specially wanted, that was what was called in the trade black Egyptian teapots. She directed me where I would get them, and they were to send the account to Mrs. Hamilton not later than noon, and she would pay them. She said in that way she would get the same discount for me that they were giving to larger buyers, which she did.

"This was my first venture to the English potteries, and a very successful one it was. We found that the goods from Mr. Hamilton had been sent off on the day that I had left. Many subsequent visits I had to the potteries, and Mr. Hamilton's house was always my head-quarters, and the connection between the families is still kept up."

Mr. Robertson contrives to throw a glamour round his friends. One might well be tempted to go into the china and earthenware trade for the sake of making acquaintance with Mrs. Hamilton, or with any one who in her stead may now be lighting up the smoky atmosphere of the potteries with an equally shining example of kindliness, honour, and courtesy.

The firm of Robertson and McDougall had a steadily improving business. One source of their success is easy to understand. The warehouse was never left without one of the partners superintending. No toil was spared late or early to meet the demands of the place. The strictest economy was observed, and all parties, wives as well as husbands, wrought with a will.

During this period of advancing prosperity, however, a sad damp was thrown over all David Robertson's hopes and prospects. His wife, having affectionately insisted on visiting her mother, who was sick of a fever, was herself seized by it, and, after a short illness, died. They had had two children by the marriage, a son and a daughter, but both died while still young, the second child being buried at the same time with its mother.

The two places of business could not now very well be carried on separately. The narrow passage between them was therefore bridged over, and by this means the two places were thrown into one. As their traffic extended from year to year, enlargements of the premises were carried out. There is little to be recorded of this period of Robertson's life. He had to distract his thoughts as well as he could by exertions, the motive for which had been so greatly and so suddenly weakened. For a lengthened period he made his home with his partner and his partner's family, an arrangement convenient for the purposes of their common work, and relieving his solitary estate by the companionship of closely-connected friends.

CHAPTER X.

A NEW BEGINNING—JOURNEY TO HAMBURG— THE HAWKERS.

IT must here be mentioned that the family of Alston in the Isle of Man were related to the family of Mr. McDougall, Robertson's friend and partner. In 1839, Mr. Alston had been left a widower with an only daughter, named Hannah, then aged thirteen. At a still earlier period this little girl had become acquainted with David Robertson's name, by being bidden to collect shells on the sea-shore for the benefit of his great conchological signboard before mentioned. That she would ever see the man himself she had naturally then no expectation, nor, for the matter of that, any curiosity to do so. In the year 1842, however, it so happened that Mr. Alston brought his daughter to Glasgow to be introduced to her relatives, the McDougalls. With them also came a cousin. Mr. Alston was a very tall man, and when he entered the warehouse with a tall young lady on one arm and his little daughter on the other, Robertson's attention was immediately arrested by the trio ; and something apparently besides his attention must have been taken captive, for he seems to have made up his mind then and there that the little girl, on whom he had never set eyes before, should if possible become his wife.

By some innocent manœuvring Hannah Alston was induced to pay another visit to the McDougalls in Glasgow, coming this time without her father. As she had won David's heart without any effort of her own on the former visit, so on this, without much trouble, he either won or completed the conquest of hers. The McDougalls, who of course thoroughly well knew and highly valued Robertson, were on their part quite content, and so smoothed the path of the lovers, that with the least possible delay they were married, on September 11, .1843.

Mr. Robertson had so far complied with the requirements of custom and propriety as to write, asking his intended father-in-law's consent, before the wedding. He received it the day after the wedding in a long letter pointing out the necessity for a considerable delay, seeing that the young lady was only seventeen, and therefore too young as yet either to marry or to know her own mind in the choice of a husband. Between seventeen and thirty-seven, it must be admitted that there is a tolerably large interval. Yet by the progress of time such a difference in age is ever becoming relatively smaller, and even its absolute limits may be wonderfully narrowed, not in fact, but in effect, by the constraining influence of strong affection. In the present instance by the event the instincts of love were justified over the dictates of prudence. Though the ages of the bride and bridegroom were so unequal, their tastes and sympathies have proved to be perfectly well matched, and the choice so rapidly made has turned out a long success in the many years of happiness 'they have enjoyed together.

Some little time after their marriage Robertson, having to make a business excursion to London, first took his wife to pay a visit to her father in the Isle of Man. When in London he went into a shop to purchase a few things to take home for presents, but was induced to buy more than he had intended, including amongst his purchases a musical box, a barometer, and a glass chandelier. On his return home a customer came in and took a fancy to the musical box and the barometer, and purchased them both, as well as one or two of the other things, and the presents were disposed of before they could be given to the persons for whom they were intended. Indeed, it seems to have become a joke against Mr. Robertson, that no present, even after it had been bestowed, was safe, if it happened to attract the eye of a customer willing to purchase it. However that may be, what happened in the instance above men- . tioned gave occasion for another order larger than the first, and the orders were repeated several times, becoming larger and larger and more varied, till at last, as most of the goods were not in keeping with the glass and china, a small separate department was made for their reception. This increased so much, that at length an independent warehouse was provided for this branch of trade. At first the goods were mostly from London, and were chiefly of a fancy character, but they soon drifted into supplying

Sheffield and Birmingham goods also. They had introduced toys among the other fancy goods, and these they still continued for wholesale customers, and they became a considerable branch of their trade for town and country orders.

In miscellaneous merchandise the element of variety is often a source of much profit, and the introduction of a new article in trade is as much to the purpose and requires the same kind of acumen as the discovery of a new species in natural history. On one of his visits to London, Robertson noticed a woman offering for sale to a shopkeeper an article that struck him by its novelty. Waiting till she came out of the shop, he then asked her the price, but she was a foreigner and could not understand a word he said. Accompanying her to find out what factory or other place of business she came from, he discovered that it was a small lodging in a mean part of the town where she and her father produced their wares. Neither of them knew a word of English. But by pointing to the articles, laying down his money on the table, and giving them his written address, Mr. Robertson was able in dumb show to conclude a perfectly satisfactory bargain.

Eventually, as the firm saw that they were trading at a disadvantage by purchasing in London many goods that were made abroad, it was arranged that Mr. Robertson should go to the Continent, and open a correspondence direct with the manufacturers. One great difficulty appeared to be his want of acquaintance with any foreign language. To meet this as far as possible, he posted himself well up in the relative values of British and foreign monies. He started off in the midst of winter, January, 1844, not a very pleasant season of the year for travelling, but he was accustomed seldom to let obstacles of that kind stand in his way. It was arranged that he should go *via* Hull to Hamburg. To his disgust, upon reaching Hull he found that the steamer he was to go by was delayed for three days beyond her proper time for starting, so that he had to spend the interval in the best way he could.

Upon going out to see the town, in the window of a stationer's shop he noticed a large phrenological chart, including an extensive commentary. This he purchased. The weather was not at all agreeable, and he had to spend most of his time in the hotel, with nothing better than the chart wherewith to relieve the tedium of the delay. On the second evening the landlady invited him to take tea with one or two of her friends. He had some scruples about partaking of hospitality, the motive for which he could not guess, but as she pressed it, he accepted her kind invitation. There may have been about a dozen present at the party. After tea the subject of phrenology was introduced. He then began to have a glimmer of the reason why he had been invited. Having been so much occupied with the chart on the previous day, he had been taken for a phrenologist. A lady in the company asked whether he would read the bumps of her husband's head. He said that he could not. She insisted that he should. He still pleaded ignorance, but noticing what seemed a rather unusual prominence where "number" was marked on the corresponding place in the chart, he ventured to ask whether the gentleman was not good at calculation. The man's wife upon this rose and clapped her hands, saying, " I knew you could do it." They then told him that this person was the most rapid calculator in the town. Nothing would do then but that Robertson must begin to read their bumps. Some men might have been led away by a first success, and puffed up by the applause which followed it, to make some further audacious attempts, thereby either losing the credit they had won or perhaps imposing on the ignorance of the company. Mr. Robertson, however, refused to comply with their wishes, and for the straightforward reason that honestly he was not able to do so. How then, they queried, could he so accurately point out Mr. L. Fort's characteristic? That was easily explained. He replied that any one who had given the phrenological chart only such a measure of attention as he had himself done, would most likely be able now and then to make a happy guess, or even to extract money by the exhibition of his supposed skill. · The company were intelligent enough to understand this explanation. From the subject of phrenology conversation drifted into a friendly dis-cussion of other matters, and he was no longer pressed to read their bumps.

The next evening the boat sailed for Hamburg. The night was stormy, and the traveller suffered. When they arrived at the mouth of the Elbe, the passengers found that the river was frozen, that the vessel consequently could not proceed further, and that they would have to take land conveyance to

Hamburg. Inquiry being made at the hotel whether they could get conveyances to proceed at once on their journey, they were assured that none could be had till the next day. A few of them, not satisfied with the landlord's statement, went a hunting on their own account. They soon found three vehicles, each of which would hold four persons inside. But there were thirteen passengers to be accommodated. It fell to Mr. Robertson's lot to join the carriage which had to take five. They agreed to take turns about outside beside the driver, but as one of the number was a lady, it was settled that she should keep her seat inside throughout the journey.

When Robertson, who had the first turn outside, was taking his seat, one of the gentlemen offered him his dressing-gown. He had a great coat, but not one lined with fur as the more experienced travellers had. He therefore thankfully accepted the offered garment, fearing that without it the cold would be too much for him. The gown was a very gay one, covered with designs of long-tailed birds and similar devices. Sitting on the elevated seat with the driver, he expected in such drapery certainly to excite the amusement of the passers-by, but in that he was mistaken. None seemed to think that there was anything unusual about his dress. He observed that both old and young lifted hat or cap as they passed. This was so different from what it would have been in any part of Scotland, where there would probably have been a crowd after them, that his interest was excited, and he felt the cold less than he expected. It is true that though the frost in the ground was very hard, the air had become milder, but, independently of that, a sensitive man might well feel rather uncomfortably warm with shame at the contrast between the good manners of the foreigner and our insular incivility.

Another peculiarity struck his attention, that when they halted to take refreshment, never anything hot was offered to them. He was led to suppose that this was from want of fire, as he had not seen a fire at any of the stopping places. Upon inquiry, however, he was informed that fuel was indeed very expensive, and that they chiefly used a long spindly grass, chopped small, in a stove for cooking, but that also they believed that cold was not felt so much after cold meat or drink as after hot.

On the way Mr. Robertson had heard of an Englishman who kept a good hotel in Hamburg. This on arriving he readily found. The landlord was very obliging, and gave him all the information he could. Not knowing anything of the language except the names of the coins, Robertson thought it best to take an interpreter about with him. But he noticed that this man, before introducing him in places of business, would have a long talk with the principals, which seemed not altogether pleasant to them. He suspected that the fellow was first making arrangements for his own benefit, and as it presently appeared that the merchant himself could speak very good English, he at once put the question whether his interpreter was acting as he suspected. The merchant frankly answered that it was so, and that he had himself intended to mention it. The interpreter being thus found untrustworthy was paid and dismissed. There was little or no difficulty in transacting business without him, for at almost all the places of any note there was sure to be some one who had more or less command of English, and even when such was not the case, when Mr. Robertson saw goods that seemed likely to suit his market, he had only to ask the price, and when that was agreed upon, the money and his address were sufficient for that transaction.

As before stated, the object of his journey to the continent was to find out where the goods were made that they had been buying in London, and to open a correspondence. To that extent his expedition had been in a great measure successful. He now therefore prepared for home, being anxious to get away, lest snow should come on and he might be kept a prisoner long enough. He had calculated as closely as he could what money would be required to carry him home, leaving a very small margin against contingencies. This he did with less hesitation, because he was going home by London and Liverpool, and he knew that in either of those places his funds could be supplemented if necessary.

As the Elbe was still frozen, Cuxhaven had to be reached by coach. They arrived there in the afternoon, but the steamer was not to start till six the next morning. After dinner, Mr. Robertson asked the landlord whether it was possible to go aboard the steamer that night. He assured him that it was not, as the vessel was lying out in the river in mid-channel, and that no one could get on board her till morning.

Remembering how this same landlord had endeavoured to detain them on their upward journey,

he settled his bill with him, and, as all his luggage
was contained in a carpet-bag, he took this in his
hand and walked to the pier, in hopes of finding some
one to take him to the steamer. Just as he got there,
a gentleman came forward, and was going down the
steps to a small rowing-boat, which seemingly he had
left there awaiting his return. Robertson asked if he
would be so kind as to take him to the steamer that
was leaving in the morning for London. He civilly
replied that he would. The traveller got safely on
board, soon went to bed, and was already a good
way on his passage when he rose in the morning.
The remainder of his journey he thus describes :—

"We were boarded by the excise some distance
before we got to London. The men were dispersed
to different parts of the boat. One of them came
to where I was, and, after talking to me a while,
he asked if I belonged to Glasgow.

"I answered that that was my native place. I
put the question to him, if he belonged to Aberdeen.

"He smiled and nodded assent. We were then
friends. I told him that I wished to get to Liverpool that night, and I feared that the boat would not
get in in time, and, as I understood that my luggage
would have to go to the custom house, there was
little hope of my getting away that night. I mentioned that I could show him what I had.

"He replied that he need not look, as he knew
at a glance the parties who were likely to have con-
traband goods, and that he would try and get me
passed. I was just to come forward to the gangway
with my bag in my hand.

"I did so. He and the supervisor were there. The Aberdonian said, 'He is all right,' and I was allowed to pass without further trouble.

"As soon as I got on shore, I made haste to the railway station, and found to my dismay there was no third class, nor would any be that night, and that the second class would take nearly all my money. I did not care to go and borrow if I could manage it otherwise. The worst was, it was Saturday night. There were but few minutes to consider, as the time of the train was just about up. The question was whether it would be best to stay over in London, or to proceed to Liverpool by second class. Could I manage by staying till Monday morning to save as much as would take me home? I thought that I could. If not, I still had resources in London or Liverpool, as before stated.

"I decided to stay till Monday. I saw that to go to a hotel and take the regular course of the house would still run me short of what I required for the journey. I went to a good hotel, as I always preferred such for many reasons, and asked if I could be put up till Monday morning, saying that I was going out early on Sunday morning, and that it would be evening before I returned.

"The landlord in the most civil manner said that it was all the same, that I might go or come to suit my own convenience.

"I had plain tea and went soon to bed, and got up on Sunday morning early and took a long walk through some of the less frequented streets. My attention was much taken up with the busy stir of open shops, butchers, bakers, hatters, shoemakers, ready made clothiers, etc., a scene so different from anything that I had ever seen at home on Sunday. I had a jug of milk and two rolls in a milk-shop or dairy, which sufficed well for breakfast. After another stroll I went to church forenoon and afternoon. Between the preachings I had a dinner similar in cost to my breakfast and equally satisfying. I went in the evening to a lecture on Death, but it turned out, as the lecturer held, to be a lecture on No Death, as he set forth that there was no death in the world, that there never had been, nor ever would be ; that it was only changes that were going on from one state to another, whatever we choose to call these changes. I had a cup of coffee and some bread in the hotel before I went to bed.

"On Monday morning the train for Liverpool with third class left at 6 a.m. It was a slow train, and it was a long tedious ride to Liverpool. The morning was very cold, and, to make myself more secure, I put on all the shirts I had, and two pairs of stockings, and cut the feet off a third pair and drew them up over my thighs. With all these and a warm great coat I was cold proof, and never felt more comfortable in a railway carriage. Having stayed in Liverpool all night, I got the steamer next morning for Glasgow, and arrived safely home with one halfpenny in my pocket, which was kept for many a year as a remembrance of a long journey finished with one halfpenny to spare ! "

Though there are no strikingly dramatic incidents in this expedition, the narrative is full of useful hints to inexperienced travellers and to those with purses thinly lined. The comical expedient of doubling or trebling the usual allowance of shirts and stockings against the rigours of a long cold journey should not be lost sight of. The journey proved of great use to the firm. Henceforward they had their goods, both of home and foreign manufacture, mostly direct from the makers. This soon gave a considerable impulse to their trade.

In consequence of increased business, as already intimated, the hardware and fancy department had to be removed to an adjoining warehouse. Of this Mr. and Mrs. Robertson took charge, while Mr. and Mrs. McDougall superintended the glass and china department. For the hardware and fancy goods they got into a good export trade, sending to India, among other things, guns, locks, padlocks by the hogshead, and bobbins of thread. In this and other respects all continued to go on prosperously.

With the itinerant dealers, the humble customers on whom their early trade had so much depended, they had now and then some amusing experiences. When prosperity had been attained, it was the practice of the firm on New Year's Day to give cake or Scotch bun and a glass of whisky to all customers who chose to come and partake of this hospitality. One time when Mr. Robertson was handing round a large plateful, an old man, instead of taking a slice as others had done, took the plate, saying, with every evidence of delight and gratitude, "Thank you, Mr. Robertson! oh, thank you, Mr. Robertson!" It was not till he had with great satisfaction

I

demolished the contents of the plate, and gone out of the house, that he discovered his mistake, from the roars of laughter and merciless chaffing of the other hawkers. Mr. Robertson did what he could to relieve the poor man's feelings by sending him out an assurance that he had been perfectly welcome.

Subsequently the flavour of the New Year's cake was further improved by having fourpenny-pieces mixed in with the other ingredients. This had, however, the disadvantage of attracting mock customers, who purchased something quite trivial to acquire the right of accepting hospitality that was not intended for them. One year, for the sake of variety, presents were distributed instead of the whisky, cake, and fourpennies; but such is human nature, that though the presents were of considerably higher value than what had been previously given, the distribution only led to envyings, jealousies, and discontent.

Some of the hawkers were none too honest. One of these, whose character was well known, applied one day to be served with a gilt Albert chain. The number of chains in the tray was carefully counted before it was submitted to him. When he had selected one and paid for it, Mr. Robertson taxed him with having taken a second for which he had not paid. "Oh no," said the man, "that was quite a mistake. He had but one." Mr. Robertson, on the other hand, said he was perfectly sure that two had been taken. The man protested his honesty and innocence, and finally offered to be searched. As Mr. Robertson had good reason to know for certain that the man must have committed the theft, he did not scruple to avail himself of the offered means of detecting it. But in this he failed. At last he said to the man, "I know you have the missing chain, and if you will tell me how you have concealed it, it shall be yours without further question."

Upon this the fellow showed him the chain lying outside his hat, but just in the turn-over of the brim, which he had held in his hand while proffering this very hat with an air of injured innocence for his accuser to examine the lining. It was either this same knave or a kindred spirit who excited the cupidity of a well-to-do butcher by showing him a real gold Albert chain, of good quality, at a price far below its real value, which he had procured for a neighbour. The butcher commissioned him to get him one at a similar price, which obviously could not be honestly accomplished. When some time after the butcher was bragging of his chain, some one pointed out to him that it was only of common metal gilt. He then wished to prosecute the pedlar, but his own part in the transaction had been of such a character that his advisers persuaded him to let the matter alone, and put up with a loss which he had richly deserved.

As Mr. Robertson by degrees acquired more and more influence, he exerted himself to persuade some of the poorer customers to save a penny or twopence a day, or other such small sums as from time to time they could well spare. These he offered to take care of for them. They did not readily believe that any good could come of such small economies, but some of them yielded to his wishes and advice, and when

their banking accounts gradually mounted up, they
became eager enough to increase them still further.
Many of these people would come to him as a responsible householder, to sign papers for them certifying
that they were without sufficient means to pay poor-
rates. There were many really necessitous cases, and
his word was always accepted on the subject by the
authorities. Among other applicants was one, Alice
Duffy, whom he had led into the ways of thrift, and
who had, in fact, accumulated sixty pounds in the
bank. Nevertheless she was continually pestering
him to sign such a certificate for her, although he
pointed out that it could not be honestly done. At
last her persistence could be resisted no longer,
and he wrote some lines for her to the following
effect :—

"Alice Duffy is a very industrious, hard-working
person, who is possessed of ample means to pay the
usual poor-rates."

Highly delighted, she carried her paper to the office,
and it was passed round from clerk to clerk, Alice
being ready with her praises to every one of Mr.
Robertson as a dear good man. At last one of the
clerks asked whether she had read the paper. No.
She could not read. So then he read it to her, and
her delight was changed into indignation, which was
not much soothed when she returned to the warehouse, and found her complaints met with shouts of
laughter from every one. In time she forgave the
jest, paid her rates without murmuring, and increased
her store at the bank. The practical joke of which
she was the victim may seem rather a severe one,

but it no doubt, in a very effective manner, inculcated a lesson of honesty among a rough set of people, and it may be questioned whether the woman's tolerably tough conscience would have been sensitive to any lighter stroke.

CHAPTER XI.

BOTANY—LITERATURE.

IN the year 1845, or about that time, Robertson became desirous of knowing the names of some of the mosses which he had long observed and admired and frequently gathered. With this object in view he called on a Dr. Rattray, a botanist of distinction and likewise an enthusiastic freemason. He arranged that the learned doctor should come to his house on one or two nights in the week, and give him an hour's lesson on mosses.

At that period shops in Glasgow did not shut so early as they do at present. Robertson and McDougall closed at 10 p.m. But the doctor made no scruples about the time of night for coming. It was often well after midnight before he went away, for when he began one of his stories, of which he had many, he would tell it out to the end, no matter how long it took, and it was sometimes one or two in the morning before he left. Of the hours thus spent, it was seldom much that was devoted to bryology. The truth was, that mosses were not his forte, and he strongly advised his pupil to give them up and study the flowering plants instead, and not, as he put it, to begin at the roof in building the house.

Seeing that there was no help for it, Robertson submitted to his instructor's authority, and gained some useful information on the subject he was competent to teach, though he had learned but little from him on the special subject of mosses. This Dr. Rattray was in some respects a remarkable man. He had risen through ʻvarious grades of life by his abilities, distinguishing himself in every undertaking by his aptitude to master his subject. Unfortunately, freemasonry engrossed so much of his time and attention that he lost much of his medical practice.

During the years immediately following his marriage with Miss Alston, Robertson's attention was necessarily much engrossed with business, nor had he yet taken up any branch of natural history for more than a passing amusement, but his scrap-book shows that he was already turning his attention to literature. Fugitive pieces of poetry he composed for home consumption, which won a *succès d'estime* among those for whose pleasure they were written. His thoughts and reflections in prose on miscellaneous subjects he entrusted to the *Scotch Reformer Gazette* and the *Glasgow Herald.*

Amongst other things, at the time of the potato famine, he ventured to argue against the unreasonable scare which made some persons imagine that "symptoms of a total extinction of the vegetable food of man" could be discerned in this calamity. The origin of it had been discreetly traced by one of the Glasgow preachers to the desecration of the sabbath. Some of his contributions endeavoured to enforce upon the minds of his fellow-townsmen in general, and his immediate neighbours in particular, the merits of cleanliness, and the high importance to the health and life of human beings of having a constant and abundant supply of fresh air. He took upon him to denounce the very inadequate arrangements of the Glasgow post-office in 1847, the unrepressed circulation of counterfeit pennies in 1849, and, about the same time, the many adulterations of food calculated to undermine health, while the very physic which might have counteracted the ill effects of those adulterations was itself adulterated likewise. Some serious discussions from his pen, on the regulation of our thoughts, and on a very prevalent hypocrisy in regard to the observance of Sunday, were deemed worthy of acceptance by the newspapers.

Of a more scientific character was an account of an experiment with leeches. It was popularly supposed that these creatures, kept in a jar, would foretell the weather—crawling up the vessel or remaining below in accordance with the rise and fall of the barometer. By prolonged observation of three of them in the same jar, Robertson convinced himself that this was a complete fallacy, since it often happened that one of the creatures would be at the bottom when another was at the top. He suggested that the truthfulness of gas-meters might in a similar way be tested, by making the supply pass through two meters instead of one, to see if the indications agreed.

In one of his paragraphs he pointed out a circumstance which he had much opportunity of observing in his line of business, namely, that each individual has a limit of capacity which is not to be passed, less from the want of power than from the want of will. Among customers who renewed their stock daily, some would regularly effect sales up to about ten shillings, others only up to five shillings, others only to three; but whatever the amount, it was uniform, unless, through some accident or sickness, loss or misconduct, the hawker was forced to begin on a lower than his ordinary scale. Then he would work up easily to his former maximum, but he would not go beyond it.

The contributions which flowed from Mr. Robertson's pen during this period of his life, though generally brief, were many in number. Whether any of his efforts were ever rejected is naturally a secret between him and the editors. Those who are prone to pry without delicacy into the innermost recesses of a literary life may fancy that he unguardedly himself supplies a clue to the mystery in the following composition, which *was* accepted, and printed under the heading : " The Scribbler's Opinion of the Editor."

" He snatches up the paper with something of ferocious greed, and scans it over with a hurried but hopeful eye. If he lights on his own production his movements at once assume a pleasing, fascinated stillness ; he becomes philosophical and humorous ; the paper is handled gently, and held in esteem. But an article in particular is a special favourite, admired, and shown to his friends. He believes the editor to be a very independent, shrewd, and clever man, and supposes the paper to have a great circulation. But should his eye fail to light on his own important piece, the paper becomes subjected to short convulsed turns, is more roughly handled; two or three more inquiring glances, and down it goes, consigned in the most unceremonious manner where chance may receive it. Left to meditate on the cause of his disappointment, he conjectures his communication may have been too late, and, in justice, could only be inserted according to precedence; may be left over another week, to adorn some seedy article that could not appear alone. If another week removes these suppositions, the cause must be an overlook, or the editor must be a very dull fellow indeed, and too mechanical to discern the merits of his piece; is convinced 'kissing goes by favour,' and wonders how some editors are patronized!"

The editor of the *Reformer* was one Peter McKensie, an able and honourable man, but his affairs did not turn out prosperously, for he refused to admit into his paper advertisements that savoured of quackery, however well they would have been paid for, and by his fearless exposure of frauds upon the community he became involved in disastrous legal expenses. With these matters, however, the present story has no concern. One night, as Robertson was passing McKensie's office, he thought he would step in with the contribution he had in his pocket. Upon his mentioning that it was a Scotch piece, "Oh," said Peter, "we don't care for Scotch pieces; our readers don't like the trouble of them." Still, he took the manuscript in hand, and, when his lips began to widen and his eyes to twinkle, Robertson knew that his effusion was accepted. If our present readers "do not care for Scotch pieces," they can skip the following account of "Jennie's visit to the Exhibition in the City Hall":—

"Mither, sic a sicht as thon is guid for sair een. Whan we entered the house near the roof,* ye'd thocht that ye war wi' Shedrach, Meshach, an' Abednego in the fiery furnace, or wi' Daniel in the den o' lions. The very lamps war red wi' heat, an' I think we war surrounded wi' every kin' o' beast in the warl. The din o' bells, and wheels, an' horns, wad hae deeved a miller. We cam doun tae a place whar they war mackin' cups an' flats,† an' bowls an' bools, an' guid kens what a', an' whirrin' them aff like prints o' butter. A bit furder yont they war printing buikes an' pictures, juist like cauin' corn throu' fanners. An', mither, they war anither fallow yoner blowin' gless in a rowe tae it was red het, an' haudin' it wi' his bare fingers. Thon chap had shurely something a dae wi' auld Cluttie. Had you seen a thing they had for makin' cards, ye'd hae thocht it was leevin'; it minded me o' twa hens pickin' out o' ae dish. An' we saw them weavin' pictures on paper. But pictures, mither! my very heed was turned amang them. Ye'd thocht they war girnin', an' gloomin', and lauchin', an' ridin', an' rinnin', an fechtin', an' fleein', an' kissin', an' clappin', an' sleepin', an' waukin', an' deein', an' leevin'— amang them I scarcely kent wha was deed or wha was alive. Mither, mither, it wad tak a moon tae tell yae the ha'f that I saw. I saw bricks made o' tea, an' a sark without a seam in't. But I thocht, mither, if we wore ours lang without seams, they wadna be lang without holes.

* In the gallery.   † Saucers.

"In the mids o' the firry-farry, a man bald out o'er the bed-head,* an rattled a girdle, an telt us we war to gang an' see anither sicht butt † the house. An' awa we crooded butt the house, up a stair, whare we got stools tae sit on. They darkened the room, an' lichted pictures on the wa', o' houses in London ; but the queer thing was how the pictures changed— creeping out of the ae thing intae anither ; turnin' kirks intae castles, an' trees intae boats. But, mither, the fleesomest thing was at last ; an' I'll think till the day that I dee that they put us asleep, an' set us a' dreamin', for it cou'd be naething else. An' then we thocht that w' saw a big fiery wheel on the wa',— an' how it trinted, and rumpled inwards an' outwards, an' upwards, an' downwards, an' backwards, an' forwards ; it stoppit, an' startled, an' freckled, an' sparkled—an' preserve us, I thocht whiles that it wad be owre the tap o' us a' thegither ; an', bless me, mither, had they no' waukened us firin' gun-cotton, I'm shure it wad hae turned out the nichtmare. But as shoon as I got out at the door, I ne'er luk'd owre ma shouther tae I was on the fair road for Lesmahago."

The above will give some idea of the lowland Scotch dialect, with which in early years Mr. Robertson himself had been familiar. It also faithfully indicates the simplicity of mind with which a girl out of the country districts would in those days have been brought face to face for the first time with the wonders and amusements of the town.

* The clerk's box suggests to her mind the box-bed of the moorland farmhouse.

† " Butt " and " ben " are equivalent to " out " and " in," or " out of " and " into " respectively.

The following anecdote, which is not imaginary, will serve as a slight illustration of the somewhat unconventional manners and customs prevailing in Glasgow itself, and which still give it something of the air of a country town now that it is exceeded in size and population by no city in Great Britain except London.

"A pet sheep, named Tom, well known in the Saltmarket, was accustomed to follow his master into the beershop, where he learned the first lesson of inebriety. Being coaxed, for the amusement of the company, to taste biscuit soaked in whisky, he soon improved and became by degrees a genuine tippler. When Tom was in his cups he was quite social; his greatest peculiarity was his epicurean fancies. He relished sweetmeats, would drink tea, eat bervies,* could chew tobacco, and was fond of oranges, and well known to the dealers in that commodity. Although at times amusing to them, he often turned out a troublesome customer, upsetting their stands at being refused his will of the fruit. At last he grew so mischievous, dunching the children and gathering crowds on the street, that his days were summarily brought to a close in the public shambles."

While refreshing his mind by thus practising his pen on various topics of more or less importance, Mr. Robertson did not allow his early faculty for book-keeping to dwindle by neglect. His triumph as a lad over the obstinate miller will be remembered. He now entered into a somewhat similar contest on his own behalf.

---

* Bervies are preserved fish, which take their name from that of a village where they are prepared.

In the early days of the income-tax the business of his firm was assessed considerably beyond the return which the partners had made. This of course implied that they had made a false return, or, to speak more politely, an erroneous one. Mr. Robertson was by no means likely to submit to such an implication, and he therefore appealed. He assured the commissioners that the expenses and profits of his firm had to come out of the difference of ten per cent. between the price at which they bought and that at which they sold. This they could not believe, and met his offer to prove it by allowing him only two hours in which to bring forward the proof.

Indignant and disgusted, he nevertheless hurried back to the shop, had the various ledgers and account-books placed on a barrow and carted off to the place where the commissioners were sitting. He showed them by the invoices that the manufacturers charged them the very same price at which they sold the goods to their customers, the margin being secured by the circumstance that the manufacturers allowed them a discount of ten per cent. on payment, whereas their customers paid them the full price. The commissioners then wanted to know how much they had at the bank, and were again surprised to find that, notwithstanding the magnitude of the business, they had nothing there. They kept a cash-box of their own without at that time troubling any bank.

In the end, as the commissioners, or inquisitors as some might feel inclined to call them, were not willing to encounter the task of examining the books in detail, there was no course left for them but to deduct the overcharge. Although triumphant, Mr. Robertson felt that it was no little grievance that he should have had to defend himself single-handed against the six official gentlemen.

So many eminent persons regard the income-tax as a masterpiece of our civilization, elastic as it is to meet the expenses of every diplomatic blunder, that it can only be the part of human frailty to feel discontent at so great a blessing. In point of fact, it was not with the tax that Mr. Robertson had any fault to find. The resistance he offered was to what he considered a petty oppression on the part of some of those engaged in levying it. That he was a very loyal citizen may be inferred from the following remarks, taken from a letter which he wrote in August, 1849, on the occasion of the Queen's visit to Glasgow :—

" We had great pleasure to-day," he says, " in seeing the Queen, and had an excellent view of her on the bell of the brae, High Street, as she passed on her way in an open carriage to the cathedral ; and the ladies had time to sum up a thousand little things that they had omitted to notice—regarding her dress, Prince Albert, and the children—by the time she returned to see the college. It was a great treat to us to see her. The pleasure far exceeded our modest anticipations. We were taken by surprise. Instead of seeing, as we expected, a formal, dazzling automaton, we were charmed, bewildered, swamped in joy, at seeing a plain, sweet, graceful, young Queen, greeting her people in the most homely and parental manner."

This period of Mr. Robertson's career may be fitly

concluded with the record that his eldest son, David, was born in the year 1847, and in 1850 his second son, Thomas, now better known in the artist world as Tom Robertson.   In the interval between these two events two little notes were entered in the father's commonplace book which seem to have an indirect bearing on the life history of David Robertson, junior. In the one, his parent remarks that the young of the lower animals utter cries while in pain, desisting when the pain is removed, but that human infants continue their lamentations long after the grievance has ceased. In the other, the question is asked, "Is the boy idle during the first three years of his life?"   To which is returned the answer, "No! he learns to walk, he learns to speak, he learns the names of numbers of things, and he compares and examines them."   This infantine precocity, in the special example on which the remark was no doubt founded, has since developed into a nice turn for mechanical invention.

CHAPTER XII.

SCIENCE BEGINS AND BUSINESS ENDS.

THE life engaging our attention has thus far been that of a struggling student and an enterprising man of business. It becomes henceforward that of a naturalist. In both periods the same moral qualities are exhibited, the same mixture of modesty and courage, the same generosity and kindliness of temper, the same unwearying and successful perseverance. Between the years 1850 and 1860 natural history pursuits and business occupations overlapped one another, but the true naturalist "has no time for money-making," and accordingly the time came when science extinguished commerce. It is probable that this result was in no small measure due to the institution of the Natural History Society of Glasgow, which took place on July 2, 1851. In the following year Mr. Robertson joined it, and by this means became acquainted with a circle of men, eminent in various branches of knowledge, willing to teach and willing to learn; by the latter readiness as much as by the former kindling enthusiasm and helping forward the interests of science. Among other intimacies thus formed was one with Mr. Roger

K

Hennedy, who for many years successfully conducted a botanical class in the Glasgow Mechanics' Institution. Not only flowering plants but seaweeds were well known to him, and as he had a summer residence at Millport, near to Mr. Robertson's, they had many walks along the shore that were fruitful in instruction to one of them and pleasant to both. With him Mr. Robertson had his first dredging experience. In dredging Mr. Robertson was destined to become an expert, and he still pursues the " sport " with great skill and ardour. His early views on the subject are thus expressed in his commonplace book for 1856 :—

" Those who have a taste for natural history will find unbounded pleasure in dredging. Every plunge of the dredge into the deep is the commencement of a pleasurable suspense till it is again hauled up, a lottery bag not just in the usual way of 'all prizes and no blanks,' nor all blanks and no prizes, for there is a kind of happy conscientiousness about our bag, that all is fair play, whatever may be our lot.

" None but those who have been at the turning out of a well-filled dredge can know anything of the glowing excitement experienced at that moment, when the contents have been brought from a surface on which, in all probability, no human eye ever gazed ; and although many of these gatherings from the deep may have been previously from time to time brought to light, yet many things that come up though not rare may be interesting, others may have been seldom seen, and the lottery is open to all to bring up a never-before-described animal or vegetable, living or dead. We may have drawn up our dredge from few fathoms or from many, we may have been trawling with great vigour and speed, or we may have been slowly floating before the tide, and under these circumstances we may have had rare things or common things or no things, but these uncertainties in no way lessen the pleasure, but rather warm and increase our enthusiasm.

"No picture is so indelible on my mind as the start for a dredging excursion one fine summer morning, when the sun was just making his appearance over the hilltops and tingeing their sides with his golden beams, the straggling clouds floating midway from the lofty peaks, the air pleasantly cool and balmy, and the sea smooth as glass, mirroring the sun in her bosom, and only ruffled by the splashing of sea-birds chasing one another and squabbling in the exuberance of their joy. Two or three kindred spirits had met and were at their posts at the appointed time. The boat being launched, the traps and provisions stowed safely away, and all seated, when the first splash of the oars in the silvery flood set us in motion, how lovely it was to look over the boat-side and see the beautiful forest of sea-weed, clumps of *Halidrys siliquosa* majestically grouped here and there, and echinoderms and star-fishes spangling as it were the firmament below!"

For a time Mr. Robertson turned his attention very eagerly to sea-weeds, and was assisted by his wife in making a collection of them mounted in the usual way upon paper.

As the smaller plants could not well be made out by the unaided eye, at first he procured a simple pocket lens of a quarter of an inch focus, with an adjusting screw for the plate that held the plant. This simple form of microscope, made by an Edinburgh optician named Bryson, he found exceedingly useful for field work, nor has he met with anything since that could answer the particular purpose better. But for closer examination of the algæ at home a compound microscope was required. His friend Mr. Hennedy had one by Nachet, the well-known French maker, which he had procured through Dr. Arnott, Professor of Botany in the University of Glasgow. Dr. Arnott kindly offered to order one for Mr. Robertson, his intervention securing for him, as was expected, an excellent instrument, although it may very well be supposed that the instrument would have been just as good if ordered in his own name.

The study of sea-weeds eventually brought him into an agreeable correspondence both with Dr. Arnott and with Dr. Harvey, the distinguished algologist, who was Professor of Botany in the Royal Dublin Society.

It so happened that, in the year 1857, a woman picked up on a rubbish heap a packet containing a collection of sea-weeds. This she carried to a Dr. Lyndsay. This gentleman, knowing that Mr. Robertson was interested in marine plants, sent them on to him. He saw at once that they did not belong to this country, and were likely to be of value to the intended recipient, but after applying to several of his friends interested in such specimens, he could find no trace of the owner. There was, however, among them, by some accident, a letter and an envelope addressed to Dr. Harvey, Dublin. To him therefore he wrote, and received an immediate answer, that he was exceedingly glad to hear of the recovery of the plants. They had been sent by steamer to Dr. Arnott, but lost on the road, having perhaps been pilfered by some one who, finding them of no marketable value, had flung them away. Dr. Arnott was pressing the steamboat company for what he considered their full value, contrary to Dr. Harvey's inclination in the matter, and the relief from this contention by the finding of the parcel appears to have given Dr. Harvey even more pleasure than the recovery of the parcel itself. He wished to send Mr. Robertson some specimens of Irish sea-weeds in return for the trouble he had taken. The reply made to this proposal, in a letter dated Sept. 22, 1857, may be quoted as characteristic :—

"Your kind offer of the plants I assure you I greatly appreciate, but it is a favour I in no way merit, having done nothing more than the common duty that fell to my lot. Therefore I respectfully decline accepting the plants. But, away from that matter, may I ask the very great favour of by times troubling you for the name of a plant that I may find unusually puzzling?"

It will be understood that troubling the kindly Professor for the name of a puzzling weed in general meant also presenting him with some rare specimen. Indeed, giving rather than receiving has been all through typical of Mr. Robertson's career as a collector, although he is not so one-sided that he cannot upon occasion gracefully and gratefully accept. One of his wife's relations, Miss Mary Ann Alston, was so obliging as to make a collection of sea-weeds

for him in the Isle of Man.   To her, on receiving this
present, he wrote the following letter :—

  " Many thanks for the beautiful book of sea-weeds
you so kindly sent to me.   I have a great love for the
book of nature.   It yields me inexhaustible sources of
pleasure, and opportunities of seeing and admiring
the beauty and extraordinary works of the great
Designer.   No one doubts the genuineness of His book.
No one ventures to aspire to the smallest share of the
work.   It has no apocryphal portions nor misunder-
stood passages.   The smallest blade of grass carries
the unmistakable impress of its omnipotent Author
on it.   The tiniest plant, far beyond the reach of the
unaided eye, demonstrates the beauty, the harmony,
the perfection of His works.   How much more interesting is a walk in the green fields or on the sea-
beach when you can recognize in almost every plant
an old acquaintance, and call them by their names.
A collection of preserved plants teems with impressive
memorials of the past and calls up associations of
happy days long gone by, bringing to memory dear
companions that shared in the pleasure of gathering
the specimens that are almost held sacred for these
friends' sake."

  When commencing naturalist, Robertson was
fairly well off for help in botany, but so far as zoology
came under his notice he was sadly to seek, as badly
off as the Germans in Greek in Porson's day.   Two
friends, members of the Natural History Society,
John Gray and Thomas Gray, first enabled him to
find his feet by giving him the names of some of his
shells.   He had not originally any express intention

of making a collection of shells or of marine animals in general, yet when they turned up in the dredge he was reluctant to throw them away, and by degrees they accumulated, and his desire to know more about them increased. At last he had to get a cabinet to hold them, as without arrangement it was clear that they would be useless for comparison or any other reasonable purpose. Also, in order to be his own instructor in these matters as far as he could, he provided himself with G. B. Sowerby's " Illustrated Index of British Shells," Forbes's " British Star-fishes," and Bell's " British Stalk-eyed Crustacea," works which may indeed have been left far in the background by the vast and rapid strides that natural history has made in recent years, but which at that time were almost indispensable to the student of the several branches of which they treated. Forbes's book in particular, by the admirable clearness of the style and the vein of humour sparkling through it, both was and still is well adapted to fascinate a beginner, and cultivate his taste for research.

The numerous visits which Mr. Robertson made to the shores of Cumbrae, and the experience he had been gradually accumulating in some of the branches of geology and botany, enabled him not unfrequently to exhibit specimens and to make remarks at the meetings of the Natural History Society. He was gratified to find that his occasional observations did not appear unwelcome to the other members. By the sympathy and approbation shown his inclination towards these pursuits was still more quickened and invigorated.

He remembers the first occasion on which he summoned up courage to offer a criticism at a meeting of the society.

A piece of rock was exhibited with a cup-like excavation, reputed to be produced by the boring powers of the limpet. Upon this he observed that if the limpet were increasing in size, as was reasonable to suppose it would be, during the process of boring so deep a hole, the hole would be wider below than above, rather of the shape of an inverted cup than like the excavation which was being exhibited. Mr. Fraser, who was at that time the secretary of the society, at once saw the point he was making, and agreed with his view. Subsequently he had to vindicate his opinion in argument with his friend, the late Dr. Gwyn Jeffreys, and had the honour of convincing that celebrated conchologist, who was not easily turned from an opinion he had once adopted. The ingenious experiments upon this same animal, the common limpet, which he carried out and described some thirty years afterwards, will be referred to later on.

In the literature of natural history perhaps no passage has been more frequently quoted or referred to than that in which Professor Forbes describes the breaking up of the Brittle Starfish, *Luidia fragilissima*, which he had all but captured, and the slipping back into the deep of its severed arm " with something very like a wink of derision." It is well known that starfishes when they lose their arms are able to grow them again, so that it is inaccurate to speak of the disintegrating propensities of *Luidia* as suicidal. The sacrifice of its arms is a life-saving stratagem, just as a wolf caught in a gin will bite off its foot and limp away on three legs rather than let itself be killed with the full complement of four. But the more anxious the starfish is to break itself up for its own selfish purposes, the more is it a point of honour with the collector to secure it uninjured. This Mr. Robertson succeeded in doing at Cumbrae in 1858. As the result of various captures then and afterwards he found that in the summer months he could rarely bring one of this species to the surface in the dredge entire. Occasionally in those months they may be found near to the shore in shallow water, and the specimens so found can be dried unbroken, but they are always thin, probably from being in a sickly state. In the spring, however, he got them in good full condition. At that period of the year a specimen was brought up in the dredge in company with several large sea-urchins that had strong sharp spines, likely enough to irritate the starfish, but even under these circumstances its temper was composed and tranquil, for "it was placed in a little water in the bottom of the boat, and lay there fully two hours, then carried home exposed to the air, and finally paid the last debt of nature, and still remained whole."

At times Mr. Robertson was willing to obtain information from humbler guides than Harvey or Forbes, or his friends Hennedy and the Grays.

His diary for March 8, 1856, gives the following record :—

"Day fine. Went over to the fireworks pond to

get a few sticklebacks (*Gasterosteus aculeatus*). I
sought in vain in those ponds which I thought most
likely to have them. I made inquiry of some boys,
whom I always consider adepts in that kind of knowledge, but without effect. Yet they did not turn out
so very unprofitable. Anticipating my course, they
took the road before me. As I had touched on a
subject agreeable to their age and likely to rouse
their curiosity, no doubt they had a desire to parti-
cipate in the adventure. As they were now a dozen
or two yards ahead, I saw them advance to a group
of children of the other sex. I heard one of the
little girls say—

"'Is it minnows? they are plenty o' them o'er
there.'

" I inquired where.

"The ready and sincere answer was, 'O'er there,'
pointing to a lot of farmers' dungsteads laid up on
some forced * earth of a freestone quarry.

" Suspecting that she meant somewhere at a greater
distance, I endeavoured to discover the particular
spot by interrogating if they were beyond or within
such and such places.

"' No, no,' was the reply, 'they are just o'er there,
at the horses' heads, there, where the men are filling
dung.'

"Still I was undetermined. There were the horses
within three lengths of myself at the tail of a huge
dunghill, but where could there be a drop of water a
fish could live in ?

"The kind little girl, observing my bewilderment,

* That is, earth that had been removed from the quarry.

did what she no doubt thought best fitted to my understanding, and what could not be unsuccessful even with a blind man—she led me to the place; and sure enough there was the pond, a flat hole, filled up at one side with a dunghill, bounded on another by rubbish, and strewed over with fragments of buckets and earthenware rejected from the manure, the unsubsided mud floating up to within a few inches of the top. Still, amidst all these impurities, the sticklebacks were there in shoals, gay, fat, and healthy. I took of them with a small net what I required, and returned home, rejoicing at my good fortune."

The previous year he had been making experiments with the common mussel—experiments the description of which is well worth reproducing both on its own account and as showing how fertile in interest the commonest objects may become to a question-asking mind:—

"I have been much interested," he says, "in watching the habits of a common mussel (*Mytilus edulis*), which has afforded me many hours of pleasant amusement. It had been in my keeping for three months. I had taken little notice of it, till, finding that it had removed from the bottom, and attached itself about two inches up the side of the jar, I became curious to know how it had got up. I observed that the fibres of the byssus were fixed at various heights, that the lowermost were fully an inch from the bottom; that by their apparent contraction it could raise itself nearly an inch; and that from this position other fibres could be and had been fixed higher up; hence the ascent. It remained in this position for eight days, during that time adding more fibres till it had twenty-one, the lowermost now appearing circularly below the shell, and the upper ones circularly above it. It was now, apparently, a permanent fixture, at least within the limits of its moorings ; by drawing the byssus towards the beak, or the base, it could move the ends of the shell alternately up and down. The movements were at times frequent.

"On the tenth day after mounting the side of the jar it detached itself, and fixed upon another place a little farther round, by four new fibres, leaving the old byssus hanging to the glass. This is an interesting microscopic object, somewhat palmate, dividing into numerous filaments, and is attached to the animal by a small peduncle, which nature has given the creature power to sever when a change is required.

"I was desirous to see the actual process of fixing the fibres, and began to watch with more care. It had now six fibres ; and, with the hope that it would require to produce more, I cut three, leaving only three, by which it supported itself and went through its usual movements with apparent ease ; the only perceptible effect was a slight jerk down at the severance of each fibre. The fewness and fineness of the filaments, and the delicacy of the attachment, looked very inadequate for the suspension of the animal ; but they proved to be strong enough and something to spare, as one of its neighbours, the hermit crab (*Pagurus Bernhardus*), mounted occasionally on the top of the inoffensive mussel without the least appearance of giving pain or oppression, although the crab used no precaution in taking light steps in ascending, nor seemed in any way doubtful of the stability of his footing. I watched all day patiently, but no more fibres ; after dark, I made my observations only occasionally, and by candle-light, the gas being too distant for minute inspection.

" Returning on one of these visits, after an absence of an hour, I found four new fibres affixed. This was a great disappointment, to lose, by this short absence, a sight I had so much wished to see. Next day there were no more new fibres, and, as it had seven, it might not be in much want of more. To reduce it again to the necessity of making a new supply, I cut four, leaving three, and I again set to watch with renewed zeal. Darkness came on without bringing about the wished-for object ; but to profit by my last night's disappointment, I placed the aquarium on the table, raised to a convenient height for inspection, bringing the gas to bear effectually upon it by means of a flexible tube ; and, so far as the facility of inspection went, all seemed right, with little probability of disappointment. Believing that it could not remain long without the support of more fibres, and to awaken it to a sense of that necessity, I agitated the water by rocking the jar slightly from side to side. But I began to perceive, to my dismay, that the water was in an unhealthy state ; I replaced it with an artificial mixture, in which all appeared to revive. Next morning all seemed to be again healthy, yet the mussel had thrown out no new fibres since I cut the four. By the afternoon I had got a new supply of sea-water, and substituted it for the artificial, which gave a renewed stimulus to the whole.

" I now observed that the motions of the mussel were frequent : after a short time it threw out with considerable force two small, well-defined streams of milk-like fluid from an aperture at the posterior margin of the anal current, which shot like two silvery wires through the water, then gradually opened and broke up into a beautiful shower of feathery-looking flakes precipitating rapidly to the bottom.   The streams continued at intervals for about a quarter of an hour, and towards the end, when more scanty, they became finer and single.   I believe the white matter to be ova.   I subjected it to the microscope, and found it composed of little transparent globules, filled with granular matter surrounded by a delicate membrane, and, when ruptured, the contents flowed out freely.   At the close of the milky discharge, the animal became more restless, and the valves opened more widely.   The foot now began to protrude and feel about, and fixed for a few seconds on the jar, then darted in with great force.   It seemed to be very sensitive, often withdrawing from a slight touch on its own fibres.   Again the foot protruded more than an inch and fixed to the jar ; the animal now began to move forcibly up and down, as if endeavouring to drag itself from the byssus ; the peduncled attachment was seen at every pull rising above the valves of the shell ; these motions lasted about five minutes, the foot still adhering to the glass, when, to my joy, I saw a very fine fibre stretched up by its side, and a white spot coming distinctly into view under the tip of the foot.

" I have since placed other mussels in separate jars, and cut all the byssus close by the shell ; in five hours

afterwards some had three, others four and five fibres;
next day one of them had eighteen fibres; and again
the following day one of them had cast its byssus, and
had attached itself three inches farther up the jar by
the new fibres before it disengaged itself from the old.
I have now often seen the fibres fixed. The part of
the foot that performs this office is at a point a little
below the apex. When more than one fibre is
attached at a time, the lower one is fixed first, then
the foot is pushed a little farther up on the same line,
and a second and a third are fixed in the same way;
but I have never seen more at a time than three,
sometimes two, and often only one."

How many a wet day at the seaside might be
beguiled of its tedium if the weary visitor would
rouse himself to repeat or initiate observations and
experiments such as these.

A wide-mouthed glass bottle or a finger-glass will
suffice for the aquarium. It matters little how common be the object examined, since a knowledge of
its manners and customs is almost sure not to be
common. The record of these in a note-book will
add to the interest of observing, and, besides the
chance of its having in itself a scientific value, will
exercise and develop the powers of attention and
description. Intimacy thus acquired with the forms
and behaviour of a few common marine animals will
make the eye and mind keen to appreciate what is
rare and strange when opportunity offers.

During the period between 1850 and 1860, Mr.
Robertson had often to carry out his experimental
courses in Glasgow amidst the distractions of business;

but his visits to the shores and waters of Cumbrae, though they might be short, were frequent, and his diary shows that he was continually searching for the treasures of the sea—shells and weeds, crabs and shrimps and other crustaceans of various orders, annelids and sea-anemones, starfishes and sea-urchins, hydroid zoophytes, naked mollusks, and fishes.

His skill and acquisitions became known, and he entered into correspondence, in regard to sea-anemones, with the late popular zoologist, P. H. Gosse. On sessile-eyed crustacea he corresponded with I. O. Westwood, the celebrated entomologist, a still living and actively-working veteran ; and also with the late Charles Spence Bate, to whom he sent many specimens of great interest for description in the work which he was then preparing in conjunction with Professor Westwood.

In 1857, Mr. Robertson obtained a specimen of the curious little fish, *Amphioxus lanceolatus*, to which reference will again be made in another chapter. Eager demands were made upon him by naturalists for specimens of this interesting animal.

His researches were not confined to aquatic objects. He did not neglect the ferns or the mosses. But he was also, at this period, turning his attention to a very abstruse subject, in which land and water were almost equally concerned, for, about the year 1855, he joined the Rev. H. W. Crosskey in what proved to be a very long and laborious task—the preparation of a paper on the post-tertiary deposits of Scotland.

For the benefit of the few who are not students of geology, it may be observed that the fossil-bearing deposits of the earth are divided by specialists into three principal groups—the primary, in which the old red sandstone and the coal-bearing series are among others comprised ; the secondary, of which the gault and the chalk are well known ; and the tertiary, this last being again subdivided into eocene, meiocene, and pleiocene. All the stratified deposits later than these are called, according to fancy, pleistocene, or post-pleiocene, or quaternary, or post-tertiary. In these the fossils have often a great affinity to organisms still existing, and often belong to identically the same species as animals now living. Though the proposed paper was to refer chiefly to the Scotch deposits, illustrative species from England and Ireland were not to be excluded from it.

In course of time Dr. G. S. Brady joined Messrs. Crosskey and Robertson, especially with a view to the investigation of the ostracoda, which are crustacea, generally of microscopic size, having their soft parts shielded by a pair of valves, which give them the appearance of tiny bivalved shells.

As the shells of mollusca were a principal group in the deposits, they had to be carefully authenticated, and, in dealing with these, they obtained the assistance of Gwyn Jeffreys. But before any help could be available in determining the fossils, the fossils themselves had to be hunted up and sorted out.

To those who have never made natural history collections and inquiries, or who have limited their efforts to picking up some worn, empty shells on the shore, and keeping them jumbled together in a box, all that has been said will convey but a very vague

L

idea of the immense activity which Mr. Robertson did in fact exert during this period in different departments of science.

That he had not altogether forgotten his medical training is shown by a long letter which he wrote, about this time, to a friend on the symptoms and treatment of croup. But knowledge of the laws of health did not enable him to secure himself against much suffering in the year 1858. The trouble and anxiety which this entailed on his wife involved her in her turn in a prolonged illness in the following year. She had a long, tedious recovery, and her medical attendant strongly advised her removal from Glasgow to Cumbrae as soon as she could be moved. He said that she must never think of returning to the warehouse if she valued either her health or her life. To be banished from a sphere in which she had always taken so active a part, as might be imagined, did not at all accord with her wishes. But necessity knows no law. Taking all the circumstances into account, they resolved to give up their share of the business. The hardware and fancy goods department was sold, and the glass and china warehouse was taken over by Mr. McDougall and his sons, the latter having already, not long previously, been taken into partnership.

The Robertsons had worked in harmony with the McDougalls for many years. The two husbands felt themselves under deep obligation to the two wives, both for their counsel and for the energetic part they had taken in practice. Mr. and Mrs. Robertson, on their part, could not but feel some regret at the moment of retiring, but by this time they had, according to their own account, as much of worldly pelf as would, with care, keep them in such a position as they had no desire to go beyond. It may be added that they apparently had enough to enable them to keep the doors of their hospitable house ever open to their friends, to come when they will, and to stay as long as the most pressing kindness can induce them. At any rate they avow that they have never had reason to repent the resolution upon which they acted.

That the adoption of such a course was in Mr. Robertson's mind some time earlier may be seen from a letter, dated June 28, 1856, which he wrote to his friend, Mr. Henderson, then in Calcutta.

"MY DEAR SIR,

"I am glad to hear from your welcome letter that you are well, and although you find much that is dissimilar both in customs and climate from what you had at home, still you are hopeful of enjoying a fair share of health and pleasant and agreeable society. Many thanks for the mica. It is just the thing I wanted, and as much as will serve me for a long life-time. Excuse me for not making the acknowledgment sooner. I had a little project in my mind of making you a pin set with Mungo Park's moss, but it was long before I could find the little plant in fruit, which caused delay. I have now the pleasure of sending the pin for your acceptance, and I hope that its appearance will never be less cheering than the moss was to Mungo Park, when he lay down in the wilderness exhausted and ready to die, but upon seeing this little plant he said to himself, 'If God cares for this little moss in the desert, He will not be forgetful of me.' Cheered with the thought, he gathered renewed courage and resumed his journey, and soon found the huts of some friendly Indians. Of the balance of my own cares and pleasures I have no reason to complain. We are all in good health, for although my head troubles me a little, it is comparatively well to what it was two years ago. I am sometimes dreaming of a retreat from business, but can never find resolution to force my way out."

Even in January, 1852, when writing to his friend Mr. Cook on the drawbacks and advantages which change, variously and at different times or even at one and the same time, presents to the human mind, after remarking that a thousand little ties and fancies tend to accumulate obstacles against change, he thus pursued the theme :—

"In this way delays are continued often long after resolves have been made, and often till some causality or other terminates the dilemna. Then change we must ; and if for the worse we blame the fates, and if for the better we laud ourselves.

"But still I long to change from the noise
    Of the bustling town and its boasted joys,
    Away from beneath the shifting smoke
    That impedes all life's currents that are under her cloak ;

"Away where the air is sporting free,
    Refreshing itself on the daisy lea ;
    Where the hum of the bees is heard so sweet,   ,
    Instead of the clanking noise of the street ;

" Where the free birds' chorus in gladness swells,
 Where wild flowers carpet the hills and the dells ;
 Where nothing's less sweet than the burnie's note
 That wimples away past my cheerie cote."

He did not in the end fix his " cheerie cote " by the side of a wimpling brook, but in a place that suited his pursuits much better, within a stone's throw of the sand and rocks that fringe a sheltered sea.

CHAPTER XIII.

ALARMING VOYAGE—IN THE WRONG BOAT— THOMAS EDWARD.

IN 1860, the year of his retirement from business, Mr. Robertson obtained a lease of Fern Bank, at Millport, in the well-loved island of Great Cumbrae. The leasehold was subsequently converted into a freehold tenure, and since 1886 this house has been his permanent residence. In 1860, however, his two sons were still at school in Glasgow, so that the family lived principally there, at 4, Regent's Park Terrace, facing the Southside Park, and at Millport only during school holidays.

When the two sons began business for themselves, on their account the family moved more into the centre of Glasgow, residing first at 108, Woodlands Road, and then at 42, Kelvingrove Street.

In the course of years, Glasgow no longer suiting his wife's health, Mr. Robertson bought a house at Uddingston, six or seven miles out of the town, to which he removed in 1882.

It was Uddingston to which nearly sixty years earlier he and his friend Hamilton had found their way when seeking work one harvest-time, and where, after being out all day in the fields, "with Thestylis to bind the sheaves," the two gentle swains had solaced their evenings with Buffon and with Homer.

At the later period the winter climate at Uddingston did not suit his own health, and for this reason he parted with the house there to his eldest son, and determined to live the year round at Cumbrae, only making excursions from it as convenience and inclination might direct. Under these circumstances some additions had to be made to Fern Bank, which the builder agreed to execute in four months, and which he managed to complete very satisfactorily in twelve. He has ever since congratulated Mr. Robertson on the good effect of his dilatory proceedings.

These migrations have here been enumerated together, not for any special importance or interest that they have in themselves, but to make the story complete in its geographical and economic details.

It will be observed that the principal place of residence was more than once determined by the requirements of the children, not by the pleasures of the parents, and it may also be noticed that a change of abode, which is a very insignificant detail on paper, may mean considerable anguish of mind to the possessor of a fine and varied natural history collection.

The inconveniences that did in fact arise from time to time by the transfer from place to place of Mr. Robertson's numerous specimens, were reduced within moderate compass by the methodical habits of a business man, and were borne with as much equanimity as an enthusiastic naturalist can be expected to display.

The frequent journeys between Glasgow and Millport were, as a rule, so many additions to the pleasures of life. Considering the charming character of the route at almost every season of the year, they could scarcely fail to be so to persons of intelligence and taste. Before the days of steamboats it is said that a sailing vessel sometimes occupied three weeks in beating up the Clyde from Cumbrae to Glasgow, but the railway and the steamer have now rather united than separated the two places by the modest limits of a two hours' journey. However, to this happy state of things there may now and then be exceptions, as will be seen by the following extract from Mr. Robertson's diary, relating to the time when he was removing his wife to Millport on account of the extremely infirm state of her health :—

"Came down to Cumbrae on January 20, 1860. Brought down Mrs. Robertson. When we left Fairlie for Millport it came on a thick snow-storm. The sailors lost sight of the lights, and in a few minutes lost all knowledge where they were. On letting down the plumb found we were in four and a half fathoms of water. The vessel was put a little south-south-west, when we were soon in upwards of fifty fathoms. We were soon in sight of rocks ahead, but no one could tell what they were. The wind was beginning to rise, and it was proposed to cast anchor as soon as water sufficiently shallow was found. They backed out a few hundred feet from the rocks, and we found ourselves in seven and a half fathoms water at the bow and nine and a half at the stern. We then cast anchor. This was about half-past nine. At this time the sleety snow was driving very hard, and no one yet knew where we were, some thinking one place and others somewhere else. A light was seen often, but none knew where or which it was. Conjectures regarding it were all equally vague, and nothing definite was ascertained till about four o'clock a.m., when the snow cleared off, and when we found that we were lying at the back of Farlane,* and the light we had seen was the lamp on Millport Quay. We now heaved anchor and were soon safely at Millport Harbour, after sailing about and lying at anchor for upwards of seven hours within ten minutes' sail of our destination."

Mrs. Robertson was carried ashore with as much tenderness as circumstances permitted, and no evil results followed from this alarming and dangerous experience. The salutary air of Cumbrae and the pleasurable excitement of the new house both helped to restore her to health.

With his time now practically at his own disposal, Mr. Robertson, with renewed ardour, indulged in dredging and shore-hunting for the animals of the sea. As already observed, on land also there was no want of attractive material for him to work upon. The carboniferous rocks round Glasgow were rich in fossils; and he found much to his liking in the microzoa of the limestone series.

Linnæus, it will be remembered, had the misfortune to marry a shrew, who, when her husband was expecting a visit from the king, took the opportunity to fling out of window all the choice specimens he had

* This is the local name of Fairland Point.

laid out for the royal inspection. Whether the outraged naturalist was tempted to fling his spouse after
his specimens is not recorded. Science in Mr.
Robertson's household was pursued under happier
circumstances. All along, he says, he had the
sympathy of his wife in his natural history hobbies,
and when relieved from the duties of business, besides
sympathy she gave him substantial assistance in
those pursuits, and after a while she chose the
recent foraminifera for her own favourite group.
Her important and valuable collection of those
minutely beautiful objects bears witness to the
scientific acquaintance with them to which she
attained.

Dredging expeditions in company with his wife,
slight of frame, but "with a heart for any fate," and
the two boys, bold, athletic lads, were generally a
source of great pleasure and amusement to the whole
party. Even the occasions in which they were caught
in rough storms or met with other disasters, which
did not prove fatal to any of them, are now looked
back upon with not a little satisfaction.

In 1865, they were at Campbelton, in Cantire, and
found themselves unable to hire a rowing boat. This
was disconcerting, as without something in which to
get out to sea the object of their trip would be de-
feated. After much inquiry they heard that the
agent of the steamboat company kept a boat for his
own private use. They called upon him and asked
for the loan of it, which he kindly granted. As their
object was to go out with the surface net after sunset,
they agreed to call again at 8 p.m. The agent then

sent his boy with them to show them the boat. It proved to be a fine one, with nice long oars. Well satisfied with their good fortune, they stepped into it, and were soon in the middle of the bay. The night was fair, and their prospects were good, so that they were in no hurry to return. It was not till about midnight that they cared to relinquish their hunting and turn homewards. When approaching the pier they were rather surprised, late as the hour was, to perceive two men at the steps. They heard one of them cry, as soon as they came in sight—

"That's her, that's her; if I get a hold of the wretches I'll drown them."

As they neared the landing a volley of curses was poured down upon them. Fearing danger, they held back a little till they could learn how matters stood. It soon appeared that they had taken away a boat they had no right to. They tried to explain how they came by it, but the man was in such a fury that he would not hearken to anything they said. It was a question whether he heard them at all amidst the noisy torrent of terrific language he was using. At last his companion seemed to explain to him how the mistake had happened. The fact was, the agent's boy had not taken the trouble to see whether he was pointing to his master's boat or a stranger's. The two men were the captain and mate of a trading sloop. They had hurriedly come ashore for a few things that they wanted, leaving their boat at the steps, and lo! when they came back, the boat was gone.

They had been watching for the last four hours,

pacing up and down, with ever-increasing disgust and impatience, and wrath surging up more and more violently in the captain's breast, their stay on shore causing the most inconvenient detention of their own vessel in the offing, and great concern to those on board of it.

The excursionists saw that they had given, if not good reason, at any rate strong occasion, for the threats and abuse that the irate seaman had showered upon them. They expressed their extreme sorrow for the great trouble and annoyance they had unconsciously caused, and explained the object they had in going out with the boat after dark. This seemed to interest and appease the captain a little, and he appeared at last to be not altogether unwilling to part with them on good terms. The boys, however, on reaching home, expressed a conviction to their mother that, had he been able to reach them when they first came within sight and hearing, he would certainly have tried to put into execution his threat of drowning the whole party. His expressed desire to consign them to a still lower deep than that of ocean may be charitably presumed to have been only sound and fury signifying nothing.

Though Mrs. Robertson, by not being present, escaped the discomfort and alarm of the last incident, of another uncomfortable one she was herself the heroine. With some friends, she and her husband had been searching for curiosities among rock-pools on the coast. Some specimens of a rare starfish were found, of which she undertook the care. Her attention, however, being in some way distracted as she was walking over the slippery seaweed, she fell backwards, starfishes and all, into a pool of water. At this unexpected collapse, her husband, not choosing his language in the excitement of the moment, ejaculated, "Oh my stars!" Upon which his friends very unjustly concluded that he was thinking more of his starfishes than of his wife. In the sequel both wife and stars were happily rescued from the rocky bath.

On one of their visits to Tarbert they were anxious to have a day or two of work with the dredge in that neighbourhood. Unluckily there were no small boats to be had on hire, and as it was the time of the herring fishery, boatmen were as scarce as boats. The herrings engrossed the attention of all the nautical population. At last they obtained leave to use a private boat. But it was small and rickety, and a short experience convinced them that it was in no way suitable for dredging purposes, and could only be trusted near shore in smooth water. The only capture worth notice made by its aid was of a fine large *Luidia fragilissima*, the Lingthorn of Forbes, a starfish that sometimes measures more than two feet across.

The difficulty of obtaining the species unbroken has been already referred to. In this instance the specimen was lying spread out in five or six feet of water. Attempts were made to bring it to the surface on the blade of an oar. It often slipped off. At last they managed to get it into the boat and to lay it out on the dredging-board. On such excursions they generally took with them glycerine, which is said to kill starfishes, and at the same time prevent them

from breaking into pieces. Their experience of its
use in this respect had been only partially satisfactory,
but it was now at once applied to the avenues of the
Luidia. Just as they were hastening to deal with the
last ray, it began to break off within an inch of the
extremity. By an instant drenching with glycerine,
its destructive propensity was put a stop to. The
specimen is still the finest in Mr. Robertson's collection, and exhibits the arrested effort at disintegration.

Finding that the boat was of little use, the Robertsons landed for the purpose of shore-hunting, and in
this the harvest was more productive. But while
they were poking about on an elevated part of the
shore between tide-marks the tide crept up unobserved
and surrounded them.

As there was no great danger, they were unwilling
to strip off shoes and stockings in order to wade
through a stretch of soft black uninviting mud. The
firmer route by which they had reached their
eminence was shut off by deeper water. On the
other hand, there was still accessible to them a stone
dyke put loosely together without mortar. This they
proceeded to scale. When on the top, it was
necessary to advance on hands and knees. Mrs.
Robertson took the lead, and her husband brought
up the rearguard. They found, indeed, that it required far more skill than they had calculated on to
balance themselves on the loose ridge of unsteady
stones. Nevertheless, they managed to outcrawl " the
cruel crawling foam " of the incoming tide, and to win
their way in safety, and dry-shod, beyond that am-
phibious region which sea and land alternately claim

and alternately forego. Yet such is human nature even in the most philosophic persons, that their spirits at the moment were not so much elated by the triumph of the escape as depressed by a sense of the comic figure they must have cut in the eyes of a few onlookers.

In several of his more distant natural history excursions, Mr. Robertson had the enjoyable companionship of his wife, who then always took an active part in the work in hand. He pays a tribute to her genius in domestic economy by expressing his belief that by their going together in most cases the expense incurred was less than if he had been by himself. When staying for a week or so at a place they used to take apartments, which with a good manager at hand were far more economical than being at an hotel, and more home-like, besides giving them more freedom for laying out and examining the treasures they gathered, and for going out and coming in at the hours which suited their pursuits.

In June, 1866, they left Glasgow for Aberdeen. Their object was to see some of the post-tertiary deposits of the north of Scotland.

While staying at Aberdeen, they took a stroll along the shore, and were amused at seeing four or five young women going into the water with a long net about six feet deep, the meshes of which seemed to be about the size used in the common herring-net. A hole was cut out in the middle, about four feet in diameter, and a long bag of white bunting, thin woven cloth, was placed in it. This was to capture sand eels (*Ammodytes lancea*). The women entered the

sandy bay till the water was nearly up to their arm-
pits, and when the waves came, they leaped up to
keep their heads above water. They went round
forming a half circle, dragging the net nearer the
shore till the under edge of the white bag was nearly
above the water, whereupon its contents were emptied
into a sort of wide-mouthed bag or apron which one
of the women wore tied round her waist for that
purpose. The little fishes were then taken ashore to
be subsequently used for bait. The process was
repeated till the women had gathered enough for their
requirements at the time.

Leaving Aberdeen, Mr. and Mrs. Robertson called
on Mr. Jamieson, of Hellon, Professor of Geology in
the College of Aberdeen, to make some inquiries
regarding the post-tertiary deposits in that side of the
country, which they were proposing to investigate.
They were courteously received, and benefited much
by the information that was given them.

As they knew that Mr. Thomas Edward, the naturalist, resided at Banff, whither they were going, they
had a wish to see him. They asked Professor Jamieson whether he could give them an introduction to
him. He said he would give it with much pleasure,
but feared it would be of little or no use, as he and a
friend had called upon him lately and received little
encouragement to make his acquaintance.

They had obtained from the professor all the particulars they needed regarding the post-tertiary deposits
of the north-east of Scotland, so they took train to
Peterhead, where their first business was to go to some
tile-works, which, they were told, were about a mile

and a half distant. When they had travelled what seemed more than a mile, they asked again, and were told that they were fully two miles away from their destination, and at their next inquiry the distance was again increased. However, at last they reached the place, took notes of the character of the deposit, and for future examination put up some of the clay in bags which held about ten or twelve pounds' weight of it in the damp state. These the tacksman of the works obligingly offered to send into Peterhead to their lodgings. He also directed them to a clay deposit in the neighbourhood of a small village called Annochie, saying that it was but a very short distance off, down a narrow pathway.

If distance in the former case had an elastic character, much more did they find it possessed of it in this. The impression was perhaps intensified by fatigue and a craving for food.

On reaching the village they asked a policeman whether there were any hotel or other place of refreshment there. He said that there was no such place in the village, and to Mrs. Robertson's modest suggestion, that a cup of coffee would be better than nothing, he could only reply by proposing the uncertain possibilities of a grocer's shop, within sight of which he civilly led them. Two carters were at the counter. The wayfarers asked an attendant if they could have a cup of coffee, as they were very tired and could not get one anywhere else in the village. The young man very readily went to inquire whether they could be obliged, and their hopes rose high as they sat and waited his return. But he soon came back, and said that what

M

they wanted could not be supplied. The only biscuits the shop could offer were so covered with red sweet-meats that they were in no way tempting to the appetite of travellers ready for a well-cooked steak or a mutton chop. The highly genial hospitality of which they were in the end partakers is thus described by Mr. Robertson :—

" I inquired," he says, "of the landlord, who had now come forward, if he had any beer.

" He said he had, but that it could not be drunk on the premises.

"' Well,' I said, 'we can drink it outside. Will you please to draw the cork ?'

" This he declined to do, nor would he allow it to be done in the house.

" I said, would he allow me to knock the neck off the bottle outside?

" We understood that we might do as we pleased outside, but that nothing in that way could be per-mitted inside of the house. We left, not in the best of humour. I brought the bottle with me, but Mrs. Robertson protested that she would not taste the beer. We came, as we thought, to guess pretty truly the cause of the snarly refusal of the grocer to do any-thing for us. He had no doubt seen us coming along conversing with the policeman, and those two carters that we found in the shop when we entered had been getting their dram, and he thought that we were a snare that the policeman was laying to entrap him, for we could not see how he could be so rude if there had not been some cause or another of that kind.

" We sat down by the roadside. I *did* break the

neck of the bottle, as I really needed something to help to carry me back to our lodgings, and I think that I got Mrs. Robertson at last to share the contents of the broken-necked bottle, as it seemed to be no punishment to the grocer to throw it away; but had it not been paid for before he refused to draw the cork I certainly would have allowed him to keep his beer."

It is fair to observe that Mrs. Robertson does not admit the accuracy of that part of the account which describes her as condescending to share the contents of the bottle. Nearly a quarter of a century has elapsed since the event. There were no independent witnesses of the transaction. An impartial historian, however, must not conceal a circumstance which indirectly bears upon the disputed question. After the example of the old voyagers, who gave names of such significance as Port Famine, Desolation Bay, and Cape Tribulation, Mrs. Robertson stigmatized the village of the churlish grocer as "Hungry Hole." Now hunger, they say, does not come into prominence in the greatest straits of the human frame until thirst has been in some measure allayed.

Little satisfied with their entertainment at Annochie, they now went in search of the clay deposit. This was not easily found, as the tile-making at the place had long ceased. But they had the good fortune to meet with the farmer in whose field the work had been carried on. He showed them the old workings, and pointed out some curious circumstances which had been observed by himself and corroborated, he said, by professional men.

He stated that about fifteen feet below the soil the workmen had come upon charred wood where a fire had been made, and that the remains of an old kitchen-midden were close by, wherein shells and fragments of bone had been plentifully met with, and a layer of peat which would have been very acceptable for fuel, if it had not been for a very offensive odour that it gave off when burning, by which its use as fuel was precluded. Peat has always a peculiar smell, one that to many persons is not agreeable. Partly, perhaps, for the sake of auld lang syne, Mr. Robertson himself, so far from disliking the smell of peat in general, has a partiality for it. Moreover, whisky with the flavour of peat was at one time very much esteemed by the drinkers of toddy. No influence of association, however, could make this Annochie peat acceptable to his nostrils. It had, he says, a noxious odour beyond any other that he had ever heard of. The charred wood, under the thick deposit of peat and clay, whatever its date may have been, evidently belonged to the human period.

While the Robertsons were conversing with the farmer upon prehistoric remains and other subjects, the gamekeeper of the estate joined the party, and hearing their object mentioned, he said that he could show them where some clay was exposed that contained shells. This proved to be clearly a patch of the same clay that lay under the peat of the old working which they had just left. After taking a supply of it, they began their return journey.

The gamekeeper directed them the best road to Peterhead, and escorted them a good piece of the way.

They passed a field in which there were rabbits in hundreds. This turned the conversation to the great abundance of certain animals in particular localities, which Mr. Robertson had had frequent opportunities of observing, so that he was in no way disposed to disbelieve the gamekeeper's statement that he supplied the Squire's house with so many dozen eggs of the peewit, or "peeweep," weekly while the season lasted. But when the gamekeeper followed up this record from his own proper employment by telling them of a neighbouring gentleman who had found a fossil head of a man with eyes and mouth and all complete, which he urged them to go and see, they excused themselves on the plea of want of time.

His account reminded them of the farmer who found a clay nodule in a brickfield and believed that it was a fossil potato. There were the eyes, and the very shape of the old red tuber, and the scar of the root by which it hung. Nobody need tell him it was not so. He had been fifty years a farmer, and should surely know a potato when he saw it.

After they had done all that they could at Peterhead, they prepared to go to Banff. Although Banff is not far from Peterhead by road, they had to go nearly back to Aberdeen to get to it by rail.

On reaching Banff they first of all went to call on Mr. Edward. He was not at home. His wife thought they would most likely find him on the shore. But there they saw nothing of any one whom they could guess to be a naturalist. On their return they found him at home. After telling him who they were, they asked to see the Museum. He replied that there was nothing there worth seeing, but if they liked he would show them some of the things he had himself.

Mrs. Robertson remarked that that was what they wished to see most of all.

His readiness to be friendly with them most likely in part arose from the circumstance that he and Mr. Robertson had a common interest in the sessile-eyed crustacea, and the parts of Bate and Westwood's work on that subject then in course of publication had shown that they were both corresponding with Spence Bate, and sending him rare specimens and new species of these little animals.

When inspecting Thomas Edward's collection they were much interested by the ingenious, primitive, and economical way in which he had the numerous small objects comprised in it put up. They were fixed by pins or otherwise to a board, the board carrying four pegs, one at each corner to support the next tier above, and so on with a goodly number of shelves thus simply constructed, forming together a cabinet at the smallest possible cost.

Mr. Robertson mentioned to Edward that their chief object in coming to Banff, apart from the pleasure of the visit then being paid, was to see some of the post-tertiary deposits in the neighbourhood ; that he had the names of the places, but that he did not know how to find the places themselves. The first name on the list was Black Pots, the second King Edwards, both near Banff, and a third was at Gamrie.

Thomas Edward said that he knew them all well, and that if Mr. Robertson could rise at 5 a.m., he would go with him to Black Pots.

The time being no difficulty, Mr. Robertson joined him at the appointed hour, with a message from his wife that she would be very pleased if after the return from Black Pots Mr. Edward would join them at breakfast. After some hesitation he agreed to do so, and in due time came very primly dressed. Speaking of their intention to go that day to Gamrie, they said that they would be delighted with his company.

He seemed to muse for a moment, and then gave his knee a slap and said that he would go; that he had a pair of boots to finish, but that he would rise and do them in the morning.

A conveyance was ordered, and they were soon on their way to Gamrie. They were fortunate in having Thomas Edward with them, since without him they might never have found the place where the shells were exposed. At the place in question beds of sand and clay rise to a height of upwards of three hundred feet above the level of the sea, and at an elevation of a hundred and fifty feet a seam occurs, but only a thin one, of shells of an Arctic type, and the seam is so little broken into that it was difficult even for Edward to find it. The place at the time was all overgrown with gorse, and they were partly indebted to the rabbits which had thrown out the shelly sand for assisting them to find what they wanted. After they had made the necessary inspection and filled a small bag with the sandy clay, Edward took them to a friend of his in the village of Gamrie, where they had tea. After spending an enjoyable day they returned to Banff. The next morning Mr. Robertson visited the shell deposit at King Edwards, having gladly accepted the guidance which Thomas Edward volunteered for this excursion.

Their task in Banffshire being now finished, the Robertsons parted with their new acquaintance on terms of kindly friendship, which were maintained till the end of his life.

When the naturalist of Banff some time after was applying for a post in a Scotch museum, he had a hearty recommendation from the naturalist of Cumbrae, but neither his own merit nor his friend's testimonial sufficed to secure the prize for him, trivial as it was. It might literally be said of him that he owed the smiles of fortune to the fortune of having his life written by the ingenious pen of Mr. Smiles. It was a surprise to the world to see how this man through all his miseries and privations had still been faithful from infancy to age to his researches in natural history.

His life and character, and the companion picture of a somewhat more commanding figure, Robert Dick, the baker of Thurso, skilfully as they have been pourtrayed, and although they excite our admiration for the men depicted, nevertheless tend to cast something of a sombre gloom over scientific pursuits. It is well that it should be seen that there is no necessary connection between an intense love of nature and a deplorable condition of a man's private affairs.

Between the careers of Thomas Edward and David Robertson there is an obvious resemblance, together with a strong and instructive contrast, which gives a rather special interest to the circumstance that the two men met as has been described and afterwards kept up a friendly correspondence.

In February, 1867, Mr. Robertson writes to Mr. Edward a letter which shows that the two men did not merely interchange idle compliments.

"MY DEAR SIR,

"Many thanks for your two valuable and interesting papers. I agree with you that much is yet to be learned regarding habitat. Too much weight has been attached to incidental observations, or to those of only a particular season of the year, or observations made (repeated) under similar circumstances, and from such vague finding permanent habitat has been fixed. We might as well set down a crow as the parasite of a tree, because we often find them congregating on it. No doubt there are many animals with fixed (special) habitats, away from which they could not exist, and many parasites which can only live on one particular species of plant or animal, and, in some cases, only on particular parts of the animal or plant ; but many, as you have clearly proved, that have been considered to belong to particular habitats are decidedly migratory in their habits, (their movements) depending, no doubt, in a great measure, on the season of the year, the state of the weather, and the age of the animals.

"In the case of amphipods and such obscure and diminutive creatures, they have to be sought for and studied the whole year round before trustworthy conclusions can be come to.

" Nothing seems more wonderful to me than the power many of these animals have of changing place ; and no way have I seen this so well exemplified as in the take of the surface-net, and particularly after night-fall, when I meet with amphipods, isopods, cumas, and annelids, in very great abundance, saying nothing of the smaller larval forms that often, from their numbers, colour the sea by day and illuminate it by night.   I meet with them on the surface from the shallow shore to over a depth of seventy fathoms, many of them characteristic of mud, sand, and gravel bottom habitats.   How the annelids and many others wriggle up through such depths is difficult to con-ceive.   In the commotion of tides and winds many of them must be often carried far from their particular homes ; and the question rises broadly before us, can they unerringly in ordinary cases regain their par-ticular habitats, or do most of these nightly wanderers perish by the way when they fail in that endeavour?"

This is not the place fully to discuss the question here propounded, but it may be observed, first, that many of the little marine animals have motions extremely rapid in proportion to their size ; secondly, that time is within moderate limits no object to them ; thirdly, that, the conditions being similar, they can mostly make themselves at home as well in one spot as in another, even if in the morning they should descend to a flat of sand or bed of sea-weed at a mile or miles away from that which they quitted overnight. But, on the other hand, it is clear that the overwhelm-ing numbers, which would result from the prodigious powers of reproduction possessed by most aquatic animals, are kept in check only by causes which ope-rate from time to time to their wholesale destruction.

To quote many of Mr. Robertson's letters on scientific subjects would not be much to the purpose unless they were accompanied by a manual of marine zoology to throw light on the names and the terms that are used in them, but two that he addressed to Professor Koelliker may be given as characteristic examples.

"Millport, September 23, 1864.

"MY DEAR SIR,

"The beautiful little amphipod you gave me yesterday along with the fine specimen of *Hyperia galba* (Montagu), I think, from the appearance in the bottle, is *Iphimedia obesa* (Rathke). I find it on the fronds of *Laminaria saccharina*. However, I will examine it with the microscope, and make sure as soon as I go to Glasgow. I will look and see if I have any specimens of the *Clymene* that you so kindly wish to associate my name with, but I fear that I may not have them; I think that it is possible that the *Synapta*, which I enclosed for you yesterday, may be new. I have not had time or opportunity yet to compare it with *Synapta tenera*. If not a variety of that species, it is none of those that I have seen. I am very sorry that I have been unable to procure for you a living specimen of *Chætophorus*.* The tide has not been so low since you came as to allow them to be reached. We leave here to-morrow morning (Saturday) for Glasgow, and will feel great pleasure

* *Chætopterus* was the name intended.

if you can find time to call as you pass through Glasgow for Edinburgh."

Some of our readers may be able to measure their own knowledge of the subjects with which Mr. Robertson was familiar by attempting to assign to their various natural orders the animals that happen to be named in this short letter. The next is of a rather different character.

"4, Regent's Park Terrace, October 31, 1864.

"MY DEAR SIR,
    "I beg to acknowledge receipt of your valuable present of Dr. Claus' book. I value it greatly for two reasons :—
    "First, as a pleasant remembrance of your short stay at Cumbrae, and the great benefit that I derived from your valuable instructions. There is one regret that I may express connected with this pleasant subject, that is, that I had not the benefit of those instructions ten years ago. A timely index to the proper path saves many weary wanderings.
    "And second, for its own intrinsic value. I find that it treats on the very objects which I am, above all others, interested in—the copepoda. We have no book, I may say, in the English language on this subject. We have, no doubt, Dr. Baird's 'Natural History of the British Entomostraca,' but it scarcely touches on the marine copepoda. Although I find difficulty in the language, the plates are so well executed (and, I believe, quite trustworthy) that I am managing to make the most of it available.

Already I have made out from it several species that have been long nameless in my collection.

"The apparent immutability of creatures so low in the scale of being seems most wonderful. I find that we have some of the same species here as are found at Messina, in all their entirety of form, independent of the difference of influences in constant operation between two places so widely apart. *Porcellidium fimbriatum* is one of the species which I refer to. It is a tenacious sucker. It often adheres so firmly to the vessel in which it is placed that I have to use a little spirits on the brush to get it removed. But so far as I can make out, Dr. Claus does not notice this fact. Perhaps he has not had the opportunity of seeing the animal alive himself.

"Mrs. Robertson and my two sons join me with kind regards. Hoping that you all got safely home and well,

"Believe me, my dear sir, yours truly,

"DAVID ROBERTSON."

The friendship and correspondence with Professor Koelliker was begun by the Professor's consulting Mr. Robertson on the proper proportion of seaweed to seawater required for the maintenance of healthy conditions in an aquarium.

The general notion at that time was that the water in the aquarium could not be kept wholesome for the marine animals unless some of the more or less bulky algæ could be induced to live in it with them. The transplanted weeds frequently died, and in consequence poisoned the water they were intended to purify.

Mr. Robertson at once satisfied Professor Koelliker's mind on the subject by asking him to consider what proportion in the ocean itself the whole bulk of the vegetation bore to the whole mass of the water. The fact is that in an aquarium the microscopic algæ which grow without any intentional cultivation on the sides of the vessel are quite sufficient vegetation for all sanitary purposes in the colony.

Some years earlier than this Robertson had been corresponding with P. H. Gosse on the habits and peculiarities of a sea-anemone and a hermit-crab which enter into a very curious partnership.

Gosse, in his " History of the British Sea-anemones and Corals," 1860, describes the cloak anemone, *Adamsia palliata*, as always selecting for its support the inner lip of some univalve shell, the shell chosen being always, he believed, tenanted by the same species of hermit, *Pagurus Prideauxii.* The only instance in which he had ever heard of the *Pagurus* being found dissociated from its friend was one communicated to him by Mr. Robertson.

He mentions that the *Adamsia* itself in early life has the power of shifting its quarters, and among the evidences of this he says, " While writing this article, Mr. D. Robertson sends me accounts of two in his possession which manifested the same propensity. Between the anemone and the shell to which it is affixed there is often a little horny film of membrane invariably extending beyond the margin of the lip, making, as it were, an adventitious continuation of the shell, and following the same general spiral direction." " From several specimens," Mr. Gosse continues, "for which I am indebted to the kindness of Mr. D. Robertson, I have been able to learn the nature and object of this membrane," and after a discussion of it he adds that, from various observations as well as from information supplied by Mr. Robertson, it appears "manifest that the membrane is a provision for the support of the growing *Adamsia*, when it has selected small or broken shells."

Still more interesting are the observations which Robertson supplied to Gwyn Jeffreys, for use in the "British Conchology," published in 1863, on the habits of *Lima hians*, a marine shell-fish allied to the pectens :—

"In confinement they build freely ; and so far as my observations go, they live longer in that state when they are supplied with the requisite materials, but failing such supply they frequently make nests of their own byssus. They also spin their byssal threads to assist them in ascending perpendicular or steep places ; and like the common mussel, the *Lima* often suspends itself by one or more fibres. Its attachment, however, is only slight ; for the least irritation or alarm causes it to detach itself from the cable and bound off. It does not seem to be particular as to the kind of building-material which it uses. At Lochranza in Arran I found their nests among the muddy roots of *Phyllophora rubens*, without the addition of any harder substance. At Rothesay the nests are made of small gravel ; and at Cumbrae they soon fill the dredge, being formed of thick and matted clusters of nullipore. On this bank I never find them free, they are all encased, at all seasons of the year, young and old, from the size of a pea to the full-grown state, each having its own separate nest. A remarkable peculiarity of *Lima* consists in the tenacious grasp of its tentacles. Sometimes when my finger touched the animal, it was rapidly seized by the tentacles, as by those of an *Actinia*, and so firmly that I have thus dragged the *Lima* round the tank. It seldom let go its hold till the tentacles were torn away, or, as I believe, voluntarily thrown off by the animal. The tentacles so detached still adhere closely to the object they have grasped, their free ends twisting about as if in conscious life, and they are with difficulty taken off. Notwithstanding this property I frequently find a small crab (*Porcellana longicornis*) in their nests, and not unfrequently an annelid (*Polynoë*),* but almost invariably a greenish gelatinous annelid.† This last kind I have noticed lying across the tentacles of a large *Lima*, which seemed to be quite at its ease, and by no means incommoded by its neighbour. I have frequently kept *L. hians* in captivity for many months. I have now, January, 1863, one which I took in May last, and it looks in good health. It commenced building in a day or two after it was put into the tank, and has ever since lived under its own roof, adding from time to time to the size of its oblong nest. This word (nest) is, in a wide sense, not inappropriate as applied to the mode of architecture ; but it must not lead to the idea of incubation, with which the structure seems in no way connected."

Mr. Robertson has also witnessed the deposition of

* *Flemingia plumosa.*   † Perhaps a species of *Siphonostoma.*

the ova, the flow continuing for about fifteen minutes, and, to all appearance, in two streams, this being one among the numerous instances above referred to of the astounding powers of multiplication in marine animals.

Besides the crab and the worms, Mr. Robertson took from among the fibres of the nest of this same mollusk a rare species of isopod, which Bate and Westwood named *Munna Whiteana.* It is not perhaps very remarkable that, when a nest or home is constructed by one animal, other creatures should take advantage of the ingenuity and labour employed, but it is scarcely a piece of common knowledge that even a shell-fish can build itself a house, and adapt a variety of materials to its purpose.

Mr. Robertson was corresponding at this period with nearly all the men of eminence whose writings were concerned with the treasures of the sea. In 1863, we find him sending a nudibranch to Mr. Joshua Alder, of Newcastle ; and in the same year he opens an intercourse with Mr. G. S. Hodge, known for his investigation of the pycnogonida, a kind of sea-spiders, so slender in body that the digestive cavity has to be prolonged into the legs. Now, too, he becomes acquainted with Dr. G. S. Brady, with whom, not long after, he was to make scientific expeditions and write elaborate scientific papers. In the following year he began to correspond with Mr. Henry Brady on the foraminifera, in the study of which it has been already mentioned that Mrs. Robertson has taken an exceptional interest.

In 1865, Dr. Baird, of the British Museum, published

N

his "Supplement to Johnston's Catalogue of the British non-parasitical Worms," and in this book numerous references are made to specimens contributed from Cumbrae.

In Bate and Westwood's work on the "British Amphipoda and Isopoda," which appeared in parts between 1862 and 1868, repeated acknowledgments are made to their kind and valued correspondent in that island, and his observations are frequently quoted. The work in question, indeed, might have been made more full and more accurate had the authors, among their numerous other avocations, found time to appeal even more than they did to his assistance and resources.

In 1862, he began a correspondence with the Rev. Alfred Merle Norman. The first subject of it was the groups of minute crustaceans, known as the ostracoda ; but, as might be expected with two such naturalists, whose sympathies ranged through the whole field of marine zoology and botany, as well as over many matters outside of that field, the intercourse thus begun soon extended to many other points of interest which they had in common, and has been prolonged through many years of ardent scientific industry and personal friendship.

An incident in which they were concerned together may bring this chapter to a close. The two, with another friend, had been out on a dredging expedition from Millport. They were delayed by a storm for some hours after their return to Fern Bank had been expected. When it was now pitch dark, the rain descending in torrents, and the wind blowing in strong gusts, at length there came a violent ringing at the bell.

Mrs. Robertson, whose alarm had long been aroused, rushed to the door, and a maid with her, but it was only to knock their shins against a bucket which some unknown hand had placed in the porch.

Presently there came a second loud ringing, and, the door being opened, this time Norman appeared, unaccompanied, but with another bucket in his hand. He had scarcely said, " Please take this in," when he was forced to add, " There goes my umbrella," the handle of that friendly protector having been at the very moment suddenly snapped by the wind. He then returned to help Mr. Robertson, who was still struggling on the road with the remainder of the apparatus, and at length they were all safely housed, and all apprehensions about them allayed.

CHAPTER XIV.

THE NATURAL HISTORY SOCIETY.

AMONG bees, the proverbial type of industry, those that are by far the best known and most admired are the hive bees that work in common and lay up their stores for the general good of a large community. But there are other species of bees, no less industrious, that work in solitude.   So, among men of science, there are some essentially hermits, who study and observe in seclusion, undistracted and uncheered by companionship in their investigations.   Others are more sociable in temper, and, no doubt, in the play of wits and in the friction of argument to men of such a disposition fresh avenues of inquiry will be opened, errors of judgment laid bare, and a sense imparted enabling them to eliminate what may be only stale and unprofitable in their own efforts from that which is useful and to the point.

It was to the latter class that David Robertson emphatically belonged.   He never stood aloof shyly or selfishly, but ever offered his capacity for others to make use of, though offering it in a manner the most modest, and often under the guise of asking for information. It will not be surprising, then, that wherever men were banded together for the pursuit of knowledge, as far as his opportunities allowed, he joined himself to them.

It has been already stated that in 1852 he became a member of the recently instituted Natural History Society of Glasgow. He was for several years a member of council, twice or thrice vice-president, and from 1887 to 1890, the president of that society. In 1859, he joined the Philosophical Society of Glasgow, of which he continued to be a member for eighteen years. He entered the Geological Society of Glasgow also in 1859. Ten years later, that is, in 1869, he was elected a Fellow of the Geological Society of London. In 1874, he published, together with Messrs. Brady and Crosskey, a monograph of the post-tertiary entomostraca of Scotland, including species from England and Ireland, in the annual volume of the Palæontographical Society; and in that year we find the secretary, the Rev. Thomas Wiltshire, thanking him for his zeal in obtaining other subscribers to the highly important series of publications which that society has so long been issuing. In 1876, he was elected a Fellow of the Linnean Society.

For many years he was one of the trustees of the Andersonian Museum, who, by the whimsical will of the founder, meet on the longest day and on the shortest day of the year, and are instructed to regard their honorary office not as a trouble but a great distinction.

In 1865, he very unexpectedly received from Vienna the honour of the following diploma :—

DIE

KAISERLICHE KÖNIGLICHE

ZOOLOGISCH BOTANISCHE GESELLSCHAFT

IN

WIEN

ERŇENNT

SEINER WOHLGEBOREN HERRN ,

DAVID ROBERTSON

ALS

MITGLIED

COLLOREDO MANNSFELD

PRÄSIDENT.

WIEN AM 31ᵗᵉⁿ *Jüli*, 1865.

DR. THEODOR KOTSCHY,   GEORG RITT. V. FRAUENFELD,

Vice-Präsident.   Secretär.

The names David Robertson, Colloredo Mannsfeld,
Dr. Theodor Kotschy, George Ritt. v. Frauenfeld,
were *written*, Colloredo in English characters, Mannsfeld in German, Frauenfeld with a small initial.
The letter which accompanied it is not without
interest.

"K. K. Zoologisch-Botanische Gesellschaft,
                    "Wien, Herrengasse, Landhaus.

"SIR,   .

"The Imp. Rl. Zoologico-Botanical Society of
Vienna has elected you a member in their last meeting, August 2, 1865.

"I have the honour to transmit you here included,
the diploma, begging leave to request your kind
assistance in promoting the society's purposes.

"Allow me, sir, to assure you of the pleasure I feel
in transmitting to you this token of the most sincere

acknowledgment of the eminent services Science owes to you, especially as I feel myself deeply indebted for all the kindness and assistance you have been pleased to bestow on me. I beg leave to profit of the present occasion for offering you again my warmest thanks for the kindness of which you gave me so many valuable proofs during my last visit to your country, and to express the hope that you will be pleased to continue the scientific intercourse begun under auspices so favourable to me.

" Believe me, sir, in highest esteem,

" For ever yours most truly,

" GEORG RITT. V. FRAUENFELD.

" Vienna, August 17, 1865."

Such a letter does honour both to the writer and the receiver. But so little was Mr. Robertson inclined to trumpet his own distinctions, that when some years later he happened in signing a scientific paper to designate himself a member of this society of Vienna, he was supposed to be joking, until he produced the emblazoned diploma itself, the wording of which we have copied above.

From his voluminous correspondence with A. M. Norman, one of Norman's letters will here be in point. It does not exemplify the valuable stream of natural history knowledge which flows through that writer's epistles in general, and an account of which would belong rather to his biography than to the present, but it illustrates the sort of appeal to which, both by him and by many others, Mr. Robertson was expected freely and readily to respond :—

"MY DEAR SIR,   " Newbottle, Fence Houses.

" I was away from home for a few days when your note arrived. I hope that the delay in consequence of this in sending back your echinodermata has not inconvenienced you, and that *Amphiura Chiajii* will still reach you in time for the meeting referred to in your letter.

"You kindly offered to aid me in a former letter in any way in which you were able as regards the echinodermata. May I then ask you to carefully collect in your dredgings this summer *small* specimens of the genus *Asterias* of all species, especially any that appeared to you to differ from common forms.

" Next, I shall be much obliged if you could add to my collection *good* specimens of *Amphiura filiformis*, *Amphiura Chiajii* and *Amphiura brachiata,*—especially the latter, should you succeed in meeting with it. The only specimens that I have (from the Moray Firth) are very imperfect.

" Keep your eyes open for the new British *Ophiuræ.* I have seen one imperfect *Ophiura affinis* from Lamlash. Look out also for *Holothuroideæ.*

" I have retained two or three small and badly preserved *Asterias*, which were in the box with the large *rubens*, as I cannot satisfy myself at present as to what they are, without further examination and comparison with other specimens.

" *I particularly want a series of young Amphiura glacialis*, the smaller the better.

" Believe me, my dear sir,
" Yours very truly,
"ALFRED MERLE NORMAN.

" May 23, 1865."

In a previous letter, dated February 16, 1864, Norman says, "Many thanks to you for your kind present of algæ, which reached me safely; fifteen of the species and varieties were new to me, and most of the others of interest."

Robertson never allowed the superior charms of marine zoology entirely to wean him from his love for the botany of the sea. The early days of the Natural History Society of Glasgow passed unrecorded, except for a pamphlet of a few pages and a short notice in *The Naturalist* for January and February, 1855. The latter contains an account of the session of 1854, and mentions that Mr. Robertson had exhibited a rare seaweed, *Desmarestia herbacea*, which had been sent him from Ireland.

Though the Glasgow Society was founded in 1851, the first volume of its Proceedings was not published till 1868. The records, however, printed in that volume begin with the eighth annual general meeting, held in Anderson's University Buildings, September 27, 1859. The very first entry is of specimens exhibited by Mr. David Robertson, and, though naturally since the foundation of the society a vast number of papers had been read, the first described in its annals is also one by Mr. David Robertson.

Many collectors and descriptive writers have to be content with dead specimens,—among the mollusca with empty shells, which are practically only husks from which the kernels have been withdrawn, and in other groups with corpses either dried or preserved in spirit, and in consequence shrivelled, contracted, discoloured. When animals are brought up from great depths of the ocean to the surface, the conditions of pressure and temperature are so greatly and abruptly changed that the creatures cannot as a rule, by any means yet invented, be observed alive or in a set of circumstances natural to them. But shore-frequenting creatures, and those living at moderate depths, can often be induced to make themselves at home with the naturalist for long periods, displaying their various beauties and singularities of habit, which could in no other way be observed. A wholesome discontent with inanimate specimens may be inspired in the rising generation of naturalists by the record above referred to and now to be quoted :—

" Mr. David Robertson exhibited a living specimen of *Corystes Cassivelaunus,* which had been in his possession upwards of seven months, during which time he had favourable opportunities of observing its habits. In bringing these under the notice of the society, he remarked that this crab, in burrowing into the sand, lies buried for weeks without seeking to change, and that the antennæ clasp into each other when the creature is so situated, forming a tube through which it breathes, and otherwise maintains a communication with the surface. Mr. Robertson also stated that he had seen the ova cast up through this opening—the inference being that the animal had placed it, by means of its claws or pincers, within the influence of the current. Mr. Robertson likewise exhibited specimens of *Nereis bilineata,* and made some remarks upon its habit of living in univalve shells, in company with hermit crabs." The masked crab, on which the above observations were made, shows on the carapace an amusing likeness to the human countenance. It is not at all uncommon, and its habit of holding the tips of the antennæ just out of the sand had been before noticed, but the meaning of this behaviour was now for the first time explained.

At the next meeting Mr. Robertson exhibited a new crustacean from Cumbrae, to which Mr. Spence Bate, on its being sent to him, gave the name *Cuma unguiculata.*

At this period the cumacea, the group of crustaceans to which this new species belonged, had been very little studied, and very little was accurately known about them. Some men of science, whose word at the time was almost law, had declared them to be creatures not full grown, larval forms, while other naturalists had rightly shown that they were adult. There was also a controversy whether they had eyes or no eyes, the fact being that some are blind, while others have eyes. Of the latter set the eye is generally single and central, whereas in Mr. Robertson's species, now known as *Nannastacus unguiculatus* (literally, dwarf lobster equipped with nails), there is a pair of widely separated eyes, which is a very exceptional character in this group.

By ordinary observers the cumacea would be considered rare animals and difficult of capture, yet by methods which will be subsequently described they may in the proper localities be taken by hundreds. Between 1859 and 1889 Mr. Robertson was able to show that there were at least thirteen distinct species in the fauna of the Clyde alone.

Dr. Anton Dohrn, now for many years past director

of the famous marine biological station at Naples, being anxious to study the embryology of the cumacea, visited Scotland for that purpose in 1867. In his "Investigations of the Structure and Development of the Arthropoda," he says :—

"Following the friendly advice of Dr. Baird, of the British Museum, I went to Millport, the watering-place on the island of Great Cumbrae, in the Firth of Clyde, on the west coast of Scotland, near Glasgow.

"Dr. Young, Professor of Natural History at Glasgow University, obliged me by his friendly introduction to Mr. Robertson, the zoologist, well known for his indefatigable faunistic researches. To my great delight Mr. Robertson, at my first visit, showed me a number of species of *Cuma*, all of which he had captured at Millport. He assured me at the same time that I could capture them myself in quantities, and that most of the females would just now be having ova. This was in fact the case."

Elsewhere he speaks of the discoveries which he had been able to make through "the favourable circumstance that in Millport I met with one of the best known crustacean faunas, and in my honoured friend Robertson obtained the assistance of an exceptionally zealous and well-informed Crustaceologist."

In regard to the localities in which the creatures are found, he says, "Very curious is the remarkable delimitation of the species each in its several habitat : Mr. Robertson had already observed the following details years ago, and I had abundant opportunity to convince myself of the complete correctness of his statements, which at first seemed to me very problematical."

With the details themselves we need not trouble the reader. Those who would take up the study of these small but remarkable animals, in which the breathing apparatus appears to be quite unique, should by all means consult the works of Professor G. O. Sars of Christiania, who, like so many other zoologists, several times makes reference to valuable specimens sent him from Millport. In 1879, for example, when re-describing the above-mentioned *Nannastacus unguiculatus* among the cumacea of the Mediterranean, as all the examples he had obtained from that sea were females, "The figures of the male here given," he says, "are from British specimens sent me by Mr. Robertson."

As the females in this group never have swimming feet, with which the males are generally provided, a difference of behaviour between the two sexes results, which Mr. Robertson was probably the first to observe, namely, that the females remain decorously at home in the sand at night time, at which period the males disport themselves in a lively manner at the surface, where they can in consequence easily be taken with a hand-net.

How highly Dr. Dohrn thought of the opportunities which had been presented him by his friend at Cumbrae is shown also in the paper which he read before the British Association in September, 1867. After stating that his investigations had been carried out some weeks previously at Millport, on the Clyde, he further says :—

"In the St. George's Channel at Millport I studied the development of palæmon, crangon, lithodes, portunus, and at last added most special researches on mysis and cuma. I am happy to say that cuma has furnished me with the material which seems to justify me in bringing out a new theory on the morphology and the homologies in the whole class of arthropoda."

At the illustrious station in the Bay of Naples princes and professors, students and tourists, from all parts of the world, pay the homage of their admiration, curiosity, or research. From it have issued a long series of works of high scientific importance. It is, no doubt, to Dr. Anton Dohrn, Dr. Paul Mayer, and one or two others, that its great success is chiefly attributable, but one might be almost justified in considering that Millport stands to it in the unassuming relation of a fairy godmother.

The first of the papers read before the Glasgow society, of which it printed anything more than the title, was called forth by what was supposed to be an epidemic among four species of sea-birds—the common gull, the common guillemot, the puffin, and the razor-bill, which had come much further up the Firth of Clyde than usual, strangely tame and ravenous for food. "They were all in a wasted condition, being almost reduced to skin and feathers, and were found floating in thousands over a wide extent of sea from the mouth of the river Clyde to the Irish coasts."

The paper in question was entitled, "A report on the mortality among the Clyde sea-fowl during the month of September last, by Mr. David Robertson."

It was read on November 29, 1859. It showed the improbability of an epidemic attacking four different species at once, established the fact that the usual food for these particular birds had been wanting from exceptional causes, and that specimens of the birds which had been examined exhibited no traces of organic disease, but that both the conduct of those which survived and the condition of those which perished negatived the hypothesis of an epidemic, and pointed clearly to the effects of starvation.

When this paper was read, "the chairman took the opportunity of saying that Mr. Robertson's ingenious and apparently satisfactory explanation might be looked upon as a final contribution towards the elucidation of the mystery which had lately attracted so much attention."

As this is not intended for an encyclopædia of marine zoology, it will not be possible here to give anything like a full and clear account of those results of his extremely active researches which Mr. Robertson from time to time laid before the society.

At one time we find him discussing the principles of architecture on which the tube of an annelid is constructed, at another explaining the advantage a hermit crab derives from having its claws unsymmetrical, one of them being very small for quickly plying its mouth with food, the other very large for holding its prey and supplying an organic door to its castle. Among various other starfishes, rare or abnormal, he exhibited a specimen of the common five-fingers, *Uraster rubens,* * which " showed a curious

* *Asterias rubens*, Linn.

feature in having a newly developed limb bifurcated."
He also exhibited a specimen of *Caryophyllia Smithii*,
from the lesser Cumbrae, an interesting species of
stony coral, frequent on the coasts of Devonshire, but
" by no means common in Scottish seas, a few localities only being known for it. This specimen afforded
an illustration of the curious reproductive power,
spoken of by Mr. Gosse, in the formation of a new
disk, mouth, and tentacles at the lower end of the
corallum, which had been broken at the base."'
At the same time he exhibited a new amphipod,
which he had discovered at Cumbrae, to which Mr.
Spence Bate gave the name *Stegocephalus celticus*.
The secretary of the Glasgow society observes, that
" this communication acquired a double interest from
the fact of the genus being new to Britain, and the
species new to science, affording another proof of Mr.
Robertson's diligence and excellent powers of dis-
crimination." Unfortunately Mr. Spence Bate forgot
all about the specimen entrusted to him, and the
animal has since been described under a different
name, the genus, in fact, as well as the species, being
new to science.
Instead of taking to himself the honour and glory
of naming a new species, as he easily might have
done by publishing a rough sketch and a few lines of
description, or the description without the sketch,
Mr. Robertson ever preferred to send his discoveries
to those who seemed to be masters in the several
groups to which his specimens belonged. He was
perfectly capable of doing good independent work, in
figuring and describing his own discoveries, had not a

modesty almost excessive restrained him. Yet, had
he been fighting for his own hand, so to speak, he
might have done less real service to science than he
has done by his ever-ready generosity in helping and
encouraging others.

Many of his fellow-members in the Glasgow society
must have marvelled at the long succession of strange
and distinct objects which he produced for their inspection—zoophytes, like the remarkable *Virgularia
mirabilis*, sponges like *Halichondria ventilabrun*,
measuring "twelve inches across the mouth of the
funnel," and withal, fishes, ascidians, shells, nudibranchs, echinoderms, sea-cucumbers, annelids, crabs,
shrimps, cumaceans, entomostraca, corals, sea-anemones and sea-weeds, not to speak of foraminifera and
fossils—these great and varied gatherings being from
the Clyde and its neighbourhood, in the fauna of
which many of the species had never previously been
recorded.

In a joint paper by Dr. John Grieve and Mr. David
Robertson, " On the Marine Zoology and Botany of
Loch Ryan, Bay of Luce, and Portpatrick, from
observations made during a short excursion in 1861,"
the two authors give a very graphic and accurate
account of those strange reefs of honey-combed sand,
which must have excited the wonder of many a visitor
to the seaside. The reefs are the work of a marine
worm.

"This annelid is the *Sabellaria alveolata*. It is
nearly allied to the *Pectinaria Belgica*, commonly
found on our sandy coasts, each individual of which
lives in a single tube formed of grains of sand—a self-

O

contained marine villa. *Sabellaria*, on the contrary, forms a colony of greater or less extent, each individual tube being joined to its neighbour, and so forming an extensive terrace, with fine crescents of self-contained houses. Each annelid has a double plume of golden-coloured bristles, and when, again covered by the advancing tide, each looks out at its own door, the reef must present a scene of great beauty from the metallic brilliancy of their coronets."

It would have been interesting to quote the whole of the account, but that Mr. Robertson disclaims having done more than observe with admiring eyes the scene of which his friend Dr. Grieve penned the description. In a subsequent paper, also of great interest, "On the Luminosity of the Sea," by Messrs. David Robertson and William Keddie, Robertson, it will be observed, was the senior partner.

At a conversazione of the Natural History Society, held on November 24, 1863, the secretary, Mr. Robert Gray, gave a short sketch of its history, plans, and progress, in the course of which he thus alludes to, without the necessity of naming, Mr. Robertson :—

"In the marine section, the society refers with much satisfaction to the successful labours of one of its members, who, by his own unaided efforts, has opened up, in a remarkable degree, the zoology of the Firth of Clyde. Many animals, hitherto accounted rare, are now known to exist as common objects, while the annals of science have received many important additions of animals altogether new to natural history records—discoveries which have caused the Firth of Clyde, and more particularly the Cumbrae Islands, to become one of the best explored and most widely-known districts of Britain."

This was no funeral panegyric, dismissing the object of it into the shades of inactivity and forgetfulness, for in the account of the very next meeting, December 29, 1863, we read :—

"Mr. David Robertson exhibited specimens of two rare fishes—Müller's topknot (*Rhombus hirtus*) and Bloch's topknot (*R. punctatus*), both from the Cumbraes ; also, a recently described crustacean—*Galathea Andrewsii*, from the same locality where it is found plentifully. At the same time, Mr. Robertson exhibited an annelid, new to the British fauna—*Clymene lumbricalis*—from two different localities in the west of Scotland. This gentleman, one of the most successful investigators of our Scottish marine fauna, was especially thanked by the president and members for his valuable contributions to the society transactions, and it was announced that among the results of his recent observations many new and important additions to the local lists would shortly be forthcoming."

By paying this singular and exceptional tribute of respect to Mr. Robertson the society certainly gave him no more than his due, but the value of the tribute consists in this, that it was paid, not by ignorant persons, incompetent to judge, but by naturalists, themselves of sterling merit, as the society's volumes of proceedings sufficiently evince.

Whether Mr. Robertson's scientific researches could really add anything to the pristine and intrinsic grandeur of the two Cumbraes, it is less easy to decide, since we are credibly informed that an old minister at Millport used ever to pray " for the welfare of the Muckle Cumbrae, and the Lesser Cumbrae, and the adjacent island of Great Britain," clearly showing the order of precedence and dignity in which the three sister domains should, at least in his opinion, properly be ranged.

CHAPTER XV

NORWAY—A BOTTLE OF MUD—THE SHETLANDS.

THE minuter details of geological investigation are important in their own sphere, but the general reader can never be persuaded to find them amusing. If two champions descending into a fossiliferous arena suddenly begin to tear up the sand and clay and fragments of rock, to hurl them (metaphorically, and through the medium of the press) at one another's limbs and features, then indeed there is a chance that some languid attention to the subject may be awakened.

We have to admit, however, that Mr. Robertson, numerous as his geological papers were, never in any of them hit the public taste by furious onslaught or biting sarcasm directed against either friend or rival. But though the scientific results of his work, both in geology and other departments, must be left to the specialist, there are several incidents connected with the attainment of those results that are worthy of notice.

In 1866, the Rev. H. W. Crosskey, who was working with him at the post-tertiary clays, had the offer of a free passage to Norway, to go to Christiania in the

North Star, a vessel owned by Mr. Seligman. The same offer was made to Mr. Robertson, who had now returned from his Banffshire expedition, and the opportunity of seeing some of the Norwegian deposits was, he thought, not to be lost. Dr. Gwyn Jeffreys gave him an introduction to Michael Sars, the celebrated zoologist.

The two friends took ship from London. Unfortunately, through an accident that happened to Robertson in his cabin, one of his ribs was broken. Saying little about it till they reached Christiania, he asked, as soon as they were come to the hotel, to have the best medical skill in the town. Dr. Boeck, brother of the able naturalist, the late Axel Boeck, was called in. He could not at first say which rib it was that had been injured. His patient, once himself a student of anatomy, was pretty sure that it was the lowest. Dr. Boeck thought it more likely to be the next or next but one above, as it was rare and not within his experience for the lowest to be broken. However, when by the application of leeches he had reduced the swelling and lessened the pain, he found that it was in fact the short rib that was broken. He paid his patient a visit every day for about a week, and generally called in a second time in the afternoon, saying that he had not come professionally, but for the pleasure of a chat. Professor Michael Sars also called almost every day. The accident retarded work at the clays considerably, but by the end of the week the invalid was able to be taken out, and when they came to any fossil banks, by being laid full length on the ground, he was able to pick out the fossils with some care. When he had to be lifted up on his feet again the pain was very great. But what is that to an enthusiast?

On reaching Christiania he had written home to his wife to say what had happened to him, for they had an understanding that when they wrote to each other they were to state matters actually as they were, so that they need not have the least suspicion that things were either more or less than what was represented, and to this agreement they claim to have always strictly adhered. The difficulty in such an arrangement rests not so much with the good faith of the high contracting powers as with the feebleness of language which cannot ensure that the words used will even denote, much less connote, to her who reads exactly what he who wrote intended.

In the present instance, although Mrs. Robertson could implicitly rely on what her husband told her, she was doubtful what might be the result, and lost no time in travelling from Glasgow to Christiania. She reached London early in the morning. The steamer was not to start till the afternoon. Nevertheless she was anxious to go on board at once, which the agent of the *North Star* line, though most anxious to oblige and assist her, did not think could be managed. He went with her to the docks to see what was possible, and the difficulty was overcome, an old fellow who took her luggage muttering as he went along, "Nothing is impossible for ladies, nothing impossible for the ladies."

On the voyage a fellow-passenger in the ladies' cabin, being much disgusted with the narrowness of her berth, amused her companions by protesting that she would have a good roll in her bed the first night in Norway. A lady already acquainted with that country advised her to wait till she got there before making up her mind to a roll. The Norwegian beds, in fact, are as restricted in dimensions as the Duke of Wellington's, in which a lady friend thought he could not have room to turn over, and the national opinion of Norway would perhaps make the same defence for them that he did for his, that when it is time to turn over, it is time to turn out.

On Mrs. Robertson's arrival at Christiania, to her dismay she was told that her husband had gone off on an excursion. Of course there had been no time for him to receive word that she was on her way to join him. She on her part could not for some time be convinced that the people were not concealing from her some very bad news, or indeed the worst, under what seemed to her so improbable an explanation.

Matters turned out very well with them in the end. They had some pleasant and interesting excursions into the country. They found the conveyances there much better regulated than at home. A book was given them, showing not any mileage rates, but the fares to particular places. At the end of the journey they paid the driver without question according to the guide-book. He took his money with an expression of satisfaction in his face, and never asked for more. Perhaps this is more than London readers can be expected to believe, but at any rate it is no garnishing of the narrative on the part of the biographer, who disclaims all responsibility for any part of the record that may appear miraculous or superhuman. Still it must be allowed that other travellers in Norway keep Mr. Robertson's report in countenance. Some of the incidents of the expedition will be best told in his own words :—

"If we sent word," he says, "from one station to another to have a conveyance at any hour, they were bound to have it for us. On one occasion we had to cross a lake in a rowing boat to the opposite side. We had written that we would require a conveyance some time between twelve p.m. and one o'clock in the morning. We arrived about the time appointed, and two horses in harness were grazing on a little green before the door ready to start with us.

"Mr. Crosskey thought that we would be better to take a sleep and have breakfast before starting, and we would then be abler to pursue our journey. We knocked at the door, and a woman came and opened it. We were rather surprised to see her in her night-gown. She did not seem to be in any way taken (disconcerted) at our appearance. She knew nothing of our language and we knew nothing of hers. However, by laying my hand on the side of my head and bending it over on my shoulder as if I were sleeping, she guessed correctly that we wanted a bed, and led the way along a dark entry * into a room with no more light from the window than let us barely see that there was something over at the side of the wall that might be a bed. She then left without saying a word. We found that our conjectures were right. It was a bed.

* Passage.

"The want of delicacy or decorum appeared to be the custom of the country. In the hotel we left before we crossed the lake, when I had got most of my clothes off, preparing to go to bed, a girl without any notice came in and lifted* my shoes that were near my feet, yet in the most modest way, and retired without a moment's delay. At another place Mr. Crosskey and I had to pass to our bedroom through an apartment where females were sleeping.

"On another occasion, my wife and I were at a most elegant little hotel at a place called Moss, about twenty or thirty miles down the fiord from Christiania. I may mention that the beds were mostly small, single, movable beds for one person, that could be readily taken from one room to another, so that the bedroom could be accommodated with just the number of beds required. In the morning a young woman came into our bedroom before we were up, and as in the other case without any notice. My wife was in her little crib on one side of the apartment, and I was in mine on the other side. The young woman came up deliberately to my bedside and lifted my trousers and thrust her hand first into the one pocket, then into the other.

"I wondered what she meant by it.

"Surely she is not going to rob me before my face in such a mild way!

"But she laid the contents down on the table. She did the same with my vest and coat, and then threw the whole over her arm and walked out.

"My wife was lying looking at her all the time, and

* Picked up.

burst out laughing as the young woman went out, calling across the room to me, 'You are done for now.'

"The maid, however, soon returned with the clothes all well brushed."

Those who have read M. du Chaillu's entertaining book, "The Land of the Midnight Sun," will be familiar with the primitive simplicity and pure-minded freedom of Norwegian manners and customs.

Mrs. Robertson on leaving home had arranged for an absence of a few weeks, as much might depend on the condition her husband was in. Mr. Crosskey, by the limits of his holiday, was obliged to leave Norway as soon as he and his colleague had finished the examination of the shell-beds that were within their reach. As the Robertsons were able to stay a few days longer, they had time to see a little of the country, free from geological cares.

Professor Michael Sars introduced them to his son, Georg Ossian Sars. The latter pleased them much by his modest demeanour, a circumstance the more striking because, as it now appears, from the youthfulness of his looks they had miscalculated his age by a dozen years. He was already, though they did not know it, the author of important works in natural history, and had given the world a foretaste of the pre-eminence in that branch of science which he was destined to attain.

One day he and his little sister came to the hotel to see the Robertsons. She was to be the interpreter, as at that date she had a better command of English than he had, though neither of them had much for conversational purposes, and the two strangers had still less of Norse. The latter feel assured that it would have been highly amusing to any one to have heard the four discussing matters in the existing state of their knowledge of each other's language, with the merry laughs of the young lady at their hits and misses of each other's meaning.

G. O. Sars, who afterwards became an excellent English scholar, has since kept up a friendly communication with them, sending Mr. Robertson his scientific papers, and, as has already been noticed, deriving advantage from specimens of the fauna of Cumbrae.

"We had," Mr. Robertson relates, "a pleasant excursion to Krolevn, where the sun was to be seen, from the summit of Kongsberg, rising shortly after it had set.

"When we arrived in the evening at the hotel at the foot of the Kongsberg, we found that every bed was taken up. The landlord had good English, and as he was a very civil gentleman it lessened our difficulty much, as we could have his advice what was best to be done. When he saw our disappointment, and that I did not yet seem very strong, and that my wife had not the most robust appearance, he said that he was sorry he could not give us a bed, but we could have the use of a room, and that he would give us blankets with a sofa, which we gladly accepted. As we had but a short time to wait till we had to prepare to start for the top of the mountain, a bed could not have given much rest.

"Unfortunately the morning was hazy, with a

drizzling rain, so the sight of the sun's rising had to be given up. As the morning advanced, the weather improved, and after an early breakfast my wife and I got a pony each and a guide. Although we would not see the sunrise, we wished to have a view of the country from the mountain, as well as to see the platform which had been prepared for the king to see the rising sun.

" On reaching fully two-thirds of the elevation, we came to a resting-place, where refreshments could be had. A number of tourists had got there the night before, to be in time for the sunrise, more than could be accommodated within. There was a wooden shed at the back of the house, with a large quantity of hay on the floor, and a head popped up out of it here (who said something) and another there, and in a twinkling the hay was studded with busts of young men who had taken up their sleeping apartment in the hay under the roof of the wooden shed. At the same time a number were busy cooking in the house on an elevated slab like a smithy's hearth. Each had his own little fire on the hearth, and his own little kettle for his party.

" Shortly after we reached this place the rain began again to drizzle, but we were resolved to push on, and although several had come from the hotel with us, they would not venture further, nor any of the others that had been there all night. We got our ponies and our guide, and off we went, my wife and the guide leading the way, and I following. After proceeding for a good way I noticed a high ridge of a rock before us, beyond which I was certain that we would have to walk the rest of the way, as no horse could scale the rock, or, if he could, no one could sit on his back when he was doing so.

"The guide (a boy) was leading the pony by a rope over his shoulder, a considerable distance in front. I was eagerly watching what was to be done when the boy came to the rock. When he did so, without looking behind him he began scrambling up over it. I had only time to exclaim, Gracious! before the pony, without the least hesitation, began to scramble up in the same way.

"It was my turn next. I thought of leaping off, but before I had time to make up my mind my pony had commenced the ascent in the most professional manner, as his brother had done.

"This over, there were no other difficulties in the way.

"It happened just at the time that we had reached the King's Stance the sun shone out brightly. The place commanded a delightful view of the surrounding country. We had now accomplished our task so far. If we had not seen the sunrise from the top of the mountain, we had seen a magnificent panorama of the country. We now retraced our steps. I had my fresh-water net with me, and had a haul or two in some of the stagnant pools for ostracoda, which are still in my collection as a souvenir of our visit to Kongsberg.

"When we reached the 'Rest,' where we had left so many cooking, we were greatly cheered, I suppose because we had first accomplished the ascent that morning. Other parties at once went off to do the same. After some refreshment we soon reached the foot of the mountain.

"I may mention one thing regarding the Norwegian ponies and their drivers. The Norwegians seem to treat their horses kindly—seldom using the whip—and keep them in good condition. The pony itself is docile and willing. They are almost in every case allowed to walk up-hill, but as soon as they reach the top they go off of their own accord with great speed down-hill. Another habit they have been taught, that is, when going into any of the stations * they do so almost at the gallop. Although docile, they are not willing to do what they seem to think is not their duty. When we were going up the mountain, a party at the same time going on foot had a little girl about eight years of age seemingly not very fit for the steep road. I asked if they would allow the little miss to be put up behind me on the pony. The offer was gladly accepted. No sooner was she seated behind me than the pony began to throw up his heels in the most frightful way. If it was a great joy to the child to get up, it was a great relief both to her and to us all when we got her safely down.

"After a short halt at the hotel at the foot of the mountain for dinner, we then got into our carioles. Mrs. Robertson had a driver. I drove my own. They took the lead and I followed. There was rather an awkwardness felt here for a stranger driving, as there is no rule of the road such as we have all over Britain. There, on meeting, it is left to each to take whatever side they choose, and each has to be guided much by

* Hotels or post-houses.

what appear to be the intentions of the other. In this case I had no difficulty, as I had just to follow. On the way, where any likely pool appeared on the roadside I had a haul with my net for ostracoda.

"Mrs. Robertson had managed to indicate to the driver that she was fond of flowers, and before we got home he had her sitting in a glory of them, that he culled from the shrubberies on the roadside. Unfortunately it came on to rain heavily. Mostly all the way along Mrs. Robertson had been driving, to let the driver get the flowers for her. His place was at the back of the cariole, where he could easily leap off and on. When we came within three or four miles of Christiania, my wife wanted him to take the reins, but he clapped his hands, saying, 'Good, good!' meaning that she could drive well, and that he would not take them. When we entered the outskirts of Christiania, she threw the reins back to him.

"She had on one of those very broad-brimmed leghorn hats. About three inches of the leghorn had been folded up on the inside of the rim and fastened down with paste. The rain had loosened the paste, and the deep flap hung down nearly to her shoulders. No description could give an adequate picture of what she was like when she drove into the courtyard of the Hôtel du Nord, amongst about a dozen army officers, with her broad-brimmed hat dripping wet, and herself sitting in a galaxy of flowers. As soon as she could be extricated from the cariole and floral adornment, she speedily made her exit. This did not seem to be any unusual sight, as none seemed to evince any surprise. We got our wet clothes changed and had a good tea and a hearty laugh at the sequel to our journey."

As to the temper and treatment of Norwegian horses, du Chaillu gives an account which very well coincides with the observations made above. "A horse," he says, "as soon as he comes to the foot of a hill, stops when he thinks it is time for the people to get out, turns his head towards the vehicle to see that every one is off, and then ascends. If all are not out, he waits, and when urged by the voice, or by a slight harmless touch of the whip, he seems quite astonished, and often during the ascent stops and turns his head, as if to say to the remaining occupant, 'Why don't you get out?' The farmers and their families invariably walk up-hill; hence the horses are disagreeably surprised when their load remains, especially when the whip slightly touches them on the back. From one station to another the driver often stops, cuts his black bread into small pieces, gives them to the horse, caresses him, treats him to a handful of hay, and then continues his route. This kind treatment not only speaks well for the people, but it also makes the horses exceedingly gentle and docile; vicious ones are seldom found." * There is a fine lesson in all that for those who care to learn it.

Another pleasurable excursion which the Robertsons took was to Dröbak, on Christiania Fiord, where they enjoyed a day's dredging in forty fathoms depth, and fished up some "good things" in the naturalist's sense of that expression. The bottom was mud, shells, gravel, and coral *débris*. The beach at this place was

* "The Land of the Midnight Sun," vol. i. p. 59.

covered with fragments of coral, *Lophohelia prolifera*
(Pallas). It was so plentiful that the garden walks
were made of it. Pieces the size of half a brick were
not uncommon, and some that were much larger could
be obtained, for they brought away with them a
specimen sixteen inches long, eight inches deep, and
seven inches broad. It is a deep sea coral, which is
washed up by the waves.

In his commonplace book Robertson gives the
following note on Dröbak :—" The fiord at this place
is held in high favour by many famed naturalists as
unusually rich dredging ground. From the many
bays and islets, channels and banks, and different
bottoms, it has all the appearance of being all that is
said in its favour.

" My experience was very small—one day's dredging of about five or six hours in a small row-boat of
fourteen or fifteen feet keel, with a pilot and an old
fisherman. The one might know very well the best
channel for the biggest ship, and the other the best
bank for haddock, etc., but of anything more or anything connected with the dredge or dredging they
knew nothing. This was their first adventure. They
were both good oarsmen, and both willing, and with
their channel knowledge and bank knowledge, and
what I could infer from this stock of information, we
were not so helpless after all. Besides this, fortune
smiled upon us with a beautiful day."

They had a letter of introduction to Mr. Parr,
English consul at Dröbak, a relation of " Old Parr,"
renowned for his longevity.

Mr. and Mrs. Parr, after showing them the sub-

stantial hospitality of a Norwegian tea, took them
over their garden, at the foot of which they had a nice
little pier, at which their boat lay and where the tide
was not felt. They had also a finely mounted sledge
for use with a pony on the fiord when it was frozen
over. The house had once been the king's palace.
Of the four acres of land attached to it about one half
was rocky; the remainder sufficed to keep a cow and
a pony.

The Parrs liked the place very much, but as their
sons were being educated in Christiania, eighteen miles
up the fiord, they had thought of parting with it to go
and live in town with the boys. Mr. Parr had bought
the place for a small sum, and the price he put on it
was still not a large one. Mr. Robertson was
delighted with it and all its surroundings, especially
no doubt with the little pier and the boat at the foot
of the garden, and would have closed with Mr. Parr at
once, as Mr. Parr was inclined to do with him. But
Mrs. Parr was by no means willing to have the bargain
concluded, till they made certain what their future
plans would be. A promise was given that, if they
made up their minds to part with the place, notice
should be sent to Mr. Robertson, but that notice never
came.

It was now drawing near the day when the *North
Star* would again be leaving for London, and it was
time for the travellers to be preparing for their return
journey.

The dredging-ropes having been all well dried in
the sun, Mr. Robertson began to pack them up,
whereupon he was seized with a fit of excessive

sneezing. It was difficult to conjecture the cause, as he was neither subject to such attacks nor had he had any exposure to cold. The fit soon passed off, and no more was thought of it till they reached home, when upon his taking out the ropes the sneezing began again with the same violence as before. It then occurred to him that before leaving Dröbak he had been dredging among medusæ, and that the ropes were covered with their stinging fibrils. There could be little doubt that it was the dry dust of these irritating fibrils that caused the sneezing. Evidently a large fortune is awaiting some one who will turn this accidental discovery to advantage in the manufacture of snuff.

On arriving in the Thames the steamer was boarded as usual by the custom-house officers. Mr. Robertson was showing some of his luggage to one of them, and Mrs. Robertson was showing the contents of a large trunk to another, who appeared to be the principal. He asked if she had any silver plate or tobacco to declare.

She answered that she had not, and volunteered to lift the things out herself, as some of them might be easily broken.

Instead of accepting her offer, he said that he would take every care of them, and bending down on one knee began to lift them up. At last he came to a row of cigar-boxes snugly packed at the bottom of the trunk. Upon this he looked up in her face with an expression on his own that seemed to imply his belief that King David, when he said, "All men are liars," might justly have extended the remark to one at least of the female persuasion.

Mrs. Robertson's countenance was by this time in a glow of mirth, and she said,

"Oh! they are my husband's crabs. They are easily broken. I will take the boxes out for you."

Lifting up one of the lids with her finger, she brought to view an assortment of various kinds of crustacea. The officer in the most confused manner said, "All right, all right," and looked at no more of her boxes.

Towards the end of the year Mr. Robertson read a paper to the Natural History Society, which is worthy of notice. A two-quart bottle of mud had been sent him by Mr. Moore, of the Liverpool Free Museum, which had been dredged by the trawlers about twenty miles off the Great Orme's Head in North Wales.

"About two-thirds of the bottle was filled with black shiny mud; above that was a thick layer of light-coloured muddy sand and shelly *débris*. This, again, was overgrown with a layer of sponge—the whole reaching within an inch or so of the neck of the bottle. The bottle itself appeared, from organisms attached to it, to have lain in the sea for a considerable time. The black mud of the lower layer was rich in ostracoda and foraminifera, but not so diversified in animal remains as the light-coloured upper portion, which contained the spines of echini, the spines and plates of starfishes in great profusion, besides the remains of other organisms of less frequency, as larval balani, the limbs and plates of two crabs (*Porcellana longicornis*), fragments of zoophytes, etc. Of the zoophytes, there were ten species met with, so far as they could be made out."

Besides these there were young shells, of half a dozen different species, that appeared to have lived in the bottle and in the black mud, and moreover the bones of a fish, the ribs of which had a span nearly as wide as the mouth of the bottle. "It is most likely that it got in alive head foremost, and not having room enough to turn, and from the smallness of the bottle's mouth, and the elevation of the fins, it would be unable to get out backwards, and consequently perished in the trap."

We may pity the stupidity of the poor little fish, but must remember that before now the skeleton of a human hunter has been found encased in a hollow oak tree, no less the victim of an unforeseen and unintentional snare.

But in his bottleful of mud what most interested Mr. Robertson was that it contained eleven or more species of foraminifera and eighteen or twenty of ostracoda. It was the study especially of these two groups that led him in the following year, 1867, to the Shetland Isles.

On this excursion also Mrs. Robertson accompanied him. Although slight in figure, she was very ready in those days, and is not unready even in these, to go out with him in the boat with "the small dredge" when other assistance could not be obtained. They often did good work by themselves, sometimes even reaching depths of sixty or seventy fathoms.

According to the accounts they had heard, the Shetlands were almost out of the pale of civilization,

the people living in huts which had to be entered by
stooping or crawling on hands and knees, the smoke
of the fire having no outlet but by the door, and the
thatch in consequence becoming so saturated that it
was taken off every year to manure the potatoes.

On their arrival at Lerwick they were surprised to
find that what they saw by no means tallied with
this description. The town was neat and clean, the
shop-windows gaily ·furnished, and the girls of the
place dressed up at least to the same style or fashion
as might be seen at this period among the same class
in Edinburgh or Glasgow.

Lerwick being the metropolis for fancy knitting of
woollen garments, they wondered to find no part of
the women's dress consisting of what was made in
the Shetlands, but on inquiry learned that it was
thought beneath them to wear any of the goods
which they themselves made for sale. This point of
honour was doubtless cultivated by the shop-keepers,
for as they obtained the knitted work from the girls
not so much by money purchase as by barter of
clothes and food, it was strongly the storekeepers'
interest to decry the use of home-made garments, and
to recommend their fashionable London goods as the
only wear.

At the hotel at which the Robertsons put up,
rowing boats could come in alongside of a little pier
close to the door, which made their getting out and
in with their dredging-traps comparatively easy.

"At this time," Mr. Robertson says, "one of my
sons was collecting eggs and the other birds. When
we left there were strong entreaties to take the gun

with me. At this time I did not wish to be troubled
with anything else than what I was specially going
for. However, they got some of the preservative
materials given to my wife in hope that something
would turn up in their way. When out with the
dredge we saw so many birds that we had not at
home, that I wished that I had brought my gun.

"We had an introduction to a Mr. Gatherer, supervisor of excise. On mentioning the matter to him,
he very kindly lent his gun. It was single-barrelled,
long, and rather of an old style, but an excellent gun,
and I never felt one with less rebound.

"We were delighted with the little piebald guillemot. We had never seen it before alive. When flying between us and the high cliffs in the distance its
mode of flight and mottled colour put us in mind of
butterflies. We bagged only three of these little
guillemots, for we made it a point never to kill more
than what we wanted for our own cabinet, with the
exception of one or two for a friend.

" Richardson's Skua, *Lestris Richardsonii*, was
another bird wanting in my son's list. They were
plentiful on Noss, and Mr. Gatherer got leave for
us to shoot over that island. As the skua was the
only bird that we were in search of, we could soon
have procured all that we wanted, but for a slight
mishap to our ammunition. Some of the small shot
had got in among the powder and forced some of the
lead into the touch-hole. The next charge would
not after several trials go off. We found what the
matter was, but had nothing with us that would force
the shot out. We had got one bird, but there was no

hope of getting more that day. However, my wife found a strong needle among some of her reserves. I broke the point off it, and with it managed to drive the lead back. We then secured two males and two females of the skua.

"We put up an eider duck, and, as she was getting off the nest, she covered her eggs with a copious evacuation. If this was intended to scare off intruders, we thought that, in most cases, it would be most efficient. The question arose, could she clean them so as to ensure hatching? In this case she did not require to hatch them. It was a bird that was particularly wanted, and I brought it down. The nest was made up of a large quantity of feathers, broadly spread on the ground. It is said that they pluck the feathers from their breasts to make their nests, and it seemed most likely, as the bird was very bare of feathers all over the under part of the body, and the feathers of the nest appeared to agree well with the feathers of that region. Among other birds obtained during our short stay at Lerwick was the tern, *Sterna arctica*. These birds were in beautiful condition.

"The stormy petrel, *Thalassidroma pelagica*, and its eggs were especially wanted. Our friend Mr. Gatherer told us that the best place to get the petrel was on a little island called Papa, a little distance off Scalloway. We crossed over to Scalloway, where we stayed with Dr. Robertson, and Mr. Gatherer joined us next day. He accompanied us to Papa.

"For this expedition we got a boat and two strong men. When we were a little way from shore the sea

became very rough and lumpy. Mr. Gatherer advised
strongly to return and run into some more sheltered
place, and take a few hauls with the dredge. His
dog, a large Newfoundland, became extremely sea-
sick. I was most anxious to get the petrels, and
urged strongly to get to Papa, saying that we
could get along the sheltered side of another island.
Mr. Gatherer pleaded hard to turn, representing that,
if we got to Papa, it might be still more difficult to
get back.

"The boatmen seemed to be of my feeling—not to
turn, and perhaps with as potent a reason as my own.
I wanted the petrels and the petrels' eggs, and, as
the men were hired by the hour, they wanted a longer
day's pay. One of the men sat at the helm ; the
other sat at the foot of the mast, with his face to the
helmsman, who, every now and again, gave orders to
the man to lower the sail, and it was down at once,
and, as soon as the circumstance was past requiring
the lowering, it was as speedily up again.

"At last we reached the island. There was only
one house on it. Mr. Gatherer had told us that the
man and his wife of this house supplied a Mr. Dunn,
a dealer, with petrels and their eggs. Mr. Dunn was
a taxidermist, and kept a small inn, and went with
gentlemen on their hunting expeditions. At Papa
we were received kindly by the fisherman's wife.
Her husband was away with his boat. We soon
made inquiries for the petrels. I wished much to see
their nests. She said that she did not know them ;
that it was her husband that got them ; but when he
came home, which she expected he would do in a

day or two, she could send some of the birds to Mr. Gatherer. She supposed that she might send a few if they could get them, but said there were some times when they could not get one. So we could make no more of her. Mr. Gatherer said that she knew quite well where the petrels' nests were, but she did not wish to let us see them ; she wished to have the disposal of them to herself, and not to let us know where to come back and gather them ourselves. This was all natural and reasonable enough, and we importuned her no further.

"We went out to the shore, which was covered with large boulders, some of them many tons' weight each, which, we were told, were thrown up in heavy storms. The sea-birds built under the stones, as well as starlings, which we saw going under them. On the steep beach, or shore, we heard the birds cheeping, as it were, under our feet. I began to roll away some of the stones to get to them. I laid my ear to the opening that I had made, but, when I held my ear to the one side of it, I thought that the sound came from that side, and when I held it to the other side I was as sure that it came from that. It put me in mind of ventriloquism. After working away at the opening, the sounds seemed to be as far from me as ever, and it was as uncertain whence they proceeded, so I gave up the search as a hopeless task.

" Fortunately, the afternoon was much calmer than the morning, and we had some dredging on the sheltered side of the island, and a haul or two on the way back to Scalloway.

" As the days were long, and scarcely at any time

dark, we never saw a star through the night, and it was often past midnight before we got home.

"On the night in question we did not leave Papa till near 11 p.m. When we got to Scalloway there was a large fire on the green at the back of the town, two women apparently in their night-dresses stirring up in it something like clothes, no one being present but themselves.

" We could not conjecture what they were burning at that time of night all alone. The scene was exceedingly weird.

" In the morning we mentioned to our landlady the fire we had seen outside of the town. She said that a bad fever was raging in the town at the time, and that when any died of it all the bedding they had used had to be burned—no doubt a wise precaution.

"We did not get the petrels till after we had left the Shetlands. Mr. Gatherer sent them to us at Kirkwall. We were rather astonished at the number, both of birds and eggs—twenty-four of each ; but we were still more astonished at the price—fourpence each, the same for birds as for eggs—sixteen shillings in all. We had left thirty shillings with Mr. Gatherer to pay for them, but we had no idea that there would be anything like the number sent. We learned after-wards, from Mr. Gatherer, that the price they charged us much exceeded what they got from Mr. Dunn of Stromness."

In the beginning of this expedition Mr. Robertson presents himself in the light of a stern parent, re-buffing the petitions of tiresome children, although, as the narrative proceeds, he seems to spend most of his time, and not only braves the tempest, but makes his friends brave it with him, in order to gratify the wishes of the lads at home.

He did not, however, neglect the purpose for which he had made the journey. There was a good deal of dredging done, but as it was chiefly for ostracoda and foraminifera, those little organisms took up little time in preservation. He only took the siftings that passed through a sieve of a quarter of an inch mesh, and these were put up in bags holding about seven or eight pounds weight of ooze, to be examined in future at leisure.

He had hoped, when planning the excursion, to do some good work with the surface-net as well as with the dredge, but he was very much baulked in this expectation, not so much by want of favourable weather as by the circumstance that frequently the small medusæ were so excessively abundant that the net filled with them as soon as it entered the water, and, even when there were fewer, they were still so many as to overpower everything else, it being next door to impossible to separate the rarer treasures from this slippery gelatinous mass. The number of jelly-fishes of various sizes cast up on the sea-shore are sometimes sufficiently striking, but they bear but a small proportion to what the ocean is capable of supplying. One day, when the boat was taken in between the rocks of Bressay and Noss, on looking over the boat-side they saw the water thick with small medusæ as far as their eyes could penetrate down into it.

It would not be safe to depend on seeing the

myriads of jelly-fish in that particular locality on any chance visit, but another sight, even more beautiful, which the travellers enjoyed, is almost as persistent as the islands themselves. Tier above tier, and hole above hole, in rows round the shelving rocks, close together sit the sea-fowl, in general, species by species at their respective elevations, the kittiwakes lowest, the foolish guillemots with their black heads next, and the herring-gulls above.

Mr. Robertson understood that the knitting industry of the Shetlands at that period brought in from fifteen to sixteen thousand pounds annually.

In reference to a statement, made perhaps more than half in jest, that neither man nor woman was ever to be seen on horseback there not busily engaged in knitting, Mr. Gatherer told him that, during all the many years he had been in Shetland, he had never seen any one knitting on horseback, although it was common enough to meet women walking along the road and knitting apparently with ease.

If it could be determined by some experiment, it would be interesting to know whether any time is really saved by doing two things at once. There are who boast that they can knit and at the same time read a book with enjoyment, but it is probable that some detriment results either to the mechanical effort or to the mental, or to both.

The Shetland women have some excuse for wishing to double their parts, for it appears that the chief portion of the drudgery falls to their share. They cut the peats and carry them home on their backs. For this purpose a creel made of straw rope, and called a keistose, is used. It is shaped something like a beehive, but longer, and is attached by a belt that rests on the carrier's bosom. The peats, brought to the town from a distance of one or two miles, are sold at twopence a creel. The women fetch and carry about four loads a day. When met with going or coming they are always knitting.

That they are hardy and willing workers may be easily judged. One striking instance was seen in the case of two women drawing a harrow in a small field near the town.

When the whalers are going to sea, the women carry the chest or other luggage of their husbands or brothers down to the ships. When asked why they do not leave the men to do it for themselves, they answer pathetically that they may never see them again ; " it may be the last service we will ever have it in our power to do them."

There is, unfortunately, another side to this pleasing picture. They have, like the rest of humanity, the defects of their virtues. As the able-bodied men mostly go to sea, and many of the young men go south to seek employment, the female population is in great excess of the male. Hence it comes about that courtship, instead of being the chivalrous devotion of the strong, degenerates into a slavish competition on the part of the more numerous and weaker sex, and, if morality does not suffer, there must be many innocent persons wronged by injurious suspicion.

That the Shetlanders were not, or, at any rate, till recently had not been, very far advanced in the arts, Mr. Robertson concluded from the character of their

mills. On the west side of Bressay he saw three mills
on the same stream not far distant from one another.
" The machine," he says, " consisted of a vertical
wooden shaft, which might be about six feet in length,
the upper end of which was connected to the grinding
or mill-stones, while the lower end had four or more
blades attached in a line with the axis of the shaft.
The water was directed so that it would only act on
the blades on the one side of the shaft, giving it a
rotatory motion, which was communicated to the
horizontally placed grinding-stones, thus avoiding all
complicated and expensive machinery. No doubt a
vast amount of the lever power of modern water-
wheels is lost in the primitive Shetland contrivance.
Still, it was simple and ingenious, and at any rate was
a step in advance of the more primitive hand-quern.
A hut was built over the mill, having its floor over
the stream. None of the wheels were large, apparently
about seven or eight feet in diameter."

Many of the natives kept a sheep or two to supply
their knitting-yarn, paying so much annually to the
farmers for "grassing" these animals. They did not
cut the wool off the creature, as is usually done, but,
at a particular season of the year, they tore it off.

One day, as Mr. Robertson was taking a walk on
the moor, an incident happened which recalled the
experiences of his own shepherd-boy life. A young
woman and a lad were bringing together a small
flock of sheep and lambs. When they had collected
them, they singled one out and laid it down on its
side, and began to pull the wool off, and in a few
minutes had it stripped bare, whereupon they let it

go free. It had a black lamb, and was itself black. As soon as it found itself at liberty it began to bleat on its lamb, which was about two hundred yards off with the others, anxiously running about in search of its own dam. It now heard and responded to the calls of its mother, and came running towards her with all speed till within a few yards of her, when it stood and looked at her in bewilderment at the strange appearance she presented. But the well-known bleat of the mother reassured it, and the next minute it was engaging as well the parental protection as a good drink of the maternal milk.

The farmers are now introducing a larger breed of sheep, but it is said that the wool is not so fine nor so suitable for the knitting work as that of the old Shetland breed.

In July the nights in Shetland are so short that practically some trace of daylight is never wholly wanting. The Robertsons, finding the nights as pleasant as they were short, were often out till after the break of day. They remarked that in these early hours the lark was never heard as they had heard it in the south of Scotland just before the grey light of coming dawn was discernible. They supposed that in Shetland, when all the twenty-four hours of the day were more or less luminous, the lark found no opportunity for greeting the sun's return with a matutinal song.

One evening, after taking tea with Mr. and Mrs. Gatherer, they had some agreeable chat with them on the customs of the Shetlanders. Among those described that of the Visors was the most striking.

Q

A number of young men of all ranks dress themselves in fantastic costumes, their apparel being in general gorgeous in appearance and not unfrequently also rich in quality. The disguise is made as complete as possible, so that one is seldom recognized by another. Between Christmas and New Year's Day they go about after dark, visiting different houses, and demanding refreshment of the best. During this period all windows and fanlights are kept closed and shuttered as securely as may be. But the inhabitants who wish to escape with the least scathe leave their doors open and their table spread with the best they have, allowing the Visors to enter and partake and deport themselves according to their own fancy.

It is an old custom, like those of mummers and maypoles and bonfire boys in England, but, as compared with the present condition of those queer survivals, it is much more arbitrary and mischievous, and is made the opportunity for paying off old scores of long standing, or at any rate grudges conceived during the past year.

When the Visors wish to display their resentment, they enter the delinquent's house, and daub the walls with tar, sometimes giving the furniture and pictures also a taste of it, besides otherwise damaging windows, garden, or outhouses. It is said that the authorities have tried over and over again to put down these detestable practices, but without effect. So well is the secret kept that they have never been able to obtain a conviction. The constables that are sworn in are said to be the most active themselves in the lawless work! When the "people love to have it so," it is difficult to save them from themselves.

CHAPTER XVI.

THE LANCELET—THE HEART-URCHIN—THE SCOOP DREDGE.

IN addition to the many foraging expeditions which he made, Mr. Robertson did much hard and solid work in natural history at home, besides carrying on a vigorous correspondence with various scientific men. Writing on November 9, 1867, to Dr. Anton Dohrn, who was then at Jena, he discusses with him some of the peculiarities which distinguish the males and females of the cumacea, and then observes :—

"I have nothing to say of myself, further than that 1 am working hard at the fossils of the clays. True, they are laborious, tedious, and at times tantalizing, with nothing to deal with but the dead, bare, dry husks of the animals, yet even there the indefinite variety of forms and figures gives an increasing desire to know more and more of them."

On the 27th of the same month he again writes, as follows :—

"November 27, 1867.

"MY DEAR DR. DOHRN,

"We have received your very welcome letter. It has thrown over our whole household that beam of pleasurable influence that attended your presence during your stay at Cumbrae. Had any intimate friend of yours at Jena come here and told us all you have said in your letter and more, it would have interested us much, but would have wanted the charm your own dictation has, wanted the pattern of your own pointed thoughts and expressions, which call up a duplicate image of yourself and doings, which makes us feel a nearness to your presence that no third party could impart.

"We had been wondering many a time if you had got the little cup. We thought it possible that it might be carried away amongst the packing paper unobserved. It was put in at the time you were packing your books. You had gone upstairs for something to tie on them, when Mrs. Robertson said, 'What can I put in his box?' She spied the little cup. It suited the fancy. The next minute it was ensconced in your box, but barely a moment before your arrival. She had difficulty to disguise her emotions that she had played you a trick.

"We are all glad to hear of your progress. The course you have laid down to be followed gives the fullest trust of successful results, that is, to take *nothing for granted*, to *examine everything for oneself.* At the first glance that may appear circuitous and tedious, but it must prove the safest and in the end the shortest way, when substantial trustworthiness is taken into account.

"I am glad to hear of Spence Bate's kindly feelings towards you. . . . I intended to have been at Edinburgh before the winter set in, to try and find *Cuma*

Edwardsii (Goodsir), but have not yet managed time, and now I fear the season is too far gone. However, I intend to take the first opportunity, and I have some hope of finding them. Goodsir says they were taken at the mouth of the Firth of Forth, and that *Cuma Edwardsii* (Goodsir) were the most common,* and further that they were of a pale straw colour, indicating, I think, a sandy habitat. Therefore, with a little perseverance and proper appliances, and with the knowledge I have of their habits, I think there is some chance of finding them.

"In regard to the tenacity of life of the *Amphioxus;* in the first place I kept one in captivity for upwards of twenty months in a small earthen preserve-pot, measuring only 3½ inches deep by 3½ inches wide, filled with sea-water, including one-third of small gravel. It was placed in a small sitting-room where gas and large fires were burning from sunset till ten or twelve at night, when they were both extinguished. This was continued in the winter months with few exceptions, causing the temperature in the twenty-four hours to be very unequal. At first the water was changed every other week or so, but, from a listless state these changes seemed to occasion, the practice was discontinued, and only at long intervals a little fresh water was added to make up for evaporation, and at last after a very long neglect it died, when we found that it had been living in water holding in solution nearly the double of the usual quantity of salt present in sea-water. But the

---

* That is, the most common of the *three* species which Goodsir discovered.

strongest proof of its power of endurance was when
under the microscope for examination, placed on a
flat piece of glass often from ten to twenty minutes
at a time, and yet when dropped into the water it
would dart off, making one or two evolutions, and
disappear in the gravel, to all appearance little the
worse for the unnatural exposure. I may, however,
mention that sometimes after examination, when
returned to the water it would sink down and lie for
some few minutes on the gravel in a motionless state,
as if it were dead. But this it often did in the water,
when repeatedly poked out of the gravel in which it
always, by preference, lay concealed.

"We all earnestly hope that you will try and force
a point to come by Glasgow on your journey, and
with some time on your hands. Could we not drop
a note to *Limulus* to lay her eggs at the suitable
time?

"Mrs. Robertson and the boys are gratified by the
cheers. Be assured of all our warmest regards and
well wishes.

                    "Yours very truly,
                        "DAVID ROBERTSON.

"Since writing the above, your paper on the
'Morphology of the Arthropoda' is to hand, for
which accept my thanks. Although only in the
embryonic state, yet all its parts are well defined,
and it is full of elements of large development."

To explain some of the allusions in this letter, it
should be remarked that Dr. Dohrn was at this time
anxious to study the development of the young of

the remarkable crustacean known as *Limulus*, or the king-crab; and, with the mother crab in an interesting situation, it would have been almost impossible for him to leave home, lest the little king-crabs should be born and pass through their early stages in his absence.

The *Amphioxus*, or lancelet, is a little fish not always to be had for the asking, but procurable in the Clyde by those who know how and where to seek it. It is remarkable, not for its high, but for its low, organization, being a vertebrate without vertebræ, for its spine is an unjointed column of cartilage. It has no ribs, no pectoral or ventral fins, no brain worth speaking of, and its skeleton is rudimentary. Had the lancelet and its immediate allies become extinct two or three hundred years ago, there would have been a missing link very difficult to supply or explain between the fishes and the animals of lowlier structure, in other words, between the vertebrates and the invertebrates.

The incident of the "little cup," an unconscious plagiarism of the trick played by Joseph in Egypt upon his brother Benjamin, serves to indicate the relations of familiar friendship established between the household at Millport and their guest, the learned but frolic-loving professor. Though work was the object of both his visits, and though hosts and guest were alike keen in pursuing it, there was a readiness on both sides to enliven labour with merriment, the whole party being thoroughly capable of enjoying a joke and happily endowed with a sense of humour.

That Dr. Dohrn, on his part, fully appreciated not only the genial hospitality but also the scientific acuteness of his host is shown by the circumstance that, at the close of one of his visits, he carried off almost by force a paper on which Mr. Robertson was then engaged, in order to ensure its being published in the *Quarterly Journal of Microscopical Science* in London.

The paper was upon a subject which has not even to this day exhausted its interest for the persistent observer who wrote it.

St. Paul, it will be remembered, upon a time takes occasion to make the memorable and magnanimous observation, " I have learned, in whatsoever state I am, therewith to be content."

Of Mr. Robertson one might fancy, from the course of his biography, that, numerous as were the changes he effected in his condition of life, there was no state in which he had either learned or found any inclination to be discontented, yet in scientific matters he has shown a most uneasy temperament, one never satisfied to let go of an unsolved problem, but restlessly renewing his inquiries and attempts to find out all about it. In one of his letters he even finds fault with the sigh of Alexander the Great that there were no more worlds to conquer, since in science there are more worlds than either our own generation, or perhaps any future generation of the children of men, is likely to subdue.

The paper which Dr. Dohrn carried off had to do with the common heart-urchin, *Amphidotus cordatus* (Pennant).

This sea-urchin is very abundant. It is said to be found in all the seas of Europe, and in all the sandy

bays of Great Britain, where, after storms, it is
frequently thrown up in great numbers. The shell, or
test, denuded of its spines, like a shorn sheep, is consequently very familiar to seaside visitors. Not unfrequently also it is met with still clothed in its spiny
apparel. The reputation of a naturalist may then be
easily earned by any one who is able to observe, with
a supercilious or patronizing air, that it is only the
common heart-urchin, or still better, that it is the
Amphidotus cordatus of Pennant. With this learned
information both the giver and receiver will in general
be thoroughly satisfied, and, insomuch as the creature
is so common, will not think it worthy of any more
notice.

The men who advance science, however, regard
objects that are common in a different spirit from
this. Professor Huxley, in writing his book on the
Crayfish, desired, he tells us, " to show how the careful
study of one of the commonest and most insignificant
of animals leads us, step by step, from every-day
knowledge to the widest generalizations and the most
difficult problems of zoology, and indeed of biological
science in general."

The fact, it may be observed, that an animal or plant
has won for itself a position in many parts of the world,
and that its multitudes give it prominence, is a sign
that it must have some quality that favours it in the
battle of life, and its commonness, instead of making
it worthy of contempt, is rather a token that, in its
own field of competition, it has won the victory.
Further, the naturalist is well aware that almost any
one species of animal, however numerically common,

would take a man his whole lifetime thoroughly to examine and explain in all the points of its development, habits, and structure. Also, for any attempt at a full investigation there is scarcely anything more advantageous than that the animal should be common.

"In the early part of 1868," Mr. Robertson says, "on the shores of Cumbrae, my attention was attracted to many holes occurring in the sand. In tracing them to a depth of four or five inches, I found an *Amphidotus cordatus* under each hole. The diameter of the hole was about equal to that of a crowquill, and often irregular, and rose straight over the long spines surrounding the dorsal impression of the test. By placing one of the animals in a glass jar with two or three inches of sand below and over it, and covering the whole with water, an opportunity was afforded of seeing how the holes were produced and kept open. Long contractile processes, with tentaculated heads —described by Forbes as 'long ringed worm-like suckers,' and by Johannes Müller as 'locomotive feet'—were thrust up through the sand, and were seen slowly, and apparently searchingly, wandering over its surface, then grasping particles of the sandy matter in their tentacles, and finally dragging them rapidly down into the hole. As these holes extend from four to five inches into the sand, and I have seen these prehensile tentacles stretch between two and three inches over its surface, the length of these instruments cannot be less than six or seven inches."

It is certainly a weird sight to watch, with the aid of a strong lens, one or more of these thread-like messengers, with a head like a microscopic sea-anemone, come cautiously peering up through the sandy funnel, and stretching and stretching itself out for the exploration of the surface sand, and to all appearance *selecting* tit-bits from a larder which to our eyes seems to be all impartially gritty. The mouth of the animal is a calcareous aperture on the under side without movable lips or jaws, but irregularly surrounded by processes which Forbes calls "short tentacula, with discs surrounded by clavate filaments." By patient attention Mr. Robertson has several times seen these descend and grasp the sand, or other material dropped from the anterior groove of the test, and convey it to the mouth. The extensile hunting filaments above described apparently convey their prey to this groove, and the small spines of the groove then pass it on. The funnel in the sand is kept open by a glutinous secretion exuded from the body of the animal, and by a set of extensile filaments which form a sort of palisading round it. Mr. Robertson carried out a series of careful experiments to determine the source of the secretion just mentioned. This source appears to be situated at the base of the spines, but it has not yet been definitely ascertained. Moreover, the great volume of this slime which the animal is able to discharge is not yet accounted for, although the quantity of it explains, what would be otherwise surprising, that a creature carrying a close armature of small spines, and with the habit of burying itself in the sticky sea-sand, is yet able to rise from it as bright and unsullied as a Venus anadyomene.

A further observation on this same urchin, communicated to the Glasgow Natural History Society in 1880, may be here quoted :—

"The common heart-urchin, *Amphidotus cordatus* (Pennant), found so commonly lying dead along our sandy shores, denuded of its spines, has a feature in its habits that I do not know has been noticed before. They burrow from about four to six inches into the sand, and when dug up and put into a vessel with sand covered with sea-water, the animał is seen at once to commence to throw the sand to the sides by the under or plastron spines. By the time that it gets down into the sand, level with the under edges of the test, the spines of the body get into motion, forming into four or five, sometimes six or seven, ridges of spines, which stretch from back to front along the sides of the test, progressing upwards in wave-like fashion, and following each other in regular succession till .they reach the superior avenue or summit. Each wave, as it emerges from the sides of the animal, brings up a roll of sand to the surface, which falls outward, and this action is continued till the animal is completely covered. When newly dug out of the sand, they often work rapidly down into it, apparently by the ventral spines, without calling into aid the formation of the lateral ridges of spines."

To repeat and enjoy these observations it is not necessary to be a philosopher or a man of science. It will suffice to have a disposition to some degree sympathetic with the lower forms of life, and to have the living specimens. The sympathy will grow and kindle with the very process of observing. For securing the specimens no other implements are needed than a spade and a bucket on a suitable shore at low water.

There is in many people a zeal for collecting which evaporates and wastes itself in the picking up of variously coloured pebbles, shining pieces of quartz, and imaginary fossils. Others more enlightened, with their attention directed to objects really worthy to be studied, are often frustrated in their pursuit of knowledge by having at their command no suitable methods of collecting. They find a coast barren of zoological interest, when perhaps it is really teeming with the objects they would most wish to obtain if they only knew how to get at them. To these it will be a real boon to learn some of the methods which Mr. Robertson has devised for gathering in his harvests from shores and sea-depths that might otherwise be found quite unfruitful.

Suppose the weather fair for shore-hunting, by preference a day or two after the moon is new or full, about an hour before the tide is at its lowest, he and a companion will sally forth, equipped with a spade, a couple of zinc pails, a couple of wide-mouthed glass jars, and a net of cheese-cloth fastened to a ring of six or eight inches diameter. Near the edge of the retreating tide one bucket will be filled about one-third full with slices of the surface sand, the other bucket half full with sea-water from any pool that happens to be near, or, if need be, from one dug for the purpose. The water from the one bucket is poured on the sand in the other, the mixture stirred quickly about with the spade or the hand, allowed to settle for about five seconds, and then the water is poured off through the net into the empty bucket. This process is repeated twice or thrice, and after this the end of the net is inverted into one of the glass jars that has been half or two-thirds filled with sea-water. Now the sand is emptied out of the pail, and, with a fresh supply, the same process is carried out, and so on till the labourers are wearied of their task or satisfied with its results.

At home the contents of the jar or jars are emptied into a basin or dish, and examined and sorted out at leisure. Amphipods, isopods, cumacea, copepoda, larval cirripedes, and small marine worms are likely to be obtained by this method, and sometimes in astonishing numbers.

A solitary worker, having far to go from his home to the tide, would be content with a single jar, and could manage with but one bucket, but then the water has to be drawn fresh for each washing, which takes up much time and greatly increases the labour. By having all the vessels of moderate size, the difficulty of weight may be overcome.

It must be remembered that while some animals frequent the purer sand, others prefer that which is mixed with mud, and in general that the more varied the condition of the ground examined, the more varied will the resulting collection be likely to be. The adventurous collector, who will scrape the sand with his bucket from under the waters themselves, beyond the lowest point to which the tide retreats, may hope for rarer species than any to be found on the uncovered shore.

It is all very well to follow the tide down to its furthest ebb, and then to strip off shoes and stockings and wade out a few yards further still ; the more you gather by these means, the more you feel convinced that by the depth of the water you are being baulked of greater treasures beyond your reach. The result is that you go out dredging. You are then independent of the state of the tide ; but, on the other hand, more dependent on the state of the weather, for dredging in a rough sea is not to be recommended. It is too apt to engender feelings of animosity against marine zoology in the breast of the student, in short, to make him sick of it. But in favourable weather there are many sheltered inlets and landlocked seas where even very squeamish bosoms may take undisturbed delight in dredging. In fact the sea animals themselves appear to love these tranquil havens.

It has been already intimated that Mr. Robertson was no sooner initiated into the mysteries of this pursuit than he became an enthusiast in it. As in his earlier days, so now, he advanced almost in one stride from being a pupil to being a tutor. He noticed that the dredge in common use with naturalists, which has a scraper on both sides, so as to be ready for action which ever side falls undermost, was very efficient, on the supposition that nothing was to be had or was wanted except what could be met with on the surface of the sea-bottom. But with this supposition, it will be seen, he did not agree.

"Believing," he says, "that many valuable objects might be obtained if a dredge could be made to dip deeper into the soil than the one in common use, I had one constructed of galvanized iron, which penetrated five or six inches into the subsoil, and reached the class of animals found burrowing beneath the surface, at the same time securing much in common with the flat-rimmed dredge. As an auxiliary to the common dredge, this form of construction is particularly useful in mud and sand, being compact with solid sides, holding no more than can be conveniently examined in a small boat, besides being clean and expeditious to work with. It sinks and takes the ground readily, and soon fills, its small size offers little resistance to the currents, and is easily pulled up. In favourable weather it can be wrought in ten or twelve fathoms by one man with ease, and in thirty or forty by two men without difficulty. It has been objected to on the ground that it dips suddenly into the soil and is filled at once, without raking over a sufficient portion of the sea-bottom, thus lessening the chance of a good haul. This, so far, is true when surface animals are only taken into account; but the special province of this dredge is not the surface, but beneath it, which will be found by no means thinly tenanted. No one who has examined mud, sand, or gravel, dug from near low water, can have failed to find them abounding with multitudes of living creatures, and we may infer that the same holds good in deeper water. The result of experience with this dredge is to prove that the subsoil round our shores is the habitat, ambush, or retreat of myriads of the invertebrate fauna summer and winter. The subsoil qualities of this dredge, instead of being objectionable, afford in reality an important advantage to the naturalist, for, by pulling it at once on the spot where it descends, he is able to establish the habitat of the animals there found, thus obviating all doubt on that point that might be caused by the dredge being dragged over many hundred yards."

The details of the construction of this instrument, known as the scoop dredge, or Robertson's dredge, will be found in the appendix. There also some notices are given of other contrivances invented by Mr. Robertson for facilitating the study of natural history, but of which the description is too technical to be included in the general course of the narrative.

CHAPTER XVII.

IRELAND—MONTROSE—THE NORFOLK BROADS.

WITH Dr. G. S. Brady, of Sunderland, now Professor of Natural History at Newcastle, and author of numerous well-known scientific works, Mr. Robertson had for some time corresponded.

In 1868, before they had ever met one another, Dr. Brady proposed that they should make a dredging expedition to Ireland in company. Their destination was to be Westport and Roundstone, both of which are on the west coast.

It was arranged that they should meet in Dublin, though neither of them knew of any particular spot in that city which they could have as a trysting-place. But as the steamer from Scotland would arrive a day sooner than the one Brady was to travel by, it was agreed that Robertson should be on the pier awaiting the arrival of his friend, whom he would recognize by the traps he would have with him.

Robertson accordingly reached Dublin on the day appointed. The next day when at breakfast he had a telegram from Dr. Brady, saying that he could not come, as one of his lady patients would not hear of his leaving till she got better, and asking Robertson whether he would return home, or venture the expedition by himself.

He at once answered that he would spend a few days in Dublin, and then, if Brady could not join him, go on by himself. He had scarcely finished his breakfast when a reply came that the doctor would leave for Dublin next day. On his arrival they proceeded at once to Westport, which they reached late at night.

Next morning they arranged with a man they met on the pier to go with them to dredge. He said he had a boat of his own. They sent him to the hotel for their apparatus. He went, and did not reappear till after a very long interval, and then, much to their annoyance and disgust, bringing only a part of what he had been sent for.

While he was away fetching the remainder, a policeman came up and asked them who had given them leave to take the boat. They explained their arrangement with the man whose return they were expecting, but were told that this man had nothing to do with the boat.

Since there were no other boats to be seen, they expressed their great disappointment at the idea of losing the use of this one. The policeman, however, said that he knew the owner of the boat, and that he could venture to let them have it for a time. This, indeed, was no more than their dilatory assistant had already ventured to do. At last they got afloat, but found their man a most unmanageable fellow. Seeing that they could do little good with him, before long they turned their course homewards. They had previously arranged with him to take them out after sunset for work with the surface net.

On the homeward course, as they passed a yacht lying in the bay, their man called to those on board that they were to take the boat up before eight o'clock and leave it at the pier for the captain. At eight o'clock the two naturalists returned to the pier, and found their man there with a nice clean boat. They stepped into it, and another gentleman who was on the pier followed, without a word being exchanged between them during the time they were out. It was not for long, because their man would not go to the place that suited their purpose.

As there was a rivulet which entered the bay close to the pier, they wanted to go further out to be beyond the influence of the fresh water. But the boatman would only row them from side to side, instead of straight out into the bay, as they desired, maintaining that if they went out the tide would be against them and too strong to allow of their getting home that night. As it was no use fighting longer with him, they returned home.

When he had brought their traps up to the hotel he asked for his money, which was handed to him, without any abatement from what had been agreed upon, although his behaviour had nearly frustrated the object of the excursion. Estimating his services in inverse proportion to their value, he cursed and swore at the payment made. Was that what they would offer him for the work he had done?

Mr. Robertson, whose kindly and generous temper is not incapable of firmness upon occasion, replied that it was what he had agreed for, that it was double of what he deserved, and that he would get no more ; he might take it or leave it.

He took it, and went away swearing at a fearful rate.

This heat of demeanour was probably assumed, for the man was evidently a very cool hand. Not only had he in the morning let out and used another man's boat as though it were his own, but for his evening engagement he had calmly ordered another man's servants to put their master's boat at his disposal, leading the crew of the yacht to suppose that the boat was wanted for their captain, while he himself intended to let it out for hire.

The " mysterious stranger " who went out in the nocturnal expedition with the tow-net, which he must have regarded with wondering eyes, and probably considered to be only a "blind," and a very childish one, belonged according to a not unlikely conjecture to the police staff. At that time a strict watch was kept against arms being smuggled into the country, and it must be confessed that, with two such ferocious looking characters as Dr. G. S. Brady and Mr. David Robertson scheming to go out after dark, upon such frivolous pretences as they had to produce, there was no little cause for the gloomiest suspicions!

They afterwards went two or three miles down the side of the bay, and met with a very decent cotter, who had a boat and lived conveniently near to the water. In this man's boat they had a haul or two with the scoop dredge, and then Robertson produced his " wee dredge," which Dr. Brady had not before seen, and in regard to which, when he did see it, he asked his friend what he was going to do with the *toy*.

The ordinary naturalist's dredge, with which Mr. Robertson was first acquainted, was generally about twenty-four inches broad at the mouth, and was heavy work even for two men in a rowing boat.

He thought to himself that a dredge one half the size would be one half easier to pull, and that by dragging it double the length as much ground would be covered as with the large one and with far less toil, and that it could be easily worked by one man. The bag too, being smaller and holding less, would be more easily pulled up. It would not, it is true, bring up so much material, but it would bring up quite enough for convenient and thorough examination. Another advantage would be that the less weight and bulk of the dredge and ropes would make them handier for transport, a matter of considerable importance in a small dredging expedition.

As soon as he found the benefit of the smaller dredge, he gave up the use of the larger altogether.

But after using with satisfaction his twelve-inch dredge, he took a further step. He made one only seven inches long at the mouth and three inches wide at the further extremity. Although this could not take in large animals, it would admit of almost all that the naturalist cares for, and as his object in making it was chiefly for microscopic forms, especially ostracoda and foraminifera, it answered its purpose beyond expectation. Being only four pounds weight it could be thrown a good way into lochs or canals, and brought out full of material rich with organisms that could not be reached with the hand-net. For this reason it was sometimes called the throw-dredge.

The first trial of it at sea was in Ireland, as above mentioned, when it soon proved itself to be no toy, but a very useful machine. Being let down into the water, it soon filled, and was drawn up with great ease. It was then found that it could supply more material than the two naturalists had time to examine, so that after that they scarcely ever took the larger dredge out again.

The expedition of the following year will be best described in Mr. Robertson's own words. In regard to some of the remarks upon the manners and customs of Edinburgh, it will be borne in mind that a Glasgow man would be thought wanting in all proper patriotic feeling if he did not endeavour to chasten the pride of "the modern Athens" by the precious balms of wholesome admonition and reproof. The journal of the excursion is thus indited :—

"On May 6, 1869, my wife and I left Glasgow for a trip to Edinburgh, Elie, Errol, and Montrose, to see the post-tertiary shell beds at these places, and to bring home clays from the various deposits for further search of the minuter organisms. Having left by an early train, we were in good time at Edinburgh. We visited the Archæological Museum, and next that of Natural History. Although full of interest, the latter had the usual defect of most of our museums, the want of the products of our own country and of our own shores. At night heard three excellent papers read at the Geological Society, one on internal heat of the globe, another on ancient river-beds between the Firth of Forth and the Firth of Clyde, and the third on ancient river-beds in general.

"Next day, called on Mr. James Rennie, of the Geological Survey, who was our guide to Portobello Westbank brickfields, where we saw some fine deposits of estuarine clays. We came back to Edinburgh, went to Granton with the dredge, had a few hauls within the west harbour from near the entrance to near the middle. The sea was so rough that we could not go outside.

"May 8. Took steamer to Boness, hired a small boat, had a few hauls of the dredge outside of harbour, brought up black soft mud, which was exceedingly difficult to wash and bring to a state in which it could be carried away. Returned to Edinburgh.

"May 9. Sabbath. We had always understood that Edinburgh was a model to the world of strict observance of the sabbath. After breakfast we had a walk down the Canongate. The streets were crowded with people walking or standing at doors, and even at the time the churches were going in men were standing about the corners of houses, not appearing in any way abashed. In other parts of Scotland of less fame for morality it was considered most degrading to be standing about the street when people were going to church, and every effort would be made to avoid being seen by the people coming from or going to it. Here cabs and dogcarts were flying about something like the everyday style. The smaller confectioners' shops were open everywhere, and shops for the sale of ginger-beer, soda-water, and milk, as well as others with fruits and periodicals for sale. Stands with drinks and cakes were common on the roadside to Portobello, and on the sands on the seashore; and on climbing to the top of Arthur's Seat, there too were copious refreshments spread out on the ground on a white sheet. We saw Holyrood Palace, and the beautiful fountain lately erected. I have the same objection here as I have to almost all other erections of the same kind, namely, that the water is made to gush or flow from the mouth of animals of various kinds, the most unnatural thing possible, a barbarous design continued.

"Monday, May 10. Left Edinburgh for Elie brick-works, where we arrived shortly after mid-day. Bagged up a good supply of the clay (fifty pounds). Sent it home by rail.

"Next morning left Elie for Errol, where there is another post-tertiary deposit. Here too, after picking out what shells we could, took another supply of clay for further examination, and proceeded to Mont-rose. When at the hotel I began to inquire about brick-fields, and clays, and bags to hold them, per-haps not in the most intelligible way, and as my wife was inquiring for the residence of Dr. Howden, the superintendent of the lunatic asylum, and was apparently taking the chief management of affairs, I imagined that the waiters were casting uncommonly suspicious looks at me. We left, to find Dr. Howden. As we had run ourselves short of bags to hold the clay, Mrs. Robertson suggested that she should sit down

on the side of the way into the brickfield and make
one or two more, while I would call on Dr. Howden.
As I left Mrs. Robertson, I saw a large funeral
coming forward. I inquired at* a bystander if it
was likely that Dr. Howden would be there. He
replied that it was, and when the procession came
forward, he pointed the doctor out to me. I went
and introduced myself to him. He left the funeral
and came with me to where we found Mrs. Robertson
busy making the bags. He kindly invited us up to
his house, where she would have a more comfortable
seat to do her sewing. After lunch the doctor took
us round in his gig to all the post-tertiary deposits
in the district, giving us much valuable information
regarding the sequence of the various clay beds and
their fossil contents. By the time that we had made
our rounds, we had all our bags and handkerchiefs
filled with clay for further inspection. For the last
hour it had rained heavily, and our besmeared
appearance (for we had all taken a share in the work)
did not accord well with that of the usual customers
of the hotel, and the waiters with their clean white
hands hesitated to take hold of the wet dirty bags
of clay, till the doctor made known his wish for
them to do so. Although the collection of these wet
clay bags appeared incomprehensible to them, yet it
seemed that I was not altogether a fit subject for Dr.
Howden, as I was still left to go as I came.

"As well as the post-tertiary clays, we were avail-
ing ourselves of what opportunities we had to collect

* Sir Walter Scott uses this idiom. See "A Legend of Montrose,"
ch. xi. : "The Rittmaster inquired at the domestic."

recent fresh-water and marine ostracoda and foraminifera. Early next morning, looking out at our
bedroom window and seeing the Montrose basin, a
large flat extent of soft mud, laid bare, I made all
haste to get to it. On reaching the edge near the
bridge, I saw that nothing could be done with my
boots on. However, that difficulty was easily overcome. I found the mud very tenacious and difficult
to lessen in bulk, but with washing and splashing I
got two bags filled. I may mention that the bags
were about nine inches long and six broad, and would
hold near a stone (eight pounds) of wet mud. If I
was badly spattered the night before, I was not
much better now, and the two bags were even more
detestable looking, being covered all over with the
soft black shiny mud. I got them laid beside the
other bags as quickly as possible.

"We had now got over with the post-tertiary
deposits of the district, and I was anxious to have a
haul with the dredge before we left. A boat and
men were difficult to get, but at last I got a boat and
two strong fishermen, for nothing less would do, as
the tide there ran very strong, they said, at the rate
of eight miles an hour. With much hard pulling we
got about a mile or so out from the harbour, where
we threw the dredge and brought up nothing but
clean small gravel without a vestige of life among it.
Two hauls more were the same. We said that it was
no use trying more there. The men told us that
sometimes there were only six or seven fathoms of
water in this place, at other times fifteen fathoms,
that it depended much on the direction in which wind

was driving storms. Speaking of fishing, they mentioned the catfish. I asked if they could procure me
one. I wanted one particularly for the ear-bones.
Some fishing-boats were coming past us, but our men
said that none of them would acknowledge that they
had one, as no one would admit that they ever tasted
one, although, they said, many of the fishermen did
taste them on the sly and used them regularly. They
said they could find us one when we got into town.
We gave one of the men what he said he thought he
would get it for. We were detained some little time
on the way back to the hotel, and upon reaching it
there was a large catfish on a stand in the hall. The
waiter said that it was for us, and inquired if anything
was to be done with it. I said that I only wanted
the head, and that he might do whatever he liked
with the rest. Accordingly we got the head packed
up as a part of our luggage. Next morning after
breakfast we paid our bill and left for home, the
waiters no doubt thinking that we were queer customers, and wondering what we could want with the
superintendent of the Lunatic Asylum, or what we
were going to do with the bags of clay from the
brickfield, and the two bags of black glair from the
river-basin, but, above all, what in the world we were
going to do with the head of the catfish!"

Had he explained that out of the whole fish he
wanted nothing but two little pointed bones scarcely
a quarter of an inch long and an eighth of an inch in
breadth, and that he regarded these as part of the
acoustic apparatus of the animal, the waiters might
still have been sceptical as to his sanity.

There are probably thousands of well-informed persons to whom it has never occurred to think of a fish as requiring or possessing ear-bones, and very few will have formed any conception of what such bones are like, or have been at the pains to search for them in a fish of any kind, let alone a catfish, a creature of ferocious aspect, with a disagreeable odour and a slime-covered skin.

Yet the ear-bones of fishes are characteristic in different species, and furnish a very interesting study in comparative anatomy. Found as detached fossils, they would be puzzling specimens to any one unacquainted with existing forms.

Robertson mounted a large number on card-board slides, some of the bones, as those of the sprat, being quite microscopic, while others are of considerable size, those of the common hake attaining more than an inch and a half in length and nearly half an inch in breadth. Thirty-nine of these slides have been photographed together, the group forming a fine plate, as unusual in appearance as it is scientifically interesting, The names of the contributory fishes are recorded in the appendix.

Those who wish on their own account to make search for these ear-bones may like to know that they are contained in cartilaginous capsules under the protection of the post-frontal bones of the skull. They are not, however, always to be met with, as may be seen by the following quotation from Professor H. G. Seeley, who says :—

" The organ of hearing is well developed in all fishes ; the membranous labyrinth in the lamprey has only two semi-circular canals, and in the myxine there is only one of these canals, but in all other fishes there are three, as in higher animals ; they communicate with a vestibule, in which are contained the bony plates called otolites ; there are usually two of these flattened, somewhat oval organs, and one is larger than the other.   But in a good many fishes, such as the plectognathi and lophobranchiates, the otolites are represented by calcareous dust.   No fish possesses a cochlea, or a true tympanic membrane, but sometimes there is a connection between the labyrinth of the ear and the air-bladder made by a chain of small bones.   In the roach the air-bladder is exceedingly small, extending under only two vertebræ, and is united with the head in this way.   The external ears of the skate are on the top of the head." *

In the month following his visit to Montrose, Robertson went with his friend Dr. G. S. Brady to the Norfolk broads in quest of fresh-water ostracoda. In working at the sides of the broads and along the banks of rivers and canals the little dredge was in constant requisition.   It could be thrown a considerable distance into the water and brought back full of the desired material.   To make this portable it had to be passed through a sieve to get rid of the coarser matters, such as stones, and decaying stems, and leaves, the residuum being then washed to clear away as much of the fine mud as possible before bagging it up.

By the dredge much was obtained that would not

* Cassell's " Natural History," vol. v. p. 12.   For a slightly different description, see the Appendix.

have been reached by the hand-net then in use, which was a small, wide-mouthed bag fixed to the end of a walking-stick.

The week's excursion gave Mr. Robertson unalloyed pleasure, although he did not much admire the scenery of the low, flat country where, he sarcastically observes, the water had to be pumped up to keep the feet on dry ground. Nevertheless the Norfolk broads and the Norfolk rivers, unlike and unequal as they may be to the grander and wilder features of Scotland, are far from being without their own picturesque delights. In the pursuit of ostracoda æsthetic pleasures may be indulged, but they have to take a subordinate place, and, on the present occasion, the merit of the scenery was that it yielded a few new species and others that were rare. The two colleagues were put in a position to give a summary of that part of the fauna of the broads which they were studying.

Nothing indeed happened to hinder the progress of their work, except a very temporary check at Yarmouth. They there hired a boat, intending to go up the river for a few days' work among the broads. They took a strong man to do the rowing, laid in a good stock of provisions and condiments, and trusted to luck to find sleeping accommodation when it might be needed. Their man said that he could shift for himself.

Unfortunately, the tide had just begun to ebb, and, before they got their boat launched and all things adjusted, the tide was letting the river down pretty strongly.

At starting the man had both oars, but, as they

appeared to be making little or no way, Mr. Robertson took one of them. They then pulled with all
their might, trying first one side of the river and then
the other ; but, after struggling for more than half an
hour, and not gaining more than two or three hundred
yards at most, they thought it best to draw the boat
up and wait till the tide turned. Why neither the
men of science nor the boatman had thought of
this expedient before starting, it might be rude to
inquire.

The boatman took advantage of the halt to return
home for something he wanted or pretended to want.
Robertson and Brady sat down by the side of a little
stream, where a great many shrimps were playing or
hunting for prey under a little cascade. There was a
little shore-crab, *Carcinus mænas*, stationed at the
corner, making many a grab at the shrimps, but they
eluded each and every attempt he made by bounding
backwards with wonderful dexterity.

The two friends now consulted whether it would
be better, leaving the boat, to go back and take a car
to Ormsby Broad, or to go on with the boat. The
tide would not be in their favour for about five hours,
and there was some uncertainty how the boat would
suit their purpose, how they might obtain accommodation at night, and whether their boatman would
return, as he did not seem by any means satisfied
with his work when he left. Determined by these
considerations, they made up their minds to go back
and take a carriage to Ormsby Broad. The sensitive
reader must be left to imagine with what a pang they
left behind them in the boat that stock of provisions

and condiments with which they had victualled their fleet for a voyage of some days.

"At another time," Mr. Robertson relates, "on the railway where we had to make a few changes before we reached our destination, as Brady knew the country better than I did, and undertook the direction of the journey, I took little notice of what station we had entered or what one we had left. On this journey Brady was the cashier, and got the tickets, and I removed our traps from the carriage we were leaving to the one we were going by. I had taken my seat in a carriage, but by the time Brady had got our tickets the train was just beginning to move, and he had to rush into the first carriage he could reach. In the one that I was in there were only myself and an elderly lady. The next station we came to the guard came to lift * the tickets. He asked for mine. I said I had none. He asked where I came from. My answer was, 'I don't know.' 'Where are you going to?' 'I don't know.' By this time Brady came forward, knowing that my ticket was wanted, and said, 'What is up?' My answer again was, 'I don't know.' The guard, in taking my ticket from Brady, gave him a look as much as to say, 'You had better keep closer by your charge.' The lady got out of the carriage, no doubt shocked, thinking that she had been riding so far alone beside a madman."

When the excursionists had returned home it was found that there were some species among their microscopic treasures which could not be made out satisfactorily without more examples. Dr. Brady was

* To take.

unable at the time to quit the duties of his profession. Robertson, being a man of leisure, was loth that any important part of their joint work should be left imperfect if any exertion of his could prevent it. Seeing that he could not have the pleasure and benefit of his colleague's company, he volunteered to go by himself. Also, with a view to the post-glacial work which he had in hand in partnership with Brady and Crosskey, he intended to operate upon the Cromer beds and some others in the neighbourhood, which there had been no time to examine on the previous visit to Norfolk.

Allusion has already been made to the small hand-net in use for collecting fresh-water ostracoda from lochs and pools. This was a small muslin bag about six inches deep and five broad, fixed to a ring with a tube for the reception of the end of a walking-stick. With this every kind of rubbish could enter at the wide open mouth, so that the gatherings had to be drained again through a wide-meshed piece of cotton stuff called bobinet. This took up much time, and to professional men, in the few days of a limited holiday, time is of considerable importance, the needless waste of it moreover being irksome to most men of sense.

Robertson's turn of mind did not lead him to acquiesce in the use of a defective instrument without first considering whether and how it might be improved.

He observed that the walking-stick handle of the net was too short to be efficient, and that one thrice the length would be far more serviceable. He therefore had a nine-foot pole or rod made of ashwood in three lengths of three feet each, which were screwed strongly together with brass joints, while the end screwed into the handle of the bag.

To obviate the intrusion of rubbish, he had a copper ring made an inch deep to fit into the mouth of the bag, the ring carrying a copper sieve of a quarter of an inch mesh, and being looped with a cord over the pole, so that it might hang freely when the contents of the bag were being emptied from its mouth.

Lastly, he lengthened the muslin bag to sixteen inches, to prevent an accident to which the shallower bag was liable, that the contents would flow out as quickly as they had flowed in.

His contrivance he found to answer exceedingly well, and when the three sections of the long rod were put into a cloth sheath they were quite portable, and the instrument was available not only for fresh-water gatherings, but also for sweeping among the sea-weeds either from a boat or along the sea-shore.

Equipped with his new invention, Mr. Robertson betook himself once more to the fens on the east of England. When in Norwich he first called on a Mr. Hamer, who was doing work amongst the clay beds, but from him he derived little information and less encouragement. He then went to see Mr. Stevenson, an ornithologist, to whom he had a letter of introduc-tion. Mr. Stevenson advised him to call on the Rev. Mr. Gunn, who had done some good work on the Cromer beds. Once more visiting Mr. Hamer, he mentioned his wish to see Mr. Gunn. Mr. Hamer told him that the clergyman had lost his wife only three weeks before, and was now away at Cromer, about fifteen miles distant, to recruit his spirits, and would most likely not care to see any stranger. When this was repeated to Mr. Stevenson, the latter remarked—

"Never mind; go and see Mr. Gunn. I am sure he will receive you kindly and give you what information he can. You can get by the coach this evening."

Following this friendly and sensible advice, Robertson reached Cromer, and called on Mr. Gunn, who, as had been predicted, received him very kindly, went with him the next morning and showed him the Cromer beds, and explained the strata that such and such fossils were to be found in.

After breakfast Mr. Gunn returned home in his carriage, taking the Glasgow geologist with him. At his own house he showed him the fossils he had collected in the Cromer beds, and also gave him much valuable information regarding the lakes that were best worth visiting.

It was on a Saturday that they returned from Cromer, so that presumably the next day must have been Sunday. As it is treading on rather delicate ground to relate what passed between the clergyman and his guest on that day, it will be safest here to quote our hero's own words, with the hope that the passage, being sandwiched in among dry details about nets and mud and ostracoda, may escape the notice of any natives of Edinburgh whose feelings have been outraged in the earlier part of the chapter.

"He [the Rev. Mr. Gunn] said that it was most likely that I would rather have a sail on the lake that was close by his house than go to church, and that I could take his boat that was down at the water's edge. I took the good man's advice, and as it was the minister's boat, and I the minister's guest, I had no dread of unfavourable criticism from the neighbours.

"On Monday Mr. Gunn sent his boy to drive me to a lake at a few miles distance. On Tuesday morning he went out with me to have two hours' work with the little dredge in the lake.

"After breakfast his boy ferried me over the lake to near to where a mail coach started that would take me a good length on my way. I was in good time for the coach and found the driver was a lady. She appeared about middle-aged, and suitably attired for her calling, and quite competent for the unusual duties that she had doubtlessly imposed on herself. It was a four-horse team. She surveyed them all carefully, to see that all was right before starting. I was informed that she was the proprietress, and that no one knew a horse better than she did. The moment she took the whip in hand it could be seen at once that she knew how to wield it, and the horses seemed to know that too. Although she used it judiciously, she appeared to be able to nip the animals with the whip on the spot she wanted with a flourish and the precision of the most accomplished Jehu."

After spending a few days longer among the broads of the fen district, Robertson returned home, carrying with him ample materials for the scientific paper on which he was engaged, and having on this expedition once more illustrated his faculty for making friends. At the end of May, 1871, he again visited Ireland,

and while waiting in Dublin for Dr. Brady, among other things he went to Phœnix Park, and obtained leave to dredge the ponds for objects of natural history. From Dublin the two friends went together to Galway, *en route* for Roundstone and Westport. The journey from Galway being by car, they took more than one opportunity to have a haul in the loughs which they passed. Upon mentioning Lough Corrib, Mr. Robertson says in his note-book, " The country between this and Galway in many places is exceedingly wild and barren, the wildness, however, not increased as in our highlands by the absence of anything like the commotion of human beings, for on the plains among the grey boulders cotters swarm like rabbits in a warren, and most of the youth of both sexes swarming round the rudest hovels, by no means inviting either to the eye or olfactory organs, are characterized by a bloom of health and happiness quite enviable."

Arrived at their journey's end, they walked from the hotel through the Marquis of Sligo's pleasure grounds to Westport Bay. Here on the shore at low water they found the profusion of life very great. Especially they observed the underside of the overhanging boulders covered as if with scarlet drapery by multitudes of a species of red ascidian. The colour of another less frequent species was light purple or peach blossom. The stones were crowded with sponges, crabs and banded shrimps were plentiful, the tube-dwelling marine worms were in enormous abundance. An extract from the notes made on this occasion cannot fail to be of service to the naturalist, who may find himself unexpectedly surrounded by a similar *embarras de richesse*.

"The material obtained between tide-marks in the bay at Westport (Clew Bay) was so abundant that it was difficult to find proper means to preserve it on the way home. The quantity of spirits we had provided for the occasion was too small, and glass vessels were too risky in transit. Salt was thought of, and although it had never been recommended in such cases, we thought that most likely, if it could preserve a barrel of herrings, it would do so with a shrimp or crab.

"In this belief a tin box was procured that would hold about an imperial gallon, with a mouth sufficiently large to admit the hand, and with a cover to fit on flush with the surface. Into this the collections were put as they were obtained between layers of salt. The gatherings were from between tide-marks and by the dredge, and consisted of crustacea, from amphipods to decapods, echinoderms, mollusks, zoophytes, fishes, and sea-weeds. We observed that when crustacea were put into the salt it did not irritate them much. They appeared soon to get sluggish and die, and were not so liable to throw off their limbs as they do when put into spirits.

"On arriving home, some of them, after six days' pickling, were found to be in good condition, with the colours little or none affected. This was very remarkable in the case of the sea-weed, of the preservation of which we had entertained no hope, but had thrown some of it in among the other things as a desperate experiment, but it also was in good

preservation ; even some of the tender *Callithamnions*
appeared quite as good as if they had been mounted
when newly taken from the water ; but I may mention
that *Wrangelia multifida* was a little brownish and
Dasya coccinea a little more intensely red.

"The crustacea were all in fine order when taken
out of the salt at eight days' end, and I believe would
have kept so for a twelvemonth.

"It would be no slight recommendation for the
salt, had it none other than the convenience it affords
in carrying these things home in a dry state, avoiding
the risk of breaking the vessels with spirits. But a
greater advantage is derived from the use of salt in
applying it to the peaty mud found at the bottom
of lakes, not especially for the preservation of the
animals found in the mud, but for the solubility it
gives to the peat when put in water, causing it to
sink after being dried, and allowing shells, etc., to float ;
whereas, without the salt, the whole peaty mass will
neither dissolve nor sink in such a way as to allow
shells, ostracoda, and the like, to be separated conveniently from the floating peat."

Later in the year Mr. Robertson paid his friend
Dr. Brady a visit at Sunderland, the two as usual
examining the rocks, dredging in the sea, and scour-
ing the pools of the neighbourhood for specimens.
When apart they often had to interchange objects of
natural history through the post.   In a letter to Brady
dated October 18, 1871, Robertson says, " The box
was well enough packed under all ordinary circumstances, but I do not think that the post-office officials
like parcels, and I believe, from the effects that we

have too often seen of the force used, that they have a wicked delight in trying how many they can damage. The floatings (I think from Seaton) had the wrapper and cover of the box punched quite through, the pieces lying loose on the material like gun-wadding. Happily the contents in this case were such as would receive little harm." How this should make corresponding naturalists relish the blessings of modern civilization and revere the inventor of the Parcels Post, for undoubtedly, even at the present day, parcels sent by letter post are liable to receive damage in a very unaccountable manner.

To conclude the Irish experiences, it may here be stated that in 1874, Robertson had another pleasant journey to Westport and Roundstone, this time in company with the Rev. A. M. Norman. An intended record of the results of this trip never saw the light, but Norman sent the sponges they had collected to Dr. Bowerbank, then engaged in describing for the Ray Society all the sponges of Great Britain. Dr. Bowerbank made out that their collection contained no less than twenty-seven new species, but Norman, to whose friendship the completion of Bowerbank's work was subsequently entrusted, formed a somewhat lower estimate of the real number of novelties. Nevertheless, the richness of the Irish locality in these organisms was well established, and in the preface to the fourth volume of the British spongiadæ, published after Dr. Bowerbank's death, and edited by Norman, the latter says :—

"A large number of the localities to which the editor's initial is attached will be found to be situated in the counties of Galway and Mayo, where a remarkably fine collection of sponges was obtained during a scientific expedition which Mr. D. Robertson of Glasgow and himself made to that part of Ireland in the summer of 1874."

In the summer of 1876, Robertson visited the north of Ireland, and upon this occasion remarks in his note-book :—

" This side of the country appears in a better state of refinement than the south and south-west, in so far as the children of the poor are better clad and not seen in such a state of rags and semi-nudity as in the south." After observing that the grown-up people, however, in the south, both male and female, may be said to be well shod and suitably clothed, and the women with a good eye to artistic effect in their red tartan shawls and striped petticoats, he continues :—

" On the other hand, the cotter houses in the north are mostly whitewashed, however humble, and on the outside they generally have neat rows of flowers along the walls and in many cases flowers in pots on the insides of the windows, and little clean white curtains a foot or so from the glass. In no case are slops or ashes thrown out in front of the house, nor in any case did we see pigs entering the domicile or about it. I believe many keep pigs, from the traffic we saw in them in Buncrana market, but I believe where they are kept they are confined in proper places. This state of things contrasts strongly with the condition of the peasantry in the south-west, where a whitewashed peasant's-house is seldom to be seen, or one without a dunghill before the door, where it often forms an island in the midst of an unsavoury pool, where the pigs as a rule, and frequently the donkey and cows, if they have any, are fellow lodgers with the family, and where floral decorations seem to be unknown. Yet in this state it must be said they are little more than one step below the peasantry in many parts of Scotland."

He observes that the peasantry in the Isle of Man take great delight in the tidy appearance of their houses, adorning them inside and out with flowers, and from his varied experience he inclines to draw the general conclusion that a taste for flowers is rarely, if ever, to be found in combination with dirt and slovenliness.

It was on one of his earlier visits to Ireland that he stayed in Belfast. Two or three years previously Gwyn Jeffreys had been staying a couple of days with him in Glasgow, looking over his shells and visiting some of the post-tertiary deposits in the neighbourhood. Gwyn Jeffreys then advised him, if ever he was in Belfast, to call on a Mr. Stewart, a saddler, and see his collection of shells.

When in Belfast, Robertson remembered the advice, but could not recall the name of Stewart.

" Believing," he says, " that there could not be many saddlers in the town, and that there could be little difficulty in finding him, I engaged a clever * young man, who professed to know the town well, to take me to all the saddlers, till I came to the one I wanted. After calling on them all, I found no one of them had done anything with shells, nor did they know any one

* Handy or suitable.

that ever had. I believed that there must be some
mistake somewhere, and that one who had made a
good collection of shells would most likely be known
to the professors of the college. I inquired at * my
young man if he knew the address of any of them
that lived in the town. He said that Professor
Wyville Thomson was often in a stationer's shop
hard by. I hurried to the place and inquired at the
stationer if Professor W. Thomson was likely to be
with him about this time. He pointed to a gentleman at the other end of the counter, and said, ' There
he is.'

"I explained to him what I wanted, and the wild
goose chase that I had had.   .

"He said, ' I know the party well that you want, a
Mr. Stewart, not a saddler, but a leather trunk maker.
I will take you to him.'"

Accordingly, he found his Mr. Stewart, saw the
collection of shells, and pleasantly made acquaintance
with the eminent professor, who took him to his house,.
Strand-town, a little way out of Belfast, to show
him some of his own natural history work,—the work
which was marking him out and qualifying him to be
soon after the scientific leader of the well-known
Challenger expedition.

* See page 250.

CHAPTER XVIII.

A GOOSE—A STRAGGLER—IT WAS CRACKIT
BEFORE—THE SCILLY ISLES.

DURING the close of 1871 and the beginning of the following year, Robertson was writing long and erudite letters to various scientific friends, Professor Young, Mr. Robert Craig, Mr. James Rennie, Mr. B. Pettigrew, Mr. T. A. Mahony, and others, on the boulder clay, suggesting improvements in nomenclature, discussing the identity of various species, asking for local details, and reporting progress. To Mr. Kirsop he writes :—

" I should be much delighted to get samples of the mud of the Nile, or from any of the Chinese rivers. I send a few opaque mounted slides, chiefly foraminifera from the Firth of Clyde, for your acceptance."

But that his correspondence did not entirely consist of geological and zoological minutiæ will be seen from the following letter to his friend the supervisor of customs in the Shetland Isles :—

"January 13-15, 1872.

"MY DEAR MR. GATHERER,

"You will think me very dilatory in replying to your kindness. As the weather had been very stormy, the goose did not arrive till nine days after it left you, and I thought it best to wait till it came, or till a sufficient time had elapsed for transit. However, it came in good time and in capital order, not in the smallest degree the worse for its long journey. You need say no more about the small proportions of the Shetland geese. This is quite a leviathan, and, besides, in excellent condition. Mrs. Robertson has had it dressed and it is now before the fire, and we just have it in time for the old new year,* which enables us to extend our festivities so much the longer.

"——And now, since I wrote the last line, I can tell you that it is nothing behind in quality to its portly and promising appearance.

"The plan you took—to free the holothurians of the water—is a good one. I never thought of it. Even with spirits it would be a great saving. Those I brought home when I was with you took a great deal of spirits, which was pretty much tinted by the time I got them home. Had the water been withdrawn, much less spirit would have done. However, the soft things do not all suit so well with the salt as the harder crustacea.

" Mr. Jeffreys' visit to America was a very fortunate circumstance, not only to science, in preventing the loss of those undescribed shells, but particularly to the Americans, who might else have been anticipated in finding them again, and so have lost the credit of the discovery.

"We were sorry to hear of Fred's illness, but hope

---

* New Year's Day according to the Old Style.

that he is now quite recovered. If he is back at Edinburgh, could he not take a race through and see us some Saturday evening and stay till Monday? There are trains at all hours, late and soon. By the end of this month we are removing to another house, 108, Woodlands Road, to be nearer our sons' place of business. Where we are it is so far to come out at night. Besides, they have always to take dinner in town.

" Now, my dear Mr. Gatherer, I have come to the most difficult part of my letter, that is, what to say to you for your great kindness, trouble, and expense. Had you even allowed me to have paid the carriage, you would so far have mitigated the difficulty. As I am thus confined to thanks, accept them in their warmest sense, in which Mrs. Robertson and my sons heartily join."

For the benefit of readers who may be inclined maliciously to recall an incident in the " Noctes Ambrosianæ," it may be proper here to record that Mr. Gatherer's well-appreciated present was the domestic bird, associated with memories of Queen Elizabeth and Michaelmas Day, not its fishy-tasting relative, the Solan goose.

Undeterred by the mixed fortune of their boating experience in 1865, the Robertson family more than once returned to Campbelton Loch. They were there in 1872, when Mr. Robertson was studying the geology of Tangy burn, in the neighbourhood of which Mr. Pettigrew resided, and where the clay deposit is only a few hundred yards distant from the sea.

On one of these visits to Campbelton they had with them a party of friends, including a gentleman from Edinburgh, then and since eminent for his truly religious character and strict behaviour.

One Sunday morning, as they were all about to start for church, a violent storm, or what they would expressively call a thunder-plump, occurred, and detained them. When the rain ceased, however, they set out and managed to enter the church just as the sermon was finished.

Their specially religious friend marched up the aisle, perhaps not altogether without an air of conscious virtue for having struggled through the mire to attend the fag-end of a service, so that his companions could not help inwardly chuckling, when the preacher proceeded forthwith very gravely to pray " for the souls of Sunday stragglers."

Had the divine known all the circumstances of the case, he might have modified his form of expression, but Scotch theologians are no respecters of persons. How little tender they can sometimes be to the hopes of humanity is shown in an anecdote which Mr. Robertson delights to tell of a Highland preacher. He was illustrating the difficulty of entering the kingdom of heaven, and thus addressed his flock on the subject: "Ye ken Alexander McDonald's coo, his brown coo. Aweel, if that coo could clim' a tree with his tail foremost and harry a bird's nest, ye might have a chance of climbing into the kingdom of heaven."

In July of this same year, Dr. G. S. Brady and his family paid a visit to Fern Bank. This was not their first visit to Millport, for a long letter to Brady, dated November 25, 1871, in which Robertson discusses the distribution of ostracoda, and the mistakes that may arise from only examining prolific ground and favourite spots, concludes as follows :—

" We are glad to hear that Florry is better, and we hope she is still progressing. We trust when the season comes round that we will again have the pleasure of seeing you all at Millport ; and tell them all, including Master Llewellyn, what a jolly time we will have in the boat on the smooth bays round Cumbrae."

Many an older friend than Dr. Brady's little boy has had " a jolly time " with David Robertson in the boat on those smooth bays. But in the interest of mariners who, like the great Lord Nelson, are liable to be squeamish at sea, it should be added that those bays are not always smooth. Let them not, therefore, incautiously make a pilgrimage from the Muckle Cumbrae to the Lesser, or they may be stranded for the night, perhaps for more nights than one, on an almost uninhabited island, with very disagreeable waves and a daunting wind interposed between them and their changes of raiment.

Even those who are superior to the qualms of sea-sickness, and who are skilled in navigation, may meet with an unpleasant experience. Thus, in 1878, Mr. Robertson's two sons had been cruising about in a little yacht belonging to the elder, called the *Ripple.* Shortly after they had landed, leaving their vessel properly secured, they were surprised, in looking from the hotel windows, to see it loose. A sudden

T

gust had torn it from its moorings, and though pursuit was made, it was never more seen or heard of.

In the following letter to Dr. Dohrn reference is made to the visit of the Bradys :—

"MY DEAR DOHRN,

"You will be thinking that I am negligent in not writing to you before now. I have been wishing to do so for some weeks past, but have been waiting till I was able to write you something definite regarding the stones for your tank. Shortly after you wrote I engaged a person well experienced in that way to procure them for me, and with the prospect of having them without delay I was very happy. After nearly two weeks' delay he sent word that he could not find the proper kind; that last autumn a great many had been taken away for garden rockeries, and that no good ones were left. However, I have lighted on an out-of-the-way place, where I have got some that I think will suit very well, and with another party went and selected the best we could find, at the same time bringing a small boat-load with us. I had to leave that night (Monday last) for Glasgow, but gave instructions that those left were to be brought over to Millport pier and laid beside the others. David is looking after a vessel to take them from Glasgow to Naples. I doubt that none will be found going from Glasgow in ballast, but we shall do the best we can.

· "We have just had G. S. Brady and family with us the last ten days. We were wishing that you had been with us. We would have had a jolly house.

"To-night Mrs. Robertson's mother and mother's sister from South Wales are coming to stay for a week or so with us. We hope to have the pleasure of a visit from you when you are over at the British Association."

Previous letters had sympathized with Dr. Dohrn in the many impediments that preceded his grand success in establishing the zoological station at Naples—troubles with the municipality, troubles with the architect, difficulties in regard to funds present and prospective. One of them deplores the severe illness of Dr. Dohrn's father, speaks of the dredged material which Dr. Dohrn had sent to Robertson from the Mediterranean, and explains that his wish for stones from Iona to place in his tank cannot be gratified, since "the only stones of that place are Druidical and sculptured stones, which would not on any account be procurable."

As the Neapolitan causes of vexation one by one disappeared before Teutonic energy and enthusiasm, the sympathy, which had been very genuine as long as it was needed, apparently became the subject of a more or less academic discussion between the two friends, to judge from the following letter :—

" September 29, 1872.

"MY DEAR DR. DOHRN,

"A day or two before I received your last letter I had written you that I had forwarded you the stones for your aquarium, which I hope by this time have arrived safe and are the kind you wanted, and as you had that letter I did not write so soon.

"You mention that I did not answer your last, but I can assure you that I did so, and it must have in some way or other been miscarried. In that answer I was going to lecture you for your total rejection of the sympathy I offered you in your hard struggles against so many difficult and opposing forces, but I did not go the length that I intended. I only pointed out to you the value nations as well as individuals put on sympathy, and how jealous they are of its partial administration, and I wished you to think more favourably of the good intentions in the remark, 'We cannot but sympathize with the noble and undaunted actions of the whale, when she often sacrifices her life in the protection of her young.' Although that sympathy is often drawn from those that are intent on her destruction, yet when proceeding from those who are most wishful that all good results may crown the labours of the object of their sympathy, it deserves a favourable distinction, and I am sure you will say with me that even in both cases the feeling is a noble one.

"It was most gratifying to us all to hear of the rapid progress you are making with the station, and the good prospects that are dawning on the whole undertaking.

"Just a day or two after I wrote you last, I got two or three of my ribs broken, which caused considerable pain for a time and interfered much with my work; but I am glad to say that I am now on the fair way to recovery, and can do a moderate day's work. I have added another branch to the scope of my researches, viz. the carboniferous ostracoda and foraminifera, these being closely connected with those of glacial deposits, and I have had some excellent speed with them.

" I shall be glad to hear from you soon."

The carboniferous fossils soon brought Robertson into correspondence with Professor Rupert Jones, and, to show the stress upon the time of a naturalist which results from investigating the microscopic organisms both recent and fossil, an extract may be given from one of Dr. Brady's letters, in which he observes, " Jones said to me the other day in a letter, that if old Methuselah busied himself among the forams. and entoms., he must have grieved to die so young! I think myself I should be tired of them before I got to his years, but one might still be far from exhausting the subject ! "

In the letter to Dr. Dohrn, it will have been noticed that Robertson speaks of having had two or three of his ribs broken. This is an accident to a man of sixty-six tolerably well calculated to impress the memory, but the occurrence was forgotten by the person most interested in it, until the letter above quoted brought it to light. When Lord Brougham as a child fell down and broke his crown, he apologized to his mother, who was scolding him for it, on the ground that it was crackit before. Robertson might excuse his forgetfulness of the second accident to his ribs on a similar score. What other breakages or batterings of his hardy frame may have been in like manner overlooked it is impossible to say. But whatever they may have been, they have left him

sturdy to row, and dredge, and climb the hill, when
on the verge of eighty-four. The only pity is that
while his ribs were "in bits," he did not secure an
annuity, like the "waesome wife o' saxty-three" in
the poem. The piece referred to is entitled, "Charge
on a Bond of Annuity," by the late George Outram,
Esq., Editor of the *Glasgow Herald*. It is a fine
specimen of Scotch humour, to which Mr. Robertson
gave a prominent place in his commonplace book.
The reader will scarcely think that any apology is
needed for the quotation of it, which may even excite
his gratitude.

> "I gaed to spend a week in Fife—
>   An unco week it proved to be ;
> For there I met a waesome wife
>   Lamenting her viduity.
> Her grief brak out sae fierce and fell,
> I thought her heart wad burst the shell ;
> And—I was sae left tae mysel'—
>   I sell't her an annuity.
>
> "The bargain lookit fair eneugh—
>   She was just turn'd o' saxty-three—
> I couldna guess she'd prove sae teugh
>   By human ingenuity.
> But years hae come and years hae gone,
> And there she's yet as stieve's a stane—
> The limmer's growin' young again
>   Since she's got her annuity.
>
> "She's crined awa' tae bane and skin,
>   But that, it seems, was nought to me ;
> She's like to live, although she's in
>   The last stage o' tenuity.
> She munches wi' her wizzent gums,
> An' stumps about on legs o' thrums,
> But comes—as sure as Christmas comes—
>   To ca' for her annuity.

" She jokes her joke and cracks her crack
  As spunkie as a growin' flae ;
An' there she sits upon my back
  A livin' perpetuity.
She hurkles by her ingle side,
An' toasts an' tans her wrunkled hide—
Guid kens how lang she yet may bide
  To ca' for her annuity.

" I read the tables drawn wi' care
  For an insurance company,
Her chance o' life was stated there
  Wi' perfect perspicuity :
But tables here or tables there,
She's lived ten years beyond her share,
An's like to live a dozen mair
  To ca' for her annuity.

" Last Yule she had a fearfu' hoast—
  I thought a kink might set me free—
I led her out 'mang snow and frost
  Wi' constant assiduity ;
But deil may care, the blast gaed by,
And missed the auld anatomy—
It just cost me a tooth, forbye
  Discharging her annuity.

" Ae day she fell, her arm she brak,
  A compound fracture as could be—
Nae leech the cure would undertak'
  Whate'er was the gratuity ;
It's cured !—she handles't like a flail—
It does as weel in bits as hale—
But I'm a broken man mysel'
  Wi' her and her annuity.

" Her broozled flesh and broken banes
  Are weel as flesh an' banes can be ;
She beats the taeds that live in stanes
  An' fatten in vacuity !

They die when they're exposed to air—
They canna thole the atmosphere—
But her !—expose her onywhere—
She lives for her annuity.

" The Bible says the age o' man
    Threescore and ten perchance may be ;
She's ninety-four—let them who can
    Explain the incongruity.
She should hae lived afore the flood—
She's come o' patriarchal blood—
She's some old Pagan mummified
    Alive for her annuity.

" The water drap wears out the rock
    As this eternal jaud wears me ;
I could withstand the single shock,
    But not the continuity.
It's pay me here an' pay me there,
An' pay me, pay me, evermair—
I'll gang demented wi' despair—
    I'm *charged* for her annuity."

That Robertson's activity was not for long interrupted by his accident will be seen from the following
letter to Brady, which is worth quoting also as an
indication of his scientific caution.

"November 4, 1872.

"DEAR BRADY,

"We have got home all right. As I wrote
you last of our intention of going to Tenally brick-
work, we went, and had a dry day, but very windy
and cold. We reached the works in good time, but
found little appearance in the clay of fossils of any
kind, nothing more than a few *very small* fragments
of shell. However, there may be more of the smaller
forms, and to make that chance as favourable as

possible, we brought away a good sample of the clay. Tenally brickfield is on the south side of the Mull. From this we crossed to Port Logan Bay on the north side, where we examined several clay cliffs along the shore containing fragments of shells. From these too we brought away goodly samples. This con-cluded our post-tertiary work. We had resolved to try the loch on Friday, if the weather would permit of it at all. Friday was both wet and stormy, but we were fortunate in getting both a good boat and a good seaman, and although the wind and rain made the work difficult and disagreeable, we got a few good hauls from different localities. But had the weather been favourable, I would have had material from many different points. However, we were glad of the progress that was made. We wished to have had a few hours' shore work in the Bay of Glen Luce, but the tides did not suit.

" We left Stranraer on Saturday at 2.30, by railway, and reached home by 10 p.m.

" In regard to the things you had from Crosskey from what is called the ' Middle Glacial Beds,' Ipswich-road, Norwich—from their singular appearance I would be quite suspicious of them, unless the locality and the exact position of the bed were given by undoubted authority. A wrong hitch of that kind would be great damage to the whole work. You remember the clay that was sent me from Eastbourne as the common brick clay, which from closer inquiry was found to be mixed with material from borings that had passed through the ' Gault,' and, for anything that has been shown, there may be something of the same kind here. There is a Mr. Taylor in Norwich, a good geologist. I will try and get his address, and write and inquire if he knows these Middle Glacial Beds at Ipswich-road. If so, I will ask him the favour to send me a parcel of it."

At the close of this same year, through the intervention of Mr. John Young, he was brought into correspondence with that indefatigable palæontologist, the late Mr. Thomas Davidson, F.R.S., to whom he writes on December 24, 1872 :—

"DEAR SIR,
        "Yours is just to hand, and I will be glad if I can in any way be of service to you, but I fear, from the vast knowledge you already possess of all the details of the subject, that I can have nothing that will be of interest to you. Last night I forwarded a list of the brachiopoda I had met with in some of the beds of Norway."

In the after part of the letter he mentions the dredging of *Terebratula caput-serpentis* and *Crania anomala* at Oban, in Loch Fyne, and off Cumbrae, with comments on their variation in size and frequency at different points.

On January 4, 1873, he writes to Dr. Dohrn, and, after fully congratulating the latter on having at last sailed into smooth waters, of himself he says :—

"I am plodding away as usual. We have now about ready our 'Monograph on the Post-Glacial

Ostracoda of Britain,' but the Palæontographical Society cannot make room for it before next year, I am sure I will be glad when it is off our hands.

"For some time past I have been going into the carboniferous ostracoda and foraminifera with considerable success, and with less labour than the clays required. At the same time I have another task on hand, that is, a list of the ostracoda of the Firth of Clyde ; and I also intend to make another of the lochs of Scotland, and another of the canals of England, Ireland, and Scotland. So you see that there is no lack of work in store for me."

In June of this year he arranged with G. S. Brady to make a dredging excursion to the Scilly Isles. Leaving Glasgow at 10 a.m. by express, he reached Penzance next morning at 6 a.m., having only had in this long ride a break of an hour and a half at Birmingham. Brady joined him an hour or two later. The steamer to the Scilly Isles was not due to leave till six in the evening.

In the interval the naturalists visited the Penzance museum, which exhibits many fine minerals, but did not show Robertson anything in his own special line of work except some little shells from the tin stream works. They were interested to observe that thus early in the year the potato-fields in that neighbourhood had already been cleared, and sown with a fresh crop. The bay also was a pleasant sight, being crowded in the morning with a fleet of about three hundred mackerel-boats. They were told that each of these had a crew of eight, none of them boys, but all strong men ; that they left in the afternoon and returned in the morning; that the fish were all packed in hampers holding one hundred fish each, and were sold by auction ; that, as this auction could not be held on each boat separately, an average had to be taken from a few samples as well as time allowed, for that all had to be aboard of the steamer by the time of her sailing ; and that a special train at Penzance awaited the arrival of the steamer, to hurry away with its cargo to the central markets ; for these enamelled silvery-gleaming fishes ill brook any prolonged delay between leaving the water and serving for the food of mankind.

Brady and Robertson went in good time on board the boat which was to start for the Scilly Isles at six, but there was no special need for punctuality, since it did not actually start till after seven. There were passengers to be waited for. The captain was fretting and fuming, but all his signals were of no avail till it suited the convenience of the superior of the Scilly Isles, with some members of his household, to embark. So fine a thing it is to be a sovereign, on however small a scale !

On this excursion the two explorers were fortunate in getting a good boat, well suited for their purpose, which was far from being a matter of course in these expeditions. They also had the assistance of two good men who understood their work. Contrary to their general custom, they used a sail, but this was of no great consequence, as they were only working with the small seven-inch dredge.

By coming to a great distance from their former hunting-grounds, they had hoped and expected to find a considerable difference in the microscopic fauna from what they had met with on the east of England or in Scotch waters. In this they were disappointed. To their surprise, the agreement extended even to the brackish water-pools.

In other respects the results were not very satisfactory. On the beach they found but few shells, and no zoophytes. The shores of granitic sand were barren, not showing various zones of life between tide marks ; and dredging in the shallow water near the shore was almost equally unproductive. Dredging in deeper water was much impeded. The dredge was often held fast, and more than once the net was torn asunder. This was not so much due to passing over rocky ground as to the presence of an annelid with a concretionary tube, which, from the abundance of the fragments that they hauled up, seemed to form a continuous floor. They obtained some specimens of the stony coral, *Caryophyllia Smithii*, with the young ones budding out from the side.

After their return home there was much work to be done in "floating" the various dredgings for ostracoda and entomostraca. In one department they had some fairly good success, for on July 28, 1873, Robertson writes to Brady :—

"Mrs. Robertson has been looking over the foraminifera. They appear to turn out very well in species. One or two may be abundant, while most of the others are thinly dispersed. In this shore-gathering twelve species are represented by one specimen each. But on the whole they are a nice group. A few agree well with figures of D'Orbigny's that we cannot find in any of the British works at our command. When your brother * gets his carboniferous paper off his hands, he will look over a few of these doubtfuls ; but I know that he does not want to be perplexed with any other work of that kind until that of the carboniferous is done. I send you a few of the prevailing foraminifera. I will now look over the shells, and send you the list as far as I can make them out."

At the same period he writes to Dr. Dickie, Professor of Botany in Aberdeen, in regard to one of the sea-weeds from Scilly, which could not be identified with any of those in Harvey's "Phycologia Britannica."

With Professor Victor Carus, who was acting as deputy professor in Edinburgh during Wyville Thomson's absence on the *Challenger*, Robertson was also now in friendly correspondence. To him he showed a young *Pentacrinus*, which was one of the rarities secured at the Scilly Isles.

To Gwyn Jeffreys he wrote on the subject of the shells from the same locality ; and Dr. Jeffreys' answer drew forth the following little note, which is of interest in regard to the eminent conchologist to whom it was written :—

"September 4, 1873.

"MY DEAR SIR,

"Many thanks for your kind and prompt reply to my queries. It was really exceedingly provoking, the way you were prevented from joining

* II. B. Brady, the great English authority on the foraminifera.

the expedition with the *Challenger*. An opportunity so favourable and important may never occur again. " Ever glad to hear from yóu, with kind regards,
" I remain yours,
"DAVID ROBERTSON."

While working at sea-weeds, shells, nudibranchs, amphipods, and various smaller fry, he was still keenly engaged upon geological studies. Writing in this same month to Mr. Neilson in regard to the carboniferous shales near Glasgow, he says, " I may mention that Mr. Young and I were very fortunate at East Kilbride. He got a fine *Dithyroçaris* and I got another. One of them is certainly a species new to science." The specimens referred to belong to a genus of fossil crustaceans, and of this very genus no less than three new species were described in the following year by Henry Woodward , and Richard Etheridge, Junr., as derived from the lower carboniferous limestone in the locality above mentioned.

To Mr. W. Percy Sladen, a great authority on echinoderms, with whom eventually he became very intimate, he wrote a letter on September 16, 1873, in regard to the discovery of a little sea-urchin, *Echinus neglectus*, in an unexpected locality :—

" An animal may be abundant, and yet, from the nature of its habitat, or the want of knowledge of the tackle proper to secure it, it may for long be considered to be rare. For example, *Pecten septemradiatus* has long been considered a rather rare shell in the Clyde district. Some years ago I was dredging in Loch Fyne. I said to my boatman, when speaking

of *Pecten septemradiatus,* that I would give him a
penny apiece for them. He asked how many I would
take. To give him a wide berth, I said I would take
one pound's worth. A few days after he wrote me
that he had procured eight hundred. He had found
out that in some places of the loch, when the herring-
nets got down to lie on the ground, they came up
with scores of this shell attached to them, and from ·
this he had learned how to secure a good haul. It is
probable the explanation is that the shells lie with
the valves gaping, and when the cords of the net get
between them the valves close upon the meshes and
hold fast. It is not unlikely that *Echinus neglectus*
may not be as scarce as it seems to be. As *Echinus
sphaera* is so variable, both in colour and form and
in the character of its spines, *Echinus neglectus* would
readily be passed over for *Echinus sphaera,* except
by those who are specially engaged in that particular
branch."

To Robertson's experience with his rare *Pecten*
there is an amusing parallel in an anecdote which
Norman relates in the fourth volume of Bowerbank's
" British Spongiadæ " :—

" When Dr. Bowerbank first commenced the study
of British sponges, the *Tethya,* etc., were considered
extremely rare. Desirous of possessing these fine
species, he wrote to the fishermen's agent at the
Out Skerries, and said he would give sixpence each
for all that he could procure. No doubt our old
friend thought the offer an uncommonly safe one ;
but in a short time a huge keg of sponges came
(300 *Tethya,* see ii. p. 84, among them !) and a nice

little bill of fifteen pounds. As he distributed his duplicates among his friends, he used to laugh over the story, which he told as a warning never to give an unlimited order."

On November 4, 1873, Robertson wrote to Dr. R. Brown the following very interesting letter :—

"My dear Sir,

"A simple way of illustrating the experiment of the precipitation of clay in fresh and sea water, is to take two small glass jars of equal size. Test glasses about four inches deep and an inch and three-quarters wide do very well. Fill the two about four-fifths full, the one with sea water, the other with fresh water. Then fill both up with clay dissolved in fresh water, say about the consistence of cream, and stir both well up. Set the jars side by side to settle, and in a very short time the precipitation in the jar containing the sea water will be seen to be going on rapidly, while in the jar with the fresh water little or no change will be observable. That the experiment be successful and true deductions come to, it is necessary to have the fresh water pure, free from salts of any kind, as a very small admixture of these will falsify the experiment to a less or greater extent. This may explain why some lakes, such as the Lake of Geneva, remain clear although muddy glacier water is continually pouring into them. The experiment may be varied by adding different quantities of fresh water to the sea water till it becomes but slightly brackish. Still, with these slightly brackish mixtures

U

the precipitation will be seen to go on far more rapidly than in the purely fresh water.

" From these results, and keeping in view the large quantity of suspended earthy matter annually carried down by rivers, and that a large proportion of it is precipitated as soon as it comes in contact with the water of the sea, we can easily understand how the courses of rivers within the influence of the tide get so branched in many cases by the precipitated mud silting up the course of the river at one place and the obstructed water at floods forcing a new channel at another—and from the same cause deltas at the mouths of rivers may in a great measure be formed.

" Whatever changes may have taken place relatively to land and sea from other causes, it does not appear that deposits from fresh water currents can be carried far seaward. It is true that the colour of the sea may be affected far beyond the *embouchure* of the river. It has been stated that the discoloration of the sea by the water of the Amazon has been perceptible three hundred miles from the shore. When such a body of water rolls forward in high floods it will keep its course clear for a considerable distance. Besides, the fresh water being lighter than the salt water, much of it may float on the surface for longer or shorter distances according to its volume and speed. Still, even in these exceptional cases we are constrained to believe that the great proportion of the earthy matter must be thrown down long before it reaches that length of travelling.

" Last night you were suggesting the desirability of trying for microzoa, etc., in the clay immediately underlying some of the great peat deposits. As peat generally contains free acid, the sample of clay to be examined should be taken sufficiently low, out of reach of the action of the acid, as most of the remains of these small animals likely to be preserved in the clay are calcareous, and would be dissolved by any contact with the acid."

During this year Robertson also renewed his correspondence with the Rev. Mr. Gunn, the friendly and liberal-minded geologist whose hospitality he had enjoyed when in Norfolk.

To him he sends a small dredge and dredging-rope, and a muslin net, and a coarse net, and canvas bags, and a tin flask of spirit, and besides these, forsooth—

"You will notice a small cotton bag attached to the rope a little forward from the dredge. This is to put a stone into when the water is any way deep, which makes the dredge work better. And there is another attached in the same way to the lower end of the bag of the dredge to keep the dredge in its proper position."

All these paraphernalia are sent to the clergyman, in order that he may forward to Glasgow two or three small bags of mud out of the Norfolk broads, where no doubt there is so ample a supply of that commodity that a little could be well spared to Scotland without sensibly diminishing the stock required for the English market.

With the apparatus, elaborate instructions are sent as to the collecting, preparing, and packing of the precious consignment. It might be natural to suppose that the flask of spirit was intended to encourage

Mr. Gunn before, and to revive him after, the various incidents of his troublesome task, but such a supposition does not coincide with the express direction that, when the mud collected has had as much of the water pressed out of it as possible, it is to be put into a jug or other vessel and have the spirit out of the tin flask poured over it. Anyhow Mr. Gunn took all the demands upon him in good part, and not only executed the commission in a most satisfactory manner, but stirred up the microscopists of his own neighbourhood to utilize the unsuspected resources that lie in the seemingly repellent mud of rivers and ponds. In these ways do genial workers not only advance the bounds of science, but largely promote the love of it.

CHAPTER XIX.

THE year 1874 may be regarded as a kind of epoch in the scientific part of this biography, for in that year the Palæontographical Society published the " Monograph of the Post-tertiary Entomostraca," by Brady, Crosskey, and Robertson.

If the credit of planning the work be due to Mr. Crosskey, and if it were the critical acumen of Dr. Brady that crowned the edifice, there is still reason to suppose that the foundations and most of the solid parts of the structure were put together by the persevering industry and skill of David Robertson.

The work and correspondence connected with bringing out the monograph made the earlier months of the year very busy ones. Nevertheless, in May, he found or made time to go with his wife to the Isle of Man to visit Mrs. Robertson's relations. The kindness of their friends in desiring to show them all the lions of the place curtailed the time that might have been otherwise devoted to natural history. Yet Robertson did not fail to skim the sand on the beach for cumacea, nor to go out dredging in the day time and with the surface net at night.

The fishermen told him that two or three miles out from the shore there were *Pecten* banks crowded with animal life, and, as some evidence that what they said was true, he noted numbers of valves of *Pecten opercularis* on the beach, and a full basket of *Pecten maximus* for sale in the market at a shilling a dozen.

He watched the people at low tide taking sand-eels for bait. The general mode of capture is to dig them up with a *grape* or pitchfork, but some have the knack of doing it with great success with an old toothed reaping-sickle, drawing it through the sand with one hand and taking hold of the eels by the other as they are brought up on the sharp teeth. But this can only be done when the sand is covered by at least a few inches of water, for when the sand is bare it becomes so stiff that the fish would be cut through before they could be brought to the surface.

The very different mode of obtaining the sand-eels practised at Aberdeen has been already described. There also they have an alternative method, for they sometimes use a peculiar long-handled spade, with which, by laying the long handle over the knee, they turn the fishes out with great rapidity. But in this operation both practice and quick fingers are needed to pick the eels up before they can make their escape back into the sand.

In obtaining lug-worms for bait there is a similar variety of custom. On the Ayrshire coast as well as in the Isle of Man the fishermen dig for them with a flat three-pronged *grape*, whereas on the Isle of Cumbrae and some other parts of the west of Scotland they take them with a flat spade.

At Douglas and Port Erin at most seasons the prevailing bait is *Buccinum undatum*, the common whelk, which seems to be abundant in many places on shelly banks. The mode of capture is by means of a basket of wicker-work shaped like a bee-hive, with a hole in the top about four inches wide having the border reflexed straight downwards, not tapering as in a lobster-pot. A few heavy weights of stone or metal are fixed at the bottom of the basket to keep it down, and some carrion or dead fish, often the unmarketable dog-fish, are put in for bait to attract the mollusks, and the whole is let down on suitable ground by a rope, with cork floats to mark its position. The basket is generally left for a night, sometimes for twenty-four hours, after which lapse of time it is frequently found full of the whelks, many of them also clinging to the outside. Besides the *Buccinum*, there are frequently a number of *Fusus gracilis*, and more rarely some of *Murex cinerea*, and as these are too small for bait, they are cast aside by the fishermen, and are thus conveniently at the service of any collector of shells who may happen to want them.

Robertson noticed that gorse was very abundant in the Isle of Man, and that it was much used as a fence on the top of the old turf dykes. Seeing that in some places it was nicely trimmed and pre-eminently ornamental, he expresses a wonder that it is not more frequently treated in this way.

In the following July we find him at work on the east coast. At the meeting of the British Association in the previous year a grant had been made to Mr. Henry Brady, Dr. G. S. Brady and Mr. Robertson, as a committee of exploration for dredging in the waters off the north-east coast of England. They were able to engage a tug called the *Bonnie Dundee*, with a captain and three men, at a cost of three pounds ten shillings a day. Robertson was agreeably surprised at the cheapness, since at Cumbrae, where rowing-boats can be had for threepence an hour, he had been asked twelve pounds for a day's use of a steam-tug.

The committee, minus Mr. Henry Brady, starting from Sunderland on their first cruise, had on board with them the Rev. A. M. Norman and the wife and some of the children of G. S. Brady. The day was fine, yet there was some swell on the sea. Although it was not great, it kept the boat in a kind of up and down motion, and was soon too much for the ladies. Even the naturalists felt more or less squeamish, which of them more and which less it may not be politic to specify, since in the biographies of those who were most unwell the question of degree might hereafter be challenged. So far as the day's dredging was concerned, however, there was nothing to complain of.

During the week the small dredge and the large one were commonly used at the same time, and Robertson was glad to observe that the heavy dredge seldom secured any species that was not also found in its smaller companion. By way of exception, on one occasion when the vessel was drifting sideways, and the two dredges were working one on one side and the other on the other side of the paddle-box, one of them came up crowded with a single species of sea-urchin, while the other had but one small specimen of that species, but a great number of a different one. In some of their operations upon rough ground the bag of the dredge was soon worn into holes or torn, especially the thin canvas or cheese-cloth bag of the "wee dredge." To remedy this a stronger canvas bag, open below, was put on the outside of the other.

On former occasions Robertson had been at a loss to get such a label as would keep quite legible on the outside or inside of the bags of wet mud. He had tried both parchment and brown leather, but the damp seemed soon to obliterate the writing. At last he thought of the plan of putting the label into a small wooden needle-case, in which he has always found the label clean and in good condition even after lying in the wet or damp for weeks together. Dr. Gwyn Jeffreys when on board the *Valorous* gladly adopted this ingenious contrivance. The plan itself, or some modification of it, might be applied to the labelling of fruit-trees. Another advantage that the needle-case had for Robertson's purpose was that, being put into the bag, it ran no danger of being torn off or defaced, as may so easily happen to outside labels. It is obvious that for the purpose of ready reference an outside label may be used in addition to the protected one.

After the first day, Norman and the ladies left, and they saw no more of them on the *Bonnie Dundee*. The custom of the dredging party was to go home every night to Sunderland. There was one exception, when they lay in Scarborough harbour for the night. It was between these two towns that their work had been carried on, generally about three or four miles off shore, in depths between forty and sixty fathoms. They did not secure many absolute novelties, but added considerably to what had before been found off that coast.

"The last day of our dredging in the *Bonnie Dundee,*" says Mr. Robertson, "Brady had a patient that he could not leave, and I had to go by myself. I had a great desire to go to the Dogger Bank. The captain said that it was about forty miles off, and that it would take us about five hours to get to it. Although there would not be too much time to dredge, and the day did not look too promising, still it was the only chance that I ever might have of getting to it; so we made straight for the bank. It did not turn out so well as I expected. The depth was fifteen fathoms, and the bottom a muddy sand, but animal life was not abundant, and nothing was met with of any consequence. As clouds were still threatening, and the wind getting a little stronger, we did not like to venture to stay longer than to take two or three hauls, but nothing was met with of particular interest. As the wind did not increase we had a haul now and again on the way home."

Success in dredging would perhaps pall on the appetite if it were not sometimes varied by a blank day. Now and then the dredger finds in his pursuit, as Punch's quarryman said of his own to the inquiring geologist, that "there's nothing to be got but muck and hard work." On the whole, however, the committee considered that they had had both a pleasant and a successful week. Their only mishap consisted in the loss of a dredge. The current was so strong where they worked that it carried the steamer along with the dredge without any necessity for working the engine. The result was that when the dredge got fast it could not be eased by steaming back to it. All the rope was let out, and a buoy attached to the end of it, but the tide was running so strongly that the buoy itself was drawn under water, and of their dredge they saw no more.

The visit to Ireland with Norman, in August of this year, has been already mentioned. In the earlier months Robertson had been corresponding with Mr. Whiteaves, who submitted to his examination the ostracoda dredged in the River St. Lawrence.

On October 15, 1874, he wrote to his friend at Banff :—

"MY DEAR MR. EDWARD,

"It will afford me the greatest possible pleasure if I can be of any service to you. I shall lose no time in making inquiries regarding the matter referred to. I have been confined to the house for the last two weeks with rheumatic pains, but I have every hope that in a few days I will be able to venture out, and I will make it my first·business to try if anything can be done.

"They are making some enlargement to the Kelvingrove museum, but whether they will require an additional assistant I do not know. There is a public aquarium being got up at Rothesay. But such situations are often ruled by parties specially interested in getting up the institution.

" However, nothing will be wanting on my part in furthering your interest."

On October 31, 1874, he writes to him again :—

" MY DEAR SIR,
        " I have just been able to be out a little, and have seen the curator of the Kelvingrove museum, who believes that an additional man will be wanted when the building is completed, but there can be nothing definite said till that time. The foundation is laid and a few feet of the walls are up, and it is expected that it will be well forward by early spring. Mr. Thomson, the curator, takes a very favourable view of your fitness for the situation. I have also seen one of the directors of the Rothesay aquarium —John Kirsop, hatter, Argyle Street, corner of Arcade—who also gives encouragement to push your application. He suggests that the best way would be for you to send in a formal application to him, and he would bring it before the board of directors at the first meeting. You should send along with it a few testimonials as to your fitness, which I am sure you could readily get at once, and a similar application to Mr. Thomson, curator of the Kelvingrove museum. I have also been to the curator of the Hunterian museum, but the prospects there appear in the mean time to be more distant."

These efforts were unavailing. The naturalist of Banff was disappointed in his ambition of becoming a subordinate servant in an obscure museum. What followed is a striking illustration of the power of literature. Dr. Smiles's book appeared. Its merits were applauded by all the reviews, and before long there was scarcely a better known name in Great Britain than that of Thomas Edward, nor perhaps was the Queen ever more fully in accord with her subjects than when she bestowed upon this forlorn shoemaker a substantial mark of sympathy and regard.

In November, Robertson was writing as follows to Dr. Dohrn :—

"MY DEAR DR. DOHRN,

"Just as I was ready to post the enclosed your exceedingly welcome letter of November 23, 1874, reached me. It truly caused as much joy amongst us as if it had been from a lost son. Although we heard sometimes regarding you, still there was the blank that it was not from yourself. We are glad to hear that your health is so much improved, and that all other matters are so much brighter, and that you are so hopefully surmounting the obstacles that had been strewn so thickly over your path. We are glad also to learn from many sources that the station is attracting the favourable notice of nations and men of science of the highest standing, and it is to be hoped that benefactors will not be long wanting to place it in perfect independence.

"Further, convey to your dear wife our many thanks for her fine portrait, which we are all highly delighted with. We claim in lieu of your (unfulfilled) promise to come and visit us on your marriage jaunt, that you soon give us the great pleasure of making Mrs.

Dohrn's personal acquaintance, and we will promise
not to tell her of all the tricks that you used to play."

In the early part of the following year, another
letter to Dohrn conveys some of the family history—

"MY DEAR DR. DOHRN,
        "Your letter of February 22 is to hand,
and it throws, as a letter from you always does,
a glow of happiness over us all, and in this case it is
doubly so, as we are to have the pleasure once more
of seeing you at Millport, and the happiness of
making your dear wife's personal acquaintance. I
hope you will be able to spare time to let us take
another 'general survey' of the bays and creeks
round the Great and Lesser Cumbraes.

"David is now a married man, and is at present in
London on his marriage trip. Thomas proposes to
enter into the same condition some time in July.
The ceremony will take place in the Isle of Man, the
home of his betrothed.

"This has been a bitter cold winter, and the mortality bill of Glasgow unprecedentedly high—sixty-five
deaths to the thousand inhabitants, more than double
the usual average. Both Mrs. Robertson and I have
had our share of illness, but mine was trifling. She
was confined to her bed for the greater part of the
first two months of the year ; but I am happy to say
that she is now much better, and in the fair way of
recovery, and we hope that in a short time she will be
enjoying her usual good health.

"We are all glad to hear that everything is going

on with you so prosperously. A little steamer would be of great advantage to you, and would further the work greatly and save the toil of the men, but I fear that it would be difficult to get one that would answer your purpose satisfactorily at the money you name. Anything of boats or engines that requires frequent repairs becomes a most annoying and expensive investment, such outlays soon doubling the original cost. I think it would be best if possible to have a good substantial thing, although it would cost more at first.

" However, except for greater distances, I would in most cases prefer the boat with oars to a larger vessel, particularly where the ground is rough, or in creeks or bays where you have to return often over the same ground, which has often to be done where we find rich circumscribed banks.

"Your letter unfolded a puzzle that we had after much guessing failed to make out, that was, who could it be who had so kindly sent so many fine oranges? At first it was at once ascribed to you, but then they came by London, and as there were boats going and coming direct between Glasgow and Naples, we conjectured that they must have been from some other source. Nothing certain could be made out till your letter came."

Subsequently it will appear that Robertson placed a far higher value on the services of a steam launch for dredging than he was at this time inclined to attribute to them. As often happens, a theoretical view was modified in the light of experience.

Robertson's zeal as a collector, and readiness both to oblige his friends and forward the cause of science, are pleasantly illustrated by an interesting little episode in the autumn of 1875. The well-known naturalist, Albany Hancock, at the time of his death, in 1873, was engaged in collecting materials for a monograph on the tunicata, that group of organisms which have been supposed by evolutionists to lead with the smallest interval from the invertebrates to the back-boned animals, and in some of which the scientific poet Chamisso first noticed the peculiar series of phenomena since described as " alternation of generations." In the course of a long letter to Robertson, dated September 3, 1875, Norman says—

" Last week I spent a couple of days with Sir W. Armstrong at Cragside (a charming place in Northumberland) and met Professor Huxley, with whom, in conjunction with Mr. J. Hancock and Dr. Embleton, there was a council respecting the condition for publication of Alder and Hancock's work on the tunicata. As a descriptive work on the species we think it may be easily got ready for the printer, and Hancock's " Anatomy and Physiology of the simple Ascidians " is very nearly fully written up, but, though he has left a vast mass of anatomical drawings, the very number of them makes a difficulty as to selection, and they are not worked up sufficiently for the engraver. Had he lived, many figures would have been worked up into one admirable illustration, but no one else can attempt to do this. I hope that Huxley may be induced to write an introduction. In order to do this he wishes to dissect a few fresh specimens of *Ascidia mentula.* I told him I thought I could get them for him through you, as the form is not rare in the Clyde."

As it proved, however, the Clyde would not, at any rate at the time, yield the required specimens. With some correspondents there would probably have been no more to be said. The objects asked for had been sought and not found, and consequently could not in reason be expected to be sent. But the following letter will show that Robertson dealt with the ascidians as Mahomet did with the mountain ; if they would not come to him, he made up his mind to go to them. Norman, writing from Burnmoor on September 21, says—

"MY DEAR ROBERTSON,

"Your letter from Oban directed to Ware has been forwarded, and reached me here this morning. It is really extremely kind, and shows a real anxiety to promote the interests of science that you should have gone all the way to Oban to get the ascidians, and I am very glad that having thus gone you were not unsuccessful in the search. Please kindly send the specimens to Professor Huxley, care of the Curator, the University Museum, Edinburgh."

On November 28, in the same year, Norman writes in regard to an invention of Robertson's, which will be found described among others in Appendix A :—

"MY DEAR ROBERTSON,

"Many thanks for your charming type-slides. They are wonderful proofs of your skill and neat-handedness, as are all your mountings. I fear it would be hopeless to attempt to get them made by a manufacturer."

A little earlier he had written to the same effect :—
" I break the tenth commandment horribly when I see your 'type' slides. I am afraid I cannot get them made for money. I have not the skill to make them myself. Could you spare me a dozen ready prepared that I could use in these *Valorous* things, if so, I should be extremely obliged."

It may here be properly and conveniently stated, that, if comparatively few quotations, or in some cases none at all, are drawn from the voluminous correspondence which at different periods Robertson carried on with George Stewardson Brady, Alfred Merle Norman, W. Percy Sladen ; with H. W. Cross-key and Henry John Carter ; with Dr. Thomas Wright, of Cheltenham, and T. Rupert Jones ; with Henry Brady, Gwyn Jeffreys, and Dr. John Murray, of the *Challenger*, and with many others, including the present biographer ; the chief reason is that the letters preserved are for the most part filled with details of natural history inquiry and research, which have either been since utilized in print, or which could not without too elaborate an explanation be made intelligible and entertaining to the general reader.

It seems to have been ever with Robertson, not so much a point of honour and of courtesy, as a matter of course to answer letters with business-like punctu-ality and unreserved frankness.

The story goes that some years ago a prelate in.

parliament expressed his wonder that his right
reverend brethren should find their correspondence
burdensome, a thing, he said, quite contrary to his
own experience and, he believed, unnecessary in
theirs ; but he forgot, or omitted to explain, that he
himself had begun by never answering letters, and
had thus ended by never receiving any.

One may safely say that it never entered Robertson's head to adopt this simple expedient for cooling
the warmth of friendship which his character and
hospitality were sure to kindle in all who became
intimate with the one or had the opportunity of
enjoying the other.

That advancing years in no way chilled the genial
glow of kindness with which he made his friends
welcome at Millport may be shown by a few sentences
taken almost at random from letters at a date later
than that which this chapter has reached. Thus Mr.
Joseph Wright, of Belfast, himself a specialist in regard
to the foraminifera, in writing to him says, " When
I look over my album it is pleasant to see the faces
of those under whose hospitable roof I spent such an
enjoyable time." On May 17, 1880, Mr. Sladen says,
" I am always looking forward to the fates letting us
meet again before long, as one of the pleasures of
life." The Rev. Thomas Wiltshire writes, on September 22, 1881, " Those expeditions in Millport
Bay, and your kind hospitality, will remain for many
a day amongst the pleasant recollections of the year
1881 ;" and again on January 13, 1882, " We
shall always remember and think over those very
pleasant and happy days we spent with her (Mrs.

Robertson) and you at Millport." Canon Norman, writing to Mrs. Robertson, under date September 11, 1888, says, " I cannot thank Mr. Robertson and yourself enough for all the great kindness and attention I received from you in every way while I was at Millport. I need not say how greatly I enjoyed my unconscionably long visit, which I shall ever look back to with pleasure. With kindest regards to Mr. Robertson and love to the young ones, yours most sincerely, A. M. Norman." Nor for this year of grace, 1890, would it be difficult to find the most satisfactory endorsement of all these cordial expressions.

CHAPTER XX.

IN the year 1876, the meeting of the British Association was held at Glasgow. In such a centre the
meeting of such a society was likely to put the local
naturalists on their mettle. Apart from the annual
report of the association, some books of permanent
value were the result.

One of the volumes called forth in preparation for
the meeting was a "Catalogue of the Western Scottish
Fossils," compiled by James Armstrong, John Young,
and David Robertson, with an introduction by Professor Young. The latter, in his preface, remarks
that "no one who has not tried it knows the labour
such lists involve," and he also observes that "Mr.
David Robertson has supplied a great want by his
complete list of glacial fossils."

Another volume consisted of two parts, the one
entitled " Notes on the Fauna and Flora of the West
of Scotland," this being a sort of introduction to the
other part, which formed the bulk of the volume, under
the title, "A Contribution towards a Complete List of
the Fauna and Flora of Clydesdale and the West of

Scotland," compiled under the auspices of the Society
of Field Naturalists, Glasgow.

The society went out of their own ranks to ask Mr.
Robertson to prepare the lists of crustacea, marine
mollusca, actinozoa, and foraminifera. He told them
that, considering the time available and the laborious
piece of work which he had to carry out in regard to
the glacial fossils, it would be impossible for him to
undertake so large a subject as the marine mollusca.
He was willing, however, that any one who undertook
it should make what use he could of the collections
in his private museum. The localities assigned to
the shells, he explained, could be depended on, but
not the names of the shells themselves, since these
had been only hastily and provisionally assigned till
a day of leisure should provide them with their turn
for exact scientific examination.

Then a curious thing happened. The gentleman
who undertook to prepare the list of mollusca readily
availed himself of the opportunity offered to examine
Robertson's numerous specimens; but, perhaps setting
down the caution to that naturalist's usual modesty,
he paid it no attention, merely entering in his list the
names and localities, just as he found them in the
drawers of the cabinet. Finally, having an honourable consciousness that the work was practically none
of his own, at the end of the catalogue he had the
name of " David Robertson " printed.

Had the work really been Robertson's own, and
been accurate in all respects except in having another
man's name attached to it, it is likely enough that he
would have passed the matter over in silence and

without any remonstrance. But as things turned out it was not possible for him to leave the matter as it stood.

At the association, where he had good reason to expect nothing but compliments and praise, he was much astonished and somewhat abashed to be accosted by his friend Gwyn Jeffreys, whose judgment and good opinion he especially valued, in a tone of surprised expostulation, that his catalogue, of all men's, should have been so slovenly. He was much pained, and, from the unexpected nature of the charge, was quite at a loss what to say. As he had no notion of the actual grounds on which it was based, this is not to be wondered at.

Like the Welsh shoemaker, he had the *mens conscia recti*, and, so far as the foraminifera were concerned, in which Mrs. Robertson was ever his faithful help-mate, he might be said, like the Welsh shoemaker's rival, to have both *men's and women's conscia recti.*

Still, troubled in his righteous soul, he hastened home to find out where he had gone astray. Then, for the first time, he became aware of what had happened. In the sequel, the Society of Field Naturalists behaved very handsomely. They entirely exonerated Mr. Robertson, and made the best amends to him in their power, as will be seen by the following notice inserted in all subsequent issues of their volume.

" The list of marine mollusca contained in that part of the guide-book for the British Association, which was compiled under the auspices of the Society of Field Naturalists, Glasgow, contained many errors. For these errors Mr. David Robertson was in no way responsible, and the society apologizes for his name being attached to the list. That the value of the guide-book may not suffer, Mr. Robertson has kindly consented to compile the accompanying list, which is as complete as the short time he had for the work would allow. It will be supplied to all those known to have that volume of the guide-book."

This was an expense to the society, and a considerable piece of labour for Mr. Robertson, since the list occupies sixteen pages of the book ; but, under the circumstances, it was a happy ending to an awkward incident, and gave to all concerned the credit which is well deserved when difficulties are met in a straight-forward and honourable manner.

Notwithstanding the slight contretemps in regard to the list of marine mollusca, the Association meeting proved to be very agreeable, giving Robertson the opportunity of seeing and entertaining many scientific friends from a distance. How pleasantly he upbraids one who did not put in an appearance may be seen by the following letter :—

"MY DEAR MR. SLADEN,

       "I am exceedingly glad to hear that you are still in the land of the living, and there in good health. Over and over we have been expressing our wonder what had come over you, that we had not heard from you. Latterly our hopes were revived somewhat, that you would be delaying till you came to the British Association meeting. But your absence from it quite strengthened our worst auguries. It now seemed quite possible that you were dead, and lying still and peacefully in your grave. Nay, this was even probable, and our chances ever to hear of the certainty seemed to depend on their passage through a very circuitous channel.

"So you see what relief your note of the 8th brought to us. Yet, although it has made us so glad, it still leaves much to regret, that is, that you are not here yourself, that we have not the pleasure of shaking hands with you and enjoying your gentle salutations and agreeable company, nor have the pleasure each of us of leading you to see our *own* collections, and to hear our own *praise* from living lips, for one half of us do not believe in one half that the papers say."

That Robertson's exhibited specimens were commended in private as well as in public, and behind his back as well as to his face, is shown by a remark of Norman's, under date September 18, 1876 : " I may tell you that the Duke of Argyll . . . .was particularly struck with the beautiful arrangement of your fine collection of crustacea."

In November of the following year, after the meeting of the Association at Halifax, where Mr. Sladen himself resided, Robertson again writes to him :—

November 6.
"MY DEAR SLADEN,
"Many thanks for your letter and newspaper. No wonder that you had no time for your wonted pursuits. The wonder is how you managed even collectively to do so much, how you managed to bring out so many different departments with such

complete success over the whole. I do not think we in Glasgow could do it. We Scotch are a contrary people, a kind of antagonistic people that do not work well together. We are split into small parties, and our strength is only known under an absolute leader. Many a time, when we had good prospects of making a great bonfire, that would have illuminated the country far and wide, the thing has been spoiled by disintegrating into small lights flickering here and there. Each, although good of itself, lost the effect, the charm of spectacle, the influence of a whole.

" I was particularly pleased with the lesson brought out by the history of your society, which showed so clearly that liberality was the precursor of prosperity, with fewer barriers and less exclusiveness. One or two may do great work, but work that is to be continued and improved, and to have its benefits enlarged through coming ages, must gather strength by enlisting the many, and to do that successfully it must be adapted to the requirements and tastes of the many."

Like that "poet of their own," who is cited as a not untruthful witness when he says "the Cretans are always liars," we have here a Scotchman, himself the most amiable of colleagues, telling us that the Scotch are difficult to work with. Nevertheless, what he says is very much in keeping with what Sir Walter Scott tells us of the character of his country-man in " The Legend of Montrose." On the other hand, those who have had much experience of societies, learned or otherwise, will be disposed to reflect that jealousies and self-assertion are nothing special to the Highlands or the Lowlands, but arise wherever the stronger find reason to claim a superiority which the weaker are unwilling to yield. It should be remembered that such disputes, which seem so ignoble when they occur among learned and wise men, do not occur among them because they are wise and learned, but because they are men.

In 1877, Mr. and Mrs. Robertson made a very pleasant expedition to Pwllheli, in North Wales, in company with Dr. G. S. Brady and his family ; but, partly owing to unfavourable weather, the natural history results were not very great. There comes, indeed, a time to most naturalists, when, in proportion to their earlier successes and industry, the chances diminish of their finding numerous novelties. Yet even here they procured a few living examples of the shell *Venus chione* in the sand at low water, this mollusk, according to Gwyn Jeffreys, not having been hitherto known in a depth less than six fathoms. On leaving Pwllheli the Robertsons stayed at Porthdinlleyn, which was a more profitable locality, and where they had, in the person of their landlord, the services of a very intelligent boatman. They admired his skill in hunting for crabs at low water. He seemed to know all the holes they frequented, and with his bare hands and arms would drag forth either crabs or lobsters from their lurking-places without the least fear. One of the evening excursions at this place is thus described :—

"After sunset with the surface net. The night was moderately calm and no moon. We row back and forward over the bay for nearly two hours. The water is not deep. The bottom is sand and sandy mud, with patches of *Zostera.* When darkness came fully on phosphorescence was seen, but not in any great abundance. The take when examined was found to be poor, mostly amphipods, and a few small isopods. What we expected and wished most for was cumas, but not one was seen. The small medusæ with eight rays were abundant, and interfered much with other things in the gathering.

"In rowing along the shore the glow-worms were sparkling like little stars along the grassy sand cliffs. They were seen distinctly at at least two hundred yards' distance."

It was two years later that Mr. Robertson went with his wife on a sort of pilgrimage to Peebles. The ostensible object of the excursion was as usual to search for ostracoda. But there was another design in view. A few miles out of Peebles, in Manor kirkyard, lies the grave of David Ritchie, the Black Dwarf, celebrated by Sir Walter Scott's novel. It was popularly believed that Ritchie had expressed a wish to have a rowan tree * planted beside his grave. Whether from heedlessness, or because there was thought to be something uncanny in the wish, it was not complied with. Mr. Alston, Mrs. Robertson's father, displeased with the neglect, took the task upon himself, and accomplished it one night in secret. The neighbours, finding the Dwarf's wish thus mysteriously carried out, were little inclined to damage or remove the tree, though they were now

* *Pyrus aucuparia*, the mountain ash.

more than ever disposed to see anything but the finger of heaven in the whole business.

"On reaching Peebles by train," Mr. Robertson says, "it being removal time, two of the principal hotels were just getting their furniture into the house. We called at one of them and hired a machine to take us to Manor. We saw the grave and the rowan tree, and took a small branch of it with us. We visited the Black Dwarf's house. The door to his own end of the house was low, just sufficient to admit himself; that for his sister, who occupied the other end of the house, was higher and suitable to her size. We had a walk through the Dwarf's garden. We were told that it was kept as near as they could in the way that he had left it. A house had been added to the end of the Dwarf's house, which detracts much from its originality. After a few turns [of dredging] among the ponds we returned to Peebles.

"When we left the hotel in the forenoon, we made no inquiry about beds, and when we returned we found that they had not a bed put up for any one to lie on. This was the time of rod-fishing, and all available places were full of lovers of the gentle craft. We hunted up and down, and could find no place where we could be accommodated. We were beginning to despair, fearing that we would have to pass the night in the open air, or apply at the police office for a night's shelter. At last we were directed to another hotel, 'The Cross Keys,' at the entrance to the town, where the mail-coaches used to put up. We were glad to hear of any hope, and made haste to the place. We were answered by a young woman, who assured us that we could not be accommodated, as they had only just got their furniture stowed into the house. My wife was very urgent that they would make some shift to take us. The young woman called to her mother, who was upstairs. She came partly down, and said that she could not possibly take us in ; that she had no place to put us ; that they would have to sleep themselves on the floor.

" My wife said that we had tried every other place in the town, and that at the place where we had most expected to get in they were in the same con- dition as herself, and that it would be hard to have to walk on the street all night.

" The woman replied that she would be very willing under the circumstances to have taken us in, but she really had no place that she could put any one into ; not a seat even to sit down upon ; that she had just been trying to get a bed put up in a room upstairs.

" We said we could put up with it in any way for a night.

" She said that we could not get up, for the stair was packed full of furniture.

" My wife said to her, 'If you can get up, I have no doubt that I can follow you.'

" We managed to get up. Here was a fine bedstead, with a spring wire mattress. My wife said that we were quite satisfied with the place, and that we would just remain where we were.

" The landlady said, what could we take our food on ?

" We said, ' On a chair, or anywhere.'

" However, a small table was soon provided. Then

another obstacle came in the way. My wife took coffee, and the coffee-pots were not yet unpacked. But a jug was at once suggested as a capital coffee-pot. All difficulties were now overcome. My wife and the hostess got into conversation about Peebles. My wife's father belonged to Manor, and though it did not appear that the landlady and the Alston family could count kin, none the less she and my wife were soon the greatest of friends."

An interesting old engraving of the " Black Dwarf's House," as it was before any sacrilegious hand had tampered with it, is still in Mr. Robertson's possession, a trophy of the pilgrimage to Manor, and a memorial of the risk they so narrowly escaped of being homeless wanderers for the night in Peebles.

Soon after returning from this excursion, they set out for a tour in the Hebrides, where the small dredge was found very serviceable even in deep water. They visited Skye, and there, from some hauls with the dredge in Portree Bay, at depths beween fourteen and eighteen fathoms, " the gathering of foraminifera was very rich, numbering above a hundred species, and mostly all being in fine condition." Some of these were new to Britain, and not many years earlier had been reckoned among the prizes of the *Porcupine* and *Challenger* expeditions.

Upon landing at Stornoway, in Lewis, the travellers noticed that the garden walks of some of the houses were laid with one species of shell, *Donax vittatus.* As this mollusk, though common enough in the south of England, happens to be very rare at Cumbrae, Robertson had a strong desire to see where these

animals were obtained.   In the course of inquiries he
learned that they were abundant at Melburt Bay, not
far from the town.   This bay they took an early
opportunity of visiting.

The day was blusterous, and the tide not far enough
out to permit of their finding the living mollusca, but,
as the shore was thickly strewn with the shells, they
gathered as many specimens with the valves together
as they cared to have.

Not far from Stornoway there is another large
expanse of sand laid bare at low water in what is
called Broad Bay.   This they arranged to visit on a
subsequent occasion.   They were warned that in some
parts of this bay there were quicksands in which they
might be entirely engulfed after the manner of the
unfortunate master of Ravenswood.   Upon reaching
the shore, they had not proceeded far before they had
to cross a small streamlet.   There was very little
water in it, and, by dropping a stone or two in, they
were able to step over without any inconvenience.
After wandering a good way across the sands, they
at length noticed that to retrace their steps was no
small distance, and bethought them that with the
incoming tide they could not so well judge the
character of the ground, and that if they chanced
upon the quicksands the danger would be greatly
increased.   Just as they were reasoning in this way,
they were seized with alarm at the observation that
they were already sinking in the sand well up on
their boots.   They at once hurried back, keeping as
far as they could on the ridges, till they came to the
little streamlet they had previously crossed.   This

was now a river several yards broad, and rising rapidly. There was no time to be lost.

Pulling off his boots and stockings, our naturalist gathered up his traps and, hurrying through the stream, deposited them safely on the other side. He then returned for his better half. He had some difficulty in getting her on to his shoulders so that her feet would be out of the water, which was now higher than his knees. There was no time to tarry. Every moment was increasing the danger. He balanced his precious burden the best way he could, and landed it in safety on the other side. Yet such is gratitude that to this day he has to put up with sarcastic compliments on the gallantry which inspired him to rescue first his traps and then his wife.

During the next three or four years, though there was much work done, and many pleasant and cheerful visits from friends were enjoyed, yet on the whole the wonted sunshine of the family was much overcast, and its radiance chequered with the shade of many sorrows. Mr. Robertson himself suffered from illness. His eldest son's wife died in 1880. In 1881, Mrs. Robertson had more than one extremely severe illness. In 1882, the younger son also lost his wife. She left him with three very young children.

For the lover of coincidences, it may be noted that just as the father lost his first wife through her imprudently visiting her friends in the Isle of Man, so did the son lose his some forty years later through her visit to the same island for the same purpose, though in the latter case the harm was done, not by an infectious malady, but by the accident of a very

Y

tempestuous voyage operating upon a frame at the time not in vigorous health. Yet another coincidence was that, just as Mr. Robertson's mother had been left a widow with a family of three little children, two boys and a girl, so was his son left a widower with a family almost exactly similar, though happily far better provided for.

It was not an unnatural thing that the grandparents should adopt the three motherless bairns, who ought, if education and example count for anything, to grow up into a group of accomplished naturalists. One difficulty at the outset was that the youngest, a boy between two and three years old, as if conscious of an irreparable loss, was often disposed to reject all the attentions of would-be nurses. On such occasions, the difficulty, it was found, could only be solved by his being taken into his grandfather's arms, where he at once lay placid and contented, with a sympathy between the two that continues unbroken.

CHAPTER XXI.

THE FISHERIES—LIMPETS—PIKE—THE *ARK.*

IN due time the clouds mentioned in the last chapter rolled by. New prospects of happiness opened for the young men, and their parents were restored to their wonted health and activity. In the following years they made some pleasant return visits to scientific friends : for example, to Canon Norman, at Burnmoor Rectory, in the county of Durham ; and to Mr. and Mrs. Wiltshire, at Lewisham. In 1883, they were attracted to London by the Fishery Exhibition. It is interesting to note the impression left on an observant and intelligent mind by these vast assemblages of the resources of the world and the products of human skill. In answer to an inquiry with reference both to the " Fisheries " and to the great world-fair of an earlier date, Mr. Robertson, in June of this present year, 1890, writes as follows :—

" Nothing notable occurred during our visit to the Great Exhibition of 1851 (it was in company with my partner, Mr. McDougall, not Mrs. Robertson), neither had it any influence on our business. Any things in the Exhibition that were connected with our trade were only productions of the highest skill of nations, beyond anything that could be available in our way. There were wonderful sights representing the improvements being made in the various industries, the result of the highest skilled workmanship, from the huge machines to the darning needle that encased a second within, and again a second encased a third, and the third a fourth, and the fourth a fifth, and, if I remember right, the fifth encased a sixth, and all in perfectly good sewing condition!

"Mrs. Robertson was with me at the Fishery Exhibition. I cannot say that my impressions of it differed much from that of 1851, except that the Fisheries, from my point of view, was greatly made up of large shops and small retailers. There was little connected with my own hobby that came under my notice, further than a few naturalist's dredges. We were much taken with the collection of the shells of Hull mounted on small tablets, an inch and a half square. They looked very nice, and brought a large series of mollusca under view in a very small space. I do not think that the whole covered more than four feet square. We were also much interested with the cooperage, where they were making herring barrels by machinery,—the staves, bottom and top hooped together ready for use in a few minutes.

"These were all matters of course, without any special interest, a sample of what could be told by each of the thousands that were there."

Although in these later years Mr. Robertson did not go skirmishing about from one end of Great Britain and Ireland to the other so freely as he had done in earlier times, he was far from letting scientific work escape him. Gwyn Jeffreys, who had previously sent him Atlantic dredgings from the *Valorous* expedition, now sent him the ooze of the Mediterranean to examine. This material had been obtained in the neighbourhood of Crete by the late Admiral Spratt. Gwyn Jeffreys searched it for mollusca, and then passed it on to Robertson to be sifted over for foraminifera and the like. Some of it eventually came into the present writer's hands ; as if any gleanings were to be expected when two such reapers had already been in the field ! But besides work from a distance, the shores of Cumbrae were an unexhausted and continual resource. It happened one day at Millport, after a considerable storm, that Mr. Robertson was fishing with a long pole from the shore for the seaweeds that were being borne in on the breakers. As he took care for this sort of work not to wear his best costume, he advanced without much fear further and further into the water, till at last, without his knowing it, his coat-tails were flapping up and down with each heave of the swell. One of his friends, seeing from a window what was happening, came down to the shore to give him notice, and, as he passed through the crowd of onlookers, he overheard a lady remark, " It is a great shame of whoever owns that man to let him go about in that way by himself."

Every one who has been to the seaside must have noticed limpets sticking to the rocks. Do they after once taking up their position retain it for life, or are they in the habit of changing their quarters? As to the answer to this question, Robertson found that naturalists were not all in agreement. He therefore put the matter to the test by an ingenious experiment, which he has thus described :—

"To ascertain the movements of the animal in its natural haunts, I placed over it an arch made from a piece of iron hoop with a wire let down through the arch resting on the crown of the shell, so that when the animal left its place the wire dropped on the rock. By this means on visiting the place at each tide, when the shell was uncovered, I could see whether it had shifted or not. To prevent as far as possible the indicating wire being acted on by the pressure of the waves when the sea was in any degree rough, a thin brass tube five inches long was fixed in the arch and the wire let down through it, by which means the lateral motion of the wire was reduced to a minimum. The observations were regularly carried on from June 21 till August 20, 1883, and were made on different limpets and on different zones of the tidal belt. It was found that no one of the limpets was regular as to the period when it went out to feed. The same animal sometimes went out for one or two tides consecutively, and at other times alternately, and occasionally not till the third or fourth flow of the tide. Those near high water were less regular than those lower down. This may be explained by those higher up on the tidal belt being for a shorter time and less regularly covered by the tide. The rocks near high water are often thickly covered with young balani * which sur-

* These may be more familiar to some under the name of cirripedes, a group which so long engrossed the attention of Charles Darwin, and in reference to which he says, " I worked steadily on this subject for the next eight years, and ultimately published two thick volumes, describing

round the limpets very closely. It was noticed that there was always a little bare space on one or other side of the shell. In these cases the animal, after being out to feed, was always found back close to the drop wire, as if endeavouring to get back to the exact spot it had left."

Since, however, limpets are sometimes found in situations from which it is impossible for them to make excursions, Robertson devised another experiment:—

"To test," he says, "whether an adult limpet subjected to confinement could live for any length of time, on August 20 I drilled a circle of holes in the rock round two well-grown limpets that were close together, and inserted wooden pegs so near each other that the animals could not get out. As I had to leave, my friend Mr. Cook, Millport, visited them occasionally and found them all right till December 20, when it was found that one of the pegs had given way and one of the limpets had made its escape to a little distance ; but the other was all right within its enclosure, having subsisted within a space of not more than a quarter of an inch beyond its shell for 124 days."

The limpet has a tongue which when stretched out is about double the length of the shell, and this tongue is furnished with rows upon rows of strong, curved teeth, forming a very beautiful object under the microscope.

all the known living species, and two thin quartos on the extinct species. I do not doubt that Sir E. Lytton Bulwer had me in his mind when he introduced in one of his novels a Professor Long, who had written two huge volumes on limpets." It must not be supposed from this that Lytton Bulwer confounded limpets with cirripedes. He was bound to disguise his professor to some extent.

The marks which the limpet leaves on 'the rock, after browsing on the film of fine seaweed, are themselves interesting. Forbes and Hanley supposed them to be "probably caused by the edge of the shell," but Robertson shows that this cannot be so, for "·I find," he says, "that whether the animal is at rest or in motion the shell is a little raised off the surface." Again, in regard to the functions of the tongue, Gwyn Jeffreys states that "this instrument is thrust out from side to side ; and, when charged with food, it is withdrawn into the stomach, unloaded, and again put forth." But Robertson observes, "After long and close watching I never could see it [the limpet] thrust out its long tongue from side to side, and I am strongly impressed that it never does so. That part of the tongue that lies behind the lips, and which is never protruded beyond them, appears to be the only portion applied to the cropping of the filamentous algæ while browsing."

The time and faculties of a man are so limited that even the most cautious philosopher must be content to owe the bulk of his intellectual store to statements which he can never test or prove. Hence it comes to pass that, in natural history, observations upon the habits and characters of different creatures sometimes gain a currency to which they have no sort of valid title. History and romance being thoroughly well intermingled, it is difficult to know where to begin the testing process. Robertson was on the look out for opportunities. He found more than one among his favourite little amphipods. It may be remembered that some time ago Ruskin wrote a note to the *Times* about the sand-hoppers, when he was very needlessly corrected for calling them shrimps. The Latin name of the species referred to is *Talitrus locusta.* In regard to this species, Bate and Westwood tell the following anecdote :—

"Upon the sands of Whitsand Bay, our friend Mr. Swain informs us that one day, at a picnic party, he saw 'not millions, but cartloads' of this species lying piled together along the margin of the sea. They hopped and leaped about, devouring each other as if for very wantonness. A handkerchief, which a lady let fall amongst them, was soon reduced to a piece of open work by the minute jaws of these small creatures."

Now, considering that Archdeacon Paley imagined that the leapings and springings of these little creatures, as in the sect of the jumpers, were so many acts of devotion, it was unkind of Mr. Swain to represent them as cannibals, eating one another out of mere frivolity! He accuses them also of riddling a lady's handkerchief, a thing so unchivalrous! Nor is it easy to believe that these creatures would prefer cambric to shrimp, or be even induced to think of the former commodity when they were surrounded, according to the story, by a glut of the latter. Whether moved by these or other considerations, Mr. Robertson determined to try the handkerchief question, and the result was that he could not get the Scotch sandhoppers in any way to appreciate or utilize such a diet.

The voracity of the pike is established by a long series of anglers' stories and weighty traditions. It

would not occur to many persons that a character so
well established could reasonably be called in question.
But Mr. Robertson, while on a short sojourn at Loch
Lomond, in June, 1887, having an opportunity of
examining some of these fish, thought that he would
like to satisfy his mind on the subject by direct
inspection. In one pike, measuring twenty-one inches,
he found indeed that the length of the narrow
stomach and intestines together about equalled that
of the whole fish, but on the other hand they were
practically empty. "Another pike (length twenty-
nine inches, weight over five pounds) was found," he
says, "to contain in its stomach a powan, *Coregonus
clupeoides*, Lacep. The head was at the bottom of
the stomach, and the tail, or caudal fins, were seen in
the throat of the pike. I was informed by the fishermen that this was not an unusual occurrence. The
powan seemed just to fill the stomach. When taken
out, the head was found to be almost completely
dissolved ; the body was less and less affected as it
neared the mouth of the pike ; and for fully two
inches the tail (exclusive of the caudal fin) was free
from the slightest marks of digestion.

"It therefore appears that the active digestive
power resides at the bottom of the stomach, which we
may assume is equivalent to a small digestive organ ;
and it seems very doubtful that the pike can be such
an insatiable glutton as he has been represented. He
may like a good meal when he can get it, but he
must have time to dispose of it before he can be
ready for another, and judging from the comparatively small means at his disposal, he may require

longer time than most of his brethren of less notoriety.
For all the great gormandizing that he has done, or
has been supposed to do, he is never represented with
that rotundity consequent on an overloaded stomach,
neither does the conformation of the body, stomach,
or intestines, admit of such."

A plea has been sometimes urged in behalf of birds
of prey that, instead of being injurious to game, such
as grouse, they may do a real service by killing off
sickly birds, which might otherwise spread infection.
Robertson was well enough disposed to accept any
sound argument that might save the life of some fine
falcon, but this particular plea he did not consider
sound. No reason, he said, had been given for believing that hawks would especially single out the
diseased birds. The most that could be said was
that they would probably take whatever they first
came across, and if we argued, not from facts but
from possibilities, the chances were that the sickly
ones would seek shelter and concealment and be
less exposed to the devouring beaks of their enemies
than the more healthy and active members of the
race.

In the controversy respecting sparrows, without
attempting to decide whether they do more good than
harm or more harm than good to our crops, Robertson
has remarked that one point which deserves to be
borne in mind is usually neglected, namely, that there
are means at man's disposal for scaring sparrows away,
whereas shouts and scarecrows and the noise of guns
have no effect whatever on the nerves of a caterpillar.

The instances that have been given will suffice to

show that Robertson, notwithstanding the extreme modesty of his disposition, was well able to hold his own when it was a question either of popular opinion or scientific authority confronting his personal observation of the facts of nature. Friends of greater learning, greater ambition, and greater prominence in the world of science, could not come in contact with his amiable unselfish temper and clear penetrating intelligence without being refreshed, instructed, and improved. How he attracted young as well as old to the eager following of his own pursuits is unconsciously illustrated by a passage in a paper " On some Marine Mollusca," in which he chronicles that his own powers as a collector had been surpassed, at least in one particular, by some very juvenile members of his family :—

" Last summer," he says, " one of my grandchildren found a specimen of *Donax vittatus*, at low water, Kames Bay, Cumbrae ; the shell had the two valves connected, but was empty. A month or two later another specimen was found, under precisely similar conditions. Although in both cases the animal was absent, yet the fact that the valves were connected together led me to believe that the species must be living in the neighbourhood, especially as it had been previously recorded from the Firth of Clyde by Mr. Smith, of Jordanhill, and the Rev. Dr. Landsborough ; and although their evidence had been doubted, the shell is so characteristic that it could scarcely have been mistaken for any other species, particularly by two naturalists of so eminent a reputation. During the present month (April, 1887), I am again indebted to one of my grandchildren, who found another of these shells at low spring-tide on the sands not far from where the other two were found. The shell contained the live animal, leaving no doubt of its living in the bay. This is all the more remarkable, as in the same bay, which has been my hunting ground for many years, I have never noticed a vestige of that shell, dead or alive; and it should warn us from thinking that we had left nothing behind un-touched, however long or diligently the ground may have been searched by us."

To be able to enter into and comprehend and appreciate the thoughts of children, is not the gift of every chance comer. To be able, like the pied piper of Hamelin, to draw children after him, a man must have music in himself. It is not by any means every teacher that can conjure even with the charm of natural history. There is an age at which young fingers handle snakes and slugs and black beetles and spiders without any fastidious prejudice, and the cool unconcern of this period of life may be utilized, by those who know how, to make zoological studies and out-of-door pursuits very attractive. But this result is born of sympathy. It comes of its own accord when there is a happy union of sweetness and light in the temperament of the teacher, so that he lures on his young companions by seeming to be receiv-ing help rather than giving it, and, instead of wearying them by pragmatical instruction, kindles their pride as his partners in research.

How easy it is to teach children a subject and yet leave their minds an almost complete blank in regard to it, is shown by a story now current of a school-inspector who was examining a class in zoology. After various more or less fruitless inquiries, he said, "Now, any of you, mention an animal." There was a long pause, and then a boy with a diffident drawl instanced "a worm." "Yes," said the inspector, "that is an animal. Can any one mention another animal?" A still longer pause ensued, and at length a boy solemnly suggested "*Another worm.*"

Had David Robertson been, not to say the master of the class in question or of the school referred to, but even living anywhere within a radius of five or six miles of it, it is safe to predict that the story would not have originated in connection with that neighbourhood.

The following little narrative seems to me pleasantly to illustrate as well the simplicity of his character as the friendliness of his dealing with young folks. Before perusing it the reader may exercise his own ingenuity in imagining what real object of natural history a small child would be likely to designate as a flying serpent.

"Often on my excursions," Mr. Robertson says, "I take some one with me as guide, generally a boy, as boys are mostly more familiar with the lakes, tarns, and ponds in their neighbourhood than older heads, and, when they come to understand your pursuit, if you go into conversation with them, they are sure to have some marvellous tale or adventure to relate, and if these do not further your purpose, they are amusing.

"On one occasion, on my way to Lochmaben, I went by Dumfries, where I wished to have an hour's fishing at a loch about two and a half miles on the east side of the town. So, to save time, I got a boy to take me to the loch. Before we got well away from the railway station he added other two to our staff, one about his own age and the other a year or two younger. Although there was no need for this addition, so far as my work was concerned, yet, as they seemed happy in each other's company, and the new comers fond-like to join the adventure, I saw little reason to object, further than that the group might be somewhat unwelcome to proprietors in forcing their way over fences and ditches.

"Finding that there was not much likelihood of any obstruction being offered, we marched along agreeably. The road lay along the side of a thickly grown plantation. The conversation soon turned upon a theme congenial to boys, birds and bird-nesting. They soon became full of the wonderful. All three had a fair share of youthful imaginativeness and were primed with tales of adventure and the miraculous. The number of the nests was wonderful, and the names that they gave to the birds were mostly unknown to me.

"Serpents came to be discussed. They all agreed that there were lots of them in that wood.

"One of the boys had seen them often on the trees, twined round the branches, beautifully striped with green and yellow, ready to spring at their prey.

"Another of the boys said that he had been nearly stung by one of them. He had gone up a tree to get a bird's nest that was nearly at the top. On looking over the edge of the nest, there was a serpent lying

over the eggs. He said that he was not long in making
his way down. When near the bottom of the tree,
he looked up and saw the head of the serpent over the
nest gerning [grinning] and hissing at him, and he
thought it had something like a horn on its head, but
he was not sure.

" The little boy, the least of the three (who might
be about eight or ten years of age, the other two being
perhaps two or three years older), said to me, with
rather an air of superior knowledge, and as if he were
speaking from undoubted fact, that there were flying
serpents in the wood.

" I inquired if he had seen them.

" He answered, ' Yes.'

" Believing that the narratives of the others were
purely myths of the imagination, or made up of stories
that they had heard told, I was nevertheless impressed,
by the way the little boy expressed himself, that he
believed what he said.

" I asked him if the creature had wings.

" He said, ' Yes.'

" Had it feathers or hair over its body ?

" He said that he did not know.

· " Had it feet ?

" He said, ' Yes.'

" I asked if it had two or four.

" He answered that it had more than two, but he
did not know how many more.

" I asked what shape it was. Was it like a mouse,
or a rat, or like what ? For I still thought that
there was something real that he was attempting to
describe.

" He said that it was neither like a mouse nor a rat; it was long and thin.

" 'How long,' I inquired, 'and how thick ?'

" 'No longer than my finger, and no thicker than a straw,' he said.

" That solved the question and left no doubt on my mind that it was one of the large dragon flies that he had conjured into a flying serpent."

Conversation with Mr. Robertson must always have been interesting, as it still is, from his habit of noticing and reflecting upon many of the little incidents in nature that ordinary eyes pass over as not being worth a thought. Thus quite recently, when a friend happened to be showing him a fine wasps' nest, he took occasion to remark that a wasp upon a window-pane is "bamboozled." You can catch it with comparatively little difficulty. The circumstances are new and strange to it. The common house-fly in the same position dodges the attempts to capture it and laughs you to scorn. While hearing him speak to this effect, I could not help thinking that almost every one would be sensible of the justness of his remarks, but that, however obvious and simple they may be, there are probably few persons who have independently made and reasoned them out.

In the year 1885, much to Mr. Robertson's satisfaction, the conspicuous merits of Millport as a station for observations in marine natural history, were acknowledged in a very public manner. In March of that year, he thus writes to his friend, Dr. Grieve—

" Your welcome letter came duly to hand. I was hindered from writing to you sooner, because I was

out with the small steamer *Medusa*, from the Granton
Zoological station, which was here dredging last
week from Tuesday to Saturday morning. Dr. Henderson from the station, and Mr. Pearcey from the
Challenger office, and Mr. Murray, joined on Thurs-
day and left on Friday afternoon. The steamer is
fitted up entirely for dredging and securing the spoils.
Dredging with such appliances is such an immense
advantage over the oars, that one would be inclined
to think that going out in a small boat was spending
the days of one's life very unprofitably. Mr. Murray
has it in contemplation to have a marine station
somewhere on the west of Scotland. Arran had
been strongly recommended, but when they saw
the extent of rich dredging ground and variety and
extent of shore, all within so short a distance of the
central point, Millport, besides an easy run to all the
lochs of the Firth, they were all in one mind that
Millport was greatly preferable to Arran or any other
place that had been thought of. Fortunately, all
round Cumbrae the dredging was exceedingly successful. Where they think would be most suitable
for the site of the station is on one of the Allans.

" In regard to the *Challenger* foraminifera; I think
that you are under a wrong impression. I did not
examine all the material. I did only a part. You
will notice that some of the figures are drawn from
Cumbrae specimens.

" When shall we have the pleasure of seeing you
here ? We were in full hope of having a fine ebb on
Monday, but a high south wind set in, and put an
end to all our hope for the present."

It was under the auspices of the Scottish Meteorological Society and the efficient supervision of Dr. Murray, of the *Challenger*, that the Marine Biological station at Granton, Edinburgh, had been opened in 1884.

The *Medusa* was a small steam yacht, specially equipped for marine research, and the *Ark*, originally moored in the inundated Granton Quarry, was a barge converted to the purposes of a small floating laboratory.

The *Medusa* had to be taken to Glasgow for repairs, and this opportunity was made use of to investigate the lower part of the Clyde off the coast of Arran. The sensation produced by the appearance of the *Medusa* in Lamlash Bay has been thus described :—

" There was one worthy butcher from Ayrshire who was specially interested. ' She'll be a pleasure-boat, yon thing?' he asked. 'No,' was the answer ; ' she's bound on a scientific cruise.' ' Ay, an' what may they do on board o' her ?' was the next query ; so an elaborate explanation was given of how creatures are hauled up from the bottom of the sea, and preserved in spirit in order to be fully studied. The butcher evidently thought it a silly waste of liquor, and meditated long. ' But what's the good o't ?' said he. A question not easily answered. Faraday once said in a similar case, ' What's the good of a baby ? No one knows what it may grow to.' So the possible bearing of dredging on the discovery of the habits of food-fishes and the improvement of fishing industries was brought forward. ' I can understand *that,*' quoth the Ayrshire man. 'Do the whole five of them go at that wark? They'll be weel paid, no doot?' No amount of argument could get this last conviction out of his head; and after hearing that one of the staff devoted his entire attention to sea-weeds, and another to the water itself, he closed the conversation with a decided, 'Weel, it's extraordinar' what queer trades some folk will follow for a livin'!'"

The Granton Report then continues as follows:—

"In March, 1885, a second visit has been made to the west coast. Dredging operations were conducted for a period of six days by Mr. Henderson, and Mr. F. G. Pearcey of the *Challenger* Commission, in Loch Long, round Cumbrae, and in Rothesay and Lamlash Bays. On three days they were accompanied by Mr. David Robertson, of Glasgow, the well-known Clyde naturalist, and to his kind assistance and guidance the short trip owed much of its success. Many rare and interesting animals were procured, not a few of which are unknown on the east coast, thus suggesting some interesting distributional problems. It is hoped that the foundation of a branch of the Scottish Marine station on the Clyde will lead to an accurate comparison of the faunæ and floræ of the two estuaries, and, in this way, clear up some obscure points in our knowledge of the distribution of British marine animals and plants."

The pleasure which Robertson derived in the summer of 1885, from the presence of the *Medusa* and the *Ark* at Millport, and from companionship with Murray and the rest of the staff, is not difficult to conjecture. In September, he writes to Dr.

Henderson, who was then on the point of leaving Great Britain for a distant appointment :—

"We are glad to hear that you got safely home. The time is going fast, and you will, I am sure, have quite enough to do before you leave. Millport now seems dull since you all left. It often comes up, the happy time we had while you were here. To keep up old associations, Mrs. Robertson and I take a walk to the *Ark* every day. We have had some heavy weather for the last few days, with high tides, but the *Ark* is keeping her ground well, which is giving us hope that she will come safely through the winter."

In April of the following year he writes to Dr. Murray :—

"I got the chain of the *Ark* tightened up a little. I am getting the rock on her west side cut away, which will be a great safety to her. I would be sorry to see any mishap overtaking the old lady. We had a pretty sharp gale last night, but she is still all right."

She is still all right at the time of this present writing, pretty securely planted among the rocks, and frequently visited by her faithful volunteer guardian. Dr. Murray, it is understood, is willing to devote the vessel to the purposes of a permanent marine station at Millport. During the summer of 1889 an experiment was made to test the interest which the public would take in it. An intelligent attendant was paid to take care of it and empowered to admit visitors at a fixed charge. A discussion took place as to what the charge should be. One of the financial committee recommended that it should be sixpence, another thought that threepence would be enough, but Mr. Robertson carried the day for his own view that only a penny should be asked. Yet so much interest was shown in the boat and its contents that five to seven or eight shillings a day in pennies were received throughout the season, without counting the larger extra donations frequently given to the attendant for his own perquisite. Mr. Robertson sometimes ventured to hint to single visitors that it would be more appropriate and in accordance with precedent if they came to the *Ark* in pairs. Since the fee was expressly intended to keep out such idlers and disreputable persons as deserve to be classed under the name of ' the Great Unwashed,' he might have gone further and suggested that clean animals should enter by sevens. He is not averse to telling the story that one day, while he was himself working in the *Ark*, with no other companions but its marine treasures, a stranger came in and looked inquiringly round. The gentleman was invited to inspect the various curiosities, and he listened with attention to all that was said about them by one who was no unwilling expounder of their various merits. When all the wonders had been duly displayed, and the tale of their virtues fitly told, the stranger ex-pressed himself much pleased, and with very polite and often repeated thanks withdrew. But this was not all, for Mr. Robertson concludes, with a pleasant twinkle, "he slippit also a shilling into my hand."

To tell the truth, Mr. Robertson would probably allow many shillings to be slipped into his hand by appreciative friends or strangers, if by such means an endowment of the necessary hundred a year could be provided to pay the wages of an attendant, to meet the expense of repairs, and so to keep the *Ark* in permanent working order. Such a compliment to the naturalist of Cumbrae would be alike appropriate, deserved, and welcome. If others far more than himself would derive advantage from it, his reward would still be in keeping with his character. Any selfish acquisition has been the last thing that his scientific work has ever aimed at. A few expressions from his correspondence during the last twenty years may be quoted as examples. When sending to one friend organisms carefully mounted for the microscope, some to be kept and others to be examined and returned, he says, " In all cases, red slides are for yourself, but never hesitate to take from the white slides anything you may require." To a friend who had asked him for specimens whenever he might happen to have abundance of a certain species, he answers, " I shall not wait for abundance, but if I have one, you shall have the others." To another friend he writes, " Never hesitate to take from any I send if there are more than one, and that one if to serve any particular purpose." To a friend who was modestly reluctant to accept specimens he writes, " It would give me more pleasure to work, believing that it might be of more use to others as well as myself." It is not surprising that one of his friends should say what many of them must feel, " But what can I do for *you* in return? For I have already so many kindnesses to thank you for, that there is a big balance all on one side of the ledger."

CHAPTER XXII.

APPRECIATIVE FRIENDS.

THE position which Robertson occupies in scientific
literature may in part be gathered from the bibli-
ography given in the appendix. Yet his services to
that literature will be very imperfectly seen, unless
we look beyond the books and papers to which his
name is attached as author, whether separately or in
partnership with others. Mention has already been
made of the foreign writers of high reputation who
have acknowledged their indebtedness to his exertions, but it is proper here also to point out how his
intimate friends at home in some of their most
prominent works have delighted to do him honour.
  A sort of forecast of the essential assistance he was
destined to render to serious workers is to be found
in *The Morning Journal* for November 5, 1865.
  Describing a conversazione of the Geological Society
of Glasgow, the report refers to numerous illustrative
specimens as "obtained, chiefly by dredging operations in the Firth of Clyde, by Mr. David Robertson."
"We know," it continues, "that natural history science
is much indebted to Mr. Robertson's labours in marine
zoology, and naturalists assure us that he is ever

ready to assist them in their efforts to complete their collections by giving them freely of his duplicate specimens." This behaviour is in itself very unlike that of the amiable tulip-fancier, who bought his rival's tulip for a large sum simply that he might trample it underfoot, and leave the specimen he himself possessed unique. But, as already explained, when it was not a question of gratifying a collector, but of forwarding a work of science, Robertson, without distinguishing between duplicates and solitary specimens, bestows the latter as readily as the former on those who seem likely to use them to the best advantage. Among those who know him, it has become the most natural thing in the world to apply to him without ceremony for any invertebrates or fossils at all likely to be within his reach or in his possession.

In 1881, Professor Ewart happened to be in want of some comatulæ, the rosy feather-star, which is attached to a stalk or pedicel when young, and drops off it into freedom when adult. He wrote to Glasgow to ask Professor Young, if possible, to procure him a supply. Almost as a matter of course, Professor Young passes on the request to Mr. Robertson, with the words, "Can he be supplied?" as much as to say, if you cannot supply him, the case in this part of the world is hopeless.

In 1876, Mr. Henry Bowman Brady, F.R.S., brought out his "Monograph of the Carboniferous and Permian Foraminifera," published by the Palæontographical Society. After thanking Mr. John Young, F.G.S., of Glasgow, for his aid, he says, "With the name of Mr.

John Young, it is natural to associate that of his assiduous colleague, Mr. David Robertson, F.G.S., the results of whose microscopical researches, always most freely communicated, have served to fill many a blank in the 'Distribution Tables.'" While giving to a new species the name *Trochammina Robertsoni*, Mr. Brady says, "For specimens of this exceedingly minute and delicate form I am indebted to my friend, Mr. David Robertson, F.G.S., of Glasgow, who discovered it in some of the carboniferous shales of the west of Scotland, and whose name therefore may very properly be associated with it." Of another new species, *Endothyra subtilissima*, he observes, " I know of only a single specimen, that from which the figures are drawn, which was found by Mr. Robertson in the rich lower carboniferous shale of Brockley, in Lanarkshire. It is not the only case in which my friend Mr. Robertson's quick eye has detected minute, inconspicuous forms that have escaped the notice of other observers."

Those who are accustomed to regard the sand of the sea-shore only as a convenient pathway for bathers and playground for children with their kirtles above the knee, would perhaps be surprised to find that among the countless multitude of shapeless grains, which are fragments of rocks and shells and various other broken down materials, the sand also frequently contains some perfect organisms, which, though not larger than the other grains, have much beauty of form in that small compass. Such are the foraminifera. They are some of them semi-transparent; others look as if they were made of fine white porcelain. The forms are various, and different species may be said severally to present the shapes of an eye, a coin, a flask, a chain, a nautilus shell, a plait of hair, or a baker's twist, a globe, or a group of globes, or simply some pattern of decorative art. The shell, or skeleton, indeed, seems, as a rule, to have a symmetry and beauty out of proportion to the very simple amœba-like soft body of the animal, which performs the functions of existence, without head or tail, without arms or legs, by thrusting out and drawing in its pseudopodia, the so-called false-feet, which are merely retractile extensions of its general substance.

While, however, a great number of these shells satisfy the eye by the definiteness and neatness of the form exhibited on so small a scale, there is, strange to say, another group in which there are species characterized by their thick, soft walls consisting of mud, or of only slighted cemented sand. These belong to the family astrorhizidæ.

In 1884, Mr. Henry Brady published his fine "Report on the Foraminifera collected by the *Challenger.*" In this he incorporated all the information that could be obtained on the subject in general. He says :—

" Our acquaintance with the large arenaceous rhizopods, which constitute the family astrorhizidæ, is almost entirely derived from the operations of the various recent expeditions, organised and equipped by government for the exploration of the deep sea. The genus *Astrorhiza* was described by Sandahl in 1857, and a closely allied type, *Dendrophrya*, by Strethill Wright in 1861, but these are amongst the few forms that inhabit comparatively shallow water, and it is to deep-sea dredging in the North Atlantic during the past twelve or fourteen years that we owe the discovery of nearly all the more important members of the group."

. It may be thought that all this, however interesting in itself, has not much to do with the life of Robertson, but it was necessary, by way of introduction to what follows, for when Mr. Brady comes to discuss the above-mentioned genus, *Dendrophrya*, he writes as follows :—

" For twenty years the genus appears to have remained entirely unnoticed by rhizopodists. As the subject appeared to be one of some importance, and there were many points concerning which additional information was required, I called the attention of my friend, Mr. David Robertson, F.G.S., to the original paper, thinking it possible that he might have met with the organism during his long and varied experience in shore collecting. This did not prove to be the case, but the subject was one that interested him so much that he made a visit to the recorded locality, Old Granton Quarry, near Edinburgh, in the hope that the species might still be found there. Unfortunately, on that occasion the search was unsuccessful ; but ere long I received from him a number of specimens gathered from similar localities on the west coast of Scotland, amongst which it was not difficult to recognize *Dendrophrya radiata.* In company with it was an erect branching modification of the same type, which, though it does not agree in all points with the figure of *Dendrophrya erecta* in Dr. Wright's paper, has the same general characters, and there can be little doubt belongs to that species."

Mr. Brady then gives notes founded on Mr. Robertson's specimens of these two species, and calls attention to the fact that all that is known of their distribution is that they have been found by Dr. Wright at Old Granton Quarry, near Edinburgh, and in pools at low water, at Cumbrae, by Mr. Robertson.

Of the species *Reophax difflugiformis*, H. B. Brady, the same author, says, " My first acquaintance with the species was from a fossil specimen in Mr. Robertson's collection, obtained many years ago from the post-tertiary college clay of Cumbrae; but I cannot speak with certainty of its occurrence elsewhere in the fossil state."

In describing *Haplophragmium globigeriniforme* (Parker and Jones), Mr. Brady observes, " I have recently received from my friend, Mr. Robertson, of Glasgow, specimens of an arenaceous foraminifer closely allied to the present species, but isomorphous with *Sphæroidina bulloides.* This interesting modification, which I propose to name *Haplophragmium sphæroidiniforme,* was found in sands dredged in the Mediterranean, at depths of seventy to one hundred and twenty fathoms."

Of another species Mr. Brady remarks, " Mr. Robertson has specimens of *Pulvinulina canariensis* from the post-tertiary beds of Garvel Park, Greenock; but with this exception the species has not been identified in the fossil condition."

In numerous other passages of the work Mr.

Robertson's name is similarly mentioned, but it may be well to refrain from quoting them all, since it is not absolutely certain that all the readers of this life will either be or intend to become enthusiastic rhizo-podists, and those who are lukewarm on the subject may ignorantly fancy that Latin names of five, six, or seven syllables are out of proportion to the merits of organisms perhaps only a twentieth of an inch in length.

Turning to another branch of the animal kingdom, the entomostraca, in another work of first-rate im-portance, we again find the name of Robertson re-peatedly occurring.

In the years 1878 and 1880, Dr. George Stewardson Brady, F.R.S., brought out his "Monograph of the British Copepoda," published by the Ray Society. In the Introduction, while pointing out the advantage of searching for these little crustaceans in the dusk or after dark, Dr. Brady says :—

"Some of the pleasantest and most profitable hours which I have ever spent have been when, after a day's dredging, I have set out at sunset on a quiet boating excursion for the purpose of capturing such prey as could be got in the surface net. Many hours of this kind spent in the company of my old friend Mr. David Robertson, amongst the Scilly Islands, on the Firth of Clyde, on the sheltered bays of Roundstone and Westport, or on the stormier coasts of North-umbria, will long live in my memory, not only by their results in the acquisition of valuable specimens, but as times of unalloyed delight in the contempla-tion of nature under a different guise from that in which we usually see her."

Again, in thanking a few of his eminent scientific friends for the aid they had given him in the preparation of his monograph, Dr. Brady says, "Especially are my acknowledgments due to Mr. David Robertson, to whom for kind and ever active help during many pleasant excursions, as well as for gifts of numerous valuable gatherings of copepoda, I am very largely indebted." The names which follow are those of Norman, E. C. Davison, Sir John Lubbock, Dr. Claus, and M. T. Thorell, a group with which most naturalists would feel it an honour to be associated.

On May 18, 1879, Dr. Brady wrote to his friend, " I have in my hands proofs of the second copepoda volume, and, as I have given one of my genera your name, *Robertsonia*, it just occurs to me to ask if you know of the name having been used by any other author. It is quite likely that some of your friends may have been beforehand with me in adopting your name, and if so, of course my genus could not stand. Please let me know."

It appeared that the name had not previously been used in science, and accordingly Dr. Brady paid his friend the compliment of instituting the genus as proposed, for a species called *Robertsonia tenuis*. In the same volume he named a new species *Mesochra Robertsoni*, with the remarks, " This I know only from Irish specimens. It occurred in gatherings taken by Mr. Robertson and myself in Lough Enask and Lough Arddery (two of the small lakes of Connemara), and abundantly in a brackish ditch near Newport, co. Mayo, Ireland, where it was found by Mr.

Robertson, after whom I have much pleasure in naming it."

During the course of last year Dr. G. S. Brady and Canon Norman jointly brought out the first section of a monograph of the marine and freshwater ostracoda of the North Atlantic and North Western Europe.

In this work Robertson took a more than usual interest, it having been originally planned, though on a less extensive scale, between himself and Brady. Thus, on September 21, 1881, Brady writes :—

"DEAR ROBERTSON,

"I think it is well to send you the MS. of what I have done at the ostracoda, that is, all up to the end of the genus *Candona*, except *Candona nitens*, of which I have no specimens, and *Candona tenella*, about which I want your opinion before calling it distinct. There may be other localities to insert, or other remarks which may occur to you as desirable. Please put in or put out anything you think proper."

In November, 1883, Brady suggested that Norman should be invited to join in the work, to which Robertson gladly assented. But this, through one cause and another, resulted in the work taking a rather different shape from that originally intended, and in its finally appearing not under the names of Brady and Robertson, but those of Brady and Norman. These authors, however, at various points of the work, show their sense of the great assistance they had derived from Mr. Robertson. He had most kindly, they say, placed at their disposal his very extensive collection of ostracoda, including some undescribed forms, and under the heading of "*Candona euplectella,* Robertson, M.S.," they observe that "Specimens of *Candona euplectella,* in fine condition, and exhibiting in perfect order the reticulated surface, tubercles and stiff hairs, excel in beauty all other European freshwater ostracoda."

Of the new species, *Erpetocypris Robertsoni,* they say, "*Erpetocypris Robertsoni* has been found only in two localities, Hayston Dam, near Peebles, and in the river at Portree, Isle of Skye. In both places it was taken by our friend Mr. David Robertson, after whom we have much satisfaction in naming it."

In explaining the distribution of the different species, these authors give the names of the writers who are responsible for the various localities, except when the responsibility rests with themselves or one other authority. In these three instances they give only initials. Some wonder might be felt why they should extend this modest reserve, natural enough in regard to their own names, to one and only one other of the numerous authorities they cite. The explanation is clear, that in using the initials D. R., which occur repeatedly throughout the volume, they are regarding their honoured friend and constant helper, David Robertson, as one of themselves and practically a partner in their work.

It is interesting to notice that acknowledgments of the same kind as those that are being made to Mr. Robertson at this very day were being made to him a

2 A

quarter of a century ago by such writers of eminence as Spence Bate and Westwood. At one time it will be of a new amphipod that they say, " This animal, of which we have only seen a single specimen, was sent to us by our valued correspondent, Mr. David Robertson, of Glasgow." At another time it will be the same story about a new isopod, or they will thank him for additional specimens of known species and notes upon them, the information enriching their work and the specimens facilitating its progress.

CHAPTER XXIII.

CONCLUSION.

MR. ROBERTSON is in stature rather below the middle height, broad-shouldered, and still muscular in appearance. To the readers of this life it is scarcely necessary to say that he has a friendly countenance. It would be a spurious phrenology that could not find in the well-marked character of his head and the lines of his face the outward symbols of benevolence, sagacity, and loyal singleness of heart. Though advancing years have slackened the rapid walk and dulled the sense of hearing, the veteran of eighty-four is still ready to climb the hill, to pull the oar, to heave in the dredge, still ready to observe and to record, still ready to start some thoughtful topic of conversation or to join in the laughter of the light-hearted.

It seems curious to think of this now venerable man of science as having once been a shepherd boy, scampering over the moor on a bare-backed colt, or as a little lad stripped to his shirt victorious in the foot-race.

The self-control by which his whole career has been distinguished is well illustrated by a story which he tells of himself when about seventeen years of age.

He had then, like many other boys, learned to smoke, and had become very fond of that indulgence. At that period, for lighting a pipe it was necessary to carry about a tinder-box with flint and steel. The process was far from being instantaneous, and as the farm-labourers, in reaping and various other employments, were often working abreast on parallel lines or ridges, the loitering of any individual was made unpleasantly conspicuous. In addition to this, tobacco was only to be obtained from shops very inconveniently remote from the farmstead where Robertson was living, and yet his finances did not allow him to purchase more than a small quantity at a time. Reflecting on all these disadvantages connected with a pleasure not absolutely essential to happiness, and with a habit which, as it had been contracted, so could certainly be broken off again, the lad one day decided to take a resolute measure of self-deliverance. He flung the tinder-box with the flint and steel over a hedge into a pit, from which he was never likely to be able to regain them. From then till now he has never had the wish to possess, at least as facilities for smoking, either those now almost pre-historic implements or any modern substitute for them. He did not at the time know Latin, otherwise, while breaking the yoke of his bondage, he might appropriately have ex-claimed, *sic semper tyrannis !*

It is not often that a single life covers so great a variety of employment. For Robertson has been herd-boy and volunteer horse-breaker, weaver, quarry-man's assistant, farm-labourer, tutor, medical student, dyer, tradesman, merchant, and finally man of science,

—not the proverbial Jack of all trades and master of none—but behaving well in all, gathering some enrichment of his mind from each, passing from one to the other by a natural transition, not out of frivolous caprice, but for some sound and well-considered reason. When he left business to follow the pursuits of natural history, he relinquished, with his eyes open and without regret, the chances or rather the not doubtful prospect of making an ample fortune. He was minded like the wise man of old, who prayed the prayer of temperance and the golden mean, 'Give me neither poverty nor riches, feed me with food convenient for me.' Those who have seen him in his own home cannot but consider him wise in his resolve and happy in its results.

The house or cottage called "Fern Bank," the scene of so much genial hospitality, is separated only by the front garden, the road, and a strip of green, from the sandy shore of Kames Bay.

On this shore, immediately in front of the house, a boulder, which is uncovered only at low water, has acquired in the family the name of "grandpapa's stone," it being with him a favourite locality at which to dig in the sand for the small marine animals that there and thereabouts abound. The rocks to the right are sometimes visited with hammer and chisel for the purpose of digging out the shell *Pholas crispata*, which there bores its hole into the volcanic ash. Between these rocks and Millport pier is Garrison Bay. About two miles further on, and on the other side of the island, is Fintry Bay. Proceeding from the house in the other direction, after passing Portloy, where at present the *Ark* is stationed, from Keppel pier the road leads on to Balloch Bay. Here the *Pholas crispata*, being accommodated with soft clay and mud for its borings, grows to be two or three times as large as its fellows in the more rugged domicile at Kames Bay. All the localities that have been named are famous among the initiated for the various kinds of animals which they severally yield to the zoologist, when, after the new moon and the full, the far-receding tides give favourable opportunities for search.

The Lion Rock, between Balloch Bay and Keppel Pier, and the De'il's Dyke or Keppel Rock, near the pier, are two celebrated trap dykes, standing out conspicuously from the softer new red sandstone. The Keppel Dyke in particular has the appearance of an artificial wall built on a grand Cyclopean scale. The other and smaller rock is locally cherished for its resemblance to a crouching lion, and so far commands respect that few pilgrim painters or knights of the camera leave Millport without having paid it a becoming homage.

The windows of "Fern Bank" face the Robinson Crusoe-like island of Little Cumbrae, about three miles distant. To the left of Little Cumbrae, but more than thirty miles further off, is Ailsa Craig, a wonderful rock, sometimes very distinct to the view, of pyramidal appearance, at other times seeming to have the base eaten away, and often entirely lost in the misty, or cloud-beset distance.

The grand hills or mountains of Arran are on the right, fifteen miles off, but sometimes looking as if their great masses were far nearer than that, at others with only their tops peering up out of the mist, at others again with their whole forms visible but cloud-like or shadowy, while yet again at times they may be completely lost as though there were no such land existing.

On the left of the view is a point of the island of Great Cumbrae itself, the point called Portloy already mentioned, beyond which may be seen, across one arm of the Clyde, the hills of the Ayrshire coast, shaped, it is said, in days of yore by glacial action.

On the projecting point of Little Cumbrae may in general be descried a strong square fortress. Far down on the opposite coast, at Portincross, is another castle, twin brother to that on Little Cumbrae point. In some prehistoric time, how far distant from the glacial age is open only to conjecture, these twin towers were erected by twin brothers, giants, who had but one hammer between them. With power equal to their fraternal affection they hurled it to and fro across the intervening miles of water, and there, on the opposite points, the two towers still stand to confound the doubts of the incredulous.

It scarcely needs romance and myth to add their interest, such as it may be, to the charms of the scenery. Cloud and sunshine, mist and storm, contrive to give to sea and sky an endless diversity, and to combine them with the forms and colours of islands and islets, rocks and mountains, shores and shipping and wooded banks, into·a hundred different attractive or imposing pictures.

" Fern Bank " itself can scarcely be entered without the attention of the visitor being called to dredges or surface-nets drying in the sun, or to some other apparatus of the master's craft.

Inside, the dining-room is hung round with pleasant pictures, all or most the gifts and work of one who is at once a skilled artist and an affectionate son. On the staircase is a cabinet of rare corals. In the library, besides many valuable books on natural history, there are other cabinets full of marine treasures in the finest order. Here, among the shells may be seen *Lima hians* in its nest. Here are strange crabs, and fine sea-urchins, and uncommon star-fishes. Here too are elaborate type-slides of ostracoda and foraminifera.

In the store-room is a great collection of amphipods and cumacea, pennatulæ, virgulariæ, copepoda, annelids, nudibranchs, and sea-anemones, with various other creatures, rare or strange, or otherwise worth preserving. Elsewhere are stored up bags of clay, waiting to be rifled of their organic contents, when, if ever, the incessant calls upon the industry of the owner give them a chance.

Amidst these treasures, which avarice will not envy, and which moreover are ever at the service of those who can use them to good purpose ; amidst these scenes of natural beauty, which likewise are open to all who can choose to visit Millport, David Robertson continues, and may he long continue, his peaceful and honoured life.

One in old times is said to have risen from being a swineherd to be Pope of Rome, ascending from a position as humble as any that there is in European society to one which in those days topped all others by its singular and conspicuous pre-eminence. In

1763, there was born near Heidelberg, to the lot of a poor German peasant, one who, emigrating first to London and then to New York, left, when he died in 1848, an estate valued at five millions of money. Many who have won distinction in literature and politics, in trade and commerce, in travel and research, or as philanthropists and teachers of morality, have risen from a level so low in the social scale that in their acquired rank and status they seem to owe nothing to fortune, but to be truly what they are commonly called, self-made men. It is not pretended, therefore, that there is anything unexampled, or even highly exceptional, in the fact that David Robertson rose from poverty to independence, and that, though left without education in his boyhood, he became in mature age a distinguished votary of science. Drudgery, self-denial, and good temper, were the humble companions of his straightforward course. No doubt, to lead a man upwards as well as onwards in the paths of worldly existence, those homely supporters will not alone suffice. When a man has done notably well, and prospered in his career, apart from any of the ordinary aids of fortune, such as high birth, inherited wealth, or influential friends, he must have had some qualities of distinction to bring about his success. This being admitted, those to whom his life is offered as an encouragement and stimulus to go and do likewise may be disposed to object that only a man of such character could have accomplished such results. For the eagle flight of some unique incomparable genius that may be true, but when the qualities and characteristics concerned are energy and perseverance, honesty of purpose, genial friendliness of heart, and openness of mind, these are not so absent from any human being but what they can probably be made to grow and flourish. They can be fostered, cultivated, brought to perfection, even from small and delicate seedlings. Each man, having them for himself in charge, may make his fortune out of them if he will ; and those who read this biography should at least be encouraged by it to make the attempt.

It has 'been cynically said of mankind in general, " if all the motives of our best actions were exposed to view, how foolish we should look ! " It has been argued that we ought not to celebrate the merits even of the departed, because the inner characters of the men eulogized may have belied their seeming goodness. Much more may it be thought improper to call any man virtuous—just as Solon thought it wrong to call any man happy—while he is still living, lest the future should spoil the past. By these general and highly genial considerations the gentle reader, therefore, is forewarned not too implicitly to trust the unavoidable ignorance of the biographer. I leave open all the reserves which the most envious or the most scrupulous can desire, when I ask those who have read this narrative to behold, in the portrait that has been sketched for them, a man liable no doubt to error, for he thought at the outset that this record of himself would be uninteresting ; a man not without the natural ambition of a superior mind, yet ever ready to esteem others better than himself; one who has been, if I venture not to say "an Israelite indeed in whom is no guile," yet surely a good son, good father, good husband, and good friend. Cruelty and fraud and selfishness may have been cunningly veiled during his fourscore years and four under the mask of gentleness and honesty, of loving-kindness and sweet serenity of temper. But if so, to all intents and purposes the mask has been the man ; and in the career which has been described it cannot be difficult or unwelcome to see an illustration of an ancient pleasant song, with some lines of which I shall take leave to close this writing, for throughout it they have oftentimes been forcibly present to my own mind :—

"Blessed is the man that hath not walked in the counsel of the ungodly, nor stood in the way of sinners : and hath not sat in the seat of the scornful.

"But his delight is in the law of the Lord : and in his law will he exercise himself day and night.

"And he shall be like a tree planted by the waterside : that will bring forth his fruit in due season.

"His leaf also shall not wither : and look, whatsoever he doeth, it shall prosper."

APPENDIX A.

Cells in Cardboard for Microscopic Mounting.

" The first mounting that I had seen of opaque objects was one that I had in 1862 from the Rev. A. M. Norman, an ostracode, *Notodromus monachus*, mounted on a hard wood slide, three inches by one, with a round cell in the middle. Finding these cells difficult to get well made, and the price high, I thought that a substitute could be made from cardboard, which I got cut into proper sizes, three inches by one. I procured a round cutter at a gunmaker's shop, with which I punched out the round cell in the slide. I then had black hot-pressed paper pasted on thin cardboard or pasteboard. This was cut the same size as that of the cell-slip, three inches by one, and was cemented to it with thin glue, which hardened sooner, and was less liable to mildew than flour-paste. Thus I had an excellent slide, that did not cost me more than two shillings a gross. I may mention that my greatest difficulty at first was to get the black slip and the cell-slip properly pressed together, till I got a little screw-press made that just took in a slide in breadth, but more than three dozen in length, which answered my purpose well. This was the first cardboard slide, so far as I know, that 'had been made at the time."

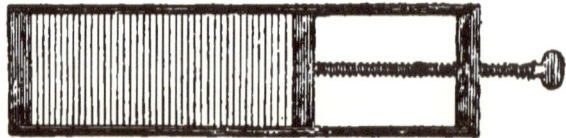

Diagram of screw-press, reduced.

TYPE-SLIDES.

"When working at the post-tertiary clays, I thought that it would be an advantage to have a slide that would hold all the ostracoda or foraminifera of a deposit, so that those of one deposit could be compared with those of another with the least possible trouble. For this purpose I made one of the ordinary slides into an oblong cell. At first I made it on the hard-wood slide, but I found the cardboard much more easily managed, and it looked better, and conformed with the rest of my slides. It held conveniently for examination, twenty to twenty-five species on each half of the slide, and this could be increased to double the extent by placing two species on one line, separating them by red spots. These slides were found very convenient when I was working conjointly with Dr. G. S. Brady."

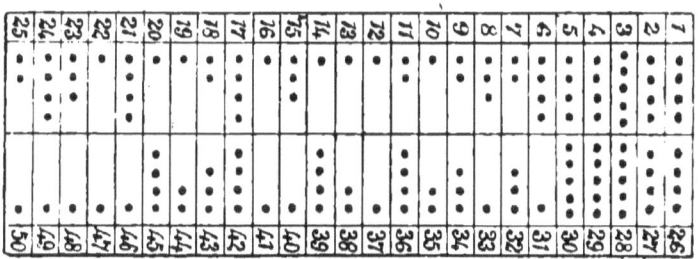

Diagram of type-slide, actual size.

RULED SLATE.

When a mass of fine material is placed under the microscope, from which the observer desires to select here and there certain minute objects, and when after careful examination of part of the field he has found and removed one of these objects, it often happens that his eye cannot again find the spot at which its search was interrupted, and much time is wasted by going over the old ground once more. To remedy this, Robertson provides himself with a small oblong slate, suitable for use on the stage of a microscope, and upon this slate he rules parallel lines and between the lines inscribes arrows which point in opposite directions on the alternate spaces. Hence in searching for foraminifera among sand spread over the slate, he has but to note the number of the space which his search has reached, and he can return to it at will, the arrow showing whether it be the upper or the lower part of the space that remains to be examined.

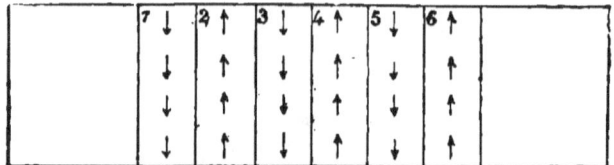

Diagram of ruled slate, reduced.

ROBERTSON'S DREDGE.

"The body of the dredge is in two pieces, which are held together by the arms passing down through the dovetailing at the sides, and each fixed at the bottom by a screw. The bottom is made of coarse canvas, stretched over a hoop, which fits into the dredge. By these arrangements the whole can be readily taken asunder and packed into very small space.

DIMENSIONS.

Length of body	18 inches.
Diameter at point of lips	10 ,,
Depth of lips	4½ ,,
Longer diameter at lower angle of lips ...	11 ,,
Shorter ,, ,, ...	8½ ,,
Longer diameter at bottom	7¾ ,,
Shorter ,, ,, ...	6¼ ,,
Circumference of arm rods	1⅛ ,,
Weight of dredge...	12 lbs.

"The rope is connected to the dredge by ten feet of small chain, which tends greatly to keep down the machine by counteracting the buoyancy of the rope. The next thing to be taken into consideration is the weight of the dredge. The ordinary weight used for a small boat is about fifteen pounds ; but, whatever the weight may be, it must be sufficient to take with ease the rope required for its use to the bottom, and to keep its place there against the ordinary speed of the boat, which has a tendency to raise the rope, and with it the mouth of the dredge. When the sea is found a little too rough, or the currents a little too strong, preventing the dredge from taking the ground, a few stones put into it will generally succeed in keeping it down, or a small bag with a stone fastened to the rope a fathom or two forward from the dredge will answer the same purpose, and not interfere with its contents."

A rope "an inch and a half in circumference answers very well, and is strong enough for any strain likely to be put upon it, and is not over half the weight of ropes usually employed for dredging purposes."

In altering the course of the boat while the dredge is down, "pull the boat back over the dredge, and the slack of the rope thus made will allow it to be done with ease."

For examining the contents of the dredge, "a board measuring four feet long by one and a half broad, having a slip of wood about an inch high along each side, will, in most cases, be found suitable." A pair of sieves, a coarse and a fine, are recommended as useful auxiliaries.

"When the more minute objects are wanted, a successful plan with dredged material, laminaria roots, shell débris, etc., is to take them home in a pail of water, and transfer them to a white basin, and in a short time many of the small animals will be seen making their way towards the sides of the vessel, and others to the surface, from which they may be easily picked up. The material may be occasionally stirred up, which will cause a new series to appear. This process may be repeated with success for a day or two. When the water has even become offensive, and many of the animals have died, a few may still be found on the surface, which do not appear at an earlier time."— "Proceedings of the Nat. Hist. Soc. Glasgow," vol. i., pp. 181-183.

FISH-OTOLITHS.

The photographic plate mentioned on page 253 represents the ear-bones of the following fishes arranged in three columns, but otherwise in the order here given.

Perca fluviatilis, Lin.	Perch	Loch Lomond.
Trigla gurnardus, Lin.	Grey Gurnard	Cumbrae.
Cottus bubalis, Euphrasen, 6 in.	Father-lasher	Cumbrae.
Pagellus centrodontus, Cuv.	Sea Bream	Cumbrae (2 slides).

Scomber scomber, Lin., 13 in.	Mackerel	Cumbrae.
Caranx trachurus, Lacep.	Horse-Mackerel	Frith of Clyde.
Mugil capito, Cuv.	Grey Mullet	Fairlie.
Anarrhichas lupus, Lin.	Cat-fish	Montrose.
Muraenoïdes guttata, Lacep., 6 in.	Spotted Gunnel	Cumbrae.
Callionymus lyra, Lin.	Gemmeous Dragonet	Cumbrae.
Atherina presbyter, Cuv.	Sand Smelt	Cumbrae.
Callionymus dracunculus, Lin.	Sordid Dragonet	Cumbrae.
Merlangus pollachius, Cuv.	Pollack, or Lythe	
Merlangus vulgaris, Cuv., 14–15 in.	Whiting	Cumbrae.
Merlangus carbonarius, Cuv., 17 in.	Coal-fish	Cumbrae.
Lophius piscatorius, Lin.	Frog-fish	Cumbrae.
Labrus variegatus, 12 in.	Blue-striped Wrasse	Cumbrae.
Esox lucius, Lin., 24 in.	Pike	Loch Lomond.
Crenilabrus sp.		Cumbrae.
Salmo sp.	Salmon fry, 8–8½ in.	
Clupea harengus, Lin.	Herring	Cumbrae.
Clupea sprattus, Lin.	Sprat	Granton.
Morrhua vulgaris, Cuv.	Cod	
Morrhua aeglefinus, Cuv., 5½ lbs.	Haddock	Cumbrae.
Morrhua minuta, Lin.	Gold-eye	Cumbrae.
Merlucius vulgaris, Cuv., 3 ft.	Common Hake	Cumbrae (3 slides).
Belone vulgaris, Cuv., 18 in.	Gar-fish	Cumbrae.
Molva vulgaris, Flem.	Ling	Cumbrae.
Motella vulgaris, Cuv.	Three-bearded Rock-ling	Cumbrae.
Platessa vulgaris, Flem.	Plaice	Cumbrae (2 slides).
Platessa limandoïdes, Jenyns, 7½ in.	Long rough Dab	Cumbrae.
Solea vulgaris, Cuv.	Sole	Cumbrae.
Conger vulgaris, Cuv.	Conger eel	Cumbrae.
Coregonus fera, Cuv.	Powan	Loch Lomond.
Silurus glanis, Lin.	The Sly Silurus	

The names adopted agree with those given in Yarrell's "History of British Fishes," 1836, except that Yarrell assigns *Morrhua minuta* to Fleming, and calls it the Poor, or Power, Cod, while in place of *Molva vulgaris*, Fleming, he prefers the name *Lota molva*, Cuvier, for the Ling.

On the slide containing the ear-bones of the Hake, which was three feet long, a query is appended to the specific name, the ear-bones of this large specimen showing some striking differences from those of smaller examples, but the differences seem to be only such as might naturally arise from great increase of bulk.

Dr. Claus, in his " Elementary Text-book of Zoology," translated by Sedgwick and Heathcote, in describing the sense-organs of vertebrates, says—

" The auditory organ, the nerve of which belongs to the hindbrain (probably derived from the sensory root of a spinal-like cranial nerve), is entirely absent in *Amphioxus*. In its simplest form it is a membranous sac (membranous labyrinth) containing fluid and otoliths. The posterior part of this sac is usually prolonged into three semicircular canals, while the anterior part, which in many cases is separated as the *saccule*, gives off a prolongation which forms the *cochlea* (fig. 578, s. c.)." In the accompanying "diagram of the auditory labyrinth (after Waldeyer)," that of the fish has a quite distinct *cochlea*, though a small one. When discussing the sense-organs of fishes, as distinct from other vertebrates, Claus says, "The auditory organ (absent only in *Amphioxus*) consists only of the labyrinth (fig. 578, i.), and in Teleosteans, Ganoids, and *Chimaera* lies partly in the cranial cavity, surrounded by fatty tissue. It is worthy of notice that in *Cyprinoidæ, Characinæ, Siluridæ*, and others, the labyrinth is connected with the swimming-bladder by a chain of small bones " (pp. 121, 139).

APPENDIX B.

OSTRACODA.

Places where to be found.—They are to be found in lakes, tarns, ponds, lagoons, canals, ditches, and often in very small patches of water, and in slow-running streams; but in the latter by no means commonly, except in weedy recesses protected from the currents, or where clumps of thickly growing plants abound.

"Nowhere, throughout Scotland, is there any want of such places either in number or variety, whether we regard the depth of the water, varying from the thinnest covering to the deepest lakes; or their situations, ranging from the sea-level to high mountain tarns; or the character of the basin in which they lie, rock, peat, clay, etc.; or, lastly, the impregnated mineral contents. Ostracoda are generally more abundant in the smaller tarns or ponds, overgrown with weeds, than in deep and large sheets of water, where the surging of the waves is unfavourable to marginal vegetation; yet I often find that places greatly overgrown with plants are not always the richest in ostracoda, but sometimes the reverse, probably in such cases by affording more suitable conditions to a greater host of enemies. Ostracoda are occasionally obtained in small tarns and ponds where the water has been nearly dried up, leaving only a little at some central depression; and even in the deep mud, where the water has disappeared, good gatherings are met with, as well as in the scanty water of furrows in old pasture land, and which are dry during the greater part of the summer. It is indeed surprising, as regards many of these patches of water, how speedily after rain they are found swarming with ostracoda and other microzoa. In some instances it has been observed that, after the rains, certain species are absent which had been present before the ponds dried up, while by next season they again become abundant. Whatever means of distribution there may be, it is very probable that this renewed life proceeds in a great measure from ova. That the ova retain vitality for a long time is certain. The late Dr. Baird, of the British Museum, showed Dr. G. S. Brady and myself a jar containing numerous forms of animal life which had made their appearance from mud taken from a dried-up canal in India during the hot season, and kept in the dry state for a considerable time after reaching this country before being subjected to water. Shortly after water was supplied, many living forms made their appearance. Where the pools are small and subject to be dried up during summer, they seldom contain many species, although in such cases one species may prevail greatly. Limestone districts are favourable to ostracoda, but all rock and clay surfaces are better than peat. Where there is nothing but pure peat, or peaty ponds, fringed with *Sphagnum*, few or no ostracoda may be expected. They are seldom searched for successfully where the lakes or pools have risen much by heavy rainfalls, nor in mill-dams, where the water is drained off rapidly, leaving broad, bare margins. It is otherwise where the water in the pools is decreasing gradually by evaporation. Then these animals appear to have time to follow the water, and may be taken abundantly when thus brought closer together in the small shallow pools left here and there. Moorland roadside ditches are more promising than those at some distance from the road. This may arise from a supply of material from the drainage of the road, which may be requisite to build up the shells of these minute crustaceans. Ostracoda are seldom absent in ditches or marshes which contain a little ochreous deposit with a metallic bluish scum on the surface of the water; they are more common in broad shallow ditches than in those more narrow and deep, and are rarely met with in springs or in ponds abounding with fish. Neither do they thrive where amphipods prevail. These little bivalve crustaceans are not always fastidious in their choice of habitat, sometimes disporting in pure fresh water, at other times revelling in water of very questionable character, while others affect brackish water, although they live in very different degrees of the saline element.

" The Govan colliery dam, which is close to the terminus

of a railway, is subjected to the dust from' loading and unloading of the waggons, and to the deleterious fumes of a range
of brick-kilns within a dozen yards or so, and is generally
covered with a sprinkling of soot from the neighbouring
factories. It is, further, the playground for the children of the
vicinity to sail their small boats upon. In spite of all these
apparent disadvantages against the ostracoda, I seldom fail
to obtain a fair gathering of them in this small patch of water,
whether in summer or winter. Their survival under all these
circumstances may be due to the fact that what is harmless
and healthful to them may be death to their enemies. The
Cypridæ proper are seldom if ever found in very deep water,
but mostly amongst the vegetation, while the *Candonæ* are met
with at greater depths. In Loch Lomond I have found them
at a depth of forty fathoms. Although these small crustaceans
appear to be greatly more abundant on the plains than on the
mountains, Dr. G. S. Brady records *Cypris cinerea, C. compressa,
C. striolata*, etc., from a pool near the summit of Mickle Fell,
in Yorkshire, at an elevation of two thousand feet.

"From the foregoing, it is evident that the abundance of
these organisms in one place cannot always be taken as an
index of their profusion in another, although the two may be of
quite similar appearance. In the one, these forms of life may
be swarming ; in the other, absent or nearly so. So little can
we depend upon apparent similarity in this respect, that, in
collecting, it is well to make trial of even the most unlikely
spots, and, although we may meet with frequent disappoint-
ments, we shall, on the other hand, often find what we shall
deem prizes where they are least expected."

As to "*time for collecting* :"— "The best time for collecting
these organisms is in summer, as they are then met with in the
greatest abundance. There can be little doubt that heat is
conducive to their increase and development. Dr. G. S. Brady
states that he has found them in the water of mill cooling-ponds
at a temperature of 100° Fahr., and the water might at times
be even hotter."

"*Mode of Collection.*"—The suitable net attached to a jointed
rod has been already described.

"To have the full benefit of the gathering for ostracoda, it
is necessary to take some of the mud, which in most cases can

be readily procured by scraping the sides or bottom of the pool with the ring of the net. In order to reduce the bulk as much as possible, all the impalpable mud should be washed thoroughly away till the water runs off clear. This can be done either in the working net, or in a separate bag of the same texture without the hoop. If the contents are to be examined in the dry state they may at once, after the water has well run out, be put into a small bag and labelled. In all cases, when the water has to be pressed out, it is better to do so in a separate bag or cloth of stronger texture, as the thin muslin working net is apt to give way in that operation. The label is best preserved when enclosed in a small wooden needle-case and put into the bag. To provide for the examination of the soft animal tissues, the whole or a portion of the material may be put into a bottle with spirits. When it is desirable to study the habits of the living animals, the gathering may be taken home in water in an eight or ten ounce bottle, and transferred to a white shallow vessel, where the animals can be well seen, and their various movements observed. In this state the life-appearance of parts of the animal can be more satisfactorily made out than after they have been either dried or preserved in spirits.

  "It may be further remarked that the washing away of all the impalpable mud is of great importance, independently of the reduction of bulk, because, where the mud is retained, it sets in drying as a cement, and becomes hard and difficult to dissolve. When thoroughly washed, the vegetable residue requires only to be dried in order to be ready for examination, thus avoiding the operation of ' floating,' which never can be done successfully where there is much vegetable matter, as is generally the case in fresh-water gatherings, which comes to the surface along with the microzoa. Therefore floating can only be done with advantage when there is much heavy material to be got rid of that will sink to the bottom, as sand or gravel. When the material requires to be ' floated,' it has first to be well dried, and then placed in plenty of water and well stirred. The heavy material will then sink, and the light buoyant microzoa come to the surface, where they can be skimmed off, and drained through a sufficiently fine sieve. The skimming and stirring may with advantage be repeated several times.

The skimmings should be well washed in the sieve and dried, when the ostracoda can easily be picked out with a hand lens and camel-hair pencil. In the dry state a series of brass or copper wire sieves will facilitate the work greatly ; a set of four, fitting into each other, suits very well, the largest being five and a half or six inches in diameter, and an inch in depth, and the rim of each projecting a little under the bottom, so as to leave space for what passes through the different sieves. The uppermost sieve should have a mesh of twelve wires to the inch, the next twenty-four, the next thirty-six, and the undermost seventy-six to the inch, which is sufficiently fine to retain all the ostracoda. The first or uppermost sieve retains few or no ostracoda, but removes all the coarse material. In most cases a great deal of vegetable fibre remains in the sieves, and may be blown off, but this must be done carefully, so as not to blow away any of the smaller ostracoda."—" Fresh and Brackish-Water Ostracoda," pp. 28–30, 33–35.

APPENDIX C.

A GENUS AND VARIOUS SPECIES NAMED IN HONOUR OF DAVID ROBERTSON.

SPONGIADÆ.

Halichondria Robertsoni, Bowerbank, Monograph, of British Spongiadæ, vol. iv. p. 100. 1882.

FORAMINIFERA.

Trochammina Robertsoni, H. B. Brady, 1876. A fossil species.
Trochammina Robertsoni, H. B. Brady, 1887. A living species, of which the specific name must be altered, having been previously used for a fossil species.

OSTRACODA.

Cythere Robertsoni, G. S. Brady, 1868. In 1889, Brady and Norman say of this, "A small but very distinct and pretty species, described first from specimens dredged by Mr. D. Robertson, at Dröbak, Christiania Fiord, in a depth of 30–35 fathoms."
Cytherura Robertsoni, G. S. Brady, 1868. This has proved to be a synonym of *Cytherura gibba (Müller),* 1785.
Erpetocypris Robertsoni, Brady and Norman, 1889. On this species see what is said at page 353.
Cytheridea Robertsoniana, G. S. Brady. This is said by Sars to be a synonym of *Cytheridea lacustris.*

COPEPODA.

Robertsonia, new genus, G. S. Brady, Monograph, Ray Society, 1878. In regard to the naming of this genus, see page 351.
Mesochra Robertsoni, G. S. Brady. Monograph, Ray Society, 1878. See page 351.

AMPHIPODA.

Bathyporeia Robertsoni, Spence Bate, 1862. A synonym of *Bathyporeia pilosa*, Lindström.

Sophrosyne Robertsoni, Stebbing and Robertson. It was by special request of his colleague that Mr. Robertson allowed the use of his name for this species.

MARINE MITES.

Cheyletus Robertsoni, G. S. Brady, Proc. Zool. Soc. London, 18 5. Dr. Brady remarks, " One specimen only of this remarkable mite was dredged off Hawthorn, on the Durham coast, in a depth of twenty-seven fathoms. I have named it after my valued friend Mr. David Robertson, of Glasgow, who was my companion on the dredging expedition when it was taken."

POLYZOA.

Sulcoretepora Robertsoni, Young and Young, 1877. A fossil species.

SPECIES DISCOVERED BY MR. ROBERTSON, TOGETHER WITH THOSE FOR WHICH HE IS JOINT-AUTHORITY.

OSTRACODA.

Cypridopsis obesa, Brady and Robertson, Ann. and Mag. Nat. Hist., 1869. See also Sars, Oversigt Norg. Crust., p. 62. 1890.

Cypridopsis Newtoni, Brady and Robertson, Ann. and Mag. Nat. Hist., 1869.

Aglaia glacialis, Brady, Crosskey and Robertson, Pal. Soc., 1874.

Bairdia Cambrica, Brady, Crosskey and Robertson, Pal. Soc., 1874.

Darwinula Stevensoni, Brady and Robertson, Ann. and Mag. Nat. Hist., 1870. This species, when first instituted, was named *Polycheles Stevensoni*, but in 1872 the authors saw reason to change the name to *Darwinella Stevensoni*, and subsequently, Professor Rupert Jones having pointed out that the name *Darwinella* was, like *Polycheles*, preoccupied, the name became *Darwinula Stevensoni*.

Cythere Macallana, Brady and Robertson, Ann. and Mag. Nat. Hist., 1869.

Cythere deflexa, Brady, Crosskey and Robertson, Pal. Soc., 1874.

Cythere cribrosa, Brady, Crosskey and Robertson, Pal. Soc., 1874.

Cythere gibbosa, Brady and Robertson, Ann. and Mag. Nat. Hist., 1869.

Cythere Cluthæ, Brady, Crosskey and Robertson, Pal. Soc., 1874.

Cythere Hoptonensis, Brady, Crosskey and Robertson, Pal. Soc., 1874.

Limnicythere antiqua, Brady, Crosskey and Robertson, Pal. Soc., 1874.

Limnicythere Sancti-Patricii, Brady and Robertson, Ann. and Mag. Nat. Hist., 1869.

Cytheridea inornata, Brady, Crosskey and Robertson, Pal. Soc., 1874.

Krithe glacialis, Brady, Crosskey and Robertson, Pal. Soc., 1874.

Cytherura pumila, Brady, Crosskey and Robertson, Pal. Soc., 1874.

Cytherura concentrica, Brady, Crosskey and Robertson, Pal. Soc., 1874.

Cytherura complanata, Brady, Crosskey and Robertson, Pal. Soc., 1874.

Cytherura compressa, Brady, Crosskey and Robertson, Pal. Soc., 1874.

Cytheropteron arcuatum, Brady, Crosskey and Robertson, Pal. Soc., 1874.

Cytheropteron inflatum, Brady, Crosskey and Robertson, Pal. Soc., 1874.

Cytheropteron Montrosiense, Brady, Crosskey and Robertson, Pal. Soc., 1874.

Cytheropteron angulatum, Brady and Robertson, Ann. and Mag. Nat. Hist., 1870.

Bythocythere elongata, Brady, Crosskey and Robertson, Pal. Soc., 1874.

Cytherideis subspiralis, Brady, Crosskey and Robertson, Pal. Soc., 1874.

Paradoxostoma pyriforme, Brady, Crosskey and Robertson, Pal. Soc., 1874.

Paradoxostoma tenerum, Brady, Crosskey and Robertson, Pal. Soc., 1874.

Bosquetia robusta, Brady, Crosskey and Robertson, Pal. Soc., 1874.

Erpetocypris tumefacta, Brady and Robertson, Ann. and Mag. Nat. Hist., 1870. This species, when instituted, was named *Cypris tumefacta*, and was transferred to the new genus, *Erpetocypris*, by Brady and Norman in 1889.

Erpetocypris Robertsoni, Brady and Norman, Monograph of the Marine and Fresh-water Ostracoda, 1889. The connection of Mr. Robertson with this species has been already explained.

Cypridopsis variegata, Brady and Norman, Monograph, 1889. The authors say, "This species occurred sparingly in several gatherings made years ago, in the English fen district, by Messrs. Brady and Robertson ; but on account of its close resemblance to *Potamocypris fulva* and *Cypridopsis Newtoni* it remained undescribed. Specimens recently obtained by Mr. Robertson in the Isle of Skye, and by Dr. Norman from a pool by the side of Lough Neagh, Ireland, by their very characteristic colouring, seem to leave no doubt as to its specific distinctness."

Candona Kingsleii, Brady and Robertson, Ann. and Mag. Nat. Hist., 1870.

Candona enplectella, Robertson, MS., Brady and Norman's Monograph, 1889. On this species see page 353.

Metacypris cordata, Brady and Robertson, Ann. and Mag. Nat. Hist., 1870.

Cythere Robertsoni, Brady, Ann. and Mag. Nat. Hist., 1868. On this species see above, page 376.

Cytheridea inaequalis, Brady and Robertson, Ann. and Mag. Nat. Hist., 1870.

Loxoconcha pusilla, Brady and Robertson, Ann. and Mag. Nat. Hist., 1870.

Xestoleberis labiata, Brady and Robertson, Ann. and Mag. Nat. Hist., 1874.

Cytherura simplex, Brady and Norman, Monograph, 1889.

Cytherura fulva, Brady and Robertson, Ann. and Mag. Nat. Hist., 1874.

Paradoxostoma orcadense, Brady and Robertson, Ann. and Mag. Nat. Hist., 1872.

Machærina amygdaloides, Brady, Nat. Hist. Trans., Northum-

berland and Durham, vol. iii., 1870. This species, when
instituted, was named *Xiphichilus amygdaloides.* Brady
and Norman, in 1889, renamed it *Machærina amygdaloides ;*
and, although its geographical range is wide, they say,
"One British specimen only known, found by Mr. D.
Robertson among sand dredged off Papa, Shetland."
Candona hyalina, Brady and Robertson, Ann. and Mag. Nat.
Hist., 1870.

COPEPODA.

Pseudocyclops obtusatus, Brady and Robertson, Ann. and Mag.
Nat. Hist., 1873.
Lophophorus insignis, Brady, Monograph, Ray Soc., 1878. Dr.
Brady says, "Three specimens only of this very distinct
and beautiful copepod occurred in a dredging by Mr.
Robertson and the Rev. A. M. Norman, six miles off the
Durham coast, near Hawthorn." In 1880, he changed the
preoccupied name *Lophophorus* to *Pterinopsyllus.*
Ectinosoma atlanticum, Brady and Robertson, Ann. and Mag.
Nat. Hist., 1873. When first described, this species was
placed by the authors in a new genus, *Microsetella,* but, in
1878, Dr. Brady transferred it to *Ectinosoma.*
Robertsonia tenuis, Brady and Robertson, Proc. Brit. Assoc.,
1875. The authors originally named this species *Ectinosoma tenue,* but, in 1878, Dr. Brady saw reason to establish
for it a new genus named after his friend and colleague.
Jonesiella fusiformis, Brady and Robertson, Brit. Assoc.
Report, 1875. This was at first named *Zosime fusiformis,*
the genus being changed in 1878.
Jonesiella spinulosa, Brady and Robertson, Brit. Assoc. Report,
1875. Changed, in 1878, from *Zosime spinulosa.*
Delavalia reflexa, Brady and Robertson, Brit. Assoc. Report,
1875.
Delavalia robusta, Brady and Robertson, Brit. Assoc. Report,
1875.
Canthocamptus hibernicus, G. S. Brady, Monograph, Ray Soc.,
1878. Dr. Brady says, "*C. hibernicus* occurs plentifully in
the Mullingar Canal at Dublin, and in a lake near Newport,
co. Mayo ; for specimens from both of these places I am
indebted to my friend, Mr. David Robertson, of Glasgow."

Mesochra Robertsoni, G. S. Brady, Monograph, Ray Soc., 1878. In regard to this species, see what has been said, page 351.

Laophonte hispida, Brady and Robertson, Ann. and Mag. Nat. Hist, 1873. This was at first called *Asellopsis hispida*, the generic name being altered in 1878.

Normanella dubia, Brady and Robertson, Brit. Assoc. Report, 1875. A new genus was established for this species in 1878, its name previously being *Laophonte dubia*.

Cletodes longicaudatus, Brady and Robertson, Brit. Assoc. Report, 1875.

Cletodes propinqua, Brady and Robertson, Brit. Assoc. Report, 1875.

Enhydrosoma curvatum, Brady and Robertson, Brit. Assoc. Report, 1875. This was at first called *Rhizothrix curvata*, but renamed in 1878.

Dactylopus tenuiremis, Brady and Robertson, Brit. Assoc. Report, 1875.

Thalestris hibernica, Brady and Robertson, Ann. and Mag. Nat. Hist., 1873.

Ilyopsyllus coriaceus, Brady and Robertson, Ann. and Mag. Nat. Hist., 1873.

Harpacticus flexus, Brady and Robertson, Ann. and Mag. Nat. Hist., 1873.

Lichomolgus liber, Brady and Robertson, Brit. Assoc. Report, 1875.

Lichomolgus Thorellii, Brady and Robertson, Brit. Assoc. Report, 1875.

Cyclopicem nigripes, Brady and Robertson, Brit. Assoc. Report, 1875.

Artotrogus Normani, Brady and Robertson, Brit. Assoc. Report, 1875. The original name, *Dyspontius Normani*, was changed in 1880.

Acontiophorus scutatus, Brady and Robertson, Ann. and Mag. Nat. Hist., 1873. The name *Solenostoma scutatum* was at first given, but changed in 1880.

Acontiophorus armatus, Brady and Robertson, Brit. Assoc. Report, 1875. This was at first named *Ascomyzon ornatum*, the specific name being due to a misprint. With this explanation, Dr. Brady described it as a new species in 1880.

CUMACEA.

Nannastacus unguiculatus, Spence Bate, Ann. and Mag. Nat. Hist., 1859. On this species see the remarks already made at pages 187, 189.

AMPHIPODA.

Amphilochus manudens, Spence Bate, Brit. Mus. Catal. Amph. Crust., 1862. "*Hab.* From roots of laminaria in a few fathoms of water, Cumbrae, N.B. (*Mr. Robertson*)." See also page 354.

Phædra Kinahani, Spence Bate, Brit. Mus. Catal. Amph. Crust., 1862. Mr. Spence Bate says, "*Hab.* Taken from a nullipore bank off the coast in the neighbourhood of Glasgow. For this and several other species I am indebted to my valued correspondent, Mr. Robertson, of Glasgow." The species has since been named *Liljeborgia Kinahani*.

Stegocephalus celticus, named in MS. by Mr. Spence Bate, but not described. It has since been described under the name *Cyproidia damnoniensis*.

Sophrosyne Robertsoni, Stebbing and Robertson, Trans. Zool. Soc. London, vol. xiii., part i., 1891.

Syrrhoe fimbriata, Stebbing and Robertson, Trans. Zool. Soc. London, vol. xiii., part i., 1891.

Podoceropsis palmatus, Stebbing and Robertson, Trans. Zool. Soc. London, vol. xiii., part i., 1891.

Podocerus cumbrensis, Stebbing and Robertson, Trans. Zool. Soc. London, vol. xiii., part i., 1891.

ISOPODA.

Paratanais rigidus, Bate and Westwood, British Sessile-eyed Crustacea, 1866. The authors say, "The only specimen that we have seen of this species was sent to us by Mr. Robertson, of Glasgow, who ' dredged it at the roots of *Laminaria saccharina*,' near Cumbrae."

Leptaspidia brevipes, Bate and Westwood, British Sessile-eyed Crustacea, 1867. They say, "The animal lives in the mud ; two or three specimens have been taken by Mr. Robertson at Cumbrae, to whom we are indebted for it." This queer little species, a twentieth of an inch in length, has been recently sent me by Mr. Robertson, he having again taken it in the month of July of this year (1890), at Kilchattan, Buteshire.

MARINE MITES.

Trombidium fucicolum, G. S. Brady, Proc. Zool. Soc. London, 1875. Dr. Brady says, " One adult and one young specimen of this species were washed from among the roots of algæ gathered between tide marks in Roundstone Bay, Ireland, by Mr. David Robertson."

Cheyletus Robertsoni, G. S. Brady, Proc. Zool. Soc. London, 1875. As to this species see page 377.

Schistostoma longisetosum, G. S. Brady, Proc. Zool. Soc. London, 1877. Dr. Brady observes, "One specimen only of this remarkable species was noticed in a gathering of entomostraca taken by Mr. Robertson in an old canal at Petershead."

SPONGIADÆ (see page 265).

The new species obtained in Westport Bay, co. Mayo, and in Galway, on the Irish expedition which Messrs. Robertson and Norman made together, were named as follows in Bowerbank's "Monograph of the British Spongiadæ," vol. iv., edited, with additions, by the Rev. A. M. Norman, M.A., F.L.S.,&c., 1882 :—

Microciona tumulosa, Bowerbank.
Hymedesmia pansa, Bowerbank.
Hymedesmia pilata, Bowerbank.
Hymedesmia pulchella, Bowerbank.
Hymedesmia tenuicula, Bowerbank.
Hymeniacidon armiger, Bowerbank.
Hymeniacidon solidus, Bowerbank.
Hymeniacidon callosus, Bowerbank.
Hymeniacidon tenebrosus, Bowerbank.
Halichondria flabellifera, Bowerbank.
Isodictya ferula, Bowerbank.
Isodictya perplexa. Bowerbank.
Isodictya crassa, Bowerbank.
Isodictya paupercula, Bowerbank.
Isodictya trunca, Bowerbank.
Isodictya coriacea, Bowerbank.

Isodictya nodosa, Bowerbank.
Isodictya involuta, Bowerbank.
Isodictya pertenuis, Bowerbank.
Isodictya scitula, Bowerbank.
Isodictya collina, Bowerbank.
Isodictya implicita, Bowerbank.
Rhaphiodesma fallaciosum, Bowerbank.
Rhaphiodesma intermedium, Bowerbank.

In the same volume the following species are described :—

Halichondria Robertsoni, Bowerbank.

Of this Bowerbank says, "The specimen in course of description was given by the late Dr. Scouler to Mr. D. Robertson, and by him to my friend the Rev. A. M. Norman, by whom it was sent to me for examination and description."

Halichondria condensa, Bowerbank.

Bowerbank says of this, "*Hab.* Isle of Man ; Mr. D. Robertson. This sponge was presented to my friend the Rev. A. M. Norman by Mr. D. Robertson, and was sent to me for examination."

Halichondria coralloides, Bowerbank.

Bowerbank says of this, "*Hab.* Firth of Forth ; Mr. D. Robertson. I received this sponge from my friend the Rev. A. M. Norman, to whom it was presented by Mr. D. Robertson."

Isodictya inaequalis, Bowerbank.

The habitat is apparently unknown. Bowerbank says, "I received a small specimen of this species from my friend the Rev. A. M. Norman, who obtained it among others from Mr. D. Robertson."

There are other departments of natural history in which Mr. Robertson's co-operation has been similarly serviceable, but from want of access to the literature of the subjects I am unable to supply the details. There is, for example, reason to believe that the Dr. von Frauenfeld mentioned in Chapter XIV. named a new species of univalve shell in honour of Mr. Robertson. On the other hand, the annelid of the genus *Clymene,* with which Professor Koelliker was concerned (see page 171), may have been the already-known species, *Clymene lumbricalis.*

APPENDIX D.

BIBLIOGRAPHY.

Showing Mr. Robertson's contributions to literature in separate or joint authorship.

THE ANNALS AND MAGAZINE OF NATURAL HISTORY.

"Remarks on the Habits of the Common Mussel." Ser. III., vol. i., pp. 314, 315. 1858.

"*Saxicava rugosa*, a Byssus-spinner." Ser. III., vol. iv., p. 80. 1859.

" Notes of a Week's Dredging in the West of Ireland." By George Stewardson Brady, C.M.Z.S., and David Robertson. Ser. IV., vol. iii., pp. 353–374 ; plates 18-22. 1869.

"The Ostracoda and Foraminifera of Tidal Rivers." By George Stewardson Brady, C.M.Z.S., and David Robertson, F.G.S. With an Analysis and Descriptions of the Foraminifera, by Henry B. Brady, F.L.S. Ser. IV., vol. vi., pp. 273–309 ; plates 11, 12. 1870.

"Contributions to the Study of the Entomostraca." By George Stewardson Brady, C.M.Z.S., and David Robertson, F.G.S. First paper : "On the Distribution of the British Ostracoda." Ser. IV., vol. ix., pp. 48–70 ; plates 1, 2. 1872.

"Contributions," etc. Second paper : "On Marine Copepoda taken in the West of Ireland." Ser. IV., vol. xii., pp. 126–142 ; plates 8, 9. 1873.

"Contributions," etc. Third paper : "On Ostracoda taken amongst the Scilly Islands," and "On the Anatomy of *Darwinella Stevensoni.*" Ser. IV., vol. xiii., pp. 114–119 ; plates 4, 5. 1874.

PAPERS READ BEFORE THE NATURAL HISTORY SOCIETY OF GLASGOW.

" Report on the Mortality among the Clyde Sea-fowl during the month of September last." [Read November 29, 1859.] Vol. i.,* part i., p. 4.

" On the Marine•Zoology and Botany of Loch Ryan, Bay of Luce, and Portpatrick, from Observations made during a Recent Excursion." By Dr. John Grieve and Mr. David Robertson. [Read March 25, 1862.] *l.c.*, pp. 21–36.

" Remarks on *Luidia fragilissima*," etc. [Read April 29, 1862.] *l.c.*, pp. 36, 37.

" Remarks on *Hippolyte securifrons, Cuma trispinosa*," etc. [Read or spoken January 26, 1864.] *l.c.*, pp. 82–84.

" On Clay Beds of Ross Arden, on the Banks of Loch Lomond." [Read May 31, 1864.] *l.c.*, pp. 92, 93.

"An Account of a Visit to the Shores of Dunbar in February, 1864, with Descriptive Notes on the Natural History of the District." By Messrs. Robert Gray and David Robertson. [Read April 26, and May 31, 1864.] *l.c.*, pp. 89, 90, 93, 94.

" Notes on *Corophium longicorne*, and on the Occurrence of *Alteutha Bopyroides*." [Read January 21, 1865.] *l.c.*, pp. 104–106.

" The Luminosity of the Sea." By Messrs. David Robertson and William Keddie. [Read November 29, 1865.] Separately published.

" Notes on Specimens from Orme's Head." [Read November 27, 1866.] *l.c.*, pp. 148–150.

" On Marine Dredging." [Read May 28, 1867.] *l.c.*, part. ii., pp. 179–183.

"On the Nudibranchiate Mollusca of the Shores of the Cumbraes." [Read February 25, 1868.] *l.c.*, pp. 204–207.

" Notes on the Herring." [Read January 26, 1869.] *l.c.*, pp. 240–247.

" Observations on a Mode of identifying certain Post-tertiary Fossils." [Read September 28, 1869.] Vol. ii.,† p. 3.

" Notes on *Cypris laevis*, and its habit of perforating the leaves of *Victoria regia*." [Read December 28, 1869.] *l.c.*, pp. 7–10.

"On the Sea-Anemones of the Shores of the Cumbraes." [Read March 27, 1870.] *l.c.*, pp. 24–30.

* The first volume of the Proceedings was published in 1868,
† The second volume was published in 1876.

" On *Petromyzon fluviatilis*, and its mode of preying on *Coregonus clupeoides*." [Read October 25, 1870.] *l.c.*, pp. 61–63.

"On the Reproduction of the Spines of *Echinus sphæra* (Müller)." [Read April 29, 1873.] *l.c.*, pp. 217–219.

"Notes on a few of the Tube-building Annelids." [Read November 30, 1875.] Vol. iii.,* part i., pp. 31–35.

"On Mounting Seaweeds." [Read April 25, 1876.] *l.c.*, p. 85.

" On *Pisidium fontinale* and *Planorbis complanatus,* two fresh-water shells new to Scotland, and *Helix villosa,* a land shell new to Britain," vol. iii., part. ii., pp. 172–175.

" On *Saxicava rugosa,* a Bivalve Mollusc ; showing an unusual mode of repair." [Read April 24, 1877.] *l.c.*, 198–201.

"Fresh and Brackish-water Ostracoda," *in* " The Fauna of Scotland, with special reference to Clydesdale and the Western District." Published separately in 1880, and attached to vol. iv., part. i., 35 pages.

"Remarks on a Few Hauls with the Dredge, in Portree Bay, Skye." [Read October 5, 1880.] Vol. v., part. i.,† pp. 11–13.

"Note on *Astrorhiza limicola* and on *Amphidotus cordatus*." [Read October 26, 1880.] *l.c.*, pp. 17, 18.

"Notes on the Common Limpet." [Read March 23, 1884.] Vol. i., part i., N. S.,‡ pp. 9–20.

"*Talitrus locusta*, Linn." [Read March 31, 1885.] Vol. i., part ii., N. S., pp. 130–132.

"Notes on *Pedicellariæ*." [Read April 28, 1885.] Vol. i., part ii., N. S., pp. 132, 133.

"*Pagurus Prideauxii*, Leach." [Read June 9, 1885.] Vol. i., part iii., N. S., p. 290.

"*Amphidotus cordatus*, Penn." [Read January 26, 1886.] Vol. i., part iii., N. S., pp. 290–293.

"The Food of Fishes." [Read February 22, 1886.] Vol. ii., part i., N. S.,§ pp. 146–150.

"*Scaphander lignarius*, Linn." [Read March 30, 1886.] Vol. i., part iii., N. S., pp. 293, 294.

---

* Vol. iii., part i., was published in 1876 ; part ii. in 1877.

† Vol. v., part. i., was published in 1882.

‡ Vol. i., N. S., was published as follows : part i., 1885 ; part ii., 1886 part iii., 1887.

§ Vol. ii., N. S., was published as follows : part i., 1888 ; part ii., 1889.

"*Purpura lapillus*, Linn." [Read June 8, 1886.] Vol. ii., part i., N. S., pp. 139–141.
"Observed Depths in Loch Lomond." [Read August 3, 1886.] Vol. ii., part i., N. S., pp. 141–143.
"*Corystes cassivelaunus*, Penn., and *Mytilus edulis*, Lin." [Read November 30, 1886.] Vol. ii., part i., N. S., pp. 143–146.
"On some Marine Mollusca." [Read April 26, 1887.] Vol. ii., part i., N. S., pp. 150–153.
"A Contribution towards a Catalogue of the Amphipoda and Isopoda of the Firth of Clyde." [Read April 27, 1887.] Vol. ii., part i., N. S., pp. 9-99.   1888.
"On the Local Distribution of *Pennatula phosphorea*, Lin., *Virgularia mirabilis*, Lam., and *Pavonaria quadrangularis*, Pall." [Read June 7, 1887.] Vol. ii., part ii., N. S., pp. 211–212.
"The Pike, *Esox lucius*, Lin., and *Isocardia cor*, Lin." [Read August 16, 1887.] Vol. ii., part ii., N.S., pp. 212–214, 215.
"*Hyas araneus*, Lin., and *Stenorhynchus longirostris*, Fabr." [Read December 27, 1887.] Vol. ii., part ii., N. S., pp. 216–220.
"On some Differences between the Marine Faunas of the Firth of Clyde and Firth of Forth." [Read February 28, 1888.] Vol. ii., part ii., N. S., pp. 220–221.
"Loch Fyne Herring." [Read November 27, 1888.] Vol. iii.,* part i., N. S., pp. 22–24.   1889.
"Notice of Thirteen Cumacea from the Firth of Clyde." [Read February 26, 1889.] Vol. iii., part i., N.S., pp. 47–49.   1889.

PAPERS READ BEFORE THE GEOLOGICAL SOCIETY OF GLASGOW.

"The Post-tertiary Fossiliferous Beds of Scotland." By Rev. Henry W. Crosskey, Vice-President Geol. Soc. Glas., and Mr. David Robertson. "Transactions of the Geological Society of Glasgow," vol., ii. pp. 267–282. Introduction and Section I.—Dalmuir. 1867.
Continued, vol. iii., pp. 113-129. [Read March 26, 1868.] Sections II.—Cumbrae College. III.—Loch Gilp. IV.—Boulder Clay, Caithness. V.—Lucknow Pit, Ardeer ironworks, Ayrshire. 1871.
Continued, vol. iii., pp. 321-341. Sections VI.—East Tarbert,

* Vol. iii., N. S., was published as follows : part i., 1889.

Loch Fyne. VII.—West Tarbert. VIII.—Crinan. IX.— Duntroon. X.—Old Mains, Renfrew. XI.—Paisley. 1871. Continued, vol iv., pp. 32–45. Section XII.—Garvel Park new dock, Greenock, pp. 128–137. Sections XIII.—Kilchattan Tileworks, Bute. XIV.—Tangy Glen, near Campbeltown, pp. 241–256. Sections XV.—Jordanhill Brickworks. XVI.—Stob-cross. XVII.—Fairfield, near Govan. XVIII.—Paisley Canal. XIX.—Dipple Tileworks.

Continued, vol. v., part i., pp. 29–35. Section XX.—Kyles of Bute.

" Note on the Precipitation of Clay in Fresh and Salt Water." [Read, April 24, 1873.] *l.c.*, vol. iv., pp. 257–259. 1874.

"Notes on the Recent Ostracoda and Foraminifera of the Firth of Clyde, with some remarks on the Distribution of Mollusca." [Read April 16, 1874.] *l.c.*, vol. v., pp. 112–153. 1875.

"Notes on a Raised Beach at Cumbrae." [Read May 20, 1875.] *l.c.*, vol. v., part ii., pp. 192–200. 1877.

" Notes on a Post-tertiary Deposit of Shell-bearing Clay on the west side of the Railway Tunnel at Arkleston, near Paisley." [Read March 9, 1876] *l.c.*, pp. 281–287. 1877.

"Garnock Water Post-tertiary Deposit." [Read March 30, 1876.] *l.c.*, pp. 292–296. 1877.

" Notes on the Post-tertiary Deposit of Misk Pit, near Kilwinning." [Read January 19, 1877.] *l.c.*, pp. 297–309. 1877.

" Note upon the Discovery of Marine Forms at a higher level than previously known in the neighbourhood of Glasgow." [Read April 20, 1867.] *l.c.*, p. 333. 1877.

"On the Post-tertiary Beds of Garvel Park, Greenock," with two sections. [Plate I.] [Read April 14, 1881.] *l.c.*, vol. vii., p. 37. 1883.

QUARTERLY JOURNAL OF THE GEOLOGICAL SOCIETY.

"Report on the Sands and Gravels and Boulder-clays, and the top Silt, at the Dock F of the Atlantic Docks, Liverpool." By David Robertson, Esq., F.L.S., F.G.S., pp. 129–132. May, 1883. An appendix to a paper on the " Drift-beds of the North-west of England and North Wales," by T. Mellard Reade, Esq., C.E., F.G.S.

PROCEEDINGS OF THE PHILOSOPHICAL SOCIETY OF GLASGOW.
"On the Distribution of Marine Algæ on the C.L.T. Buoys in the Clyde." By John Grieve, M.A., M.D., and Mr. David Robertson.
"On the Uses of the Antennæ of *Corystes Cassivelaunus*, the Masked Crab," with an illustration.   1861.
"Notes on the Post-tertiary Geology of Norway." By the Rev. H. W. Crosskey and David Robertson.   1868.

PALÆONTOGRAPHICAL SOCIETY, VOL. FOR 1874.
"A Monograph of the Post-tertiary Entomostraca of Scotland, including species from England and Ireland." By George Stewardson Brady, C.M.Z.S., the Rev. Henry William Crosskey, F.G.S., and David Robertson, F.G.S.

THE QUARTERLY JOURNAL OF MICROSCOPICAL SCIENCE.
"Notes on *Amphidotus cordatus* (Penn.)." vol. xi. new series, pp. 25–27.

REPORT OF THE BRITISH ASSOCIATION FOR THE ADVANCE-
MENT OF SCIENCE FOR 1874.
"Preliminary Report of the Committee on Dredging on the Coasts of Durham and North Yorkshire." Drawn up by David Robertson and George Stewardson Brady.

REPORT OF BRITISH ASSOCIATION FOR 1875.
"Report on Dredging off the Coast of Durham and North Yorkshire in 1874." By George Stewardson Brady, C.M.Z.S., and David Robertson, F.G.S. pp. 185–199.

WORKS CONNECTED WITH THE MEETING OF THE BRITISH
ASSOCIATION IN 1876.
In the "Catalogue of the Western Scottish Fossils," the paper on "Post-tertiary Fossils," is by David Robertson. 1876.
In the "Fauna and Flora of Clydesdale," published by the Society of Field Naturalists, Glasgow, the paper on "Recent Marine Mollusca, Actinozoa, and Foraminifera," is by David Robertson. 1876.

TRANSACTIONS OF THE ZOOLOGICAL SOCIETY OF LONDON.
"Four New Species of Amphipoda." By the Rev. T. R. R. Stebbing, M.A., and David Robertson, F.L.S., F.G.S. [Read Nov. 5, 1889]. Vol. xiii., part i., pp. 30–42, plates v., vi., January, 1891 (separate copies, 1890).

INDEX.

PRINTED BY WILLIAM CLOWES AND SONS, LIMITED, LONDON AND BECCLES.

www.ingramcontent.com/pod-product-compliance
Lightning Source LLC
Chambersburg PA
CBHW051510100726
47898CB00005B/1400